Don Kenefick is the ultimate late-developer. Having suffered a stroke at the age of thirty-nine, years of indifferent health followed until he attempted a programme of self-improvement. He put himself through university leading to a master's degree, and engaged in politics and acting to improve speech. Here now is his first book – a lifelong ambition – and others will follow.

THE CAPTIVE SHADOW

For Rita, Tracy and Phoebe

Don Kenefick

The Captive Shadow

Copyright © Don Kenefick

The right of Don Kenefick to be identified as author of this work has been asserted by him in accordance with section 77 and 78 of the Copyright, Designs and Patents Act 1988.

All rights reserved. No part of this publication may be reproduced, stored in a retrieval system, or transmitted in any form or by any means, electronic, mechanical, photocopying, recording, or otherwise, without the prior permission of the publishers.

Any person who commits any unauthorized act in relation to this publication may be liable to criminal prosecution and civil claims for damages.

A CIP catalogue record for this title is available from the British Library.

All characters appearing in this work are fictitious. Any resemblance to real persons, living or dead, is purely coincidental.

ISBN 978 184963 381 9

www.austinmacauley.com

First Published (2013)
Austin Macauley Publishers Ltd.
25 Canada Square
Canary Wharf
London
E14 5LB

Printed and Bound in Great Britain

Chapter One

London 2001. Trash everywhere. Discarded trash littered the streets, trendy trash stuffed the shops, sophistic trash buried the wisdoms, self-indulgent trash filled the cemeteries. Today's tagging trashed walls caringly dressed up by yesterdays' stonemasons; tenacious concrete weeds of trash strangled the architectural flowers. What was once a World City was now a trash city.

The city's inhabitants injected trash into their veins, sniffed it up their nostrils, inhaled it into their lungs, poured it down their throats, and spewed it into the gutters. Trash swelled waistlines, balance sheets and egos. Trash evicted news from Fleet Street, art from Piccadilly, science from South Kensington, discernment from Downing Street. When Britannia was cooled, Londinia was loused. If Charles Dickens could have witnessed the scene, he'd have preferred the fog.

Among Londoners, a tiny number remained steadfastly trashproof. One of them was Peter Goodwin, whose immunity owed much to his meek personality and humble life, which together inoculated him from the bacteria of sensualism.

Peter stood, with April behind him and the High Street in front of him, scanning the odd-numbered premises on the other side of the road. He glanced bashfully at a trade card cupped in his left hand, and read 'The Starlight Introduction Agency. Proprietor, Angela Richards. Truly personal and confidential. 163 High Street, Plumham, London'.

Locating number one-hundred and sixty-three was not easy. Few shop fronts confessed their succession. 'The Garden of a Thousand Noodle Delights' admitted to being 139, but the rest were reticent until 'Davidsons, Funeral Directors', broke their cover at 187. Peter counted along the plastic fascia boards until three flickering neon tubes under lighted 'Nico's Kebab Palace'. In the shop window, a hunk of reconstituted lamb waltzed before hissing gas jets and sooted ceramic radiants, and a chubby man in a greasy apron held a steel in his left hand and sharpened a knife the size of a cavalry officer's sword. It didn't seem to be the place where Miss Right might be introduced.

The adjoining shop looked just as unlikely. An old canvas canopy on rusting iron supports concealed the shop sign, but the front pavement's vista was not romantic: stacks of plastic washing-up bowls in the three primary colours; extended families of garden gnomes; a range of Disney cartoon characters printed on the sides of pedal operated waste bins.

He counted again and arrived at the same spot. Peter was innately careful when venturing anywhere new, not that he did go anywhere new very often; but here he was inhibited by a dilemma of embarrassment. Should he chance crossing the road to find this reclusive place? Risk being spotted by someone he knew? And then be ridiculed? Looking for a partner? At his age? Or should he remain longer at a safe but difficult distance, and perhaps arouse suspicion that he might be a loiterer, a pervert, a terrorist, an evil-doer? He glanced about him as casually as he could, knowing that furtive looks attract distrust, but nobody was scrutinising him, so he chanced another count.

The third tally also ended at Nico's, and he was about to turn away when he noticed a drab, recessed doorway, between the meat vendor and the stack of plastic bowls, through which lay a staircase to the upper floor, and the possibility of a new life for Peter. The sun warmed his face, beckoning him to emerge from a lifetime of social hibernation, and he started to cross the road without another thought.

His pace quickened as he looked towards a future, but his toe caught a rift in the road's surface that now revealed the seam where tram rails had run sixty years earlier. Tarmac splits were common in the London Borough of Plumham. Providing necessities for the community already overstretched the council's slender budget: replacing public lavatory signs with new ones in eleven languages; sponsoring the eco-spiritualism awareness festival; funding a new evening class syllabus to include lessons for sexual deviance. Little was left for low priority highway maintenance.

Peter's balance was lost. Bent double, he scrambled forward to regain it, but failed as he reached the gutter, and had to climb the double kerb on all fours. Brushing the dirt from his hands and knees, he stole a look about him, and was surprised to find that nobody had noticed his humiliation. The world was busy at that moment: a mother was slapping her erring toddler about the head; a twelve-year-old concentrated on rolling her joint; a man scraped dog's excrement from his shoe onto the seat of a bus shelter; Nico levelled his sword and prepared to charge a singed left flank.

His unexpected isolation gave Peter the courage to glance over the building. The two sash windows above carried no trade signs, although the polychromatic Victorian brickwork of the upper story spoke appealingly of homely promise, in spite of one hundred and ten years of grime. Looking upwards, away from the plate glass, plastic and extruded aluminium, his eyes found warmth, but no assurance that this was the right place.

Three generations of birds' nests in the hopper-head had given the rainwater downpipe a broad back curtain of green fungus, and at one spot the dampness had rejected the thin skin of ground floor modernity. Glazed tiles now dared to claim kinship with the upper story as they peeped from behind a split and warped plywood panel, and it was here that Peter found what he sought. The disunited timbers that twisted towards him carried the letters 'ST----LIGHT ---CY': those which disagreed bore the absentees.

He started towards the door hesitantly. Doubts began to crowd his mind. Was he too faint in the heart? Too long in the tooth? Too weak at the knees? Too soft in the head? It was then that Peter's unique defensive system was activated. His mother had a pile of old gramophone records that he had listened to since a child. When he was bewildered, memories of those old words and melodies sometimes comforted him, steadied him, motivated him.

Now, the pulsating rhythm of a samba swelled from his unconscious, and a refrain danced from his memory:

'En-joy your-self! It's la-ter than you think.
'En-joy your-self! While you're still in the pink'.

Even though Peter's 'pink' had aged to vascular dulled purple, the impetus of the palpitating tempo carried him lightly up half the staircase; but the forlorn look of each uncarpeted, well-worn stair changed the melody, and Cole Porter's 'Love for Sale' filled his mind. In his mother's collection of cherished records, with dulled and scratched surfaces, that one alone still wore its pristine gloss: she had found it embarrassing to listen to a plaintive lyric concerning a prostitute. The song's line about climbing the stairs chilled Peter's incentive, and he might have abandoned this future had not an eccentric thought struck him. Why was the composer's name 'Cole'? Was 'Cole' an American spelling of 'Coal'? His wandering thoughts pushed his doubts over the top stair, and 'Welcome – Please Enter' on the ill-fitting door eased his apprehensive feet across the threshold and into the Starlight Introduction Agency.

Through the door lay a middling sized room with two desks; one fairly tidy, but with no occupant. The second desk was smaller, further from the door, was littered with screwed up paper and empty drink cartons, and behind it sat a girl in her late teens. Her grey-blue eyes looked over Peter as a gourmet might look at mouldy bread.

"Miss Angela Richards?"

"She's out, having an early lunch. And probably an expensive one. I'm left to do all the work, and this is all I get for my trouble." She tilted back her head, opened her mouth wide, and emptied half a packet of crisps into it. Peter's mind, still partly in the past, recalled a childhood sight. Opposite his mother's little house was a larger family home. They had a cellar. Twice a year the coalman lifted the cast-iron cover from the coal shoot set in the front garden path, and emptied sack after sack of coal into it.

"Perhaps I should come back later."

She crunched the crisps two or three times and swallowed the whole mouthful with a single gulp.

"I'll help you. I'm Modesta White, the new assistant. Sit down." She nodded towards a khaki painted tubular steel chair with a riveted canvas seat which confronted her desk, and pulled open another packet of crisps.

Peter had expected a gentler baptism to the rite of being introduced to the opposite sex, but he did as he was bid. He always did as he was bid, whether gentle or not. He crossed the floor softly until he reached Modesta's working zone, then his feet crunched through a space carpeted with discarded cigarette ends and biscuit crumbs.

He unzipped his quietly toned anorak and was about to remove it; but Modesta's emasculating gaze inhibited him, so he sat down obediently.

"Thank you, Miss White."

"It's Mzzz White."

Peter's awkwardness was already in surplus, without the struggle to articulate a vowelless word, so he smiled and nodded.

"Well?" she asked in a voice as silky as carborundum.

"I'd like to join your agency."

On top of the desk rested a large plastic container in the form of Pooh Bear, filled with pens and pencils; but she ignored it and pulled from under a celebrity magazine her personalised pen in the shape and colour of an erect penis.

"Name?" she asked, sliding an application form from the pile at her left.

"Peter James Goodwin."

As Ms White lowered her face to write, Peter saw the full effect of her hairstyle. Above each ear a perfectly parallel swath had been shaved bare, and her remaining hair, dyed the colour and tone of traditional blue-black ink, seemed to have been flattened with used sump-oil, and then pulled out into spikes like the outer shell of a chestnut. Her head bobbed as she wrote, and Peter was reminded of old wartime films of naval contact mines floating in the ocean. He instinctively drew back in his seat, as if worried that her head might explode if touched, and then earnestly tried to adjust his eye to a trendy image of beauty.

"Address?"

"Thirty-six Brunel Terrace, Plumham, London. I can't remember the postcode exactly. It's something like –"

"Sex?" interrupted Modesta, looking over Peter as if in doubt.

"Male," replied Peter uncomfortably.

"You're the first one who hasn't given me a filthy answer to that question."

"I don't make jokes very often."

Modesta cast a critical eye over Peter's forlorn figure. "I can believe that." Her frost pushed his April heart back into January. "Age?"

"Fifty-eight."

"Telephone number?"

"Actually, I'm not really on the phone."

"What do you mean 'not really'? Either you're on it or you're not."

"I'm not."

"Then how do you expect our clients to get in touch with you?" That handicap he'd not considered. While he tried to think of a solution, Modesta unearthed her tolerance and placidly spread her left hand to repair the black lacquer on her fingernails, slightly worn from frequent scratching of an untreated syphilitic condition.

"I'm not sure," said Peter at length. "Perhaps they could leave messages with you."

"Perhaps," shrugged Modesta, waggling her fingers dry. "Colour of hair?"

"It used to be dark, but there isn't much left now. Some of it is still dark, but most is a sort of greyish colour. If I call it 'silver', does that sound attractive?"

"Male pattern baldness," said and wrote Modesta, dismissing Peter's suggested euphemism.

"Classical hairline is that Mrs Jessop calls it."

"Who's Mrs Jessop?"

"The lady who lives next door to me."

"She's a traitor to her sex."

Peter did not understand that judgement, but decided not to mention any friends again in case their treachery debarred his membership.

"Height?"

"Five feet ten inches."

Modesta was now finding it difficult to conceal her despise for the limp brute she saw in front of her.

"You're going to find it hard enough to find a partner, without making yourself an imperialist reactionary as well. We're all Europeans now." She prodded some buttons on a calculator. "One metre, seven hundred and seventy-eight millimetres. Sexual orientation?"

Peter hesitated, pondered and looked about him. At his left hung a large print of Millais's *Hearts Are Trumps*, faded at one side by the sun's trespass and unsympathetically framed in bevelled ramin. The painted image of three Victorian sisters, demure yet engaging in their chaste pink and grey satins, restored his wilting icon of femininity, and he found the nerve to look back at Modesta.

"Er, what does that mean?" he asked eventually.

"Do you want us to find you a man or a woman?"

"Oh, I see. Well, a lady of course."

"Why 'of course'? Are you homophobic?"

"Well, no, I'm not. I just, sort of, like ladies."

"You're not going to help yourself by using the language of conservative male oppression. We're not ladies, we're women."

She had plucked another feather from Peter's wing of understanding. Had his mother's intuition been wrong all those years when he had dutifully raised his school cap and surrendered his seat on a bus? If the *Titanic* sank today, who would leave the ship first? Had ladies never existed? A gramophone record in his mother's hoard declared one to be a tramp; another coaxed a lady to be good. Until the little black silhouette figures appeared, toilet doors had admitted them. Even the Plumham Working Men's Club had, for many years, considerately displayed a notice 'Ladies Not Permitted Unless Accompanied by a Man'.

As Modesta wrote 'heterosexual' on the form she asked, "Been married before?"

"No."

"Have you had a lot of sexual partners during your life? Or only a few?"

Peter recalled his one previous attempt at sexual union, many years earlier. Buoyed up by fine weather, a pleasant meal and a small wage rise, he had approached a street walker, who eyed his neatly pressed but aging suit, his outdated starched shirt collar, and said, "I don't take luncheon vouchers.' He then raised his hat, left her, and never tried again."

"Well, actually, I haven't had any."

"Are you telling me that you're still a virgin?"

The canvas seat of Peter's chair had been asymmetrically stretched by battalions of overweight bottoms, and now offered restricted comfort to only one buttock at a time, while the tubular steel frame bit into the other. For most people, frequent fidgets were essential. Peter's endurance levels had been enhanced by self-consciousness, but even he now found it necessary to rearrange himself as his left leg went numb.

"I suppose I am."

The fact that Peter 'supposed' rather than knew infuriated Modesta, and the tightening grip and rising temperature of her right hand inflicted a mild dose of Peyronei's disease into the plastic tubing of her personalised pen.

"Why are you looking for a partner now, at your age? What stopped you before?"

"I spent most of my life looking after my mother. She died recently."

"Why didn't your father take care of her?"

"I never knew my father."

"You mean, you're a love child?" For the first time she seemed to take an interest in him.

"No. I'm legitimate."

"So, your father ran off and left your mother to cope with you alone. Typical male!"

"It wasn't like that. He was sent aboard, on military service."

"Oh, I see. I suppose he joined up because he enjoyed killing and raping."

The piano of his passion had an outsize muting pedal, but none for the liberty of forte. A cloud of purple anger enveloped Peter's brain. His mother had lovingly sculpted his father's remembrance as the world's kindest man. Peter still clung to the remnants of the father he'd never known: a few treasured photographs; his apprenticeship certificate; a school prize he'd won; the tie he'd worn on his wedding day. Never had Peter understood how anyone could want to murder another, until that moment. His fingers dug deeply into the palms of his hands; then he slowly started to unwrap them as he looked towards Modesta's neck to estimate its size. His blood vessels screeched with irritation, the room looked clouded and clear at the same time, frozen fire covered his skin, black sound filled his ears, the fierce intakes of air scratched his dried mouth.

Then, as if soothed by the spirit of his father's tender hand, Peter's brain dialled its own emergency service, a cerebral black disc started spinning at an obedient seventy-eight revolutions per minute, and the voices of Bing Crosby and the Andrews Sisters came to his rescue as they urged him to:

'Ac-cen-tu-ate the pos-it-ive...'

Peter looked at Modesta's eyes until the contemptuous blue weakened, and he spoke in a calm, measured voice.

"He wasn't a professional. He was conscripted. Just a civilian in uniform. And he was killed on the day that I was born."

The profundity and assurance of what he'd said left Peter in a void of astonishment. For the first time with Modesta, perhaps for the first time in his root-bound life, he sensed ascendancy. She too was temporarily stunned. He had derailed her train of conceit. Each sat for a while cocooned in quietness. Peter broke the silence.

"The truth is, I feel lonely."

Modesta's dented arrogance swiftly straightened itself, and she returned her attention to the application form.

"Taste in music?"

"Actually, I rather like Dick Haymes."

"What's that?"

"The name of a singer."

"What sort of music? Is he like Garage? Like Handbag? Like Indie?"

"I don't know much about music. He's someone that my mother used to like."

"I asked about music, not boredom."

"Pardon?"

"Never mind." She wrote 'Not applicable' in that space, and passed to the next section on the form.

"Profession or occupation?"

"I've had several. Mum didn't have much money, so I had to leave school early. I had a nice steady job in a factory, but the factory closed down. So I became a bus conductor, but then bus conductors were scrapped. After that I got a job in an office."

"And that's what you do now?"

"Unfortunately, that firm did a thing called rationalisation. Lots of people lost their jobs, including me."

"So now you're out of work?"

"That's right."

Modesta's left hand was raring to write 'pathetic wimp', but her right hand was bridled by the need to earn money to support her drug habit, so she reluctantly entered 'varied and interesting career, now seeking employment' on the form. That morsel of fawning hypocrisy filled her momentarily with self-loathing, and she looked back at the man who'd caused her ethical downfall with a sneer which curled her lower lip and lifted the chunk of metal that pierced her left nostril.

Peter noticed her disdain, assumed that she might suspect him of being a fortune hunter, and so he swiftly explained.

"But I've got some money saved. I can pay my way. Well, up to a point." The final remark was added for security. He, in turn, didn't want to attract the avaricious. What he didn't disclose was that his nest egg was by no means small. An early life of involuntary scrimping had schooled his prudence; love for a parent without money had inspired him to respect it and treasure it. By humbly avoiding the vicious treadmill of trendiness, by meekly abstaining from the epicurean and bacchanalian delights, he had stretched his meagre income into an abnormally roomy piggy-bank. Unlike most of his generation, he had saved all his life for a sunny day; but the sun had yet to break through.

"What do you do in your spare time?"

Peter thought for a while.

"Do you go pubbing and clubbing? We've got lots of girls on our books who like to go pubbing and clubbing."

"What's clubbing?"

"It means going to clubs, of course."

"What kind of clubs? Golf clubs? Cycling clubs?"

"Of course not. Proper clubs. Where you do this." She rose from her chair and started to punch the air viciously. For the first and only time during Peter's visit her eyelids lifted above their droop of boredom and her mouth's line of scorn fractured into a wild and frenzied smile.

"Boxing clubs? Oh no, I don't do that. I don't like the idea of hurting anyone."

"Not boxing clubs, dummy. It's dancing, isn't it?"

"Dancing? No, sorry, I can't dance. My mum and dad used to. Quite a lot."

She stopped assaulting the air, resumed her seat and eyed the worthless Peter slowly.

"No, I don't suppose you do. So, what do you do?"

She pushed back her chair, and Peter noticed how the lower hems of her camouflaged combat trousers rested, rather incongruously, on gilded stiletto heeled shoes.

"Well, I'm –"

"We don't want to hear about stamp collecting or building model railways. They're not going to turn anyone on."

"I suppose that –"

"Forget about pigeon fancying and plane spotting. Tell me something cool."

"Do you think that –"

"And nobody will want to know that you like to dangle hooks in the water to torture fish with. Perverts aren't in fashion just now."

Peter sat silently for a while. He was going to mention photography and family history, but now wasn't sure what reception they'd get. Modesta lost patience.

"Look, go away for a while, and try to think up something interesting. Something impressive."

"All right," agreed Peter, not altogether sorry that the interview was over. "Thank you for your assistance. Goodbye for now."

Modesta didn't return his thanks, so he made his way to the door and closed it quietly behind him.

"Fucking wanker," said Modesta, in a voice just loud enough to penetrate the closed door.

"That's an oxymoron." Modesta turned swiftly to see Angela, the proprietor, who had returned quietly via the rear stairway.

"How long have you been there?"

"Long enough." Angela stood, with arms akimbo, her Marks and Spencer cardigan stretched over a more than classical bosom, her kindly brown eyes annealed to agate. "Why did you talk to him like that?"

"He's a rat."

"A mouse maybe, but not a rat. You shouldn't treat a lifelong bachelor that way."

"He's not a bachelor. He's a male spinster."

"That's spiteful bunk. And even if it wasn't, you don't handle a client that way."

"He's a wimp! He's a chauvinist pig!"

"And you're unsuitable for this job," asserted Angela, ignoring Modesta's self-contradiction.

"I can't help it if I'm a deprived orphan," Modesta scowled, and the metal through her nose drooped.

"You lying, spoiled brat. Your father is a successful solicitor and your mother is a music teacher. I've just had lunch with someone who knows you; your last employer."

Modesta started to snarl, her drawn back lips revealing eye teeth that had been filed to points, but carefully capped and finished by one of London's most exclusive dental surgeons.

"You're a nosy, interfering old bag."

"And you're fired. Go, and take your ugly political correctness with you."

Angela suddenly remembered Peter, and hurried towards the door to rescue him, leaving behind a faint trail of perfume that was soft blue, with quiet pink overtones. Her sensible shoes descended the stairs as quickly as her bouncing bosom allowed.

"You poxy old cow! You frustrated old dyke! You're jealous of me because you're not getting any cock," Modesta shrieked from the top of the stairs.

"Bollocks!" shouted back Angela, astonishing herself with a word that had never passed her lips before, and had only abided in the mouths of builders whose ill-fitting trousers exposed their bottoms.

Angela reached the street, but could not see Peter. She guessed that he had turned left, towards the centre of Plumham, and sped after him, anxious to draw out the shard of rancour that Modesta had driven into his crumbling confidence.

Peter, unfortunately, had gone in the opposite direction, in a brown haze of bewilderment. Anaesthetised with failure, his empty soul dragged a wet rag of hope behind him, and he vacantly turned into a side street that was new to him. There, he edged carefully along a narrow pavement past a man kneeling to repaint a pillar box. Post boxes he had always liked. They seemed solid, dependable, paternal, friendly, ready to accept letters without complaint. His childhood friends hadn't liked them; they thought that ghouls lurked inside waiting to grab their hands if they tried to post letters. But Peter felt otherwise; he'd have hugged them if he hadn't been so self-conscious.

He saw the man's brush smooth paint across the Royal Cypher cast into the bowed metal door, persuading the scarlet coating into its outline. Then he noticed the emblem's form; it was the insignia of a fleeting monarch razed by a divorced American. A connoisseur of pillar boxes might have been captivated by its rarity, but for Peter it had blurred intimacy. He had a hazy recollection of King Edward the Eighth being somehow significant to his family's history. It was an omen; for good or bad he did not know, but it braced his resolve. He was not going to abdicate.

Chapter Two

"Paper, paper. Read all abaht it. *News; Star; Standard.* Paper." The news-vendor's threadbare voice penetrated the December evening fog of Plumham High Street, coaxed by lungs limp from forty years of London life, twenty years of cheap tobacco and three distant years of trench warfare. As the voice's owner loomed into view, Christopher Goodwin took a penny from his pocket and thrust it into a hand vinegared by dearth.

"Ta, Guv," responded the vendor, peeling a newspaper deftly from the bundle under his left arm, and moved his head aside to discharge a round of thick yellow sputum over his right shoulder into the gutter.

Christopher was surprised. Men of that age usually called him 'lad' or 'son'; but 'Guv' was definitely new. Having grown appreciably taller than his father and elder brother, he could no longer be dressed in hand-me-downs, so for his eighteenth birthday his mother had taken him to the Plumham branch of Fifty Shilling Tailors and bought him his first suit; quietly and modestly handsome in clerical-grey herringbone. This evening he wore it for the first time, with his only white shirt and a carefully pressed tie; and its aura of maturity clad him with much needed assurance as he apprehensively stepped towards his first encounter with the Plumham *Palais de Danse.*

He walked across the remains of a pavement artist's chalked gallery, between the aluminium studs of the newly installed Belisha crossing, mounted the double kerb at the other side of the High Street, and made his way to the tram stop.

Most of the shops were still open. Few closed before eight o'clock even on a Thursday night, and their affable window lighting gave cheer to a pavement forsaken by the fog-veiled street lamps. The grey-green murk around the tram stop was softened by the glow from a tobacconist's shop, and Christopher looked into its elderly bow window at an extensive display of pipes. Not seeing what he wanted, he pushed open the shop door, which had been scumbled and grained by a craftsman into an authentic semblance of English oak, and entered the warm and spectacularly neat interior.

At one side of the shop's crimson carpet stood a small scale colonnade of herma, each crowned with a turned thuya bowl of loose tobacco: Old English Spun; Colonial Curly Cut; Old Crusted; Honey Dew; De Luxe Empire Flake; their gentle fragrances radiating a welcome balm for the clammy corruption of London fog. Behind them rested an impressive display of Havana cigars: Don Pepin, Hoyo de Monterrey, Ramon Allones, Romeo y Julieta; the romantic artwork of the labels on their boxes defaced by excise duty stamps.

Christopher glanced across the glazed tops of three cigar display cases, with their regimented ranks of coronas, cheroots, manilas, Jamaicas and Burmahs, to where Mr Mubby, the short and balding proprietor, stood and smiled from behind his counter.

"I'm afraid that I'm only a beginner," confessed Christopher, as he looked over the bewildering tiers of cigarette boxes that covered the longest wall of the shop.

"Then you're in the right place, sir. I'll be delighted to help and advise, in any way I can." And that was no empty promise. Mr Mubby's commercial philosophy was simple: help a novice as much as possible, and there's a customer for life. He'd built his reputation and his business on it, and it gave him the chance to air his lifetime's store of tobacco knowledge.

"I'd like a packet of cigarettes, please, but I don't know what type."

Mr Mubby's diplomacy gagged his primary conviction that cigarette smoking was effeminate. His veiled strategy was to secure a customer, and then gradually wean him into smoking manliness. He noticed that Christopher's eyes were scanning the shelves at the far left.

"Those are Turkish, sir. Abdulla, Sultan, Brutus, Ghiree, Khremona. Popular with the ladies, sir; and certain theatrical gentlemen." The intimation of the final remark was not lost on Christopher, so his eyes travelled to the next section.

"There we have Egyptian cigarettes, sir: Salonica, Dimitrind, Kyriazi Freres. Poets, and women with short hair who wear trousers, usually smoke those." Mr Mubby felt it his duty to add sociological guidance when navigating newcomers around the complex world of tobacco. He thought it was time well spent, and he continued the rundown of his immaculately stocked shelving.

"Here are American brands: Lucky Strike, Chesterfield, Camel. But one needs to be a frightful show-off to use those." Mr Mubby ran an eye over Christopher's quiet suit. "I don't think they're really you, sir. Then there are the French: Gauloises, Elegantes, Boyards. They're smoked by arty types and revolutionaries who need a haircut." My Mubby extended his tour through Russian, Brazilian, Cuban and Balkan varieties, and Christopher began to feel embarrassed at the amount of the tobacconist's time he was taking. He had only budgeted to spend sixpence on cigarettes, but his mentor's attentive civility made him feel obliged to be more lavish.

"To be practical, sir," continued the tobacconist, "I rather feel that a domestic brand might favour one who is poised on the threshold of discovery. What did sir have in mind? A box of twenty-five or fifty?"

"Actually, I only wanted a packet of ten."

"Well, sir, the popular ones start at sixpence, and they include Player's, Goldflake, Capstan, Astorias and Kensitas." Christopher was cheerfully surprised to find that the tobacconist seemed in no way vexed by the humbleness of his needs. Mr Mubby's unchanged tone not only remained pleasantly helpful, but he continued to call him 'sir'. It was a fine start to the evening. Christopher felt that adulthood really had arrived.

"What about a slightly better quality?" Christopher asked, wondering if the tobacconist's 'popular' should be interpreted as 'common'.

"Certainly, sir. We have Three Castles at eight pence, Garrick at nine pence, Du Maurier at seven pence."

'Du Maurier' grabbed Christopher's imagination. The name seemed exciting yet safe. The sophistication of an exotic sounding name for only an extra penny was a bargain, and he handed over his seven pence and pocketed the cigarettes, departing the shop with a gush of thanks for the tobacconist's help. Mr Mubby was also delighted. He thought that he now had another fledgling smoker whom he could nurture into finesse; but the future would disappoint him. That customer would never again buy any tobacco goods, from him or anybody else.

Christopher now stood at the tram stop with reinforcement in each jacket pocket; the slick nonchalance of a cigarette to cloak his gaucherie; and a newspaper to unfold and hide behind should awkwardness become critical. He was fully insured for the evening ahead.

The street brought Christopher's consoled nostrils back to a sulphate reality. The fog's status mantle forcefully imprisoned London's traditional stench of horse dung, now challenged by the odour of inefficiently burned petrol, to which it added its own acrid smell of sulphur dioxide. But it could have been worse. Had the tram stop been two hundred yards to the west, it would have been within smelling range of the tannery, where leather was still steeped in animal excrement for a month before being processed.

Christopher peered into the ochred blackness, which had thickened considerably, and the road's centre was now lost. Most of the traffic could only be heard, and what was visible had only evanescent outlines. His eyes tried to focus on the fugitive silhouettes, but could only discern a sandwich board man who dutifully trudged by in the gutter, intent on earning his five-shilling fee, even though nobody could now read his placards.

Ears instead of eyes seemed the solution, and he listened intently for the distinctive whine and clatter of an approaching tramcar, but the fog was a masterly illusionist. Sharp sounds were muffled: familiar ones disappeared. The thunder of passing trains on the nearby overhead bridge was reduced to a cough; the rattle of shunted couplings from the neighbouring marshalling yards vanished altogether. The newsvendor's congested lungs could no longer contact this side of the street, neither could the costermongers' yells from the market place; although the high pitched voice of a street preacher still managed to reach many of Plumham's sinners to reassure them of their place in hell.

But disappearance wasn't the only trick up Fog's misty sleeves; it could exaggerate as well. Small, personal, insignificant sounds, usually crushed under the weight of London's clamour, were now reborn with an uncanny sovereignty. The creak of a baker's basket; the squeaking instep of a new shoe; the scrape of a red-topped match along its abrasive sided box as a man paused to relight his fog-mist pipe. While the harsh shriek of a locomotive's steam whistle became a whisper on the lips of the night, so the murk echoed to the rhythmic slapping of a skipping rope against the pavement while its owner chanted:

"Salt, mustard, vinegar, pepper.
Salt, mustard, vinegar, pepper."

Christopher stood alone at the tram stop in a world of fading footsteps, surreally isolated from other flesh, eerily cut off from other souls. Adulthood could be a lonely business, and he began to shiver.

He should have worn his overcoat that night, but it was now three inches short in the sleeves and its tattiness would spoil the appearance of his new suit. Even a scarf and hat would have improved his comfort, but he was not sure if the dance hall charged for cloakroom use, and he'd already exceeded his budget by a penny that evening. He could have gone home and tried again another day, but Thursday suited his slender resources. On that night they only charged a shilling for admission. On other evenings it was raised to one and sixpence, and two shillings at weekends. What's more, Christmas and New Year were approaching, and prices were always raised over that period. His salad days lacked mayonnaise, and couldn't wait until prices went down again.

Although he was in his final year of apprenticeship to Durham and Company, Plumham's premier firm of toolmakers, Christopher's wages were still meagre, and most of the money he surrendered to his mother for her housekeeping. Not that he begrudged it; his parents were kindly and caring, but they were also hard pressed. His father's income as accounts clerk with the local co-operative society was frugal. Although the family were grateful for the job's security when many of their friends joined the dole queue during the darkest years of depression, the gap between want and supply always needed bridging. Christopher's mother had managed that for the early years, toiling over her ancient treadle sewing machine with alterations, repairs and dressmaking commissions for neighbours; but then cataracts started to form over her eyes, and she could no longer cope with close work. It had been a devastating blow to the family's hopes. Christopher had been the only boy in their street to pass the grammar school's entrance examination. He'd shown promise there, and his proud parents had dreamed of the day that he might be a doctor, a solicitor, an architect. Then fate had shown her ugly hand, and he'd been withdrawn, to his headmaster's dismay, to find work at the age of fourteen.

Now, with a tiny amount of copper and silver in his pocket, he waited with benumbed patience for a new chapter to begin. As disembodied voices floated by at one side and unseen traffic crawled past on the other, his teeth began to chatter. He was trying to revive his flagging circulation by thumping his arms about himself, when he thought he heard a welcome sound. He strained his ears, and there was the unmistakable discord of an approaching tram; the rumble of bogies on rail joints, the scrape of a plough in its conduit slot, the creak of an ash frame.

The tram halted just short of where he stood, its only visible token being the firefly twinkle of the back-lit glass studs in its destination number; and Christopher ventured into the road vigorously waving his white handkerchief. The nearside inching traffic was headed by two cyclists who fortunately saw him, and adjourned what little progress they were making.

As its single headlamp came into view, Christopher realised that he'd approached the wrong end of the tram. It was an old car, originally built for the Plumham and District Electric Tramway Company, now repainted in London Transport's red and cream livery, but yet to be refitted, which meant that the driver's platform still had no windscreen. The driver looked down at Christopher with an amused twinkle in his eyes, the only part of his frozen body that was visible behind a high-buttoned greatcoat, and two scarves and a balaclava helmet under his official peaked cap. Christopher smiled back, thankful that he wasn't the coldest person in the world, ran the length of the tramcar and mounted its rear platform.

He intended to climb to the upper deck to practise smoking his first cigarette, and had one foot on the iron tread of the spiral staircase when he remembered that these old cars still had upper seats of slatted wood, which could have creased his fog-dampened suit, so he passed through the mahogany bulkhead door into the upholstered safety of the lower saloon.

The front seats seemed to hold the best prospect for spotting landmarks, as the view through the side windows had resigned; so Christopher sat in one and stared through the glazing of the front bulkhead. There the driver stood, feet apart, skilful determination pouring from his chilled hands into the two massive polished brass control handles as he coaxed his burden through a wall of blackness; but beyond the dashboard there was nothing to be seen.

The tram lurched forward at the pace of an arthritic tortoise, the aged twin motors complaining fitfully. Christopher bowed to the certainty that he'd be there for some time, and took a bundle of pencilled notes from an inner pocket to revise his dance steps. His ballroom dancing tuition had been patchy. Workmates had given occasional demonstrations of basic steps, but their advice hadn't seemed altogether reliable. An advertisement for Madame Rose's 'celebrated' dance academy then caught his eye, and he'd spent a precious half-crown on an hour's individual instruction. The academic location turned out to be the parlour of Madame Rose's Victorian cottage, equipped with a wind-up gramophone and a few fatigued records; but her teaching had been effective, even though she smelled of gin.

Spare half-crowns, however, were not plentiful in the Goodwin household, so Christopher then got a book from Plumham's public library, borrowed his young sister's hopscotch chalk, marked out the foot positions on the linoleum covering of his bedroom floor, and practised alone; taking care to polish away the chalk after each session. His mother's diminishing eyesight probably wouldn't have noticed it, but he respected her pride, sympathised with her affliction, and loved her motherliness.

The 'ting' of the approaching conductor's ticket punch disturbed his studies. The displayed fare table told him that his journey would cost two pence-halfpenny in each direction, but he decided to speculate an extra penny and bought a sixpenny all-evening ticket. Before the night was out, that would prove to be a sound investment.

He again peered past the driver in his unsheltered hardship, but still saw only a swirling void. Although the vents were closed, fog had seeped into the unheated saloon, and clung close to the ceiling, obscuring the 'No Spitting: Penalty £5' notice written in varnish-gilt on a cross-member. Christopher pulled his jacket closer around him and resumed his learning.

From the library book he'd copied some basic steps for the waltz and quickstep only, hoping that they'd see him through the evening. Forward right foot, sideways onto toes with left foot starting turn, close toes of right to left continuing to turn, back and side with left lowering heel, back right starting to turn left, sideways onto toes of left foot continuing turn, close toes of right to left, sideways with left lowering heel: then repeat. He was fairly sure that he'd mastered the quickstep chassé, so he put that page to the bottom of the bundle. On the next sheet he'd written the sequence of the lock-step, but he'd always got in a muddle over that one, even under Madame Rose's watchful eye, so he put that page back in his pocket. Embarrassment came to him all too easily: there was no point in giving it an open invitation. Instead, he spent some while concentrating on a natural turn, a spin turn and a reverse turn before moving to his waltz pages. Counting a slow one – two – three in his mind, he tried to visualise a natural turn, then moved to a right closed change, and was about to revise the reverse turn when he realised that the tram's motor speed had increased.

Through the side windows he could now see the pavement, and the fog continued to lift even as he watched it. As the tram gathered speed the joints of its elderly wooden frame creaked. Down Plumham Hill it went faster still, its jaded motors grateful for the co-operation of gravity, and its speed set the car into a pitching motion like a giant rocking horse. At the bottom of the hill the road snaked around the public lavatories, and the tram tore through the chicane adding sideways heave to its composite motion. The Odeon Cinema, a gaudy amusement arcade, the police station, Lyons's restaurant, three pawnbrokers and countless shops blazed past until the squeal of magnetic brakes and the scrunch of a slipper brake on the track brought the tramcar to a shuddering halt; and there, in all its glittering glory, was his palatial destination.

"Who's for the hop?" sang out the conductor, and Christopher alighted happy, but still cold.

In the foyer, he approached the ticket office, where sat a time-worn woman who displayed peroxided hair, heavy make-up and too much wrinkled cleavage. She continued to count change from bankers' bags into her till as he waited.

"We don't open for another 'alf hour, love," she cautioned, then glanced at Christopher's grey pallor and shivering body, and sympathy rose in her bosom, in spite of its exposure.

"Here, Bert. Let this poor bugger in; he's frozen solid," she called over her shoulder to a uniformed doorman, as she accepted the proffered shilling and surrendered a ticket.

Christopher walked past the cloakroom, bar entrance, balcony stairs and into the main hall, where he crossed the sprung, polished hardwood floor, freshly dusted with French chalk, and sat on a gilded chair with maroon upholstery close to the bandstand. He looked about him with a mixture of awe and elation. Similar feelings welled up in him when he visited luxurious cinemas, but here the mood of opulence was exhilarating. Ornamental pilasters carried crystal wall lights and supported a faux marble entablature; the neo-Rococo walls had apple-green grounding, inset with dusky pink panels outlined by gilt mouldings, but sullenly interrupted with red fire extinguishers.

The ceiling had extensive plaster ornamentation, two elaborate chandeliers and the ubiquitous mirror-ball. Spotlights were schematically hung to accent decorative features, the most powerful being aimed at the bandstand. The sumptuous surroundings raised his self-esteem slightly above its nervous base. As he looked about him he started to absorb some of the glamour, and then realised that he was not alone. On the stage sat a musician, looking even more tense than Christopher as he improved the symmetry of his alto saxophone's reed by gently scraping it with a razor blade.

Ted Hooper had reached a crisis in his musical life. For some while he had been the linchpin of the saxophone section, his sensitive lips having developed an embouchure which gave a full and sweet tone throughout the instrument's range, and was the essence of the honeyed voice of a three-alto and one-tenor line-up. He was able to achieve an impressively smooth lip glissando, could use unorthodox fingerings for creative densities and, when improvising, he was at vogue's leading edge: he could swing. In all, he was an outstanding semi-professional, and would have turned to music as a full-time job had not four hungry mouths at home dissuaded him from taking chances. Now, though, he faced turmoil.

As with many of his generation, poor diet during childhood in the Great War and his parents' inability to afford toothpaste had been the authors of premature tooth decay. He had clung to his rotting teeth for as long as possible, but extensive pyorrhoea had loosened them to the point that he could no longer control the pressure on a mouthpiece. A succession of guest celebrity bands had played the *Palais* for the past week, and Ted had taken the opportunity to have all his teeth extracted. Now, ill-fitting temporary dentures lurched over sore and rapidly shrinking gums, and he was dreading their first trial that evening.

A group of six teenaged girls entered ahead of time and took seats at the far end of the hall. They all seemed to stare at Christopher, who tried at first to ignore them, but then self-consciousness got the better of him and he again took out his dance notes to study them.

Ted, having finished smoothing his reed, took a cigarette lighter from his pocket and carefully warmed and expanded the cork on the crook of his saxophone before pushing the mouthpiece home. Then he turned to his personal needs. He was slightly annoyed by the early arrivals in the hall, so he took cover behind the open lid of the grand piano to parget a fixative cement over the pink plates of his dentures before pushing them firmly into place, and then practised biting on two fingers to check their underpinning.

The girls now seemed to find Christopher a figure of fun; looking at him continually while whispering to each other and giggling. He glanced over his clothing to see if anything was improper, but their amusement puzzled and embarrassed him, so he furtively changed his seat to another, behind a plaster Corinthian column, where he escaped their view. He looked over his pencilled notes for a while, but then other musicians started to arrive, and he watched their preparations with fascination.

Most of the band kept their overcoats and hats on while they unpacked and thawed out. The bassist slid the canvas cover from his instrument, extended its steel spike, and then crossed to the piano where, with a cigarette dangling from his lower lip, he dabbed a few keys and manipulated the pegs of the bass to tune its strings. The trumpet player inserted the mouthpiece and slapped it home with the palm of his hand, producing a plopping noise from the trumpet's bell; and the drummer, having assembled his kit, inserted a sixpence into the slotted ends of the tensioning rods of his snare drum and tried to coax the fog out of the taut vellum.

The trombonist's priorities were different. He had a prodigious thirst that could not wait for the interval, so he firstly smuggled in a quart bottle of brown ale and a glass, which he hid behind his music desk. As the other saxophonists arrived, the mutilated Ted negotiated with them and relegated himself from first to third alto.

Suddenly, the main doors of the hall swung open, and a river of brilliantined heads and swirling skirts swept in. The lady with the exhibited bosom had opened the floodgates; the musicians hastily removed their overcoats, threw them out of sight behind the wings, and took their seats, Ted pushing three fingers against his top plate as a final precaution.

The pianist gave a quiet count, the band played an introductory chord, and from the wings strode Grant Sinclair, whose real name was Cedric Mudge, with arms outstretched, clarinet in hand, resplendent in white tie and tails to trump the rest of the dinner-jacketed band. At centre stage he bowed to acknowledge applause that was disappointingly restrained, and began to shovel charm into the microphone.

"Ladies and gentlemen of Plumham, thank you for your gracious greeting, and welcome to the dancing centre of the universe. This evening, yours truly, Grant Sinclair, and his talented orchestra will lift your feet and carry you on a rhythmic journey of rapture and delight. As always, we'll start the evening with a swing, so take your partners for the first quickstep as we bring you, all the way from the United States of America, Benny Goodman's hit, 'Stomping at the Savoy'."

The pianist played a four bar introduction and the band then riffed its way through the first chorus, the rearranged saxophones sadly lacking Ted's robust lead. The bandleader took, as usual, the clarinet solo spot, a habit previously resented by Ted, whose technique was superior even though it was his secondary instrument. Tonight however, for the first time, Ted was grateful that his clarinet remained on its stand peg.

The number ended to polite applause from the dancers, and Christopher realised that he'd been so captivated by the experience of live music that he'd forgotten to get up from his chair. Previously he had sampled an amateur brass band in the local park, and an organ at the cinema; but after Madame Rose's scratched and faded records, this rousing and warm sensation left him stimulated. He now felt ready to plunge into the world of dancing.

"We'd like you to continue now with another quickstep; but first, ladies and gentlemen, will you welcome the lovely, the talented, the wonderful – Carmita!"

Carmita, whose birth certificate claimed her name to be Cynthia Stebbings, entered from the right, her silver dress revealing an even greater expanse of cleavage than that shown by the ticket office woman, which explained why she received more applause than the bandleader had got. Christopher watched the band play the first chorus, and then got to his feet as Carmita started her vocal refrain:

"Some-body-y loves me, I won-der who…"

Most of the dancers had stayed on the floor after the first quickstep, and the girls who remained at the sides mostly stood in small, closely knit cliques, talking to each other. Christopher slowly approached one group, but none turned to look at him, so he passed them by.

Two girls stood together, and one of them accepted the invitation of a young man in a tweed suit, leaving the fair-haired girl in a pale blue dress standing alone. As Christopher drew near, she caught his eye and seemed amenable. He listened to the band, and suddenly thought that the tempo seemed fast; certainly faster than the quicksteps on Madame Rose's scratched records. Carmita continued asking George Gershwin's question about who loved her, and Christopher concentrated on its pulse.

He tried to remember his dancing notes and mentally fit the steps to the rhythm. Forward with left foot, starting to turn to right. No, that couldn't be correct. It must be right foot first turning to right. Then what? Was it forward left? Or sideways left?

He was now almost at her side, and her face wore a welcoming look, but at the last moment he panicked, passed her by, and eased himself behind a column to revise his pencilled pages. He surveyed the dancers on the floor from behind the column, thought he recognised their steps and mentally fitted them to the music's tempo.

By the time he emerged, a muted trumpet passage was over, and Carmita was starting a fourth chorus. She liked to show off the education she'd received at Plumham Central School, the only one in the borough where French was on the curriculum, and gave a proficient delivery of Gershwin's exotic "Quel-qu'un m'ai-me-ra…"

With renewed confidence he approached a rather plump girl with a large bow in her hair and thick spectacles.

"Would you care to dance?"

"My mum says I mustn't dance wiv nobody what I don't know, an' I don't know you."

The refusal sent Christopher around another group of disinterested girls, and he hurried past the spot where the gigglers had gathered, although he could no longer see them. Carmita concluded her French excursion, and the band remained with the same composer and at the same tempo for 'Oh, Lady Be Good!', Grant Sinclair now exercising his singing voice.

Christopher had circled almost half the hall by now, and he resolved to be courageous and try to make his approaches less hesitant. He asked an auburn-haired girl with freckles, who replied, rather abruptly, "No thank you."

A woman in her thirties with a cigarette in a long holder responded with, "Can't you see I'm smoking."

A girl with a short haircut and a long black gown shrugged; and the next one he moved towards turned her back and disappeared into the crowd as the bandleader sang, not inappropriately, about being "...aw'f'ly mis-un-der-stood..."

A girl in a pink cardigan had her back to Christopher. She turned on hearing his question, and there was one of the gigglers, who burst into tears on recognising him and fled into the ladies' cloakroom. The chain of rejections now began to erode his nerve, which was saved from further damage by the quickstep sequence closing. Although he was far from being vain, he nevertheless realised that he was not bad looking, and his lack of success puzzled and worried him. What he didn't twig was that the folded newspaper, which he'd brought for refuge, projected clumsily from his jacket pocket, giving him an eccentric appearance, and was conspicuous long before his wholesome looks were in focus.

A succession of foxtrots was announced, and as he knew nothing about that dance, Christopher thought that he'd reconnoitre the hall and watch the *modi operandi* of other men in the hope of finding the doorway to womanly acquiescence, or to gain insight into the social graces; or perhaps just to discover his own faults.

As he moved swiftly through the bystanders he wasn't lucky enough to be within earshot of any accepted invitation, so his skill with the spoken overture remained limp. He did, though, manage to study body language, but could see no common tactics in use by the successful. Some men looked straight at their target, some lowered their eyes, others looked to the side, as if disinterested, and two even closed their eyes. Gesticulations of heads, hands and arms were used by many; but the limbs of others remained inanimate. Some smiled politely, some grinned extravagantly, a few appeared grim, and the rest remained expressionless. Many raised their eyebrows, a few wrinkled their noses, and one seemed to waggle his ears.

Christopher's tour did confirm that he'd been right about one thing. Everywhere smokers used cigarettes, and pipes were nowhere to be seen, even though they still dominated in the street. His hunch had been nourished at the cinema. Females in films seemed to go for cigarette smokers. In American movies women inevitably fell for the man who coolly flicked a cigarette from a packet whilst pushing his trilby hat onto the back of his head with the other hand. He wondered if only cigarette smokers went dancing, or if pipe smokers changed their habit as they entered the dance hall. Whatever the answer, Mr Mubby would not have been pleased.

The foxtrots continued, and it seemed an unhappy omen that the melody played was the Gershwin brothers' 'But Not for Me'; the words cheerlessly hinting that 'songs of love' might not be for him.

As he passed a long wall mirror, he quickly glanced at his reflected face to see if anything was wrong. A pallid skin was epidemic among sun-starved Londoners. A quilt of smoke above a blanket of fog guaranteed that most remained ashen; and anaemic diets and tuberculosis bleached others still further. In earlier decades, that could sometimes be put to use. Budding Eliza Doolittles might accelerate their upward mobility by passing off their pastiness as a ladylike pallor; but times had changed. Parisiennes, led by Gabrielle Chanel, had made a suntan fashionable. Plumham's chic women now resorted to the use of toned face powder, and 'powdering one's nose' was no longer just a euphemism. But for men there was no remedy, unless, to use Mr Mubby's word, they turned 'theatrical'.

Christopher looked about him at other men's faces, and noticed that a moderate number of them now sported moustaches, with varying degrees of success. Since Clark Gable had captured cinema screens, reputedly making girls' hamstrings tremble, a number of Plumham's roving young men had hirsute upper lips. He asked himself if one might improve his chances, but it was a futile question. A moustache could not be grown in an hour.

The music ceased. The bandleader had noticed that the slow foxtrots had not been completely popular, decided to follow them with a set of waltzes, and quietly called the orchestration numbers to his resting musicians. Ted took the sheets from his music pad, noticed several sustained high notes, and disappeared behind the piano lid to apply another layer of mortar to his dentures.

Christopher was awkwardly placed in a corner of the hall when the slow waltzes were announced, and was astonished at the speed with which couples found each other and swept onto the floor. With determination he made a beeline for several girls, but other men beat him to it every time. The dance began, and he found himself almost alone on the perimeter. Frustratingly, some girls were dancing with each other, but he doubted the etiquette of intervening. Looking across the room, the only unoccupied female to be seen was the tubby girl with the bow in her hair who was still following maternal guidance and waiting for someone she knew to show up.

It became particularly disheartening as he watched the dancers. The band played at the tempo he was used to, and he was now certain that he could cope with the footwork of this dance. After the evening's promising start, the mood was now depressing. When he had confidence, either he could not find a partner, or he was bafflingly rejected.

At the close of the waltzes, Grant Sinclair proclaimed an 'old time interlude', and asked the people of Plumham to 'journey back with me, to a time of chivalry and serenity, and take your partners for a military two-step'. Few accepted his invitation. Christopher had never heard of such a dance, and drew back into the foyer, where he climbed the stair to the gallery with leaden feet. He needed to be alone; to watch from a distance; to gather his thoughts.

Once in the upper gallery he moved to the front, leaned on the brass rail and watched the dancers for a while. Quite a few older people were there. A number of them stayed for the whole evening, and were content to watch the dancing as entertainment.

After a while he retreated to a quiet spot at the rear, slumped into an armchair and tried to tidy his cluttered mind. He couldn't, so he took the London evening newspaper from his pocket and unfolded it. At the top of the front page a brief weather report read: 'Cold with local fog'. He couldn't argue with that. Immediately below it, in very bold type was the headline:

THE KING ABDICATES

In the hall below another batch of slow foxtrots had begun, and Carmita was singing Jerome Kern's 'Smoke Gets In Your Eyes'. As he sat, her narrative of true love, blind love, doubted love and departed love floated up to him, and he continued to read his paper.

This afternoon, to a hushed and tense House of Commons, the Prime Minister, Mr Baldwin, announced that King Edward VIII had signed the Instrument of Abdication at 10 a.m. that morning; in the presence of the Duke of York, the Duke of Kent and the Duke of Gloucester. A copy of the Instrument has been issued. It reads:

> *I, Edward the Eighth of Great Britain, Ireland and the British Dominions Beyond the Seas, King, Emperor of India, do hereby declare my irrevocable determination to renounce the Throne for myself and for my descendants...*

The band were now playing Vincent Youman's 'Time On My Hands', the arrangement featuring a fine legato solo by their thirsty trombonist, played muted at first and then open. As the expressive melody swam through Christopher's awareness, his eyes absorbed page after page of resignation.

Between the reported facts lay a string of opinions from those who claimed insight into the abdication. The outspoken George Bernard-Shaw alleged that the true reason for the King's departure was because he hated the job; and Gipsy Lee was said to have foretold the event in a prophecy made years earlier. Each page added melancholic torrents to a lake of low spirits; the Prime Minister's poignant speech, the heavy-hearted responses from across the world, the pensive comments of statesmen, dignitaries, celebrities and lesser mortals. A monarch who was said to have been the champion of the people, an advocate of modernity, a war veteran and the 'Empire's ambassador' had abandoned everything.

From the bandstand, the plaintive strains of Duke Ellington's 'In My Solitude' painted the atmosphere a dismal blue. Carmita's skill blended the ballad's pigments into a deep shade of sorrow, and as she sang about sitting in her chair being 'filled with despair' her intonation spread Christopher's chiaroscuro. It glazed his nerve ends and darkened his spirit. With abdication in his eyes, solitude in his ears, and a sense of failure in his soul, life had returned to being cold and foggy.

Perhaps he was too responsive, too impressionable, too sympathetic; but from somewhere in his unconscious a resistance movement was forming against the disheartening invader. Why despair? he asked himself. And almost at once the world seemed to answer back. The final columns of his newspaper carried details of a new king and a new queen, with two little princesses. From the floor below, the band broke into a lively tempo and through his octagonal microphone Mr Sinclair declared the world to be 'S'Wonderful'. It was time to go forth.

Christopher tossed his newspaper aside and descended the stairs two at a time. In the men's washroom he rinsed solitude from his face, combed abdication out of his hair, straightened his tie, brushed his jacket's lapels, polished the toecaps of his shoes down the backs of his trouser legs, and looked in the mirror with fresh resolution. This time he'd not give up.

He emerged just as the trombonist concluded one of his rare vocal spots: Jimmy McHugh's 'On The Sunny Side Of The Street'. He had a pleasant voice and a punchy delivery, but he didn't sing very often. He claimed it made him too thirsty.

As Christopher made his way down the side of the hall towards the bandstand, he saw a group of young men from his neighbourhood. Although they were a friendly bunch, he needed to avoid their company. None of them shared his critical financial state, and would probably ask him to join them in the bar for a drink during the interval. It was an embarrassment he wanted to avoid. For that reason he'd gone to the dance hall alone: almost all of his friends had some money to spare.

An about-turn took him again past the tearful giggler. This time she neither cried nor laughed, but kept her distance as he passed. The dance floor had now cleared, and Christopher eased his way through a substantial crowd at its edge. Most were chatting, in pairs or in groups; some with companions they'd arrived with, while others listened to new voices. It seemed that he was the only singleton left.

Before him a sizeable party of dancers left to go to the bar, and through a now clear path he noticed two girls whom he'd not seen before. Perhaps they were latecomers, or perhaps they had been continuously on the floor; but his attention was drawn by the dress which one of them wore. It was strikingly elegant, and at fashion's summit. Its fluid lines were sculpted from floral patterned imitation silk, the large fanciful pink leaves of the motif being veined with a hint of pale green and set against an indigo ground. The stylish mid-calf length, slightly lower at the back than the front, with godets let in below the knee, gave prominence to her slender figure; the skirt attached to the bodice by diagonal seams harmonised with her smoothly rounded hips; and softly pleated sleeves cut slantwise revealed tender arms.

A young man with crinkly red hair, whom the girls obviously knew, asked one for a dance, leaving the girl in the eye-catching dress standing alone. Another dance was announced, but Christopher didn't hear it; his mind was filled by the picture in front of him. As he moved towards her, men streamed by and whisked girls onto the floor; but miraculously she remained alone. As he got near, he wondered if she was an untouchable goddess, or perhaps a mirage that only he could see. Why hadn't anyone asked her to dance? He presently stood next to her, and she appeared to be flesh and blood; and mortal. Now he was there, it seemed discourteous not to ask her to dance, although he was prepared for certain disappointment. His mouth opened, but the words refused to emerge. Then, wondrously, she looked at him, smiled and nodded, and together they walked onto the floor.

Still close to the edge, they turned towards each other; he offered his left hand for the interlocking hold demonstrated by Madame Rose, and gingerly cupped her left shoulder blade with his right hand. The music started, he listened to its tempo, and then a calamitous thought struck him.

"Is this a foxtrot?" he stammered.

"Yes, it is."

"Oh dear."

"What is it?"

"I'm very sorry. I'm afraid I don't know how to dance a foxtrot." He expected her to march off, but she didn't; so he made a desperate suggestion. "If we dance a waltz, do you think that'll work?"

"No. It won't fit the music. Can you quickstep?"

"Sort of."

"Well, try those steps, but dance them slowly."

They clumsily danced the length of the hall, Christopher concentrating hard to transpose half-remembered steps into a slower rhythm, and then struggled through a semi-improvised turn to dance across the front of the bandstand. There, Grant Sinclair dazzled Plumham with his suavity by singing the latest hit 'These Foolish Things', and narrated a nostalgic list of airline tickets, telephones and a 'tinkling piano'.

"There, it's going well now, isn't it?" she encouraged. Actually, it wasn't going at all well, but her words added magic to Christopher's elation. Not only did he have a member of the opposite sex in his grasp for the first time, but she was attractive, considerate and helpful. He could hardly believe his fortune.

As they blundered down the third side of the hall, he got the uncomfortable feeling that he ought to be making conversation, but he had no idea what he should talk about. He laboured to think of something congenial, but most of his mind was taken up with trying to remember his dance steps, so he just blurted out his most recent memory.

"Did you know that the King has abdicated?"

"Yes, I heard it on the wireless before I left home," she replied, and then threw back her head and laughed joyously.

"What's funny about a king abdicating?"

"Nothing, really. But it's a very original way to open a conversation. It makes a change from hearing 'Do you come here often'?" He saw the humour and laughed too; which was good. It relaxed him a little, and took some of the stiffness out of his legs; but the dress she wore convinced him that he was dancing with one who was very affluent, and he couldn't lose much of his tension.

The bandleader liked the song he was singing and, after a piano solo, started on the rarely sung second verse, extending his mementoes to include daffodils, silk stockings and railway trains.

As Christopher fumbled his way around a crowded floor his back collided heavily with another dancer. Turning his head to apologise, he recognised Colin, an old school friend, who looked at the girl in the glamorous frock and gave him a knowing grin and a long slow wink. Colin had benefitted from no less than twelve sessions in Madame Rose's academy, and he deftly led his partner out of Christopher's faltering path.

Silently he concentrated on his steps, trying to improve their flow, and his thoughtful companion sensed that he needed to talk and unbend a little more.

"What's your name?" she asked with a smile.

The question startled and flummoxed him. He did not know the protocol. Should he answer 'Mr Goodwin', or 'Christopher Goodwin', or 'Christopher', or just plain 'Chris'? His failure to give an immediate reply added to the awkwardness: he now thought that he must appear completely stupid not knowing his own name. She came to his rescue.

"Don't tell me. Let me guess. Is it David? You look like a David."

He shook his head.

"It can't be Derrick. I don't like that name. Derricks are horrible," she proclaimed with mock prejudice, and the look on his face told her that she had guessed correctly.

Grant Sinclair now began the almost unheard of third verse of his current favourite, and added wild strawberries, roses and mouldering leaves to his wistful list. A few people began to look bored by the melody's prolongation, but Christopher was boundlessly grateful.

"Could it be Peter? I like that name best of all. Peter is the nicest name in the world."

He toyed with the idea of pretending that his name was Peter, but the scheme had endless pitfalls, and he had more than enough on his plate already, so he resisted temptation and replied that it wasn't.

"You don't look like a Charles, or a Henry."

He smiled and nodded.

"All right, I give up. What is it?"

She had resolved his quandary by only using forenames, so he admitted to being a Christopher.

"What a coincidence. That's my name too."

"Your name is Christopher?"

"Almost. It's Christine. But my friends call me Chris. I expect yours do too."

He happily agreed. It was cosy to know they had something in common; but he still couldn't overlook that dress. Her social standing was probably a million miles from his own, and he couldn't imagine that he'd ever become one of those friends who called her 'Chris'. He formed a mental picture of her leading an old-fashioned life of leisure, not having to work, being still owned by a father who'd one day transfer his right of possession to a young man who could 'keep her in the manner to which she'd been accustomed'.

The lengthy succession of 'Foolish Things' had now closed. The pianist played an eight bar bridge as the musicians changed their orchestration sheets, and an arrangement of Ray Noble's 'The Very Thought Of You' gave the newly appointed first alto a lengthy saxophone solo which he tackled bravely, but without Ted's finesse.

Christopher soon felt that it was long overdue for him to say something, but ideas still failed to percolate, and he inadvertently set free the thought that was uppermost in his mind.

"I don't suppose you have to work for a living?"

"Yes I do. I'm a typist."

"I didn't know that typists earned a fortune."

"They don't. What makes you think that I'm rich?"

"That dress. It looks like the latest Paris fashion. It must have cost a mint."

"It doesn't come from anywhere near Paris," she laughed. "That material was bought in Plumham market, and my mum ran it up on her new sewing machine."

"I can't believe it. It looks terrific. Is your mother a designer?"

"No. But she's a terribly good mum."

Like Christopher's suit, this evening was the first trial for Christine's new frock. On her rare previous outings she'd worn her elder sister's cast-off brown and moss-green organdie cotton dress, but its Wall-Street-crash colours were long out of date, even in Plumham, and for some while she'd gently hinted to her mother that she'd like something of her own. Mum had found a picture of the perfect creation in a copy of *Harper's Bazaar* she'd been reading in her dentist's waiting room, and quietly tore the page from the magazine and slipped it into her handbag: probably the only dishonest thing that she'd ever done. With gums still numbed by anaesthetic, she went straight to Plumham market, where she found printed French crepe de Chine, which would retail for at least six shillings and eleven-pence a yard in a drapers or a department store, at only three shillings and nine-pence. Ever resourceful she set about persuading her husband to buy her a second-hand sewing machine, and spent hours with sheets of brown paper and scissors, between nightly fittings of Christine, until she had a satisfactory pattern. After accidentally cutting her husband's football pool coupon in half, she shifted her task from table to floor, where she completed her highly ambitious *haute couture* premiere.

Christopher was heartened to find that the girl before him was not a wealthy heiress or a slumming socialite, and he felt the vice that had gripped his tongue start to loosen. His limbs began to relax, and he was about to think of something to say when the melody ended. He expected the usual coupling passage to be played into the third number of the sequence, but instead the bandleader made an announcement.

"For our third dance, ladies and gentlemen, we give you an exciting variation. While the lovely Carmita sings that captivating song 'Temptation', the orchestra adds the exotic rhythm of a bolero."

Grant Sinclair didn't like doing this, and he was sure that the dancers wouldn't care for it either, but he gave in to Carmita's bidding. She loved this song because it gave her the chance to display the power of her voice; and he complied for his own protection. Carmita had a vengeful temper when she was crossed, and he didn't want to run the risk of their relationship being divulged to his wife. As it happened, he needn't have worried. Mrs Mudge already knew about her husband's affair with Carmita, and about his liaisons with the seven singers who'd preceded her. What's more, she didn't care. As long as he earned enough to keep her expanding fifteen stone body well stocked with chocolates, cream gateaux and cherry brandy, he could have had fifty mistresses if he'd wanted.

The bandleader's intrusion was not wholly welcomed by Plumham's dancers. Most had never heard of a bolero, and nobody knew how to dance one. Many left the dance floor, and it could have given Christine a sound excuse to unload the millstone of Christopher's awkwardness. He fully expected her to make a polite exit, but to his delight she lingered.

"Shall we risk it?" she asked with a smile in her voice.

"Yes please," he replied, overtly grateful.

As the unfamiliar rhythm started, some tried dancing a rhumba, a few experimented with a tango, one or two virtuosi attempted a beguine, but most soldiered on with foxtrot steps; and for all, feet didn't synchronise with music. The two Chrises persevered with their retarded quickstep and, for them only, there was gain; in an eccentric picture, their eccentricity was less conspicuous. For them too, a cautious affinity was being sown: he valued her warmth; she sensed his unexpressed tenderness.

"I am yours..." the not inconsiderable power of Carmita's lungs trembled the chandeliers, and two now talkative young people began to discover a little about each other. Both had kept cats as pets, now deceased; neither liked porridge; but they could not agree about Wallis Simpson. She felt sorry for her; he didn't.

Although inconvenienced, the audience gave Carmita a cordial ovation at the close of the song, and Christopher escorted Christine from the dance floor.

"I'm sorry that I was such a bad dancer. Was I the worst you've ever met?"

"Not at all. I don't think that I'd die if you were to ask me to dance again."

"You really mean it?"

"Of course I do." Christine had rejoined her friend by now, and they went in the direction of the tea balcony, both giving Christopher a friendly wave as they left.

The evening's interval was then upon him, and it was at that point he promised himself that he'd devote the second half to dancing with her again, even if it was only once more. He could hardly believe what had happened. This was his very first encounter, yet it was somehow immaculate, complete, sublime. Here was a girl who was pretty, tolerant, responsive, kindly; and she'd been content to be in his company for all of twelve minutes. Someone might live for a lifetime and never know anything like that. With uncharacteristic presumption he already began to think of her as 'his' Christine. He felt his veins tingle with anticipation and elation. If he hadn't been so reserved, he'd have jumped in the air.

The men's washroom was crowded as he entered; all the cubicles were filled, and there was a long queue to use the urinal. Oddly, most of those present weren't dancers. The *Palais* had one type of patron who stayed in the bar all evening, and only emerged during the interval when there was no danger of having to dance with anyone.

After a tedious wait to relieve himself, Christopher was washing his hands when he heard a voice from behind.

"So this is the place where the nobs hang out."

He turned to find the group of lads whom he'd avoided earlier. The speaker was Dusty Miller, who had finished his apprenticeship as a plumber a year ago, and was now earning 'real' money.

"Hey, Chris; I saw you dancing with that posh skirt," said Keith, another of the group, who was a telegram boy and soon to become a postman. Christopher was about to tell him that she was not well-heeled, but, by happy chance, Keith continued. "I wouldn't want to dance with a toffee-nosed dolly like that. I'd have to talk all la-di-da like." The others nodded agreement, and Christopher realised that it was to his advantage to preserve that image of her. At least part of male Plumham was being kept at bay by that luxurious looking dress.

As they all re-emerged into the foyer, Christopher's former friend, whom he'd collided with, happened to be passing.

"Hello Chris, haven't seen you for ages. That was a real stunner I saw you dancing with. You'll have to go a bit ritzy to keep up with her. Get yourself a swanky tie, that's my advice. How about this?" He indicated the impressive silk one that he wore, which pretended to be in the colours of an exclusive club, or a public school, or a prestigious regiment; but actually signified nothing.

"I bought it up West last week for five and eleven."

"You paid six bob for a tie?" cut in Dusty, who loathed all forms of self-aggrandisement. "They must have seen you coming. You can buy 'em down the market for one an' a tanner. If you've got that sort of cash to throw about, then you can come to the bar with us, lob out the fags, an' stand us all a pint of wallop."

"I don't smoke or drink, which is why I can afford a decent tie," retorted Colin, and left the group to find a more appreciative audience.

"Doesn't smoke or drink? That ain't natural," commented Keith after he'd gone.

"Can't be a real man," explained Cyril, who worked in his father's butchers shop, which he hoped to inherit one day. "He must be queer."

"What's he doing here, then?" asked Christopher, coming to his schoolmate's defence with a little logic. "Did he ask you for a dance?"

"You're dead right, Chris mate," said Dusty, putting a hand of agreement on Christopher's shoulder. "A bit poncey, maybe, but not a poof. And we know you're not an iron-hoof, so how about coming to the bar with us?"

It was the question which Christopher had been dreading, and his mind sprinted to think of an excuse. He gave a white lie, saying that he'd promised to meet someone on the tea balcony, intimating that it was a girl. It must have sounded convincing. They responded with a cheer and the customary "get in there" clichéd ribaldry, and he headed off in that direction. When they were out of sight, he changed his route and again climbed the stairs to the gallery, where he secluded himself in a quiet corner and waited for the interval to finish.

The band reopened with an up-tempo flag-waver. Christopher descended into the hall immediately, and slowly circled the dance floor looking for a sight of Christine's dazzling frock, but she was nowhere to be seen. He continued his dawdling tour throughout an unusually long set of four numbers, but there was still no sign of her pink and indigo elegance. Paradoxically, a number of girls now looked compliantly towards him as he passed. Even the plump girl with the bow in her hair seemed to show some interest, possibly because the many times he'd walked by qualified him as a known person; but he faithfully stuck at his quest.

The next dances were a series of slow waltzes, the perfect opportunity for him to make amends for his earlier clumsiness; but still she didn't appear. As he'd failed to respond to the encouraging glances he'd received from several girls, he began to think of himself as a conspicuous oddity, and again climbed to the gallery to escape attention and to watch for her from above.

As the melodies rippled by so his anxieties grew. Where had she got to? Had she gone home? Become ill? Met another man? He would have ventured into the tea balcony to look for her, but the money he had left wasn't sufficient to play the host, especially if others were with her. He toyed with the idea of dancing with another girl, but if he did that and missed a chance of meeting Christine again, he'd not forgive himself; so he stayed with a one-woman mission. He started to wonder if there might be a way to find her that he hasn't tried, but the bandleader interrupted his thoughts.

"And now, good people of Plumham,. We take you on a magical trip to up-town Manhattan, where the classiest people are dancing the rhumba. And what better tune to dance to than Cole Porter's latest, and perhaps greatest hit: 'I've Got You Under My Skin'."

Ted's aching gums welcomed the news as he replaced his saxophone on its stand, picked up a pair of maracas from the floor and swallowed a little of the blood that had started to seep from a ruptured tooth cavity.

As the last of Grant Sinclair's words rang out, Christopher caught a glimpse of that enchanting dress, and he bounded down the stairs, apologising to an older couple midway for almost knocking them down. Then his pace slowed. What was he hurrying for? He couldn't dance a rhumba. What was he going to say to her? He still moved towards the hall as he kneaded the problem. Perhaps she couldn't dance one either. Could he then suggest that they try their misbegotten dance yet again? He'd find her and work on it.

He pushed his way slowly through the bystanders, but couldn't find her. The sophisticated triplet notation of the melody line of Cole Porter's middle section gave him an uneasy feeling. Where was she? He'd completed an almost full circuit of the hall now, and she had vanished.

"Don't you know, lit-tle fool; you ne-ver can win…"

Carmita's words were full of foreboding. He fully expected to find Christine waiting somewhere. Then his gaze drifted towards the dancers and he saw her, already dancing with a man in a wide-lapelled suit who held his right hand questionably low, in spite of his tallness.

Christopher watched for a while, and as they moved through a 'Cuban Walk' and a crossover, he realised that she was quite an accomplished dancer. He'd like to have watched for longer, but was slowly steeped with the thought that if she caught him looking, she might cast him as a voyeur; so he took refuge in the gallery once more.

At the dance's conclusion, the owner of the wide lapels did nor remove his hand from Christine's waist, but manoeuvred her towards the bar where they stayed for some while as Christopher's watchful uneasiness grew.

Eventually she did reappear, by herself, and he hared downstairs, but was again too late. Now she danced with a rotund man, somewhat shorter than her sixty-five inches, who wore a heavy gold watch chain across his expansive waistcoat.

An anxiety ridden routine grew ripe. He'd tuck himself away until he saw her alone, then he'd hurry to be with her, only to find that someone else always got there first: a man with excessively brilliantined hair and a pencil moustache; another who wore a tweed jacket with leather patches on the sleeves; yet another with a centre parting and a large nose. Sometimes he continued to prowl around after missing her, in the hope that she might reject her partner, but he didn't do it for long. He worried that if she noticed, he might appear to be spying, or jealous, or interfering, or covetous.

The evening was passing. He wearily climbed the stairs to the gallery for the umpteenth time and stood at the front looking down at the dancers as they cleared the floor. What Christopher hadn't realised was just how much of the evening had slipped away. He was so absorbed in his aim that he'd been deaf to Father Time. Then, with devastating unexpectedness for Christopher, Grant Sinclair's voice tolled the knell of parting: the last waltz was announced.

At that moment, he saw Christine standing below, quite alone, and he tore towards the staircase. He descended so quickly that his feet couldn't keep pace with his body, and he tripped and fell down the last few stairs and crashed onto the foyer floor, face down. As he pulled himself up, most of the little amount of money which he had left rolled out of his pocket, and across the polished parquet, but he didn't have the time to stop and try to find it. When he got to his feet he felt a sharp pain down the inside of his left leg, and he suspected a pulled muscle. He limped as fast as he could across the dance floor to where Christine stood, and then saw a man, proudly overdressed in an inherited and somewhat moth-eaten white tie and tails, bearing down on her. The man, who doubtless held the opinion that his formal attire would fittingly complement Christine's sumptuous dress, looked certain to reach her first. Christopher tried to put on a spurt, but the pain in his leg made him stumble, and he almost fell again.

The man in the immoderate finery did close on her first, and seemed to be giving her a long-winded invitation, presumably formal to match his outfit. Christopher continued to hobble towards them; there was nothing else that he could do. She seemed about to accept the lengthy proposal, when her eyes glanced to the side and must have noticed his ungainly approach. With tact, she excused herself, turned to Christopher with a smile, took his arm, and guided him back to the dance floor.

"Hello again, Chris. I was wondering when you'd show up," she said with obvious warmth in her voice. "My, you have been in the wars."

"I had a bit of an accident; but I'm alright now," he explained between panting breaths, as he quickly tried to straighten his dishevelled appearance.

It may have been the gentle exercise of the slow waltz, or the relief to know that his effort had not been for nothing, or his happiness to be with Christine again, but the discomfort in his leg gradually eased, and his dance steps became less constrained.

"I noticed you dancing earlier," he said, with considerable understatement. "You were very good. You must have danced here a great many times."

"Actually, I've only been twice before. My big sister taught me at home; and one of the girls at work showed me lots of steps. There's a half empty basement below our office, and we both often practise there in the lunch hour."

A new worry now loomed in Christopher's mind. His happiness was fleeting, and he wanted it to stay. At the close of the dance they were due to part. How could he prevent it? Or even delay it? He'd like to ask if he could see her again, but he didn't know how to contrive such a question. He mustn't scare her off by seeming too bold, too presuming, too familiar; but neither could he let his only chance go by.

"I know that you're a Christopher," she interrupted his thoughts. "But what's your surname? There are too many for me to guess this time."

"Goodwin."

"That's another coincidence! Mine is Groves. We're both cee-gees." As she spoke, they were moving past the bandstand during a crescendo and he thought she said 'gee-gees'. He wondered why they were horses, and assumed it was because of his inept dancing.

"I'll have to get a few more dancing lessons."

"Don't worry. You've done well for your first time."

"How did you know that it's my first time?"

"It's a bit obvious. You're supposed to lead me in the dancing and in the conversation." She laughed joyfully, with no trace of derision. He was glad that she'd accepted his ungainliness so light heartedly.

"I could do with more tuition, though."

"You ought to ask someone who can help you."

Christine's lightly veiled invitation went unnoticed. His mind was so busy trying to think of how he could broach the matter that an opening door hadn't been seen, let alone entered. And she had ambivalence about him. His pronounced shyness was exasperating; but his lack of brashness was attractive. On balance, the attractiveness seemed to be winning.

The last chorus of the last waltz ended, but the band gave Christopher's addled thoughts a temporary reprieve. Instead of the final chord of the melody being sustained, the drummer gave a four bar break in quickstep tempo to usher in the evening's leave-taking number, and Grant and Carmita stepped up to the microphone together for a farewell duet: 'Goodnight Sweetheart…'

Christopher found unexpected confidence in the last dance, and their feet harmonised willingly. The speed of the dance also nudged his sluggish imagination, and an idea dawned; he'd invite her to the bar for a drink.

That final dance was very short, and Grant Sinclair rounded off the evening with a brief speech to his 'wonderful audience' wishing them a safe journey home. Few listened to it. Many moved quickly towards the exit to be at the front of a bus or tram queue. As they walked slowly off the dance floor together, Christopher put a hand in his pocket and furtively counted the few coins which hadn't rolled away when he fell. He used his thumbnail to try to detect the serrated edge of silver, hoping to find a florin or half-crown, but he only felt the smooth rims of copper. His total resources were down to a few pence only; he'd have to abort his plan.

As they reached the floor's edge, she turned to him as if to say goodbye, and the crisis prompted another idea.

"Would you like a cup of tea before you go? It'll fortify you against the cold." Even as he said them, the words sounded stiff and chilled; but now they were out, and couldn't be thawed.

"I think that the tea room is closed now."

"May I offer you a cigarette then?" In desperation, he pulled out Mr Mubby's packet as a last resort.

"I don't smoke, but you go ahead and have one."

"Actually, I don't smoke either."

"Why have you got cigarettes then?"

He explained, as best as he could, why'd he'd bought them, and she gave a laugh which shook her shoulder-length waved brown hair. But her laugh disguised her feeling. His admission was probably the best thing he'd done all evening. It laid open his sensitive vulnerability, which she now found increasingly attractive, and it decided her to take the initiative that he'd been striving for.

"May I ask you for a favour?"

"Of course," he replied enthusiastically.

"I came here tonight with a friend, Janet. But she met her boyfriend, and I think they want to be alone, so I'll have to go home by myself. Will you walk with me to the tram stop? You can protect me from all those peculiar men."

"Of course. And you can protect me from those peculiar women." His instant repartee surprised him, and it pleased Christine. She had broken through his shyness at last. "Where do you live?"

"On the new estate, at Plumham Wood."

"Does the tram go all the way?"

"I have to change to a trolley-bus for the last part."

"Then I'd better come on the tram with you. There might be some peculiar men at the bus stop." He was gathering courage by the minute, and was now certain that he could find the nerve during their journey to ask her for a date.

From the cloakroom she collected her raincoat, wrapped an emerald green chiffon scarf about her hair, and pulled on her most important accessories, her gloves. Her mother always insisted that no young lady should be seen in the street without gloves; it was highly improper.

Out of the hall they walked past a few bedraggled weather-beaten Royal Jubilee decorations which still hung from Plumham's soot soiled brickwork: perhaps forgotten; perhaps awaiting a coronation. She gently slipped a gloved hand under his arm, gave him a smile which attractively wrinkled the top of her nose, and together they walked into the night.

Chapter Three

It would be another eight years before the tectonic plates of credit crunched; but in 2001 Cyril Nudwick was already above his plimsoll-line in debt and was sinking fast, dragged down by the lading of his cravings.

Three decades before, his Uncle Henry had quenched a similar thirst very cheaply: for the cost of a tape measure. Uncle Henry had listed the names and addresses of the newly wedded from the *Plumham Gazette*. When he was sure that a husband would not be at home, he'd call on a young bride, pretend that he was an official from the local health department and ask to take personal details, including her measurements. Many of his interviewees noticed how his hands lingered over certain parts of their bodies as he measured them, and how he had to recheck those areas more than once.

Emboldened by three months of success, he chanced an inside leg measurement, and that was his downfall. After he penitently confessed in court that his services were intended to be a well-meaning, if misguided, supplement to the NHS, liberal magistrate Julia Hedgebury concluded that he was 'over enthusiastic', gave him a mild ticking off, and an even milder fine; which immediately encouraged similar practitioners to install themselves in the area. And they flourished, until Hector Grant, JP, ascended the bench and doled out illiberal prison sentences to several misunderstood carers, which closed the pathway to one form of alternative medical care.

On reaching a solitary adulthood, Cyril thought of following his uncle's clinical practice, but then opted for a safer career in research instead. Although his income as a shop assistant was not generous, his lonely lifestyle enabled him to save for the deposit on a roomy three-storied Victorian house, which had a deflated asking price because of its sad need for attention and maintenance. A venal estate agent and a co-operative mortgage consultant used highly creative arithmetic to broaden Cyril's slender income to match the mortgage benchmark; so closing the deal, but opening the doorway to their client's eventual insolvency.

Once installed in his new house, Cyril then quartered himself next to the single communal bathroom, carefully drilled observation holes in the wall between the two rooms to facilitate his studies, and then let all of the other rooms as bed-sitters.

The house was conveniently close to a local teaching hospital, and Cyril offered generous rent discounts to the more nubile student nurses who now occupied all of his rooms. Luckily for him, although the London Borough of Plumham spent a great deal of their ratepayers' money investigating and defeating the prejudices of race, gender and sexual orientation, they had not yet got around to discrimination on aesthetic grounds, and so Cyril was able to offer very low rents to the most attractive young women whilst dissuading the ugly with large surcharges.

Cyril's dedication to his studies took priority over commercial prudence and left him financially anorexic; so he could not afford to buy himself a wide-screen television set, designer clothes, a well-stocked wine rack, nor any of the basic creature comforts necessary to raise him above the extreme poverty level as generously defined by the sociology department of Londinium University, formerly the Plumham Polytechnic. He thought that he ought to find a fellow researcher with similar interests who might be willing to contribute to his costs in return for the shared use of his facilities. But his brand of research was a delicate business, and he needed to be sure that he'd approach the right person. For some while he'd had his eye on Peter Goodwin, who lived nearby, as a potential colleague. He knew little about Peter, but the loneliness of the man gave Cyril the impression that he might be a possible contender for the post. He had resolved to carefully sound him out the next time that they met.

The fervour of Cyril's research programme left him no time for food preparation, and he relied on takeaways to keep body and soul together. But popular consumption and Cyril's upbringings had walked in different directions. His mother had devotedly protected him from the dangers of ingesting foreign food: 'It's always prepared by foreigners, dear; and they don't wash properly or use toilet paper'. Catastrophically, those bastions of English culinary virtue, the cooked meat shops, the pie and mash shops, the pease-pudding purveyors, the saveloy steamers, had been ruthlessly razed by invaders from China, France, Thailand, India, Greece and many other places.

For him, there was now only one safe nutritional harbour in the whole of Plumham; Miriam's fish and chip shop. Miriam had inherited the shop from her father, and had lived there all her life. The food that she prepared looked highly eccentric. Chips could be any thickness, some as thin as matchsticks, others as fat as sausages; but, like everything she cooked, all tasted delicious. Her quality control was impeccable; she sampled everything frequently, rather too frequently, which was why the girth of her body resembled a gasometer.

"Hello Charlie," she sang out as Cyril entered the shop. She called everyone 'Charlie'. It saved having to clutter up her memory with people's names, and left it free for her favourite recollections: those about food. When not eating, she liked to reminisce about meals of the past, or dream about those of the future. "What are we having today?" she asked Cyril.

"Scampi and chips please."

"Scampi! Oh, I do love scampi," she rhapsodised as she twiddled each piece in a bowl of batter-mix and dropped it into the sizzling oil. "They're my favourites, they really are. I could eat them all day, I could. I really could."

Miriam's obesity placed her well outside Cyril's field of research, but such lost opportunities wouldn't have worried her. She was one of those rare and fortunate individuals whose work and interests coincided perfectly; and the job suited Miriam in other ways. The powerful smell of over-used cooking oil was one of the few fragrances that could mask her body odour. Her skin seemed to have an obstinate resistance to soap, and her ample folds of flesh were too weighty to penetrate anyway, which somehow seemed to challenge Cyril's mother's theory about the quality of national hygiene.

"Do you want salt and vinegar on them when they're ready?"

"No thanks. I've got some tartare sauce at home."

"Tartare sauce! Oh, I do love tartare sauce. I could eat it with anything, I really could."

Cyril heard the scrunching noise made by the shop door as it opened. Hinge drop and rain-swollen timbers of the ill-maintained door made its leading edge scrape heavily across the unevenly quarry tiled floor. Miriam preferred it that way. It took an adult's strength to push the door, which deterred local kids from opening it and shouting 'Oi, fat arse', or similar little quips that made these children so endearing.

"Hello Charlie. What's for you today?"

"A meat pie and chips, please," requested the newcomer.

"A meat pie! Oh, I've got some lovely pies today. Delicious flaky pastry, all golden brown it is. Melts in your mouth, it does. I could eat them all day, I really could."

Cyril looked across at the new arrival, was pleased to see Peter Goodwin, and they nodded their usual greeting. Peter mostly fended for himself, but the bruising he'd received that morning from Modesta White left him too enervated to prepare his lunch for that day. He visited this shop occasionally because he liked the food. Even for the undemanding Peter there was no amatory attraction in the place; which was just as well. Only food could trigger Miriam's romanticism, even though her grandfather had been a licentious clarinet-playing bandleader. Her mind was content to dwell on her nourishment, and caress every imaginary mouthful.

Finding a possible way to open a quiet conversation with Peter occupied Cyril's thoughts, when a crash interrupted them. Two of the aging wall tiles, which formed an Art Deco sunburst pattern above the frying range, had fallen onto the floor. Most of them had fallen off at some time, and Miriam always reaffixed them using evaporated milk: everything that she used had some food value. She would have left them where they lay, but that nosy health inspector was due to look in again soon. At this moment, though, she scarcely seemed to notice what had happened. She appeared to be half mesmerised by the hypnotic scent of the frying batter, and Cyril decided that this was the right time to open negotiations with Peter.

"I'd, er, like to ask if you might be interested in a little project of mine?" he asked in a low voice, his head inclined towards Peter's left ear.

"What sort of project?"

Cyril was about to give a tentative outline when the shop door scraped open, a man they both recognised as an off-duty policeman entered, and the memory of Uncle Henry stayed Cyril's tongue. While Miriam exalted the glories of her fried plaice to her latest 'Charlie', Cyril drew the only piece of paper that he could find from his pocket, jotted his telephone number on it, and passed it to Peter.

"Give me a ring on that number. I'll let you have the details," Cyril whispered, with a knowing look on his face which Peter didn't understand.

Miriam dropped Peter's meat pie onto its bed of chips, fighting bravely against the temptation to take a bit out of it, and started to wrap the paper.

"How about a pickled onion as well?"

"No thanks."

"I love pickled onions, I do. I like the soft ones best. Most people like them crunchy, but I like them soft. More flavour. I could eat them all day, I really could." Miriam wiped the saliva from the corner of her mouth with the back of a podgy hand, finished wrapping Peter's lunch and gave it to him.

"Don't forget to phone me," reminded Cyril, still waiting for his scampi to cook, as Peter nodded and left the shop.

Peter sat alone in his late mother's little house and slowly ate his lunch. He was never bored at home; he was surrounded by walls steeped in memories of love and sorrow, but seldom joy. During his life he'd tried to find solace by sometimes holding imaginary conversations with the father he'd never known, but they only took place when he'd some good news to tell. Modesta White had ensured that there wasn't any for that day.

He still felt unsettled by the morning's events, and would do so for some time to come. After stress, his heavily inhibited passion always left a sizeable charge of unburnt adrenaline smouldering in his bloodstream, and it would be a while yet before his throat lost its aridity, his skin lost its tautness, and the barbed wire unwrapped itself from around his brain.

At times like this, Peter sometimes softened the torment by bandaging his mind with old remembered memories. He found comfort by thinking about his mother's reminiscences, when she had sighed for the happy days she'd shared with his father. And that reminded him of a task he'd been evading since his mother's death. There were a number of little boxes in which her most personal and treasured possessions lay, and he had yet to open them. Ambivalence checked his hand: he dearly wanted to share in her precious moments; but he felt uneasy about prying into his parents' intimacy. There was one box in particular, on which was written 'These Foolish Things' in his father's handwriting. The box, his mother had told him, held a collection of mementoes of their earliest meetings. His father had started it on returning home after their first dance together. At first, he'd been too shy to tell her about it, but when they got engaged he had shared his secret with her, and they'd laughed lovingly over it. During Peter's lifetime, though, he'd only seen her cry over it.

Peter also had to decide on how he was going to preserve her 'special frock', an exquisite creation in pink and dark blue crepe de Chine which had always hung in her wardrobe protected by layers of tissue paper. The dress seemed to hold distant dreams for her, and he had promised his mother that he'd never part with it.

On finishing his meal, he remembered the piece of paper which Cyril had given him, and he pulled it from his pocket. It advertised a literary discussion group who were to meet that afternoon in the Alderman Mubby Memorial Hall, and at the top a telephone number had been written. Peter assumed that Cyril might be a member of the group, and was perhaps going to recommend it to Peter. He wasn't to know that Cyril had merely used a handbill which he'd been given in the street, and which had no personal significance; but the idea of trying something new, meeting fresh people, broadening his horizons, appealed to Peter.

He washed the memory of Miriam's meat pie from his plate, and decided to telephone Cyril straight away, as there was only an hour left before the meeting was due to start. After locking up the house, he made his way to the nearest public telephone.

Considerable force must have been used on the phone booth. Its door had been torn from the top hinge and now leaned at a drunken angle with its lower corner resting on the pavement. The handset had been ripped from the wall and lay, stamped into fragments, on the ground.

"Is it broken?"

The voice came from behind Peter, who turned to see a slightly built elderly man. He wore what appeared to be a well preserved demobilisation suit, although his extremities broached flair with a baseball cap and trainers.

"It's all the phone company's fault, you know," he explained to Peter. "Everything used to be all right when we had proper phone numbers. They used to have letters in front of the number. You knew where you were then. If you wanted a Plumham number, then you dialled P-L-U. They had to change them because the kids today can't read. The schools these days only learn 'em how to smoke hash and pinch things."

Peter smiled and nodded. He didn't want to spend time debating the social merits of telephone numbers with this ageing reactionary, and he hurried away to find another phone box.

The next one smelt overpoweringly of urine, and the one after that had its mouthpiece clogged with dried vomit. Peter had a long walk to find another, which took him down streets he rarely visited.

A corner premises caught his eye. On its fascia was written 'The Nova Introduction Agency', and out of curiosity he stopped to look through its glazed door. Bills and advertisements pasted over the door made viewing difficult: posters for discotheques; the Trotskyist Action Party; an acid-house event; a sale of reproduction antique baths at amazing discounts. The Plumham Anti-Foxhunting League had done especially well with three sheets displayed, although no one had seen gentlemen in hunting pink gallop down Plumham High Street. He found a small gap to peer through, and saw that the place was empty, apart from three and a half months of mail strewn across the worn vinyl flooring: unpaid bills; a misdelivered result from a pregnancy testing service; and over fifty neglected applications from the friendless of Plumham. He was about to turn away when Peter felt a tap on his shoulder.

"Looking for a bit o' skirt, mate?"

The speaker was a man slightly older than Peter, dressed in the most incongruous collection of clothing that charity shops could supply. A pair of widely flared trousers, from an era of psychedelic flower-power, were too short in the leg and too tight at the waist: a T-shirt that loudly commemorated an American rock concert was partly covered by a shabby double-breasted Edwardian waistcoat; and his feet were clad in a pair of well-worn tap-dancing shoes. Everything about him was deliberately second hand. Even the elastic band, which trussed his sparse lank greying hair at the rear of his head, had been found in the street, having been discarded by a postman during a delivery round.

"I could fix you up, good and proper, I could; if you was to cross me palm with silver, so to speak." The oddly dressed man continued, with a meaningful leer. "I'm Maurice Slupp, I am; but round here they call me John, Honest John," he added, giving a number of furtive glances up and down the street, which didn't look at all honest.

"No thanks. I'm just looking."

"Want a nice bloke, then? I cater for all tastes."

"Oh, no. I'm not that way."

"No mate, I didn't think you was. Bit of a ladies' man, I thought, when I saw you. No need to be shy with me, mate. Man of the world, I am. I could get you a good bird, I could. Nice and clean. No rubbish."

"No thanks, I don't really –"

"No need to worry, mate. You'll get a straight deal from me. Ask anyone around here. 'Honest John is dead straight'. That's what they'll tell you."

"But, you see –"

"And you can exchange her for another one if she's no good. I can't say fairer than that, can I?"

"Well, I'm sorry, but –"

"You can trust me, because I'm one of those caring people. Customer care, that's my motto." He noticed a slight look of annoyance on Peter's face, and added, "Only trying to earn an honest crust, Guv."

"I don't really need your services just now; but have a cup of tea on me." Peter thrust a pound coin into the man's hand.

Honest John's appearance, manner and speech were, in reality, entirely phoney, but he succeeded in fooling most people. He used theatrical make-up to give his skin the look of one who slept rough, but he actually owned a semi-detached in the select suburb of Plumham Heights. His face wore a convincing half-crazed gloat which had been perfected with long practice before a mirror, and although he smelled strongly of methylated spirits, none ever passed his lips. He kept a sponge soaked with it in his pocket, which he squeezed from time to time with his elbow. Almost everybody who encountered him felt uneasy, and usually gave him money just to be rid of him. On a good day, he could clear over a hundred pounds, undetected by the tax man, which nicely supplemented his dole money and a dubious disability benefit.

"I can't drink tea, because of me dodgy guts. I can only drink coffee, and that costs at least a couple of quid around here."

Peter dredged the depths of his trouser pocket, drew out a handful of cupronickel and dropped it into Honest John's awaiting hands.

"Ta Gov., that'll do nicely. Now remember, if you need my 'elp, you'll always find me round here. Anyone will tell you where Honest John is." Before leaving, he gave a crooked wink with an eye which appeared unwashed and sleep-encrusted, but which had been faked using sawdust and spirit-gum.

Mr Slupp shuffled off in search of more fruitful clients. Peter at last found another telephone box, and this one was obviously in sound order because its inner surfaces were wallpapered with a mosaic of postcard sized advertisements. Several were from women who yearned to confess their naughtiness and looked forward to being well spanked; while others proudly listed the torture equipment they had available. If only one of them had offered love and kindness, he might well have been tempted to telephone.

Peter dialled the number written on the paper, but at that moment there were only two people present at Cyril's research centre; one was taking a bath, and the other was secretly watching her, so neither answered the phone as it rang. It was mistakenly assumed by Peter that Cyril had left home to attend the advertised meeting, so he decided to catch a bus and join him there.

A newly enfranchised single-decker bus pulled up, and Peter found that he was its sole passenger. He sat at the front, close to the driver, who looked bored and desperately in need of conversation.

"Where are you off to?" the driver called across to Peter.

"The Memorial Hall."

"What's on there, then?"

"A literary meeting. I haven't been before. I thought I'd give it a try."

"Take a tip from me, mate, I don't think you'll like it much. I don't mind a bit of a read now and then, but it has to have a bit of action in it. You know, blokes bashing each other, an' women taking their clothes off. I keep away from all that arty-farty stuff. Bloody boring if you ask me."

The driver's experience of literature being exhausted, he then turned to football and talked continually about it. Peter had a number of life-cramping oddities, and the most isolating was that he could see no point in spending time watching men run up and down a field kicking a ball. In his unenlightened darkness, it all seemed futile. But that awkward quirk distanced him from most male company, who'd probably have lynched him if he'd ever dared to voice such ignorant heresies; so he politely nodded and murmured sounds of agreement as the driver alternately lauded and defamed a list of names unknown to Peter.

He was relieved to reach journey's end, although he must have put on a fairly convincing act, because the driver said that he was sorry to lose Peter's company.

"Hi," said a young man with shoulder length hair, a broad smile and varnished fingernails, who sat behind a desk just inside the hall. Peter responded, and so betrayed another of his enfeebling eccentricities. He was burdened with a stubborn streak of Englishness which refused to bow to American primacy. He improperly said 'hello' while others used 'hi'; and he'd never been in the right ballpark, taken candy from a baby, earned big bucks, bet his bottom dollar, given anyone a bum steer, been behind the eight ball, realised how his cookie crumbled, had a bad hair day, nor asked anyone to read his lips. He just couldn't be sure of a sure thing. Most of the time he thought of himself as a bloke, sometimes as a chap, but never a guy; and he was probably the last person left in Plumham to say 'gosh' instead of 'wow'.

Peter was told, with a charming smile, that there was nothing to pay for his first visit; but if he enjoyed it and decided to join the group, then a minimal subscription was payable to cover expenses. It sounded a fine scheme, so he took the proffered leaflets and entered the conference room. There, a gathering of about thirty people sat in small clusters, each distancing itself from the others. Cyril wasn't to be seen. Several people looked towards Peter as though eager that this incomer should join their coterie, but, not wishing to ruffle any of them, he sat by himself.

The people all seemed to be talking about exotic holiday experiences, the ones relating the most expensive having the loudest voices. As Peter had not been on a holiday since childhood, and had never been abroad, he was glad that he sat alone. From their mannerisms, most seemed to be from a small, fashionably gentrified area in the north of the borough; the only part of urban Plumham where dog owners carried plastic bags. There, the exteriors of the Victorian terraces had been scrupulously cleaned to reveal the fabric's original bloom, whilst their interiors slavishly followed the insincere dictates of the fashion gurus in the glossy magazines. There, house buyers thirstily paid exorbitant prices for the privilege of living in an area where, statistically, they were most likely to be mugged.

The chatter eased as the group leader entered, took his seat, announced himself as Doctor Robert Crupp, but invited everyone to call him 'Robbie'. There was good reason for him to be pleased with himself. He had recently gained a PhD for a study of the social and cultural significance of graffiti written on the walls of public lavatories, and had spent a great number of pennies in the course of his researches. His thesis had been published under the title of *Ballads From The Bog*, but had sold only one copy, to a customer who mistakenly thought that it was about Irish folk music. Then the publishers changed the title to *Lyrics From The Lav*, and it became a runaway success.

"And now, to boldly split infinitives where no man has split them before," Dr Robbie proposed, tossing back his long blond hair, which he did whenever he spoke. His joke received only polite laughter, because he made the same comment at the start of every meeting.

"Firstly, I'll read an extract from Tristan Makepiece's new novel *Slow Train To Southwark*. This is how it starts: 'Two or three generations ago, when LSD meant pounds, shillings and pence, when gay meant carefree, and when women wore sensible knickers'…" Peter was enjoying this reading. To him, the words were apt and humorous. He particularly liked the comment about 'sensible knickers'. Having travelled the London Underground all his life, he had witnessed the gradual change in women's lingerie advertisements which always bordered the escalators, and he had seen female torsos evolve from corseted rigidity to near nudity. The author, he felt, had been honed on the same stone, and he was about to register his appreciation when he heard mutterings from others.

"Reactionary!" grumbled one voice.

"Liberal basher!" murmured another.

Peter was taken aback. He couldn't imagine himself bashing anybody, so he kept his opinions to himself.

"You don't seem to like this, do you?" commented Dr Robbie, in his self-consciously casual way. "But I'll read a little more. 'The streets were filled with young people, wandering aimlessly with a mobile phone in one hand and an opened can of lager in the other; gobbing on the pavements as they went'." The voices of protest grew louder.

"Fascist," was heard frequently.

Peter earnestly searched his wits, but could find no connection between this book and Fascism. Eventually the group leader set the novel aside and abandoned that reading.

"That ghastly book could only be appreciated by people who live in those frightful suburbs, where neatly trimmed minds live behind neatly trimmed hedges." The speaker was a slender man in late middle age, who sat forward on his chair and bolt upright, with his knees tightly together. As he spoke, he clasped the palms of his hands together as if praying; and then concluded by spreading his hands before him. Others made similar comments, and Peter began to wonder if he was somehow misplaced. He didn't live in the suburbs, and his late mother's little Victorian urban cottage had no hedge before it, but faced directly onto the street.

"What does our new friend think of it?" asked Dr Robbie, looking straight at Peter, who felt all eyes turn towards him. He tried to think of something non-committal.

"I really couldn't say. I'm far too 'umble," said Peter, with a vague recollection that 'humble' without the aspirant was a literary quotation from somewhere. To his surprise, he got a better laugh than the group leader had received for his split-infinitive gag, and a few even gave him a brief clap.

"For our next book, then, we'll turn to Alther Redwing's latest novel *Deep Purple*." This time a hum of approval arose from those familiar with this author's work. Peter hadn't heard of her, but the book's title recalled for him a song from his mother's ageing record collection, so he started to listen cheerfully.

During the next twenty minutes, the group leader read extracts from various parts of the novel. The plot was narrated by a character who'd spent his adolescent years sniffing the saddles of unattended women's bicycles. His twenties were devoted to having sex with dogs; and then he found true fulfilment in middle life when he got a job as a mortuary attendant and turned to necrophilia. The lurid and explicit descriptions started to make Peter feel sick. He looked round fully expecting others to start protesting, but to his surprise they all appeared intrigued, even captivated. His discord was that he still clung to hopelessly outdated ideals that coupled sex with affection, and could not begin to imagine it as a remote and lustful act. As nausea rose in his gullet, he found temporary relief by switching off his ears and escaping to the antiemetic solace of old remembered melodies; letting a 'Blue Moon' eclipse purple carnality.

"I'm sure that some of you, at least, feel that this text calls into question the dynamics of power and subjection," said Robert Crupp, having finished reading the extracts and looking around with carefully practised nonchalance.

"Absolutely," began a middle-aged man who resembled a bank manager of the nineteen fifties. Every inch of his appearance spelt convention. His Oxford pattern shoes had mirror-like toecaps, his suit boasted knife-edge creases down the trousers, and the rigidly starched collar of his white shirt was closed with a mutely knotted tie. "The book's narrator represents the quintessence of capitalism, and its plot symbolises the tragedy of the oppressed classes. Smelling the bicycle saddle is the impulse of greed that distances itself from work, the kinship between dog and underdog is obvious, and the corpses are the defeat of internationalism and the crushing of the trade unions by a capitalist conspiracy."

"Interesting," said the group leader, tossing back his hair vigorously. But for Peter it was baffling: doubly baffling, in fact; as if his eyes and ears were in separate worlds. He couldn't fathom how pornographic fiction became political fact, and he couldn't credit that leftist words came from a rightist image. If the man had worn a beret with a red star on the front, it might have been less surreal. But that was only the start. As further comments flowed, so his bafflement turned to bewilderment.

"You're wrong," said a woman in her thirties dressed in dungarees and industrial boots with heavily reinforced toe protection; although her expensively styled hair rumoured that she presented herself in other guises at other times. She glared at the previous speaker with the disdain that fine furniture has for woodworm. "You're forgetting that this was written by a woman. It is womanhood that is oppressed. The non-human dog symbolises the distancing of feminine Otherness; and the silence of the corpse is the repression of female sexuality by the male establishment. The whole work aches from Lack."

"You both relish symbols, but we need to look deeper than that," said an earnest looking young man, whose exorbitantly expensive designer clothing could only be distinguished from the shoddy schmutter sold in Plumham's street market by its prominently displayed labels. For the wearer though, it shored up his askew idea of superiority. He kidded himself that, by spending a great deal of money on something that poorer people bought for a lot less, he was distinguishing himself from the common herd: although those clothes betrayed that it was only his gullibility that was a cut above the others. "We must recognise that duality between person and self. The book just has to be an outward expression of some inner state," he added.

"That is certainly true," agreed a man of indeterminable age, who wore a long beard, a garment that resembled a Victorian nightgown, and open sandals. "Sniffing the bicycle saddles is the signifier of an expanding consciousness."

Although the erudite words seemed impressive, Peter suddenly started to doubt their value. The thought entered his mind that this was all as purposeless as the men who kicked footballs about, but he quickly squashed that idea and tried pliantly to yoke with his betters.

"You can't just go deeper, you must also go upward and outward," declared a woman in a sequined headscarf, who wore large conspicuous rings on every finger of both hands. "This divine book is so full of re-evaluative energy. It redefines respectability. It contemplates notions of a respectability that transcend respectability; and at the same time subverts respectability with respectability." In his ignorance of trendsetting intellect, Peter thought that sounded triple Dutch, but the woman's view had its supporters.

"It is, I'd say, a harmony between freedom and cultural imprisonment," said a woman whose hair was as closely cropped as that of a rookie US Marine, and who had a massive rectangle of glossy black plastic suspended from each earlobe. To the newcomer her opinion may have seemed learned, until it was realised that she said the same about almost everything.

"We are all seduced by the eternal quest for the sublime," agreed a woman who appeared to be gazing into the distance while her hands moved as if outlining a crystal ball; and the state of her nostrils hinted that she powdered her nose from the inside.

"I'm not taken in by that pretentious mud," a woman in a formal suit said firmly. "I am looking for a clear verdict, the *quaestio quid juris*."

Dr Robbie had looked towards Peter a couple of times as if inviting him to make a comment. Fortunately, Peter had brought a small notebook and pencil with him, so he evaded attention by pretending to take notes. Not being sure what to write, he started by setting down his name and address.

"Then you're missing out on at least ten layers of meaning," suggested a man who liked to pass off his neglect of shaving as 'designer' stubble. "You're ignoring its cryptic dialectic."

As tensions mounted and histrionics loomed, Peter began to wonder what all the fuss was about. It was as if a furnace was being stoked to boil an egg: an egg which, in his innocent opinion, was rotten to begin with.

"Oh! How can some people be so stiff?" asked the upright man with a dislike of suburban values. "One simply has to surrender oneself to the intuition of ontic flux," he added, affectedly brushing a hand across his immaculately coiffured blue-rinsed hair. His hollow comment was part of the idiobabble that he regularly used to camouflage his lack of lore: first-rate packaging around second-rate wisdom.

"Why don't you take your heads out of those post-structuralist clouds?" asked the Red man in the grey suit. "That section of the text where the dog defecates on its debaucher. That can only represent the brief triumph of nineteen sixty-eight. If that interpretation doesn't inspire you, then you're a traitor to the class struggle."

Between all the sophistry, a few brave souls proffered opinions that were peppered with the words 'you know', 'really' and 'sort of'; but they were all flatly ignored. Whilst the artilleries of the class struggle, the gender war and the claptrap conflict had ammunition aplenty, the common view had sadly lost its firepower.

"Your gearboxes are jammed in metaphorical mode," criticised the man who wore overpriced rags. "Why ignore the metonymical side of your brains?"

"Why drive at all when you can fly?" questioned a woman who wore a diaphanous blouse over her conspicuously unfettered bosom. "This glorious book simply strains to free itself from the contamination of social meaning. It is a crime to imprison this beautiful writing. We must set it free. You must throw open the doors of your structuralist dungeons and let the work romp in the meadows of plurality; frolic in the fields of diffusion. Why don't you throw off your strait-laced corsets and fly with me?" As she said 'fly' for the second time, she flung out her arms melodramatically, three buttons on her blouse sprang open, and one full and somewhat pendulous breast fell out into full view. She made no attempt to cover it, but left it exposed. For Peter, it added to his already considerable embarrassment; but nobody else seemed to notice. He was not to know that she had deliberately enlarged the buttonholes on her blouse, and that this display occurred at most meetings.

"That's all very well; but while you're flying away, you're deserting your sex," said a young woman in a black leather jacket on which the words 'The only good man is a dead man' had been written in silver Saxon-Gothic lettering. "These shadowy ideas are too limp for the Cause. To get anywhere, you must be militant."

"Let's not get bogged down with all that leaden-footed stuff, sweetie," countered the man with the blue rinsed hair and the tightly pressed knees. "Why must we walk through this book when we can dance?" Peter felt that he didn't want to walk through the book, let alone dance. So far he had written down his name and address seventeen times: and he continued to do so.

"That's right," agreed a man in a denim jacket with dyed green streaks in his greying hair. "All that metalanguage is too heavy."

"Why don't you all come back to earth?" said a young man whose ears, nose and eyebrows were pierced with a haphazard collection of metal lumps, who wore cotton trousers with the words 'The Waste Land' embroidered across the fly in mauve silk, but who spoke with received pronunciation that could have graced a British film soundtrack of the nineteen forties. "This book is a potentially meaningful discourse of freedom and pleasure. It encourages the readers to ask questions of themselves and their relationships to this day and age. It challenges the norm. It is simply a desire to seize the present." Although Peter was not at all comfortable with this man's enthusiasm, he could at least see a vague connection between his comments and this lewd novel.

"Now you've destroyed the sublime," cried the woman with the exposed breast. "How can I fly again? How can I find myself?"

"You can find yourself by looking between your legs," replied the immaculately suited Marxist, with undisguised contempt.

"You can't speak to me like that!" she shouted, stamping her foot, which made her breast wobble. "I had an uncle who was working class."

"Don't take any notice of that Stalinist bastard," consoled the woman in the dungarees, intensifying her glare towards the left-wing antagonist.

"Shove your penis envy up your Lacanian Gap," he snapped back.

The overalled feminist slowly rose from her chair with burning coals in her eyes, and single-mindedly started to slowly advance on a now cringing Bolshevik. From deep in a pocket she drew a large flick-knife, pressed a button on its side so that its finely honed steel blade sprang into view, and holding it with both hands she aimed it like a bayonet at his crotch and loomed towards him.

"You've been asking for this for too long. Now you're going to get it," she hissed with slowly paced menace. "You're going to be gelded."

Her look of grave unswerving resolution horrified most of the other people, and they froze in their chairs. Paradoxically, the self-proclaimed militant in the leather jacket looked most frightened of all. Peter stopped writing his name and address, felt that he ought to do something, but couldn't think what it might be. Deviantly, the eyes of the man with the blue rinse widened and his slim body started to shiver with excitement; and the exhibitionist woman cupped a hand under her exposed breast.

"I think perhaps we ought to calm down," stuttered the group leader with hands visibly trembling and his composure vanished; but nobody heeded him. Although he commanded respect as an authority on lavatorial lyrics, his influence during a crisis seemed sadly in want.

As the glittering steel blade resolutely closed on him, the blenching Marxist started to perspire freely. His iron curtain, it seemed, had fallen; demolished by a thumping tachycardia.

Dr Robbie had two worries uppermost in his mind: if blood got spilt on the floor, the charge for hiring the room might increase; and if a scandal broke loose, it might affect the sales of his book. Wretchedly, he felt powerless as the feminist avenger hovered above her target. She extended her arms, locked her elbows, massed her weight behind the unwavering weapon and looked as if she was about to lunge forward.

"Cutting thrills you, does it?" The voice was that of a man in his late twenties who hadn't spoken before. He wore a T-shirt covered in printed quotations from the works of T S Eliot, and sat slumped in a chair with his legs stretched before him looking remarkably relaxed. His words halted the descent of the knife. "I reckon you fancy him, and you want to turn him into an honorary lesbian. Aren't your girlfriends butch enough for you?"

The knife remained poised inches away from the carefully pressed trousers for what seemed an eternity; then she withdrew it, returned to her seat, and burst into tears.

The paralysis of fear gradually fell away from the targeted man and colour started to return to his face. Most people began to relax, especially the group leader, and the leather jacketed activist stopped trembling; although the man with the *blueté* hair looked somewhat disappointed. The woman with the exposed breast rearranged and rebuttoned her blouse, but did so with an extravagant flourish which ensured that she displayed the other breast for a lingering moment.

Dr Crupp thought that he ought to move swiftly on to his next topic to get the meeting again under his control, and to take minds off what had just happened. He managed to find his voice, although his speech sounded like a kettle about to boil over.

"For our final item today, Ursula has a special treat for us. She is going to read us a brand new poem by the wonderful Margaret Nudding."

The woman with the almost shaven head and the massive plastic earrings got to her feet.

"I take this poem from a new collection of Nudding's work which is not due to be published until next month, but I'm privileged to have an advance copy, and this is the first public reading. The whole collection is marvellous, but I think that this one is the best. It is entitled 'On a Snowy Morning in July'.

"Mrs Cunningham was dancing,
Slowly, slowly.
Though it couldn't be a dance,
Because it was a 1947 vintage wine.

Mrs Clutterbuck was dancing,
Not so slow, not so slow.
But it wasn't really a dance,
More like a hypnotised pink blueness'."

On the poem went, through five more stanzas, each of which, for Peter, seemed to gather more and more absurdity. He assumed that it was meant to be comical, like Edward Lear's rhymes, and was about to show his appreciation by laughing when he glanced around him to see that the rest of the audience looked intently serious, and at least three were taking notes.

As Ursula's voice skipped along, through a lengthy list of oddly named married women whose dances resembled a disabled sergeant major, a bowler hat full of dead promises, a divorced oak tree and many other Delphic images, Peter found it increasingly difficult to stop himself giggling. He returned to writing down his name and address, but that was not enough, so he took out his handkerchief and, while pretending to wipe his face, stuffed the end of it into his mouth.

The poem galloped through a crescendo of apparent incongruity, until finally Mrs Wibbly's dance voted for an existential sculptor who suffered from dysentery, and the thunderous applause that followed thankfully drowned the laughter that Peter could no longer contain. Eulogies poured from the audience.

"Magnificent! It has a structure that could withstand an earthquake..."

"It takes us farther than infinity and…"
"Captures the very essence of oblivion…"
"Thinks beyond the ultimate…"

As the praise faded, Dr Robbie closed the meeting as swiftly as he could: he didn't want to run the risk of another confrontation. The soberly dressed Marxist was the first to slip away, no doubt still worried that a knife might reappear. Others departed in chattering groups, but Peter continued to write in his notebook. Whether conversation remained at a literary level, or returned to the topic of expensive holidays, Peter would have felt excluded, so he ducked notice by keeping his head down until they had all left. He then folded his notebook, and was about to rise from his chair when he twigged that he was not alone. A woman in her mid-thirties still sat in a chair against the far wall. He hadn't noticed her before because she'd been seated directly behind the large woman with the sequined headscarf. A sunbeam invaded the room through a skylight, ricocheted off the bevelled edge of a mirror and splattered the opposite wall with seven colours, the violet intruding onto her cheek, and it was there that Peter noticed a tear slowly falling.

He couldn't be sure if she was in distress, or if she wanted to be left alone; he wasn't certain if she knew of his presence, or if his silence concealed him. He was about to ask if she needed help, when she arose and started to make her way slowly forward, a white stick in her right hand sweeping the ground before her, her left arm groping cautiously. As she edged forward, Peter noticed a book on the floor immediately before her which the white stick had missed, and he called out a warning. His unexpected words ploughed into her unguarded solitude, she responsively twisted in the direction of the startling voice, caught a foot behind a chair leg and pitched forward, striking her forehead on the edge of a table as she fell. The white stick scudded across the floor, and her stunned body slumped onto the polished wood floor and lay motionless and crumpled.

Peter was at her side within a second of her hitting the ground, and immediately regretted never having taken first aid lessons. He tore into the foyer hoping to find help, but everyone had gone; and the street outside was deserted. Back in the conference room, he knelt beside her, took off his anorak and turned it inside-out, intending to place it beneath her head. Then he remembered that for fainting patients, the head had to be kept low. He wasn't sure if the same applied to concussion, but he straightened her legs as best as he could and slipped the coat under her feet.

The thought then occurred to him that she may not even be alive. He placed fingertips on her wrist but could feel no pulse. He reached for her handbag hoping to find a small mirror which he could place beneath her nostrils to detect breathing; but then realised that a blind woman was unlikely to carry a mirror.

He was just thinking of trying to find a telephone to call an ambulance, when she let out a soft groan and her eyes flickered open.

"Are you alright?" he asked anxiously.

"I'm not sure. Who are you?"

"I'm Peter; Peter Goodwin. You've had a nasty fall. You'd better lie quite still."

"There's something under my feet."

"Yes. It's my coat. I'll rearrange it for you." He took up the folded anorak, gently lifted her head, and placed the coat carefully beneath it.

"There's no need for that. I must get up and go home. Can you find my stick, please?"

"You mustn't try to get up," he said soothingly. "You hit your head as you fell. You've been unconscious for a while. There might be internal injuries. You lie there quietly, and I'll go and call an ambulance."

"I don't need an ambulance. I'm sure I'll be all right."

Peter noticed that a slight swelling had already appeared on her forehead and he redoubled his efforts to persuade her to get medical attention.

"You don't look at all well. Do you have a headache?"

"It feels sore, but it doesn't throb."

"Do you feel dizzy?"

"I won't know until I stand up."

"Is your – er –" he was about to ask if her vision was blurred, but checked himself in time. "Look, I feel very guilty about this. I was the one who startled you and made you fall. I'd feel much better if we got a doctor to look you over."

"All right then, if it makes you happy," she said at length, with a slight smile. "But no ambulances mind. I don't want any fuss. I'll take a bus to the outpatients' clinic. It's not far."

Peter helped her to her feet and she stood for a while as he recovered her stick.

"I'd very much like to go to the hospital with you, if you'll allow me. I don't like to leave you like this. May I? Please?"

She didn't really want any company at that moment, but his voice sounded so kindly that she couldn't bring herself to refuse.

"All right, then. Do you mind if I take your arm? We'll get along faster that way."

"Of course," agreed Peter, and guided her hand over his elbow.

"I'm Alice, by the way," she said with a reassuring nod, and together they walked carefully into the sunshine.

Chapter Four

The unwrinkled surge of four electric motors, the velvet grasp of airbrakes and the compassion of a sprung steel underframe carried the Goodwin family towards the suburbs of Plumham Wood. Eighteen months had sprinted past since Christopher had first made that same trip with Christine, a journey that had been repeated every week afterwards. This evening, though, was different: his parents, little sister and elder brother were with him. This evening was special, very special: it was Christopher and Christine's engagement party.

Jim Goodwin had suggested using the Co-op hall for his son's party. Although his wages were still meagre, he did enjoy a few perks from his employer, and free hire of the hall was one of them. But Christine's parents knew of Ruby Goodwin's failing eyesight, were concerned about her trying to prepare the food, and tactfully insisted that their house be used instead.

Christopher now sat next to his sister on the generously spaced seating of a newly designed tramcar, the herald of luxury travel. It was a pleasantly warm, cloudless June evening; and as the world whispered past on the other side of the car's air-operated doors, his mind slid into his favourite daydream: a second-by-second recall of his first journey with Christine. He ran the memory like a film: prolonging the tension with slow motion; re-running the dramatic reversals; freeze-framing the sweetest moments. His quest had come so close to failure that he needed to reassure himself of the present. He relived its narrative whenever he couldn't sleep, or while he was bored, in fact, at any time when he wasn't with Christine. His chronicle of missed opportunities had been privately edited and re-edited a thousand times, but it engrossed him now more than ever.

***

"No seats outside. Standing only inside," the young conductor had announced, aping the language of his older colleagues who really had served on open-top tramcars. Christine and Christopher pressed their way into the packed saloon, heated only by the density of human bodies. A slightly built man in a trilby hat had offered Christine his seat, but she politely refused and remained standing next to Christopher, whose mind was so busy trying to think of a suitable way of asking her for a date that he hadn't recognised the significance of her gesture.

He was tall enough to hold the polished brass handrail that traversed the ceiling, but she could only reach the suspended leather strap, and she softly fell against him as the tram lurched into motion. The warmth of the crowded car awakened her *Sans Adieu* perfume, which drifted upwards and toyed with Christopher's nostrils as he strenuously urged his disobliging brain to deliver an opening line: "Would you be agreeable to…?" Too formal. "May I have the honour…?" Too pompous. "Will you…?" Too abrupt.

***

"What does engagement really mean? The question interrupted his reverie and brought him back to the present.

"Pardon?"

"Being engaged. What's it all about?" asked little sister Anne, who no longer played hopscotch or skipped because her budding breasts now bounced embarrassingly.

"It means being trapped," commented Jack from the seat behind. Although a smile crossed his face, his words were only partly in jest. Jack now earned a substantial wage, far more than his father did, and he saw himself as the family's guardian. He had quietly pledged himself not to marry while they were short of money, which was not too difficult for him, as he did not find himself particularly attracted towards women. But at times, his concern for the family seemed too intense. He had obtusely suggested to his brother, more than once, that he ought to follow his example, and since Christopher had dated regularly, an unsteady edginess had wavered between them. Which was a pity. If only the Plumham Cooperative Society had paid their father an adequate salary, an otherwise loving family would have been free from such friction.

Christopher gave Anne a less cynical reply to her question, and gazed out of the window as the Victorian yellow brick of central Plumham gave way to Edwardian red. The tram stopped at a change pit for a few moments, where its urban plough was shed and the suburban overheard wire was coupled to the trolley pole. Recollection of that spot again triggered his best-loved narrative.

***

"Do you ever go to the theatre?" Christine had asked, as the allure of her perfume intensified. "There are two now in Plumham."

"They cost quite a bit. Two shillings, I think. The cinema is only sixpence, and they change their programmes three times a week now. Besides, I still have to watch my pennies. I haven't finished my apprenticeship yet."

"How much longer have you got to go?"

"Just under a year."

"That's not so bad. All you need is to find a friend who's sympathetic. I think that girls should always pay their way, especially when they're earning more than a boy." Her soft brown eyes dilated to their warmest and she smiled sweetly up at him, but again her invitation was not harvested. Christopher's distant mind still sweated for inspiration. "Do you think you could possibly see you way clear to…?" Too wordy. "Why don't you…?" Too patronising. "A friend of mind has this problem. He'd like to ask a girl out, but…" Too spineless.

***

"End of the line. All change." Christopher's main feature was now disturbed by the conductor as he strode impatiently down the aisle flicking over the seat backs for the return journey. The family stepped down from the tram and walked a little way up the road to where the double overhead cables denoted a trolley bus route.

"What are these electric buses like?" asked Anne, who hadn't been to this part of Plumham before.

"Very quiet. Very smooth," replied Christopher.

"That's right," agreed jack. "I travelled on one last Saturday when I went by myself to see Tottenham play at home."

To a bystander, Jack's remark would have seemed pleasant enough, but for Christopher it was another mild rebuke. His elder brother often hinted that too much female company emasculated young men, and that he shouldn't neglect 'manly' pursuits, like going to watch football matches together as they used to do.

Christopher felt his mother slide a hand around his arm and give it a reassuring squeeze. Although she'd never admit it, Ruby had a closer bond with her younger son than with anyone, including her husband. They shared cherished hopes and confidences that were hard to say to anyone else; and each tasted the other's griefs and joys piquantly. She held dear the thought of Christopher getting married and raising his own children. For her, family was a precious river: the only thing that made sense of life; the one thing that remained after death. Not that she didn't appreciate what Jack was doing for them, but she quietly wished that he'd dampen his earnestness.

As a trolley bus coasted around its terminus loop and halted by them, Christopher sensed his mother's need, and felt the weight of the future upon him. Several times recently she had tenderly assured him that he was not deserting her, but was giving her fulfilment. Nevertheless, he still felt for Jack, who was benevolently working his way into a blank tomorrow.

The placid comfort of London Transport's latest innovation soothed Christopher's concern, and its softly spoken engine carried his thoughts back once more to abdication day.

***

"When are you going dancing again?"
"I'm not sure if I'll be able to."
"Why's that?"

"My friend Janet, the girl I usually go with. She might be getting serious over her boyfriend, and won't have the time to go with me anymore."

They were surrounded by the smells of humanity. A loosely wrapped pack of fish and chips oiled the air; but the infrequently washed clothing of a tallow worker was less savoury. An aromatic kaleidoscope of camphorated oil, liquid paraffin, eucalyptus, mindererus spirit, sal volatile, creosote and wintergreen betrayed an array of ills, seasonal and chronic; and a man returning from a funeral had the pockets of his solitary conserved suit stuffed with mothballs. But Christopher's nose was oblivious to them all. For him, Christine's perfume filled the world, defined it, and left him tongue-tied as it wafted around her chiffon headscarf. Her favourite uncle had jauntily given her the little bottle of scent last Christmas, her first and only encounter with luxury, and she had made it last ever since.

"Can't you go to the dance alone?"

"My mum wouldn't like that."

"I went by myself."

"It's different for boys."

"Yes. I suppose it is."

"She might let me go though, if she knew that I was going with a boy who's reliable. Someone respectable. Someone nice."

Each syllable that she voiced fluttered appealingly, but they fell on stony ears. Only half of Christopher's mind was alive to his surroundings and, unfortunately, it was the wrong half. His psyche still toiled to compose. "How about...?" Too offhand. "Might I enquire...?" Too grandiose. "May, perchance...?" Too poetic.

***

"Has Christine's house really got an inside toilet?" Little sister Anne's inquisitiveness again intruded on his reminiscence. For the artisans of urban Plumham, a back yard and an outside privy were the status quo, for which they counted their blessings. In some other communities, back-to-back housing meant a communal lavatory. What's more, all the people of Plumham now had water piped to their homes; whereas in Shoreditch, two out of three still used the street pump. For Anne Goodwin, boiling a kettle on a frosty morning to melt the ice at the bottom of the lavatory pan had never seemed a hardship; until recently. A number of girls at her school had moved out to the new estates, and a fresh *crème de la crème* boasted of their improved facilities. Since then, Anne had imagined herself to be at the bottom of the pile. Not only was her family lavatory outdated, but she had never visited a house that was any different. Now, her trip to Plumham Wood was going to remedy that indignity. There, she would experience an indoor lavatory at first-hand, and then she'd be able to look her school friends straight in the face again.

"Yes, it has," answered Christopher, a little bemused by the question.

"Will they let me use it?"

"Of course."

"That's wonderful," she concluded, with a vigour that took him aback.

Christopher pondered the wisdom of her questions for a while, and watched through the bus window as new rows of brindled red bricks, regimented by neat lines of lime mortar, marked the frontier of Metroland. The disciplined lines of, as yet, unsoiled buildings augured cleaner, better times to come; and the thought of a bright tomorrow swept him back, once more, into yesterday.

***

The final scene of Christopher's epic daydream found them both standing at the trolley bus stop for the last leg of her journey home. Christine suggested that she should now travel alone, because the buses on this route did not run late, and he might find himself stranded. Her idea left him with mixed feelings. It would avoid embarrassment, as he almost certainly didn't have enough money to pay the fare; but it also meant that he'd have to untie his tongue before the bus arrived.

She sensed his quandary, and eased the air with snippets about her family's recent past. They moved to Plumham Wood nine months ago. Her father had been reluctant to take on his first mortgage in mid-life, but her mother was the family dynamo, and now he was pleased that she had egged him into it. Perhaps, if Christine had remained silent; then Christopher might have found his voice, but as a trolley bus swung into the kerbside, he still hadn't put the right words together.

As the two people in front of them boarded the bus, Christine stood on tiptoe, brushed her lips softly against his cheek, whispered "Goodnight" in his ear, and then mounted the platform as the conductor rang the bell. She had pressed a trigger. A bullet of ice-hot frenzy shot from his feet to his head, where it instantly defrosted his brain and then hurtled back down again to electrify every nerve ending in his body.

Christine gripped the chrome handrail as the bus pulled away, looked back over her shoulder to wave, and was immobilised by the sight of Christopher starting to run after her. His long legs pounded at an incredible pace, and for a while he closed to within five or six feet of the bus's rear.

"Will you... let me... see you... again?" he panted. She nodded vigorously, her face wearing an unusual contradiction of both anxiety and relief. Now it was her turn to be speechless.

The conductor looked from one to the other with unconcealed amusement, and a number of passengers in the rear seats had also noticed. As it accelerated, the bus started to pull away from Christopher, but Christine's reassuring kiss had unlocked remarkable reserves of energy, and he managed to close the gap again as his arms hammered desperately to pump the oxygen that his muscles screamed for. She wanted to jump down onto the road to join him, but by now the speed was too great.

"This... Saturday?" Again she nodded eagerly, leaned from the platform to be closer to him, and looked for a moment as if she'd lose her balance and fall. Most of the lower deck passengers had realised that something was happening, and many rose from their seats to watch.

"Seven..." The pain from his leg from the dance hall fall had now returned, but he endured it doggedly. "...o'clock..." It was a cruel irony. As the bus drew away, he needed to shout louder, but his vital, gulping need for breath almost stopped him from saying anything, "...outside the..." They were the last words that he could manage. The massive draughts of breath that he now dragged into his lungs paralysed his larynx, and the torrents of freezing night air sandpapered the walls of his windpipe and blurred his vision. It was like sailing around the world, only to sink outside the home port. He had found life's fortune, and lost it again. As his blood pressure soared, the world started to turn red.

Then, suddenly, Christine found her voice and, not for the first time that night, reacted to his distress flares. She slung her arms around the upright handrail to steady herself on the swaying bus platform, cupped her gloved hands to her mouth and shouted louder than she believed possible,

"Outside the cinema!"

At first she thought that he might be out of earshot, then he raised both arms with thumbs extended and waved wildly.

Her joy sank as she turned inwards to find everyone staring at her, and she escaped embarrassment by climbing the stairs and spending the last leg home wrapped in a cloud of other people's tobacco smoke.

Christopher, meanwhile, staggered to the side of the road, tried to support himself on a lamppost, missed it, and slumped into the gutter as his heart slammed against the inside of his ribcage and felt as if it was almost about to jump up his throat and out of his mouth. He lay there, doubled up, for a full five minutes, frantically guzzling air, and then climbed painfully to his feet. He carefully checked every inch of his precious new suit, and was relieved to find it undamaged; so he limped back to the tram stop, exhausted and bedraggled, but elated beyond words.

***

Wake up, dream boy. We're here." Christopher felt Jack's forefinger prodding his shoulder and, with his family, he alighted from the bus, just a little breathless from the exertions of his wandering thoughts.

"Oh! Aren't they lovely," exclaimed Ruby as she noticed the select number of agreeably spaced detached houses set away from the road by lengthy gardens, their Tudor pedigree stretching back at least nine years. She slowly focused her failing eyes on the solidity of their oak doors carved in a stylised version of linenfold panelling; the idealised Romanticism of dormer windows; the apparent antiquity of jettied upper storeys, half-timbered with unseasoned elm infilled with herringbone pattern brick nogging.

"You deserve to live in one of those, Mum," commented Jack with good intent, not realising the concealed humiliation his father felt.

"Does Christine's family live in one of those big places?" asked Jim Goodwin to deflect his awkwardness.

"No, Dad," replied his younger son. "Those houses cost a small fortune. Theirs is at the back, and much smaller."

The exclusive properties which they were looking at were originally flanked by extensive woodland, and the purchasers bought them in the belief that their surroundings would not be disturbed. Then a pitiless firm of builders acquired the adjacent land, and proposed a large development of lesser quality homes for lesser quality people. It was even rumoured that some of the designs included flush faced interior doors. How could civilised life be preserved without door panels? The Plumham Wood pioneers were up in arms, a bitter struggle ensued to repel the invaders, but they lost the day. Now, the view from their rear windows was no longer virgin forest, but defiled vapidity. Sycamore, oak and chestnut had capitulated to an undulating, unvarying and unending desert of roofing tiles. There were, though, two minor windfalls. All of the roofs had gables of some sort, which distinguished them from council housing; and none of them was flat. The developers had no time for Le Corbusier or Walter Gropius, which thankfully deterred those *frightful* people who read Virginia Wolf novels and refused to hang net curtains at their Suntrap windows.

"Perhaps film stars live here," said Anne, remembering that Cedarwood Film Studios were only a few miles down the road. "Hollywood must be like this."

The houses' occupants were, in fact, mostly dentists, solicitors and higher grade civil servants, infiltrated with a sprinkling of bank clerks whose subsidised mortgages and contractually delayed marriages enabled them to perch above their economical stations. But, whatever their position, they all had one thing in common: dislike of the new neighbours who had devalued their property, deflowered their landscape, degraded their locality, deflated their self-esteem.

"I think it's more like Park Lane or Mayfair," suggested her mother, who had never been to either place, but remembered the names from the new board game which Jack had brought for the family last Christmas. "It's so English," she added, with selfless pride and a sense of unassuming affinity. Although her eyes were declining, they had never been green.

The family group made their way reverentially along an access road between the highly desirable residences, and entered an avenue of second-grade properties. Here, four walls still stood independently, but the gables were not hipped, exposed bricks only peeped through the rendering at door surrounds, the porches were supported by spiralling pillars of tiles, and the houses were christened with numbers instead of names.

In one modestly sized garden, a cast concrete birdbath had been placed at its centre, and a small area of paving encircled it. A little toddler peddled a shiny red and green tricycle around it at remarkable speed. As they passed, he rang the enormous bell on the handlebar, and gave them a broad smile which displayed all of his six teeth. Anne waved back, and returned his grin with an even wider one.

The affable evening air was sprightly with the sound of lawnmowers and handsome with the scent of newly cut grass, two encounters that were unlikely in urban Plumham, apart from the park and the cemetery. The Goodwins had passed the gold and the silver, and were now in a chromium crescent where pairs of houses embraced, their joinery painted in grime-resistant cream and their steel framed windows paying homage to antiquity with leaded fanlights.

Geniality heartened their walk through the estate. A man forking over a flower bed removed the Vulcanite briar pipe from his mouth and bid them a cheerful "Good evening"; a chubby nervous-looking woman in a floral apron looked up from polishing her brass doorstep plate, and gave them a shy nod; a studious looking man walking in the opposite direction with a pile of library books under one arm stepped courteously aside, raised his hat and paid tribute to the fine weather. Whatever Plumham Wood's early settlers might have feared, these barbarian hordes were not impolite.

They had now reached the other ranks of housing, where terraced lance-corporals and privates stood in regimented straight lines. Indifferently laid stock bricks were now cloaked with pebble-dashing; and iron-studded oak had given way to Swedish redwood for front doors, which discordantly flirted with Art Deco in the sunray motifs of their glazing. The lawnmowers here had a budget quality sound, although the grass smelled as sweet as elsewhere. The boys who played in the traffic-free road all wore belts with snake buckles to draw in their grey flannel trousers which had been bought two sizes too large to accommodate future growth; and the girls who performed handstands all revealed navy-blue knickers with a handkerchief tucked into one leg.

Halfway along the road Christopher opened a front gate, ushered his family down a short garden flanked by roses to an already open door, where Christine's parents stood with open arms.

Greetings were affectionate and sincere. Harry Groves, who was only faintly less shy than Jim Goodwin, shook hands warmly, while the resourceful Sally Groves, maker of Christine's posh frock, hugged and kissed everyone.

"This is a lovely place you've got," blurted out Jim Goodwin, who'd spent two weeks rehearsing his opening line, knowing that he'd remain voiceless if he didn't. "Everywhere is so clean here."

"That's because it's all brand new," smiled Christine's father. "It won't be long before it's as grubby as everywhere else."

They filed into the sitting room through a door which was not flushed as the established had feared, although it was panelled in mass-produced Columbian pine and fitted with a lock set in cheap marbled Bakelite.

"Oh dear," fell from Ruby Goodwin's lips as she glanced around the room. "We're too early. There's no one else here. Whatever must you think of us?" she added, and her whole family shrank into its shell of embarrassment.

"No, no. It's just what we wanted," eased Sally nimbly, having been well prepared for the legendary Goodwin solicitude. "Now we can all get cosy before the rest arrive. Harry, why don't you take Mr Goodwin out the back and show him your workshop?"

Jim Goodwin thankfully followed Harry out into the small back garden, and together they entered the newly erected shed, with its bouquet of creosote. On a little bench at one end stood a three-sided black iron last, where the family's shoes were mended. On the wall above was hung a modest range of tools, mostly second-hand; and on two shelves stood rows of cardboard boxes preserving Harry's carefully catalogued 'might-come-in-handy' collection: the salvaged innards of several worn out electrical appliances, a set of developing dishes, although he didn't yet have a camera, the movements from three broken clocks; and a lifetime's accumulation of part-worn hinges, locks, screws, nails, horseshoes, broken tiles and a number of oddments that he could no longer identify.

"Welcome to the workhouse, Mr Goodwin," said Harry, chuckling, as timid men do, at his own joke to avoid misunderstandings.

"Call me Jim, please."

"Of course, old chap. Of course. And I'm Harry." They both shook hands again, and Christine's father looked furtively out of the shed door, then closed it quietly behind him. "You know what, Jim? I think we both need fortifying for the evening ahead."

After taking a second cautionary glance through the shed window, he then crossed to a small wall-hung cupboard which he'd made, at the age of twelve, during his second term of school woodworking classes. It had seen sterling service. His mother had used it to store home-made medicines; then both his daughters had commandeered it for a toy box; and now it housed his possessions that he liked to think of as most secret, although all the family knew about them.

He opened the cupboard door, took out two small cups and a bottle of Great War vintage rum: the official issue used in the trenches to embolden the troops before they went 'over-the-top'.

"I didn't know that you could still get that stuff."

"You can if you know where to look."

Two generous measures were poured, and they toasted 'The Future' and took discreet sips of the liquid courage. They then drank to their wives, to their children, to the forthcoming marriage and 'the good of days' before their cups needed recharging.

Within the house, Sally had lubricated Ruby Goodwin's social stiffness with a glass of port, and now talked her through a brief tour of her new home. Ruby marvelled at the convenience of having electric power points, a gas cooker, and a fixed bath in a little room of its own with running hot and cold water; and, as was her nature, she admired it all without the slightest trace of envy.

Meanwhile, little sister Anne had given the coveted indoor lavatory a leisurely and luxurious trial, and Christine's elder sister, Janice, had pushed back the sliding doors between the two small reception rooms, and now stood alone with Jack, awkwardly trying to make conversation. If anything, she was even less impressed with the opposite sex than he was. She had endured the past company of several lukewarm boyfriends, and had now quietly decided to become a career woman.

By the time they were halfway through their second cups, the two fathers had revealed large reservoirs of confidences. Christopher's father never drank because he couldn't afford it, and Harry Groves rarely did so because he preferred to spend the money on his family; so the distilled sugar opened two floodgates of restraint almost at once. Jim confessed to feeling guilty about not contributing to the party, and Harry reassured him that his offer of the Co-op hall was generous, but perhaps this way was more homely. Harry, in turn, showed concern that the Goodwin family had invited none of their friends or relatives, and Jim unfurled his unease about being a burden to others. Hesitantly, Harry let on that he was worried about having taken on a first mortgage so late in life, and Jim admitted to a sense of failure for never having had one. But as the viscous liquid sunshine warmed their thoughts, so talk about a brighter future effloresced, and the duologue finally blossomed with ideas about having grandchildren, and bouncing babies on knees once again.

When they re-entered the house twenty minutes later, it was full of guests; but the fathers' convivial handbrakes had been released, and they felt ready to face them.

Jim strode up to his younger son and placed a confident hand on his shoulder. "When you're wed, Chris, don't you waste your money paying rent, like I've always done. You buy yourself a nice place like this one." Then looking his future daughter-in-law straight in the eye for the very first time, he added, "And you, my dear, must make sure that he does."

This was a Jim Goodwin neither of them had seen before, and they could only nod in astonishment.

"What do you suppose they've been talking about?" whispered Ruby to her new friend.

"Old husbands' tales, I expect," replied Sally, who not only knew about the hidden rum, but had prompted the manoeuvre in the first place.

Jim's newly adventurous eye scanned the scene. The men wore suits, and the clerical workers could be distinguished by the shiny seats of their trousers; all, that is, except Uncle Archie. He had given Christine her bottle of perfume, and had graduated to owning a best suit, which he wore for weddings, funerals, christenings and hospital visits.

One man stood alone, and empathy took Jim to his side and discovered him to be Christine's Uncle Larry.

"What do you do for a living?" enquired Larry.

"Oh, I've just got a dull job with the Co-op. What about you?"

"Me? I'm in shipping." Uncle Larry stood alone because his pretentious replies made most think of him as snobbish, but they were wrong; his seeming pomposity masked an acute sense of distress over his closeness to the breadline. He was, in fact, a poorly-paid clerk with a stingy shipping company in the City of London, but had been nurtured in the belief that appearances had to be maintained, at all costs. For him, a visit to the pawnbroker was not an option; not that he really had anything worth pawning. To save money he walked almost everywhere, and frequently had to line his worn shoes with cardboard until he could afford to have them mended.

His only windfall had been the inheritance of a suit from a deceased cousin, which he'd worn to an old friend's retirement party. But the cousin had been smaller than Larry, whose hands had then to be used to hold down the ill-fitting waistcoat and jacket sleeves, and so he'd missed out on the proffered food and drink at that event. Not wanting a repeat of that headache tonight, he'd climbed into his working suit, after having carefully doctored the fraying cuffs and trouser turn-ups with black ink.

At first they could find no common interests, but the shipping man had a low Plimsoll line when it came to alcohol. His glass of stout painted Jim as a kindred spirit, and when they discovered that their fathers had both kept poultry in their backyards, the conversation took off. Their trip down memory alleyway savoured Rhode Island, Wyandottes and Buff Orpingtons; nest boxes and entry traps; fertility testing and incubators; crop binding, gapes and scaly leg.

When Jim moved away from him to circulate again, they shook hands as if they had been life-long friends. Neither could have guessed that they were destined never to meet again. The cost of daily travel to the City by train was too much for Larry's paltry income, and he left home very early so that he could buy a cheap workman's return tram ticket which demanded journey's end by eight that morning, then he'd sit in a central London park for an hour waiting for his office to open. That December was to have an unusually cold spell, Larry's morning exposure would lead to pneumonia, and by Christmas he'd be dead.

Jim's next encounter was with Great Aunt Flossie, and it took only a couple of minutes for him to realise why she was by herself. She spoke as if she had news of stellar importance to reveal, but she only offered endlessly tedious trifles about deadly dull people. He endured it for nine or ten minutes, then broke away with the excuse that he had to help out in the kitchen.

He reached the kitchenette door as Christine emerged, carrying a tray of ham sandwiches, followed by Christopher with a dish of pickled onions and a bowl of mustard, and then Harry Groves holding a new bottle of port to top-up the ladies' glasses.

"Are all your guests here now?"

"All except those awful people who live next door," answered Christine.

"Why did you invite them if they're not very nice?"

"Actually, old Arthur Screep is quite a pleasant chap, but he's very ill. We only remain friendly with them for his sake," explained Harry. "His wife though, she gives me the pip," he added with a rare dash of disdain.

"And there's their ghastly son," reminded Christine.

The family's sorrow for their neighbour was under constant reminder. Mr Screep was in the late stages of cancer. The inadequate analgesics that could be prescribed were no longer effective, and his screams of agony could be heard most nights through the thin party wall.

"Why is your neighbour's son so awful?" asked Christopher when he and Christine had finished handing round the food.

"I've not mentioned him before, but I suppose I ought to tell you now. I went out with Malcolm Screep for a short while before I met you, and he's pestered me ever since to go out with him again. His mother is very pushy too, and I can't stand the sight of them."

"Is he so bad, then?"

"He's so slimy and spooky. Those are the best words I can think of. You'll be able to judge for yourself soon. He won't miss a chance to come here."

Christine looked as though she was going to say more, but the door opened and into the room loomed a baleful matriarch, trailing an unctuous young man in her wake.

"This is Mrs Screep and her son, Malcolm," announced Sally, and a frost settled on the gathering as the newcomer stood in her thick brown stockings and scrutinised the other guests with her lead coloured eyes.

"Is your husband coming?" asked Harry.

"He is unfit," she replied with an inflection of arctic indifference. For Mrs Screep, her husband was just a lingering nuisance who stood in the way of collecting from his substantial life assurance policies.

As she folded her arms across her chest and hoisted her sagging breasts into a confrontational stance, Malcolm moved out of her shadow, stepped up to Christine, bowed his heavily brilliantined head and said, "Watákushi no sekkusu wo suru ka?"

"I'm sorry, I don't speak Chinese."

"It's Japanese, actually."

"What does it mean?"

"It means welcome and good fortune," lied Malcolm. The question, in truth, asked if Christine would have sex with him, although the grammar was solecistic; and he bowed again kneading a dough of sour smarm.

Christine smiled and curtsied, thinking that she had been complimented; but Christopher eyed him cautiously, and had an uneasy feeling that he'd met Malcolm Screep somewhere before.

"Isn't he wonderful!" pronounced Mrs Screep, stepping forward so that she looked at her son to admire him. "He taught himself, you know. He's so clever. He has a frightfully good position at the Foreign Office, and he assists them in their dealings with the Far East. They think the world of him. One day he'll make the perfect husband for some very lucky girl." With that closing remark she looked Christine steadily in the face and nodded, as if to say 'Look what you're missing'.

In actuality, her Malcolm had quite a lowly job in the civil service, and they didn't think much of him. He'd learned Japanese in his spare time hoping to secure a post that was soon to fall vacant, but in spite of his efforts, he'd been turned down for the promotion.

"And you must be Mr Goodwin," said Malcolm, giving Christopher a limp and clammy handshake. "You are a very lucky fellow."

"Indeed I am," replied Christopher, and as he released the dank hand, he suddenly remembered where he'd seen that face before, and his mind was thrown back, once more, to the night when he'd first met Christine.

***

During the tram journey back to central Plumham, Christopher had eased his sore limbs while his mind still danced with divinely unbelievable memories. The extended rendition of 'These Foolish Things' swirled around the sweet recollection. The stretch of the melody had drawn him and Christine together, and he would show his gratitude by building his own souvenir collection. There was an empty shoebox at home, and he'd fill it with memories of her. He'd start with the evening's tram ticket, and the packet of cigarettes that still lay untouched in his pocket.

When he alighted from the tram, the pubs were turning out and London's gutters began to flow with urine, adding another aroma to the City's fragrance. As he waited to cross the road, a friendly hand fell on his shoulder.

"It's young Goodwin, isn't it?"

Christopher turned to find half a dozen men from his works, fronted by the machine-shop foreman. Their unusual friendliness had obviously been minted by an evening's heavy drinking. Skilled hands didn't usually socialise with apprentices, and Christopher felt honoured by the attention he was receiving.

"So, what have you been up to, my lad?"

"I've been dancing."

"Been to the local hop, eh?"

"Do you know the official definition of ballroom dancing?"

Christopher shook his head.

"It's a navel engagement without loss of semen."

Although they'd heard the joke before, all roared with laughter, and Christopher felt that he ought to do the same, even though the innuendo was beyond him. After all, it wasn't every day that he was treated as an equal by the machine-shop's hierarchy.

"And where have you gentlemen been?" asked Christopher, anxious to return the conversation.

"Gentlemen? Us? That's a new one."

"He'll go far, this lad."

"Flattery will get you everywhere."

"We've been celebrating Chalky's stag night. He's getting hitched on Saturday."

Christopher's lowly status and slender wages had kept him away from stag nights; although he'd heard wildly exaggerated tales about them.

"Is Thursday unusual for a stag night?" asked Christopher, searching for something to say.

"He needs a day to get over it."

"Otherwise, if he doesn't show up at the church, we'll get the blame."

"So, how did you make out tonight, young Goodwin?"

"Did you get your end away lad?"

Christopher's esteem for his elders clashed with his respect for Christine, and put him in a fluster. He put his hand quickly into this pocket for the emergency kit he had not yet used.

"Er, would anyone like a cigarette?" he stammered.

"Du Maurier. They're a bit posh, on an apprentice's wages."

"Have you had your hand in the till?"

"I can only afford Woodbines."

"You've got a wife and eight kids. He hasn't."

The Woodbine man was already smoking, and the rest were pipe smokers, having been successfully groomed by Mr Mubby, so Christopher put the cigarettes back into his pocket.

"Aren't you having one, lad?"

Haltingly, Christopher explained that he didn't smoke, but had bought the cigarettes to improve his image and to mask blushes of distress. His audience collapsed with laughter. Two were physically doubled up, and looked as though they'd never be able to straighten. Then, the zephyr of alcohol blew mirth into geniality.

"That's the best laugh we've had all night," said the foreman, wrapping an affable arm around Christopher's shoulders. "You deserve a reward for that. How about coming with us for some supper?"

"I'm sorry, I can't. I've no money left."

"Don't worry about that, my old son-of-a-gun. The treat's on us."

They made their way, still chuckling, into Market Street, and approached a sea food stall.

"Now then, my lads, we'll all buy a round," began the foreman, with mock assertiveness. "Except you, my old cock sparrow," he added, slapping Christopher on the back once again. "And the order of the day is –"

"Whelks!" they all chorused.

"Whelks?" queried Christopher.

"If you want to be a member of this club, you've got to eat whelks."

"Whelks put lead in your pencil. I should know. I've got five kids."

"Five that you know about."

Christopher had seen whelks once, and their ugliness flooded his memory. It was doubtful if he could bring himself to eat any, but he was basking in the warmth of unexpected friendship, and he wanted that to abide. Although, in a sober tomorrow, it was probable that they would again pay him little heed, some might be less aloof. So it was worth the labour, and he smiled and nodded.

They spaced themselves along one side of the stall, with Christopher at the far end. The foreman bought the first round, and the little white ceramic dishes were passed along the counter flap. Christopher drenched his portion in vinegar, but, unlike the others, alcohol had not blunted his taste buds, and as he took a deep breath and sank his teeth into each twisted chunk of gristle, he could only swallow it after a monumental struggle with his feeling of revulsion and a sensation of nausea.

Before he had finished them, someone else had bought a round, and another dishful appeared before him. For the others, the conversation became solemn, as fermented hops and distilled grains worked their way through a medley of emotions. The foreman gave Chalky some well-meant matrimonial advice about finance; and an older man became nostalgic, recounting how he'd supported a family of five on twenty-nine shillings a week during unemployment in the Great Depression; and another reminded the bridegroom-to-be of the harshness of means testing for 'extended benefits'. Christopher took the opportunity, while their attention was off him, and deftly tossed the contents of the dish up onto the canvas canopy which topped the stall. Then he did the same with the next dish, and the next.

On the other side of the stall, a few people stood. Opposite Christopher was a young man with a bowler hat and a rolled umbrella, and as he looked across he saw, to his alarm, that the curly brim of the bowler hat was filling with whelks. He had supposed that the canopy was flat, but looking up he now saw that it was ridged at the centre, and his discarded whelks had been rolling down the other side. The spotty-faced young man was eating a bowl of prawns, and as he concentrated on peeling them and picking away the inedible parts under the dull light of a hurricane oil lamp, so he was unaware of the decoration being added to his hat. To Christopher's relief, the man finished his last prawn, shouldered his umbrella and left before he, or anyone else noticed.

***

Now, eighteen months later, the same face looked again at Christopher, who had no idea if this oily young man remembered him, nor if he associated him with the whelks that he must have later found around his hat.

While Christopher pondered, Sally Groves, ever purposeful, judged that the Screep family presence had already refrigerated her gathering for long enough, and attempted a defrost.

"I think it's about time some of you sang for your supper. Who would like to do their party piece?"

For most, they hadn't yet drunk enough to loosen their stays, and all hung back, except for great Uncle Cedric, the brother of Flossie. His age demolished inhibition; he was too close to the end of life to wait for anything.

"I've got my cards, and a few other things with me," he said buoyantly, pushing himself forward. Sally sat on her disappointment, and bravely showed a face of approval. Old Cedric had performed conjuring tricks for years, and used to be quite good; but his fumbling hands, dull eyes and leaky memory now prompted giggles rather than gasps.

He settled at one end of the room, and took out a white handkerchief with an arthritic flourish.

"And now, before your very eyes, I'll make this scarf disappear," he confidently announced; but his fingers were as inaccurate as his declaration. In his right hand he clutched the outer case of a matchbox that had been fastened to a length of taut elastic which passed up his jacket sleeve and was tied at the far end to his braces. As he spoke, he thought that he'd been pressing the handkerchief into the empty box, but he'd misjudged it. With a magic word and a showy gesture, he spread open his hands to show them empty, and the matchbox cover shot up his arm without the handkerchief, which merely floated to the floor. "There. That's magic!" he proclaimed triumphantly, not being aware of his blunder.

"It's on the deck," muttered an old workmate of Harry, whose speech was still salted by his duty in the navy during the Great War; but most of the others politely applauded, pretending not to have noticed.

He then took out a coin, palmed it successfully, and regenerated it from behind Christine's head and out of Christopher's nose. He looked, for a moment, as though he was going to do the same from the cleavage of Mrs Screep's hoisted bosom, but her permanent glare of disapproval dissuaded him, and instead he went for the safer option of her son's left ear.

Flushed with success, he produced playing cards from his pocket and tried to shuffle them; but he'd drawn out the wrong pack. This one had been drilled through and fitted with a rubber band, so that the card inserted into its middle would rise up again, as if bewitched. It took Cedric a while to realise that he was trying to shuffle the wrong pack, and after he'd found the right one, his humiliated hands sent the next two card tricks disastrously wrong.

Sally Groves rescued him. As he prepared for another probable calamity, she stepped in front, clapped enthusiastically, thanked him for a wondrous show, and most of the others followed her lead. Almost instantly, Cedric forgot his errors, gave a series of deep bows and retired contentedly to the back of the room.

"So, who's next?"

"What about the happy couple doing a turn?" leered Malcolm Screep.

"Oh no. There's nothing that I can do," pleaded Christopher.

"Yes there is," persuaded Christine. "We can demonstrate our dance."

Her commandeering of the foxtrot as exclusively theirs warmed him to the idea. It was the dance that had first entwined them: it was fitting to celebrate it. Before he had a chance to decline, everyone else pushed themselves back against the walls, Sally wound the gramophone and lowered the needle onto Roy Fox's 'Touch Of Your Lips'.

During the past eighteen months Christopher had had plenty of practice, and now gave a good account of himself, in spite of the tiny floor space. Sally's head swayed with the rhythm as Denny Dennis sang the romantic ballad. She was particularly fond of this record, although she wished that Sid Buckman had set aside his trumpet and taken the vocal.

"Why don't you join in, Malcolm? I'm sure that any of the ladies will be pleased to dance with you," suggested Christine's mother, still uneasy about the detachment of the Screeps.

"My Malcolm wouldn't dream of doing *that* sort of thing," decreed Mrs Screep, as if dancing the foxtrot was the depth of depravity. Her Malcolm was not at all worried though, as he looked fixedly at Christine's slender body and mentally undressed her for the tenth time that evening.

As they finished their dance with a swirl, great Aunt Flossie suddenly tottered across the floor towards Christine, and apprehensive looks crossed the faces of those who knew her. She hadn't found anyone to talk to for a while, so she'd passed the time drinking out of any unattended glass that she could find. Now, a mixture of port, eggnog, gin and brown ale swilled around her stomach, bleariness veiled her face, and a turbulent inner woman drew breath. The transformation was phenomenal.

"I must give you a warning before you marry," she loudly spluttered to Christine, whose eyes widened in surprise. "I was the only girl in our family. I had eight brothers, and he was one of them." Her finger pointed accusingly at Cedric the clumsy conjurer, who tried to make himself inconspicuous. "One by one, they all got around to asking if they could see my private parts. And they all wanted to show me theirs. Put me off for life it did."

Older members of the Groves family knew of Flossie's erratic disposition, and they swiftly surrounded her to isolate the eruption. But she wasn't to be silenced that easily.

"Men's things are horrible, they are," she shouted through the human wall. "That's why I never married."

"With a face like that, she probably didn't have any choice," muttered Jack, at which the misandrist Janice uncharacteristically raised a slight smile.

Old Cedric sidled apologetically over to the Goodwin family. "You'll have to excuse her. She's a bit tenpence-ha'penny."

"Tenpence-ha'penny?" queried little sister Anne.

"Not the full shilling," explained Jack.

The elders of the Grove family consolidated their encirclement of Flossie, and hustled her towards the door.

"Would you get us out of a tight spot, Bill?" said Harry Groves to his old workmate. "You're the only one with transport. Can you run her home? She doesn't live far away."

Bill obligingly took down his cap and coat from the hallstand while Flossie was being edged down the front garden path towards a motorcycle combination which stood at the kerbside. The saloon sidecar door was opened, and she was pushed inside without ceremony.

After turning on the fuel tap and prodding the carburettor float chamber, Bill lunged on the kick-starter; but in his hurry he hadn't noticed that the magneto was too far advanced, and the heavy single cylinder engine backfired powerfully in mid-stroke, twisting his foot and compressing his Achilles tendon. He sat back and nursed his smarting ankle while the uncles looked on anxiously; then he cautiously limped up and down the pavement to see if it would take his weight again.

While all the attention was on him, nobody noticed Flossie experimenting with the door catch to see if she could open it. By the time he'd returned to his machine, he found the sidecar empty, and Flossie was dancing a Viennese waltz down the centre of the road. As the custodians of family decorum ran up to her, she started singing a rude song at the top of her voice:

"Aunty Mary
Had a canary
Up the leg of her drawers.
When she –"

Now she was pushed back into the sidecar even more hastily. Harry Groves, having a very practical bent, unhooked the family washing line and lashed it around the sidecar to prevent another escape. Somebody volunteered to start the engine for Bill, who still limped painfully, and with relief Harry watched as the red hand of Ulster on the gold-lined rear mudguard faded from view.

"Oh dear. I'll never live this down. I should have known better and not invited her," confessed Harry Groves as he walked back up the path.

"Don't you worry, old lad. I'll soon take their minds off it," consoled Archie. Uncle Archie, giver of perfume, was a natural organiser after he'd had a few drinks. "Now, then. Who's for a party game?" he sang out as he re-entered the house.

Archie's persuasive personality and easy patter coaxed even the reluctant into a docile guessing game, then he nimbly pressed them through a series of relay races: passing an orange under the chin, blowing up paper bags and bursting them, and pushing a matchbox cover from one nose to another. He knew tensions were best unwound when people happily made fools of themselves. Even the ultra-shy Jim Goodwin felt the benefit.

Only two sat aside: Ruby Goodwin, reluctantly, sat on her chair as a martyr to her cataracts; and Mrs Screep resolutely stood on her plinth as a monument to purity. Even Malcolm Screep took part, but only in the hope of rubbing himself up against Christine.

The organiser next ventured into amiably suggestive territory. He pushed everyone out into the garden, and allowed them back one by one with a tall story that he had borrowed the Blarney Stone for the evening, and each could have a wish granted after kissing it. The participant would kneel, be blindfolded, and guilelessly kiss a woman's fleshy upper arm; but removal of the blindfold revealed a vision of Archie's rear as he pretended to pull up his trousers. Reactions varied from screams to howls of laughter, but none was without humour. By the close of the charade, though, Mrs Screep's censorious face turned bright purple, her teeth were bared and she looked as though she was about to explode; so he decided to tone down the next event.

Archie's imagination stood him in good stead for a round of forfeits, and his ingenuity charmed his audience as he thought up whimsical stunts to genially embarrass one guest after another. The entertainment was frothing merrily by the time it got to Christopher's turn, and Archie shrewdly cast his performance jointly with Christine. It was announced that Christopher was to be a horse, and Christine had to ride him into the next road, where she'd probably not be recognised, knock on house doors and ask, 'Will you please give my horse a drink?' and their task would not be fulfilled until someone produced a bucket of water and Christopher drank from it. To add spice, Archie appointed Malcolm Screep to go with them as observer and referee; and ruled that if the 'horse' collapsed and could not go on, then Malcolm was to take his place.

Christine climbed on her fiancé's back, and together they trotted across the road with Malcolm Screep in close attendance while the others cheered them on their way. Dusk had fallen, and wispy clouds were gathering to change the full moon from Cheshire to Stilton.

Into the next road, the first house they reached was a lone Victorian cottage which the developers had not been able to demolish due to complex legal covenants, and now looked quaintly out of place. The trio pushed their way up a rickety garden path, through heavily overgrown shrubs, and Christine leaned over her horse's head to knock at the front door. After a lengthy spell, swollen finger joints were seen to disturb the faded curtains at one window, but the door was not opened, so they started to retrace their steps.

Navigating the neglected garden was not easy for the novice horse, and halfway along the path he trod on a loose paving stone which tilted under their joint weight. Christopher's left foot slid into some soft soil, he hopelessly tried to regain his balance, and then tumbled into a mildewed laurel bush, taking Christine with him.

Malcolm danced with glee, and drooled incontinently as he caught a glimpse of Christine's stocking top.

"The horse is down! It's my turn now," he chirped.

"No it isn't," countered Christopher, as he pulled Christine out of the shrub and bushed himself down. "The rule is that the horse has to give up. I'm going on."

"He's right," agreed Christine when it looked as though Malcolm was going to argue, and she remounted.

Christopher didn't let on he'd twisted his ankle as he fell, and now he had difficulty walking. Leg injuries seemed to be in vogue that night; first Bill's motorcycle and now this. But he took heart remembering that he'd hurt the same limb at the dance hall eighteen months ago. He'd succeeded then; he'd do so now.

At the next house, the door was opened rather rapidly. A startled woman glanced at them, and it was closed even faster. Christopher disguised the limp as well as he could, and they reached the next house. Christine's knock was answered by a slender man in a dressing gown, who listened to her question and answered,

"Not today, thank you. I never buy from hawkers."

Going down the next garden path, Malcolm noticed the limp. "I think I ought to take over. You might injure yourself permanently," he gloated, but the covetous offer was refused.

"We can't do that. We're Methodists," was the curious reply Christine received at their next stop. Now Christopher was experiencing a great deal of pain, and he could feel his ankle swelling and pressing against the side of his shoe; but the thought of Malcolm Screep's clammy hands wrapped around Christine's legs kept him going.

The next door was opened by a friendly looking woman who raised a questioning eyebrow.

"Please, will you give my horse a drink?"

"Is he a good horse?"

"He's the very best," replied Christine, patting Christopher on the head.

The woman, fortunately, was a spirited party goer, and guessed what was happening. She brought a white enamelled bowl filled with water to the door, Christopher drank from it, thanked her warmly, and hobbled back to the party where they were applauded, and Malcolm brooded.

Archie noticed Christopher's limp, and wisely decided to lower the heat. "Now, we're all in good spirits," he announced, "we'll give our voices some exercise."

Sally Groves had invited Tinkly Tom to her party. Tinkly Tom got invited everywhere, because his piano repertoire seemed boundless. He was 'Old Tinkly' to everyone. Although a mere thirty-eight years, he looked much older, and nobody could remember ever having known a Young Tinkly.

Christine's mum was a not unaccomplished pianist herself, but like many of her generation she was too inhibited to follow her ear, and needed to see music before she could play it. When alone, she enjoyed playing the melodies of Ivor Novello, or selections from *The Desert Song*; and when she could persuade Harry to chant The Monk's Chorus, they would roam together through 'A Monastery Garden'. But she could never bring herself to thump out raucous accompaniments as Old Tinkly could.

Archie got the sing-song underway with an old London favourite, 'Down by the Old Bull and Bush'; and a fairly new one 'The Lambeth Walk'. Then the music seemed to take control, and they swayed through old music hall songs, army ballads and the latest from Tin Pan Alley.

As the singing swelled, Sally Groves made her way into the kitchenette to prepare warm drinks, and Ruby Goodwin followed her hoping to help. Behind the closed door, the two mothers hugged each other with relief at the party's success. As the kettle warmed, they chatted confidently about the engagement, and how happy they were that their children had found each other. Gradually the conversation embraced their other children, and they both showed anxiety about the outward lonesomeness of Janice and Jack. Waveringly they toyed with the idea of trying to foster friendship between them, and they were just getting down to making serious plans when the door barged open and in marched Mrs Screep.

Malcolm's mother examined the kitchen like a commanding officer conducting a billet inspection. Her eyes fell on a little shelf where Sally's home-made pickles and sauces paraded in jars wearing paper hats. Marrow pickle, Harvey sauce, damson chutney and mushroom ketchup all stood obediently to attention as she ran a fastidious eye over them.

"I'm glad to see that you make your own relishes, Mrs Groves. That one at number twenty-five, her with the peroxided hair. She's one of those lazy modern women. Doesn't even make her own jam. Buys it from the grocer, she does. Whatever is the world coming to?" The two mothers didn't attempt an explanation of the world's wrongs, so Mrs Screep strode through a captious overview of the neighbourhood's imperfections. Even when she didn't have anything derogatory to say about a woman, which wasn't often, she'd speak her name as if it was charged with sinister innuendo. Her review finished with... "That Smith woman at number twenty-four. She wears those wanton liberty bodice things. It's not natural, a woman not wearing corsets. I ask you, has the world gone mad?"

Fortunately, at that second, the water boiled and the two mothers busied themselves with cocoa, coffee essence and beef tea.

As the guests rested their voices and sipped their drinks, a few started to talk about the times of last buses home, so Archie moved to bring down the curtain with a fanfare. He led three rousing cheers for the hosts then, using a skill gained as a youth in the Boy's Brigade, he upended a large saucepan and improvised a drum roll with two wooden spoons. An elderly man produced a mouth organ from his jacket pocket and, together with Old Tinkly, they played a passionate rendition of the National Anthem.

Everyone stood respectfully for The King. Those who had seen military service threw back their shoulders, straightened their elbows and instinctively aligned their thumbs with the seams of their trousers.

In spite of his throbbing ankle, Christopher was at the pinnacle of life's happiness. He was enraptured by his love for Christine, enchanted by affection for his family, entranced by the joy of the evening, enriched by a glow of delight. He was elated with life, content with his surroundings, at ease with the world; and, as he noticed Malcolm's crestfallen face, triumph crowned his bliss.

If only he'd known, at that moment, of the malignant part which Malcolm Screep was to play in his future life, he'd have felt very differently.

Chapter Five

Peter's anxious hand pulled open the entrance door of St Agatha's Hospital, and he guided Alice carefully into the out-patients' wing.

Their trip from the Memorial Hall had been distinctive. As they reached the street, there were no buses in view, so Peter had gallantly hailed a passing taxi, in spite of Alice's protests about the extravagance. On seeing Alice's white stick and the swelling on her forehead, the driver switched off his meter, and insisted that there'd be no payment. These were first experiences for both Peter and the cabby: one had never been in black cab before; the other had never been called a saint.

Peter was now warming into his knight's tunic. He persuaded the hospital's reception clerk that Alice ought to have priority attention, and they were ushered in for a preliminary examination straight away: but the assessment nurse judged the case non-urgent, and they joined about a hundred other people in the waiting area. An electronic notice board carried the message that waiting time for low-priority patients would be at least three hours. Peter decided not to dishearten Alice with that news, and kept it to himself.

He steered her into an empty chair and sat beside her, rummaging around his brain for topics of conversation that might divert her for a hundred and eighty minutes.

Views about the weather lasted only moments, and then he looked for inspiration. He brushed away the mothballs of his memory and recollected being treated here for several childhood accidents, but since then the glazed wall tiles had been transformed with laminated plastic surgery, and the overwhelming odour of disinfectant had vanished.

"I remember this place from when I was a young boy. It used to have a strong antiseptic smell then."

"My memory doesn't go back to those days."

"There are lots of people here," he added as an afterthought.

"I know. I can smell them."

Peter sniffed, and found that she was right. A baby with an overfilled nappy crawled beneath their seats as his inattentive mother talked about her last holiday experiences to another woman; five varieties of aftershave decorated the air; four people ignored no smoking signs; and about a third of the waiting patients vented the spiced complexities of curry.

"Haven't you been here since you were a boy?" she added.

"I'm afraid I have, but not in this section. My mother died here a few months ago."

"I'm sorry. Was it sudden?"

"Not really. She seemed to gradually fade away ever since my dad died."

"Did he die recently?"

"No. He died about the time I was born. It was during the war." The hunger of loss still gnawed Peter. His mother had born a fitful depression bravely through life, but at its close he'd grieved to see the yellowed skin and glazed eyes bled by a lifetime of sadness.

"Neither of us seem to have had much luck recently."

Peter wasn't sure if she meant her blindness, or if fate had failed her in some other way, and he was about to ask when a massive woman descended on the seat in front of them, turned her head and gave them a broad smile which displayed a mouthful of grey teeth.

"Why! Hello you two," she exclaimed in a stentorian voice. Peter assumed that she must have been a friend of Alice, and nodded a greeting in return.

"This is the second time I've been here this week," she continued, turning up the front brim of her large felt hat. "Only just got over the operation on my veins, I have, and now they tell me that I've got a hiatus hernia, and I'll have to be cut open again. It's been one thing after another for ten years. It started with the fibroids, and they made me anaemic, so I had to have them done. Then I had stones, and they had to come out. After that my tubes started playing up, the bronchial ones, and I kept coughing up this nasty stuff, and all the coughing gave me a prolapse in the personal area, so I had to have that seen to. I'm a walking miracle, you know. All the doctors say so. They marvel at me, they do. 'We don't know how you keep going, Mrs Trim', they say." Peter was beginning to wish that she hadn't 'kept going', but he politely smiled and remained attentive for Alice's sake. "And all of the time I've had to put up with the palpitations, and this ringing in my ears, and hot flushes, and lumbago, and the shingles just won't leave me alone." She had the unfortunate habit of projecting her voice like an actor on stage, and many people now took notice of them, which multiplied Peter's discomfort.

"Of course, I have to count my blessings. The eczema has cleared up, so has the fungus between the toes, and that green coloured discharge from the nipples doesn't bother me any more." Then, as she started a vivid chronicle of the post-operative treatment she'd received for haemorrhoids, Peter started to feel queasy, and looked hurriedly about for a toilet door and the shortest route to it. Mercifully, as Peter felt stomach acid rising in his gullet, the woman was halted in full flight by a nurse calling her name.

"It's been lovely talking to you both," she concluded with a grateful smile. "It's so nice to meet a caring couple. These days most people just don't want to know."

"Your friend wasn't very reserved about her personal particulars," remarked Alice when the woman was out of earshot.

"My friend? I've never seen her before in my life. I thought that she was your chum."

"I don't know her, I assure you." Alice gave a sprightly chuckle. It was the first time that he'd seen her laugh, and it immediately reminded him of his mother. Now, for the first time since the panic began, he took a long, slow look over her, and realised how much she wore the hallmarks of the mother he'd known before the claws of despair tore away her freshness. The naturally waved hair, the slender figure, the sensitive face, awoke memories of a fragile beauty whom destiny had forgotten.

"What are you dreaming about?" she asked, with a threshold of awareness that was at Peter's doorstep.

"I've just realised how much you remind me of my mother."

"Come off it. I've heard that one before."

Peter wanted to plead that he meant it sincerely, but realised that his claim would only seem phoney to her. He delved the dusty cellar of his mind for another topic, and a man trundling past with a trolley of magazines and books prompted one.

"Did you enjoy that meeting we went to?"

"Not much."

"Neither did I. Why did you go?"

"I made a mistake. I thought it might be a creative writing class."

"You write?"

"Not very well. My one extravagance was to sponsor the publication of a book of my poems. But it couldn't have been much good. It didn't sell." Alice's natural modesty widely misjudged her work. She'd poured her soul into a beautiful collection which she'd entitled *On Her Blindness*; but it had emerged stillborn from the publishers' office. No one bought it, no one read it, no one cared.

"It's very brave of you, though. How do you manage it? With your disability?"

"There are special typewriters, but I use an ordinary one and memorise where the keys are."

"That must take some doing."

"It's nothing special. All professional typists learn the keyboard off by heart and don't look at it when they're working."

"But how do you know if you've made an error?"

"My mum checks my work after I've finished it. She's been very good. She encourages me no end."

Peter wanted to ask more about her family, but a noisy rumpus had broken out. A student nurse had discovered the baby with the overflowing nappy crawling across the car park, and had brought him back into the hospital: but his mother, bursting with maternal indignity, was shouting at the nurse for not having discovered the baby sooner. It was the student's first encounter with the logic of liberated parenthood, and the girl broke into tears and fled the waiting room, leaving a staff nurse to pacify the mother by offering to change baby's nappy.

"Now that it's gone quiet," said Alice, "I think I ought to phone my mum. She'll be wondering where I've got to."

She took a mobile phone from her shoulder bag and pressed its keys skilfully. Peter had noticed a sallow young man with long hair standing to one side, and his wide unblinking eyes furtively surveyed the crowd. He'd spent a long time looking at Alice's handbag, and now she'd produced her phone, his attention intensified, so Peter moved protectively towards her.

When she finished her call, Alice sensed Peter's closeness, and asked, "Would you like to borrow this, to phone your wife?"

"I'm not married. I live alone."

"And why didn't some nice girl snap you up?" she asked with a twinkle in her voice.

Peter sketched an outline of his family history. Although his mother hadn't asked him to stay with her, he'd always wanted to look after her.

"Where did your father die?"

"In the Far East. I think he was a prisoner of war, but I don't know the details. My mum was always too upset to talk about it."

"I've always felt sorry for the people who suffered then."

"That's unusual, for someone of your generation."

"I suppose it is. Maybe I'm just eccentric. One of my poems was concerned with the London Blitz. I symbolised it by writing about falling rain. Probably nobody would have realised that, even if it had been read."

"It sounds very clever, though. And we might say that these days it's stopped raining."

"If this is sunshine, then it's a sham," her voice echoed profoundly, and he was suddenly alive to her intellect. But he was not humbled by it. For the first time in his subdued life he didn't feel intimidated by another's insight, but wanted to embrace it.

"It's only a paper sun," crooned Peter in a rusty voice, the words tumbling out through a crack in his reserve. The songs in his mother's record collection had always been armour against the outside world; but with Alice the visor was raised.

"Very witty," she commented.

"By the way, how was your mother?" he asked, remembering her phone call.

"Oh, not so bad," she answered, but her face stiffened with concern, and Peter guessed that her sight was not the only thing that troubled her. He was about to ask her a few cautious questions, when another commotion erupted.

A man started bellowing at the hospital staff for intimidating his son. Apparently someone had stopped the boy from skateboarding along a hospital corridor, and the infuriated father pointed out that this was an infringement of civil liberties, it would arrest his child's development, and demanded compensation for the outrage.

Peter took advantage of the interruption to look over Alice again. She sat placidly wearing the most elegant clothes that her mother had been able to find in charity shops, and contrasted starkly with the cultivated discordance of her compeers. To Peter, it seemed a curious anomaly: it was as though the gift of sight guaranteed unsightliness.

The aggrieved father, his protests unsatisfied, now threatened to expose the hospital to the press, and report them to the NCPCC, the Commission for Human Rights and, for good measure, the RSPCA: and he stormed out of the building tyrannously pushing his son before him, demonstrating his post-modernist philosophy of parenthood by clipping the boy around the ear.

"What are you thinking about now?" asked Alice, as relative tranquillity descended.

"Oh, just something silly."

"You might as well tell me about it. There's nothing else to do."

"Are you sure you want to hear it?"

"Of course."

"Well, at home, in my mother's wardrobe, there's this most beautiful dress. I think that it was a ball gown, which she had when she was young. She always treasured it, and said that it was special to her. It's very pretty, and it would fit you perfectly. Would you like to have it?" As Peter looked at Alice, she now seemed more a woman, and less like a victim.

"Thank you for the offer, but, no, I don't think that anyone should have it. If you mum's memories are locked away in that dress, then it ought to be hers, for always."

That sensitive reasoning convinced Peter that Alice's blindness gave her better vision than most who were sighted, and her kindly understanding gave him the will to move closer.

"When I said that you reminded me of my mother, I really meant it, you know."

"Yes, I believe you did." Alice had slowly inclined towards Peter's naïve charm, and she now knew that he wasn't on the make.

"Would you like me to get you a cup of coffee, or something?" The shifty young man with the covetous and narcotic dilated eyes had gone, and Peter felt that it would be safe to leave Alice's side for a while.

"I don't like coffee much. But I could murder a cup of tea."

"Really? I thought that I was the last person in Plumham to drink tea."

"Well, you're not. There's at least one other."

The drinks machine wore an 'out of order' badge, so Peter followed an intricate series of signs and found the patients' canteen. A gaunt woman in her fifties with heavily dyed hair stood behind the counter, and a half-smoked but unlit cigarette dangled from her lower lip, as if glued there.

"May I have two cups of tea, please?" asked Peter.

"I'm the lady what does the food. That's the lady what does the drinks." She indicated a teenager who stood at the other end of the bar.

"What?" enquired the drink lady, adjusting the safety pin which pierced the side of her nose with ladylike refinement, and leant forward just enough to display the words 'fuck off' tattooed on the top of her left breast.

"Two cups please."

"What of?"

"Tea."

"The 'ot water thing has broken down. You can 'ave a cold drink. We got Kooky Kola, or Bubble Up, or Fizzy Bizzy, or Tangy Express, or Taste Explosion."

"No thanks." Peter smiled apologetically.

"Fucking snob," commented the drink lady as Peter left. "Who's he think he is? Someone important? Like a celebrity from the telly?"

The food lady nodded, with ladylike delicacy, and the cigarette dropped from her lower lip onto a dish of Yummy Chummies.

Empty handed, Peter returned to the room where the malaised, the maltreated, the maleurous and the malingerers waited, patiently and impatiently.

He resettled himself next to Alice, apologised for being tealess, and noticed that the cast of concern had returned to her face.

"Are you worried about something?"

"No. Nothing."

"Sure? It might help to talk about it."

"I don't think so."

"Are you worried about your mother?"

"She's not very well. It's nothing much."

"Perhaps I could help?"

"No, you can't. Just leave it alone, will you."

"OK; I'm sorry. I understand."

"No you don't. How could you? You don't have to put up with all this." She banged the end of her stick on the floor to emphasise her words.

Peter fell silent, then noticed a tear running down her cheek, as it had done at the literary meeting. She brushed it away quickly, and they sat without speaking for two or three minutes.

He wanted to help, but couldn't think how, when suddenly, with uncanny accuracy, she placed a hand onto his.

"I'm sorry about that. You'll have to excuse me. I get a bit ratty at times."

"Of course. Of course," he comforted, and spontaneously placed his other hand around hers, squeezing it reassuringly. They sat with hands entwined for two or three seconds, and then she withdrew to wipe away another tear.

"Do you get out much?" he asked, keen to rekindle the conversation.

"Not so much now. Humphrey used to take me everywhere, but he died last Christmas."

"That's tragic. Was Humphrey your boyfriend?"

"Humphrey was my guide dog."

"Oh, I see. Can't they give you a new one?"

"I have to wait my turn. Training takes a long time."

"So, how to you manage now?"

"I've remembered many roads in Plumham. Bus drivers are very good. They always help me on and off."

"Do the public help?"

"A few are very nice, but mostly they don't care. To some I'm just a nuisance, to others I'm an easy target. I've had three handbags snatched."

"That's awful. Would you like to get out more?"

"Of course."

"Perhaps I could help?"

Again Alice fell silent, and Peter realised that he'd pushed his luck too far. In front of them now sat a young man wearing headphones that exhaled an intermittent hissing noise, and the youth twitched rhythmically. His presence was fortunate. Another woman seeking an appreciative audience for her medical history passed them by, and then managed to corner a tolerant looking woman with a baby. Within moments she had begun an interminable catalogue of past calamities which had blighted the present, and Peter was thankful for a narrow escape.

Peter decided to chance a risky question. "Have you ever thought of getting married?"

"That would heal one irritating sore," she said with a slight smile. "I'd get rid of my ghastly surname."

"I noticed that you had an unusual name when we registered."

"Unusual is hardly the word for it. Screep is ugly, it's hideous, and it's embarrassing."

"Is it an English name?"

"Apparently there have been Screeps in Plumham for over two hundred years; but I don't know where it originated. I don't really want to know. I've often thought about changing it, though."

"Wouldn't your father be upset if you got rid of the family name?"

"I'd be glad if he was."

"Really? What is your father?"

Alice hesitated. "A bastard," she said after some time.

"Why? What has he done?"

"He ran off with another woman when I was twelve."

Over the next hour, Peter gently coaxed Alice to open her life to him. Scenes of her mother striving to make the most of very little filled centre stage, and then as the narrative unfolded he saw what he understood so well: the respectable face of poverty; the devotion of the vulnerable; the unsung courage of prudence.

Although he and Alice were so different, their biographies were off the same shelf, and each read the other's words with empathy. They were kindred spirits, but material strangers.

As Peter's and Alice's worlds plaited, so the lives of others parted. A little boy sat on the floor nearby, innocently tearing pages from an outdated magazine which, puzzlingly, he crumpled and pushed down the front of his trousers. His elder sister practised her ballet steps, while their mother sat, ashen faced, and listened to a junior doctor stammer out the news that her husband's wounds had proved fatal.

All the while, Peter was gaining confidence and Alice was growing pliant, and he had just found enough courage to ask again about her mother's health, when a nurse called Alice's name.

"Are you the lady's partner?" asked the nurse of Peter, who was agreeably surprised. He'd expected her to say 'father'.

"No, but he's a good friend," replied Alice. "I'd like him to stay with me." It was another tribute for Peter, who now felt elated.

They were shown into an examination booth, where stood a stocky man wearing a white coat and a broad smile.

"I am Doctor Vladimir Kozhevnikova," he announced. "And in case you had not guessed it, I am Vlussian." The doctor theatrically exaggerated his lumpy Russian accent, which was an immediate ice-breaker for his patients, and both Alice and Peter responded with a grin. "Please be seated, will you? And now, whatever has happened to this lovely lady?"

"I feel a bit of a fraud, really," replied Alice. "I've just given my head a bit of a lump, but my friend here insisted that I get it checked."

"And he's absolutely right. A famous man once said 'No head injury is so trivial that it can be ignored'. Do you know who that man was?"

"I've no idea."

"The great Hippocrates himself. And what was true two thousand and four hundred years ago is true today."

Using his quaint charm and large hairy hands, Doctor Kozhevnikova gave Alice a conscientious examination, and then sent them off down labyrinths of corridors to the X-ray department.

"I've not heard of a Russian doctor before," commented Peter, as they waited for the film to be developed. "Have you?"

"Only Doctor Zhivargo," grinned Alice.

After the wearisome initial wait, they now moved through the system rapidly, and soon they were back with the good doctor.

"This is good news," declared the doctor as he looked over the X-ray film. "The lovely lady has no broken bones or cracks. Now, she must go home, get plenty of rest, use a cold compress, take Aspirin if there is a headache. And you, sir," he said, turning to Peter, "must make sure that the lovely lady does as she is told. The swelling should go down in about a week, but if there is any drowsiness, or nausea, or confusion, then you must come back and see me at once. Tell the reception peoples that you are my special patient, and I'm always at your service."

He concluded his advice with a polite bow, shook Alice's and Peter's hands affectionately, and they both gushed their thanks to him.

They left a waiting room that was even more overcrowded than when they had arrived. The hospital continued trying to repair the damage of fast driving, fast living and fast food; but the outside world seemed bent on delivering harm, both to others and to themselves.

"Now we must see about getting you home," said Peter as they left the building which supplied Cyril Nuddwick with his nubile tenants.

"You haven't bought me that cup of tea yet," said Alice, with the sparkle back in her voice, and Peter responded joyously to her unexpected invitation.

"Actually, I do know a little place that's just around the corner. It's nothing special, but they brew a fine cup of tea."

"So, what are we waiting for?"

Peter's destination had nourished locals for a long as he could remember. It had started life as a coffee house, where the office workers of Plumham spent their luncheon vouchers. Then, as youth culture split the community, the owner added chromium plate and a juke box, and it became a cafeteria where the ton-up lads congregated. When the interests of young Plumham turned to a different type of speed, the proprietor found it more profitable and secure to offer lorry drivers some no-nonsense English breakfasts with a mug of Rosy Lee, and the place became a caff.

That was how Peter remembered it, but as it came into view, he saw that there had been another change. The council's enthusiasm for yellow street lines had frightened the lorry drivers away, and a new owner had converted it into a café, and was determined to retain the final acute accent.

A new fascia board spotlighted 'Chez Nous – Cuisine Français', and in much smaller print, 'Proprietor – S K Patel'. On the pavement outside stood an ill-matched unoccupied selection of weather-beaten bentwood chairs and cast aluminium garden tables. The early evening sun still gave a little warmth, so they made themselves almost comfortable at one of them, and Monsieur Patel burst forth immediately, wearing a bow tie, and with a crisp white cloth draped over one arm.

"Welcome, mam'sell, m'seiur," he greeted, flicking dust off the table with an exaggerated flourish. His timbre was a curious hybrid. Born and bred in Plumham, his normal tone was that of a Londoner with a slight inherited Asian lilt; but for business purposes he had grafted onto that a continental affectation which he'd developed by listening to Hercule Poirot television dramas.

"Would you like something to eat?" Peter asked Alice.

"No thanks. My mum will have a meal ready for me by the time I get home. Just tea will be fine."

"Just a pot of tea then, please."

"Tea?" recoiled Monsieur Patel in horror.

"That's right."

"But m'seiur. We 'ave zee finest coffee in *Londres*. Our *Café au lait*, eet ees renowned throughout *l'Angleterre*."

"I'm very sorry, but we're not coffee drinkers. Could we please have tea?"

The proprietor gave a Gallic shrug, disappeared into the café to reappear moments later with two cups, a milk jug and a coffee pot filled with hot water on which floated a teabag tied with string; and then left again with a superfluous, "*Bon appetit*."

"Shall I be mother?" Alice offered, her hands already groping their way across the table. "I can do it, you know. As long as you don't mind me putting a finger into your cup to gauge when it's full."

"Not at all, I'll be honoured."

Alice coped with the task remarkably well, and they both winced at the pallid taste of the tea.

"I'm sorry it's so crummy. This used to be a really good place. It's got a different owner now."

"Was the previous owner an elderly man with red hair?"

"That's right."

"I remember him from when I was a child."

"How did you know that he had red hair?"

"I saw it."

"Really? So, you haven't always had your disability?"

"I could see until I was sixteen. I suppose I'm only ninety-five percent sightless now; I can tell the difference between night and day, but not much else."

"So you can remember what things look like?"

"Precisely. That's why I like people to describe what they can see. It helps me to visualise the world. Actually, you're quite good at that."

To Peter, that was an unmissable open door, and he was about to take advantage of it when a voice intruded from behind.

"I see you've got yourself fixed up, then." Peter turned to see Maurice Slupp, alias Honest John, as he was taking a sidelong leer at Alice's pretty face. The imputation of the remark gave Peter instant unease, and he determined to be rid of him as vigorously as possible.

"That coffee we 'ad was real nice," continued Honest John, "but it made me a bit peckish, like. Can't afford these posh places meself, but there's this other place what I know. They do you meat and taters, an' a bit o' bread an' butter, an' a cup of tea, an' then you gets yer afters; an' all for five an' 'alf quid." His dodgy gut seemed to have found a miraculous cure.

Peter drew a turquoise engraved portrait of George Stephenson from an anorak pocket, and another of Charles Dickens in sepia, decided that the expense was worth it, gave a farewell glance at Pickwick's cricket match and handed the higher denomination to the phoney tramp.

"Ta, Guv. That'll do real nice, that will. You're a real toff."

"Why did you do that?" asked Alice when he'd gone. Her sharpened hearing had detected the crackle of paper money.

"Because he's down and out," answered Peter, and then added with a touch of honesty, "and to be rid of him."

"I think he's a fake." Alice's ears had also heard the sound of a mobile phone from the rapidly departing figure.

Intermittently, due to a wiring fault, French accordion music scraunched from a small speaker placed beneath one of the tables; and Alice and Peter unenthusiastically finished their tea.

"Another pot for m'seiur? Mam'seil?" asked the chef de cuisine. "Eet eez on zee 'ouse," he added as they shook their heads.

Peter added a generous tip to the bill. As they departed, Monsieur Patel gave Alice a long, slow wink. Evidently, white sticks carried little identity in the French quarter of Plumham.

"I think I ought to see you home."

"No. No. You've been very kind. Just see me to a bus, and I'll be fine."

As they waited by a bus stop, dusk began to fall, and Peter found courage more quickly than his father had done sixty-four years previously.

"May I ask you something?"

"Of course." Alice's voice held no deterrent.

"I was wondering. Until you get your new guide dog, would you let me take you to one or two places, I could describe things to you. I could also buy you a decent cup of tea."

"What did you have in mind?"

"Well, we could –"

"Yes?"

"I was about to say we could go to the cinema. But that's silly."

"Unless you're prepared to describe the whole film to me."

"I don't think that the other people in the cinema would like that."

"I'll tell you what. I'll think of something, and you can take me there. How about that?"

"Wonderful! When?"

"Give me a while to get over this bump. Let's say, same day next week. At around one o'clock?"

"Shall I call for you at home?"

"No, don't do that." Alice's face froze momentarily, and Peter knew he'd touched a fragile spot. "I'll meet you by this bus stop. Don't worry about me, I can find my way around." A bus had stopped by the kerbside, the door chuffed open, and he helped her mount the step.

"Until next week," she called over her shoulder.

"Until next week," echoed Peter, still unable to believe what had happened. As the bus drew away, he waved until it was out of sight, and then realised the futility of waving to a blind person.

Enchanted, Peter started to walk home. He was transformed: he was a born-again hero, a reborn Galahad; an unborn Romeo. The two ends of the day could hardly have been more different: a morning squirming under the glare of Modesta White; and an afternoon blessed by Alice's gentle company. All at once the world had meaning, life had purpose, and he had a future; even though that future might only last for a week.

As day faded into night over London, the city's depleted sparrow population went to sleep, its swelling community of drug dealers and imported prostitutes started to awake, but one of its citizens was set apart: he had hope.

He passed through streets where an unbrave new world had discarded half-eaten hamburgers, once used condoms and overused hypodermic syringes; but decay didn't trouble him: he had peace.

Music entered his head, no longer as a barricade to the world, but as a celebration of it. He started to hum a little tune: if he'd know how, he'd have danced. He had joy.

When he reached home that night, he'd have something really special to tell his father.

Chapter Six

Flight Sergeant Stone was a firm but kindly man, and he strode into hut seventeen on the air-wireless training section at RAF Wickstead carrying a message scented with success.

The trainees in the billet sprang to attention at their bedsides as he entered, and he glanced around at the expressions of apprehension.

"At ease, men. I'll settle your worries firstly, and tell you that you've all passed your final tests. Some of you only just scraped through, but I won't go into details."

Looks of relief appeared on every face, and the men were now fully at ease.

"There'll be a parade at o-nine hundred hours tomorrow morning, and before then, get these sown on your sleeves. They're proof that you're qualified. Make sure that you live up to it. Place them at four inches below the shoulder eagle. Tomorrow you'll find out where your postings are." He handed out badges of a clenched fist clutching at blades of lightning on a dark blue background. "I'm glad that I won't be seeing any of your ugly mugs alongside the next intake," he lightly added with the ghost of a smile as he left by the door.

The whole billet relaxed. "We've all passed. What a relief."

"And that means a good piss-up tonight. What about we all go to The George?"

They mostly whooped agreement, took out their 'housewives' and extracted a needle and thread from between the folds of cloth.

"He said four inches below the shitehawks. How do we measure four inches?"

"Use your dick."

"His cock isn't that long."

"You speak for yourself."

As they left for their evening of farewell boozing, two remained behind; the only ones who were married and had to conserve their slender incomes. In the far corner sat Christopher Goodwin using a Bakelite button-stick and carefully upending a tin of metal polish onto a blackened duster to shed lustre over the crowned eagles on the tunic of his Best Blue.

"Do you think they'll expect all this bullshit at our operational stations?" asked Christopher of his remaining comrade.

"Of course they will. The Air Force thrives on it. The only good thing is that's it twice as bad in the army, three times as bad in the marines, and four times as bad in the guards."

Bob Oxley sat polishing his boots next to Christopher. Previously a plumber and self-taught trumpet player, he had supplemented his civvy-street income by playing with a swing quintette at gigs around his home town of Rochester. When he took a solo it was solid, and his rideouts had drive; but he'd never mastered the dots, so his applications to join the Central Band and then the Squadronaires had both been turned down.

Most of the others weren't very fond of Bob. He often sidled down the centre of the floor clicking his syncopated fingers and would then break into jitterbug steps. They thought him extrovert or eccentric, but Christopher knew otherwise. He realised that the casual manner was just a façade behind which was a sensitive soul and, although they'd only know each other for a ten-week training course, it was the equivalence of a life-long friendship.

"I'm very worried about where I'm going to be posted," confessed Christopher. "I don't want to be too far from Christine."

"That's natural enough. I feel the same about my missus."

"But there's more to it than that for me," said Christopher, and decided to take the wraps off his innermost concern. As the billet was otherwise empty, and as they'd probably never see each other again, this was the juncture to confide. "Christine is desperate to have a baby. And I'd very much like one too."

"Don't you know how?"

"A couple of years ago she had a miscarriage. She's been more than a bit depressed ever since. We keep trying, but it doesn't seem to click."

The smile vanished from Bob's face. "I'm sorry, old chap; I just didn't realise. Forgive my clumsiness, won't you?" This was the Bob whom Christopher knew and liked.

He explained how the hopes of both families seemed to be pinned on them. Christopher's brother and Christine's sister were still allergic to the opposite sex, and Ruby Goodwin's blurred eyes could see only a grandchild as her salvation.

"That's rotten luck, Chris. As you know, I've a couple of little ones myself. They can be buggers at times, but I certainly wouldn't be without them. Have you thought of seeing a doctor about it? They can help at times, you know."

"Yes we have. He only told us to try and relax, and let nature take its course. So far, nature hasn't been very obliging."

They continued to talk late into the evening, Bob doing his best to console Christopher, until the revellers roared back and peace was shattered.

As Christopher slept fitfully that night, Oberleutnant Wolfgang Gildner guided a Heinkel III towards Plumham, its two Daimler-Benz twelve-cylinder engines deliberately desynchronised to confuse the British sonic tracking system.

The moon which shone that night had yet to enter the lyricist's lexicon. It was not the romantic harvest moon, nor the wistful blue moon, not the lovers' moon that rhymed with June, spoon and croon; but a bombers' moon.

"Flugzeugführer an vorderen Borschützen. Laβt sich schon etwas von der feindichen Verteidigung wahrnenmen?" Gilder asked, and the gunner replied that was yet no sign of enemy defenders.

"Ausgezeichnet. Es scheint fast als könnten wir einen ungestörten Flug haben," replied the pilot, thankful that they might have a quiet flight.

Oberfeldwebel Friedrich Hager, the navigator, disliked the inconvenience of his cramped seat, where the absence of a chart table meant that he had to spread the maps on his knees. He despised the Bordfunker who sat behind because of the amount of room that his equipment occupied. In fact he loathed many things; the English in particular.

"Flugzeugführer an Luftschifeer. Stimmt der Kurs?" asked Gildner, and Hager replied that they were on course.

As the fires of a blitzed London filled the horizon, the navigator moved into the glass nose cone, Gildner repeated his gratitude for the lack of opposition, but was surprised when Hager retorted that he'd rather see action.

"Warum?"

"Ich würde gern ein paar Engländer vernichten."

Gildner was taken aback by the acrimony of Hager's hatred for the English, queried his reasons, and was told that it was personal.

"Die Engländer sind die zivilisiestesten unserer Feinde. Eigentlich, hätten sie gescheite Führer würden wir nicht mit ihnen kämpfen," Gildner told his malevolent comrade, trying to assure him that the English were the most civilised of their enemies.

"Die Engländer haven im letzten Kreigmeinen Vater umgebracht. Er ist gelfallen bevor ich geboren war; ich habe ihn nie gekannt. Jetzt habe ich die Gelegenheit seinen Tod und meinen Verlust zu rächen."

Gildner wasn't convinced that losing a father in the distant Great War should arose such venom, and hoped that using his bombsight soon would dilute some of the navigator's malevolence.

As Plumham approached, Gildner passed stewardship of the aircraft to the now prone navigator.

"Zielzone nähert sich. Kontrolle an Sie."

Hager took the temporary loan of authority with the enthusiasm of a manic annihilationist. "Ein wenig nach Steuerbord. Noch ein wenig. Jetzt Kurs halten. Ziel voraus. Kurs halten. Bombe weg!"

Eight vertically suspended two-hundred and fifty kilogramme bombs fell from the chutes in the belly of the Heinkel, their four fins catching the air and somersaulting them to fall nose downwards.

If this was Plumham's finest hour, it was also its darkest. As the fires from the earlier waves of incendiaries raged out of control, the deluge of high explosives now rent the oxygen-starved air.

In the next century, liberalists living in Erehwon might believe that those bombs were the zenith of unbiased democracy.

They were prejudiced against nobody and selected their victims with total equality. They didn't distinguish between sex, age, class or race. There was no religious preference. Christian, Muslim, Jew, Hindu, atheist and agnostic all had the equal opportunity of being blasted into the hereafter. But that latitudinarian idea was certainly not shared by the people of Plumham on that night.

The parade now stood easy as Flight Lieutenant Parnell addressed them, clipboard in hand. The list of home postings pleased all of the men, and the now hopeful Christopher Goodwin and Bob Oxley grew impatient until their names appeared at the foot of the administration officer's roll.
"And now for the overseas postings," he announced. "2753648, Goodwin, P."
"Sir," responded Christopher, and his heels snapped to attention.
"Your unit is RAF Segaulon," concluded the officer.
"Where, sir, is Segaulon?" Christopher looked mystified.
"It's in Malaya, lad," explained the flight sergeant, with more than a touch of sympathy.
"Of course," echoed Flight Lieutenant Parnell, secretly thankful for Stone's help, and was careful not to disclose that he'd never heard of the place before.
Christopher's crestfallen face was soon to be matched by that of Bob, who learnt that he was destined for Egypt. The posting clerks at Adastral House seemed to exercise a cynical callousness towards their rudderless but distant comrades.
"I'll come to the billet shortly to give you your travel passes," confirmed the flight sergeant. "Those posted abroad will be given forty-eight hours embarkation leave." The shiny-trousered in Kingsway held, perhaps, a sliver of compassion after all.

As sirens wailed, the London-bound train made an unscheduled but compulsory stop at the next station. A guard ran the length of the platform as fast as the frugally coarse material of her new uniform and the perished elastic of her underwear would allow, and informed passengers of their right to alight and take shelter. A few accepted the invitation, and the train once more lurched into motion.

As Christopher Goodwin stood in the corridor, he now saw a vacated seat in a compartment; entered, and hoisted his kitbag onto the luggage rack. He still felt crushed by the revelation of a foreign posting: the present and the future now seemed buried in a cellar of concern, despair and disillusion.

"Honoured to have you on board, mate," an elderly man in a worn tweed suit paid homage to the sight of Christopher's uniform. "I take my hat off to you. You go into the sky and give 'em hell, just like they're doing to us."

"You do more than that, my love," said a stout woman in denim overalls as steam curtained the window. "You give 'em a whole lot more. Serve the buggers right, it will."

"Yeah. Give that bleeding Hitler what for."

"Don't stop at Hitler, chum. Kill off all the Jerry bastards while you're at it."

"That's the way. If there are any left, they'll only start another bloody war in a few years' time."

"And while you're about it, get rid of the Eyeties as well. Sod 'em all, that's what I say."

A studious vicar sat in a corner of the carriage and now leaned forward. "I don't think that we need go that far. The Germans are all God's creatures, after all." The Reverend Cholmondeley was travelling to Blitz torn London from his quiet rural parish for the first time, and was taken aback by the torrent of bitterness and hatred.

"Fat lot of good your God has done for us. Just a load of conchies and pooftahs in the congregations these days."

One woman sat in the opposite corner who had not spoken. The lady wore a large floral hat, carefully preserved, but now showing signs of fading and wear; and the empty shopping basket on her lap suggested that her expedition for unrationed goods had been in vain. She seemed to be the only surburbanite among the great unnumbered, and looked like the type who'd get out her best china and make cucumber sandwiches whenever a vicar called on her. His religious dogma now had less effect on the proletariat than the political slogans and comedy catch phrases which affirmed their national unity. He was not used to being without the obedient weather vane opinions of his parishioners; so he appealed to her for support.

"Madam, I'm sure that you'll disagree with these good people," he started, sure that her silence had been fostered by true English seclusion. "If we all put our trust in God, then enemies can become friends. If we pray for them, then they must see the light. Their heads have been turned by a minority of evil doers. If we appeal to them, in a truly Christian spirit, then goodness will surely rise up and triumph."

His potential stanchion looked placid for a while, then opened her lips to liberate a cascade of unanticipated acid. "Piss off, you sanctimonious old tosser. What the hell do you know about it? Last week my sister Lilly was torn to bits by a bomb. My only son had his guts ripped out by a grenade before he could reach Dunkirk. My old man was in the Fire Service and had a leg crushed by a falling wall. A bomb hit my daughter's school and now she's a bag of nerves. I ought to be wearing black, but I haven't got any bloody clothing coupons. Clear off, and take your cruel God with you."

It wasn't the polite 'Amen' that he was expecting. None had turned to God but had turned the other way. Urban religion had withdrawn into a background of uncertainty and uneasiness. The Reverend Cholmondeley looked very flustered, then took down his suitcase and hurriedly left to try to find a less barbarian compartment.

The home front had brought about an amazing transformation. In railway carriages there was the extraordinary spectacle of the British actually speaking to each other without being formally introduced. Fellowship, companionship and unfamiliar familiarity had been kindled by mutual danger, hardships and stress, and now liberated tongues and emotions found sympathetic ears.

The train crawled on its way, its speed restricted by new regulation to a mere fifteen miles an hour during an air raid, but that only lubricated the savoir vivre of Christopher's temporal companions. They willingly confided accounts of terror, pain, relief, blackout, separation, loneliness, queuing, digging for victory, love, hatred, spam, dried eggs, ITMA, Workers' Playtime, holidays at home with a deckchair and a pot of tea in the garden, shortages, suffering, and confessions of a personal nature. Even fashion got a brief review: make-do-and-mend; liquid stockings; substitutes for face powder and lipstick; the disappearance of pleats, flounces, low hemlines and double-breasted coats; and last but not least the lack of glamour in the standard issue gas mask. Lack of sleep had now replaced the weather as the foremost topic of conversation, and names and details of jobs were exchanged freely: but the only subject absent seemed to be the gossip and scandal which would have appealed so much to Mrs Screep. Their sentiments now had solid foundations.

At last the unwavering wail of the all-clear siren enervated the train, but the locomotive's worn and leaking cylinders lost much of their stream pressure, and its speed was far from dashing.

When they arrived at the central London terminus, Christopher's fellow travellers gave him a hearty slap on the back, and the women kissed him on the cheek, except for the one in overalls, who pressed her lips to his and wriggled her hips sensuously; then gave him a long slow wink as she left.

Christopher's revitalised contentment didn't last. By the time he'd crossed to the suburban line platforms his anxieties again rose. Most of all, he hadn't yet told Christine about his foreign posting. He knew that those sent to the Far East usually didn't return for three years or more, and the notion devastated his hopes. His thoughts grated as if he had broken piston rings on all cylinders. In all his life he'd never felt so wretched, weary and defeated.

Christine now waited at Plumham Station, having received her husband's telegram that morning. His arrival was more than two hours overdue, and she sat in the overcrowded buffet looking at her third drink in a cracked cup. It was a curious liquid which passed for tea, and she stirred it with an unattractive utility spoon made from a light, brittle alloy which was chained to the edge of the table.

She'd had nothing to eat since yesterday, and looked at the counter where the drying slices of National bread were beginning to curl to reveal their mean contents. The soup looked as thin as workhouse gruel, and the sight staunched her appetite.

The experience of the previous night meant that she'd also been without sleep for almost thirty hours. Now an auxiliary nurse, she'd spent the night at St Agatha's Hospital trying to help the qualified staff to cope with the heaviest flow of casualties that they'd ever experienced.

Some hospital porters spent much of that night in the loft spaces trying to extinguish the roof-piercing incendiary bombs with stirrup pumps or smother them with old blankets. But they were losing ground. Two fires had spread across the rafters, but later a fire tender arrived to boost their heroic but slender efforts. At last the struggle had been successful, but not before extensive structural damage had been inflicted, and parts of the roof groaned threateningly. But that wasn't the only sound that contributed to the hospital staff's worries.

As the frequent explosions then grew louder and closer as waves of Heinkels vomited their bomb loads and the jarring symphony of anti-aircraft guns rose to fortissimo, so the emergency team now ushered increasing numbers of injured into the cellar, where makeshift allocations of mattresses were placed between the boilers, the coal stores, the heating pipes and the reserve power generators.

The women ambulance crews brought in stretcher after stretcher of tragedy, and the Red Cross and St John's Ambulance supplemented the official services. Patience, tact, gentle humour and many doses of morphine endeavoured to pacify, but the stifled anger, weeping and pleads for lost family increased hour by hour.

Christine carefully picked splinters of glass from the face of a fireman, but the elderly woman who sat next to them trembled uncontrollably while she waited for attention.

"It's me nerves, they're all used up," she sobbed. "It's the horror and the shock and the worry and the fear. I just can't begin to tell you about the fear. I never know what's going to happen, I don't. Each and every night it gets worse, it does. It's more than flesh and blood can stand, it is. How can I go on? I just don't know any more, I really don't."

"There, there, my old Dutch," consoled her husband. "Try not to worry."

Three of the staff were occupied trying to restrain an epileptic in a violent fit, and Christine moved to the next patient who lay unconscious on a blood-soaked mattress. She pulled back the blanket to catch her first glimpse of a deeply gashed abdomen and exposed entrails, and she blacked out and collapsed on the floor.

A heavy rescue worker, his head in a bandage, scooped her up in his stalwart arms and carried her inert body into the stairwell away from the smells of vomit, fear and surgical spirit. As her eyes blinked open, a mobile canteen worker with her arm in a sling bent over her and said, "You ought to rest for a while, dearie. Go and get a bit of fresh air."

But Christine knew that the air outside was heavy with the grit of shattered bricks and the dust of shattered lives from where humble homes lay broken and death still fell from the skies; so she took three deep breaths, and re-entered the stopgap clinic.

Several patients had just been sick, and so before the floor became hazardous Christine cleared the remains of meagre part-digested rations, hydrochloric acid and digestive enzymes off the ground.

A man, his skin dry and brittle like the pages of a neglected, ill-used Victorian book, grated his toothless gums as he watched the life recede from his grandson. "Is he going to live?" he asked a passing sister.

"Sure," she replied, but he read her taut mouth as a minus sign, and his mind retreated behind a moat of solitude.

For others their compasses of fate also pointed towards a grave. "I told her not to go. I told her to stay put," sobbed the mother of a six-year-old girl who had run from a shelter to retrieve the doll that she'd dropped, but as she reached it a shard of shrapnel had sliced through her neck. Now the woman cradled her daughter desperately as a little heart stopped beating, never to know the flutter of romance. Another innocent infant's soul had been crushed under the jackboot of liberticide and robbed of a future.

The rain of hopelessness didn't fall everywhere. The stiff upper lip of one woman told a neighbouring patient, "I used to complain about my man's snoring. Now I could sleep through anything."

At the other side of the room a trembling man screamed, "We can't go on like this. We just can't. I can't stand it any longer."

Christine then knelt beside a fireman with a damaged leg. Using a cobbler's knife with a curved blade she cut through the length of his long boot, and the man's anxious wife sat beside watching. As Christine pulled away the waterproofed leather it exposed the milk-white barb of a fractured tibia as it pierced the skin, and now it was the wife who fainted.

As the ink of night drained from the sky, the all-clear sounded, and a calm descended like that of an audience as the theatre lights dim. But the tranquillity didn't endure. Immediate danger had passed, but they all knew it would return, and a grasp of the misery yet to be faced from the night's destruction rapidly brought down the curtain on hope.

Later that morning, an off-duty Christine turned the latchkey of her home as a telegram boy parked his cycle by the roadside and handed her the news of Christopher's homecoming. Her exhaustion was set aside, and she quickly washed her face and tidied her hair, but not knowing the time of his arrival, she didn't change out of the starched chastity of her uniform but hurried to the railway station instead.

In the compartment of the Plumham bound train the silent refrigeration of English reserve had also been thawed, and friendliness and conversation surrounded Christopher once again. But now the talk centred on the night's bombing raids with a sense of participation, and that only added more pounds to the weight on his mind.

As he hoisted his kitbag onto his shoulder and approached the ticket barrier at Plumham Station, he was relieved to see Christine hurrying towards him. She wrapped her arms around him and held him in a rapture of joy, love, hope and deliverance.

She did not yet know that Hera's bower of bliss would be pitilessly severed so soon. There were so few moments to be together, but so many to be apart.

They made their way to the High Street and boarded a tramcar where war modifications included masked headlights and reduced interior lighting that had removed half of the lamps and hooded the remainder.

The conductor made his way along the aisle, but refused Christopher's proffered fare. "Have this one on the house. You're doing a great job."

The anti-splinter mesh stuck to the window glass made it impossible to see where they were, so Christine had to stoop to look through the small diamond shaped clear section at its centre. They passed the dance hall where Christopher had first performed his cross-threaded foxtrot, but its roof now yawned open and a 'Closed due to bomb damage' notice sealed the entrance.

Within a few more yards the tramcar stopped, the driver slid back the bulkhead door and announced, "Sorry, everyone. The road ahead is closed. Looks like an unexploded bomb. You'll have to walk it now, I'm afraid."

Christine and Christopher walked a short way to where the road had been roped off, and there a parachute mine hung from the ladder-arm of a lamppost by its green silk canopy. There the Bomb Disposal Company of the Royal Engineers worked to defuse a ten-foot monster capable of delivering damage over a half-mile radius, and a policeman ushered them along a side road.

Turning into Jubilee Street they found another barrier just being dismantled. There the Bomb Disposal squad had worked through the night to dig up unexploded bombs that had buried themselves fifteen feet deep in the soil of Plumham Cemetery. From the disinterred and now disintegrating departed a furious and nauseating stench had risen that churned the stomachs of the crew and forced them to retreat. Then a helpful builders' merchant had brought cans of timber preservative from his store and it was poured generously over the site to try to mask the smell. The humiliated dead had now been recommitted to the ground, but the fetor lingered, and pedestrians held threadbare handkerchiefs to their noses as they passed.

A woman pushing an empty pram looked scornfully at Christopher as she passed and shouted, "Why don't you get up in the sky and get rid of these bastards? Look at what they're doing to us." The rebuke stunned him, but Christine noticed a strip of blackout curtaining tied around the woman's arm, and restored his balance. "Don't you worry, my darling. She's upset. She's out of her mind with worry. People say things they don't mean when they're like that."

Through Mason Street little had changed, but entry to Radley Road left Christopher open-mouthed. It was the place where, only a fortnight before, during Wings for Victory week, a parade headed by the Women's Voluntary Service, cadet forces and the Home Guard had lugged a large piece of a crashed Dornier bomber on the back of a fishmonger's cart like a Roman triumphal march. They were followed by an amateur singing group and the crowd roared and clapped as they sang:

"Red white and blue,
What does it mean to you?
Surely you're proud
Shout it aloud…"

Now it seemed that there wouldn't always be an England. In a cruel irony the trophy had taken revenge. Two 'Herman' thousand kilogram high explosive bombs had broken the homes and the people. Stretcher parties, fire engines, mobile canteens, wardens and the Heavy Rescue Service were still labouring.

The two-and-a-half inch rubber-lined hoses of the Auxiliary Fire Service snaked across the dampened road, and were overlaid by the three-and-a-half inch type used by the professional fire service who'd joined them later. Three London taxicabs were still parked, having been commandeered to draw the Auxiliaries' pumps into place. In the rear seat of one of the cabs a young mother had taken refuge while she shyly suckled her young baby. A small group of exhausted and bedraggled fire-fighters sat on a collapsed wall, one eating a very thick cheese sandwich and drinking cold tea from a milk bottle. One other had fallen asleep, while two others lay dead beneath a tarpaulin.

On the other side of the road, an ARP driver gathered the torn remains of a baby that had been blown through a window and then burst as it hit the ground. She then tenderly wrapped the piteous bundle in a torn curtain.

The only morsel to have escaped the attention of the impersonal bombs was the street pig-food bin chained to a decapitated lamppost; its contents still as sour smelling as ever. Even if human welfare was at a low, at least the pigs were being well cared for.

Christopher and Christine picked their way cautiously along the broken road as building after building groaned open. The gaping rooms denuded twisted doors and tortured window frames. A wooden staircase still defiantly stood where most of the walls had collapsed, and an enamelled bath tottered perilously close to an abyss.

Many Englishmen's castles now exhibited their pathetic secrets to the world. In one windowless front room sat a young woman amidst the debris of her possessions, crying her heart out: it was her birthday.

Beside a pile of rubble a woman wearing a chintz overall tried to retrieve some of her home, but could only find a buckled galvanised bath, a flattened birdcage, some grubby ribbons and a broken picture frame. Her treasured ornaments were now dust being scattered by a cruel wind.

A few homeless souls seemed compliant, but they were only in a temporary daze. When they awoke the nightmare would take command.

A man stood weeping for all to see, his bare arms unaware of the late autumnal chill. He looked at his humble achievement built from a lifetime of hard work: now totally destroyed. Yet his plight was not absolute. Beneath the wreckage of other buildings the owners lay pulped. The adjoining home had fallen like a pack of cards: clubs uppermost; hearts turned downwards.

The afternoon before a small local grocer's shop had received a rare and valued delivery of goods still unrationed: tins of boot polish, combs, razor blades, toilet paper. The proprietor had expected a lengthy queue to form the next day, but all lay in ashes. The customers who still lived would remain in want.

A mass of roof tiles had been shifted by wheelbarrow at one site, and the rescue team now desperately hacked at the fallen bricks and crumbled plaster only to reveal the silent body of a young girl. Her right arm, still clutching a teddy bear, had been severed, and would no longer know a mother's loving touch, a suitor's hesitant caress, nor one day the small hand of her own child. Teddy was unscathed, apart from one missing eye; but he'd lost that months before due to the carelessness of an elder brother. The unbiased nature of the Luftwaffe's bombs did not overlook teddy bears.

In happier days children had gleefully sung 'London's Burning', but now those words carved a sinister message.

As Christine neared the end of the road, a rescue worker noticed her auxiliary nurse's uniform and ran to her.

"Sorry, nurse, but I wonder if we might ask you for a bit of help. Me and the lads have a spot of trouble. Could you help us please?"

The rescue crew had managed to make a small hole above the cellar of a collapsed building, but were concerned that if they tried to enlarge it without shoring the remainder might cave in.

"We think that there might be life down there. A baby was heard crying a while ago. All of us are a bit on the plump side, but you might get in. You're a lot slimmer than we are. Would you give it a go?"

Christine nodded, and one of the team pulled away a length of lath from a pile of plaster and placed it across the gap, marking its width carefully with the stub of an indelible pencil. Then he handed it to Christopher and asked him to measure his wife's hips and shoulders.

The crew leader studied the result carefully. "You should have about three-quarters of an inch to spare at either side, perhaps a little more. We'll hold you tightly. You won't come to any harm. Still willing?" She again nodded, and he turned to Christopher. "I hope you don't mind us handling your missus. But you see, we've trained for it. She'll be safe in our hands."

Christopher reluctantly agreed. He'd heard rumours that rescue men could be callous and indifferent. It was even said that some took advantage of the women they were rescuing and artfully fondled their amatory regions. But he needn't have worried about this squad; they were chivalrous to perfection.

"I think it might help if I removed this," said Christine, indicating her uniform.

"I agree, only I didn't like to mention it myself in case it embarrassed you," replied the foreman. The men hastily took hold of tarpaulins and blankets and held them as a screen around her while they conscientiously averted their eyes.

Christine removed her uniform, rolled down her precious stockings, kicked off her shoes and stood in her regulation black underwear and utility brassiere. The largest and most fearsome of the men noticed a group of passing youths who now loitered in the hope of seeing an undressed woman.

"Clear off you lot, and don't come back." The menace in his voice fell on guilty ears, and they departed the scene rapidly.

One of the rescuers gave her a torch, Christine moved to the side of the hole and the modesty screens were lowered. Following their instructions, she raised her arms above her head in a diver's stance, two of the men grasped her thighs, upended her and painstakingly lowered her through the scarcely accommodating gap.

As she hovered above the floor, she switched on the torch and then fought fiercely against the urge to vomit. A large number of friends and neighbours must have squeezed into that cellar, and now their twisted, blackened and shattered bodies lay in the water that leaked from a split lead pipe, water now heavily rouged with blood and befouled with urine, faeces and gastric flotsam. Fragments of flesh floated on the surface and sundered limbs and organs sank below. The smell, and the blood rushing to her inverted head as she hung suspended by her thighs put her on the brink of shouting to be raised, but then she caught sight of a small cot below her in which lay a seemingly sleeping baby boy.

She extended her arms and found that she could just touch his chubby tenderness, so she discarded the torch, wrapped her hands around him carefully and called to the squad above in a voice now faint from the ordeal.

They lifted her with utmost care, but the back of her brassiere caught on a length of rusted reinforcing rod. She needed both hands to hold the baby, so she let it tear away the shoulder straps. Then the fastening broke, and the garment fell into the pit of human slaughter.

Christine held the baby close to her as she was helped to her feet. One of the men had found an old wooden stool for her to sit on, and Christopher held out her uniform. But she ignored the dress and clung to the little one resolutely, so the men swiftly held the tarpaulin screen around her again.

She examined the little chap closely and carefully, but he now seemed limp. No pulse or breathing could be detected, then she saw a bruise spreading at the side of his head and her spirits floundered as realisation dawned.

"This is not the time of year for sunbathing, Nurse Goodwin." The voice was that of Doctor Turner who'd just arrived, but as he noticed Christine's flowing tears he awoke to his blunder.

He knelt beside her and attentively scrutinised the babe, then shook his head. "I don't think that there's anything that anyone can do for him. Seems like a cerebral haemorrhage. Poor little mite. I'm sorry." The sympathetic doctor carefully prised the child from her arms and passed him to a woman stretcher bearer who stood nearby. "I think you've had enough for one day, my dear," continued the doctor. "You've been on duty all night, and we don't want you cracking up, do we? Now, I think that I ought to run you home. My car's just over there."

Before he could receive a reply, Christine ran to one side and vomited repeatedly. It was not lessened by the fact that she'd not eaten for so long, and spasms of acidic bile fell from her lips.

The doctor stood by her, and noticed the cuts and abrasions on her back from where she'd rubbed against bricks and splintered timbers. "Look, I don't want to lose the best auxiliary girl that I've got. You need to get home and rest as quickly as possible."

Christopher helped her on with her dress and shoes, and put her stockings in his pocket.

"Thank you for your offer," she said at length, "but I'm worried that I'll be sick again when I'm in your car."

"Now don't you worry about that. Just sit in the back seat with your husband to look after you, and tap me on the shoulder if it feels like happening again. I'll just pull into the side of the road, and all will be well."

The rescue men poured out their thanks to her as she left. One declared that she deserved a medal, and the rest agreed.

On the road home, Christine did have to tap the doctor's shoulder and quickly open the car door; three times. At last they reached home and Christopher expressed his appreciation profusely.

"I'm sorry I can't come in to look after you, but I've got many, many patients waiting for me. Now, Mr Goodwin, what she needs is attention to her sores, a lot of rest, plenty of liquids and a little nourishing food," he advised, and left with a cheery wave.

Sitting on their sofa with a bowl of water, Christopher washed the dust from her back tenderly, picked away the splinters with tweezers and applied antiseptic amply. Then he sponged her arms, shoulders and chest, and was thankful to see that her soft breasts had escaped harm.

He encouraged her to drink two large glasses of water, left a bowl beside her in case she felt sick again, and entered the little kitchen to make a pot of tea and prepare the only cooked food that he knew how to put together: buttered toast. But when he had returned, she slept soundly.

He paused for a while, then consumed the humble offering himself, and waited an hour to see if she would wake; but her slumber was deep-rooted. Her slender physique was slumped uneasily across the rigid arm of their bargain-basement settee, so Christopher carried her gradually up the narrow staircase and placed her gingerly on the bed. After covering her with a sheet and blankets, he sat and looked at her for the remainder of the evening. For him, living that should have lingered for years would now be crammed into fragile moments; and as those moments haemorrhaged he lacked a bandage.

The pale light of an early November morning fell on Christine's eyes as they blinked open, and minutes later Christopher entered with another tray and toast; this time crowned with marmalade. He'd already placed a glass and a large jug of fresh water at the bedside, and now he coaxed her into taking the food, although her appetite was still off the menu.

She stayed in bed for another hour at his insistence and he sat on the edge holding her hand and tried to exorcise her memory of yesterday with carefully edited reminiscences of their most valued moments together. A little brightness returned to her face, so he hesitantly broke the news of his departure the following morning, and then of his overseas transfer.

Her disaster flares lit his pity but darkened her flickering spirit. She clung to Christopher as the sting of helplessness pierced her torn fibre. Nostalgia turned to melancholy; dreams became waking nightmares; her longings atrophied, the bitterness of her cup overflowed. Her fingers dug trenches of anguish into his arms, her body shuddered like a loose sail in a storm, her tear ducts spilled once again.

Then, from deep within her vault of suffering, an ingot of courage rose slowly. A thought gradually appeared like a photograph in a developing tray. How could she send her man into battle burdened with more worry? She owed the future a debt of hope, so she shut away her fears behind a thin door of mettle and inwardly vowed to rewrite the endlessly overwritten palimpsest of her emotion.

Little by little her body obeyed her veiled commands, and she managed to smile at Christopher, assure him that she could take it and kissed him lovingly.

Kneeling beside the bath he again cleaned and soothed her back, she donned an ageing skirt and blouse, and set about preparing a featherweight lunch.

Christopher suggested that they might go to the cinema that afternoon: watch romantic make believe beneath the tobacco-smoke blueness of the projector's beam and listen to the reassuring newsreel voice of Bob Danvers-Walker. But Christine easily convinced him that it would be nicer to spend their last hours in their little home. They sat pressed close to each other on the sofa, listened to their favourite records, and Christopher opened his precious shoebox of souvenirs still topped with an unsmoked packet of cigarettes and a tram ticket. They tried to relive happiness once more, looking at yesterday in the broken mirror of today.

In late afternoon Christine prepared the most elaborate meal that her slender rationed larder could surrender, found a single candle to add romance to the table, laid out her best china and found half a bottle of Madeira in the cupboard below the stairs. As the food warmed in the oven she climbed quietly to the bedroom, carefully unwrapped the tissue paper from around the glamorous dress that her mother had made more than five years ago. It seemed fitting to do all she could to present herself as Christopher had first seen her. She didn't want him to leave with only the memory of sorrow in his kitbag.

She was glad to find that she had a dusting of face powder left, and dabbed the last of Uncle Archie's pre-war perfume behind her ears. Then she descended to the living room, gave an elegant twirl and curtsied before an amazed but delighted Christopher.

They lingered over their meal, savouring each mouthful and every moment of each other's company. The food was cold by the time they'd finished. Christine insisted that they'd leave the washing-up until the next day, and they snuggled on the sofa and finished the Madeira.

Getting to her feet, Christine held out her hands to Christopher and pulled him to his feet. "I seem to remember that you weren't very good at asking this question, so I'll do it. Shall we dance?"

In that confined space they lost themselves in a final foxtrot to the words and music of Sammy Fain and Irving Kahal:

'I'll be see-ing you
In all the old fa-mil-iar plac-es
That this heart of mine em-brac-es
All day thru...'

The poignant lyrics made it difficult for Christine to sustain her brave face; but she managed to hold the door firmly closed on her sadness.

To lighten the mood she turned to Ray Noble for the sprightly rhythm of a quickstep, but again the taste of parting strained her resolve.

'Goodnight sweet-heart,
All my prayers are for you.
Good-night sweet-heart,
I'll be watch-ing o'er you...'

As the song unwound, it seemed to offer hope.

'Sleep will ban-ish sorrow...'

But at its close they were both privately reminded of the escaping minutes.

'Till we met to-mor-row;
Dreams en-fold you
In them dear, I'll hold you...'

That 'tomorrow' could be a long way off. A very long way off. They both knew that they had to make the most of their last remaining hours. Christopher had filled his box with memories of the past: now it was his last chance to sow memories for the unborn years.

They retired to bed early. Frost crystallised on the bedroom window, so Christine put a match to the little gas fire and blue-capped flame gradually reddened the cracked teeth of the ceramic radiants as the jets plopped and grumbled to themselves.

As their kisses lengthened, they entwined passionately, and for a while Eros overpainted their fears, longings and desolation. As the wake of ecstasy receded Christopher fell into a deep sleep, but Christine didn't. The alarm at the bedside and the nearby inverted nurse's watch spelled out the passing minutes, and it was now her turn to spend the night devotedly watching Christopher.

She was already a sleep debtor, and now the left column of her account fell further into the red; but few of the people in bomb-torn Plumham were in credit.

As the first light of day dusted stars from the slate of the night, the steel tips of Christopher's heels disturbed the sleeping pavement. In the early November fog the High Street seemed to be on an inadequately developed film taken by an out-of-focus camera, and Christine clung to his free arm.

At the railway station they hoped that there might be the usual delays or cut services due to bombs on the line or priority shipments. It might have delayed their parting; but, remarkably, the timetable's schedule was perfectly intact that day.

Christine bought a one-penny platform ticket to be near him until the final second. They stood on the platform and clasped one another closely to shut out the cruel world that surrounded them, and it was not until the guard's whistle blew and the train jolted into action that Christopher jumped aboard. Shrouded in steam, she ran to the end of the platform holding his hands as he leaned out of the carriage window, and they continued to wave long after each was out of sight.

Her sealed door of sorrow finally burst open, and she cried as she heavily retraced her steps to the barrier. She would now have to patiently wait at home for yesterday to return, while he faced an unknown tomorrow in an unknown land.

But, unbeknown to them both, one ache of yearning had been answered. Perhaps it was the pathos of holding a dying baby in her arms, the thought of a population being destroyed, the pain of parting, the memory of Ruby Goodwin's clouded eyes or the desperate need for fulfilment, but the previous night sleeping genes had been roused, and baby Peter was conceived.

Chapter Seven

The bleak mid-winter of Peter's life seemed to have lasted since the age of ten. Now, at last, spring had sprung. Defeatism evaporated through every pore in his body. He was uphearted.

As he walked back from his first meeting with Alice, he was now heedless of the dross strewn about the streets of Plumham. He strode around blue-bottle covered heaps of chunder unloaded by last night's binge drinkers; salt and vinegar soaked chip bags routed by the obese battalions; aluminium foil boxes with the remnants of tikka masala, vindaloo, Madras, jalfrezi and phall; the abandoned spillages of man's best friend. Only the stub ends of spliffs and joints had been diligently preserved to be recycled another day.

He was no longer perplexed by anarchic attention-seeking architects sweeping away the classical disciplines of Vitruvious; nor a community sweeping away the classical disciplines of humanitas. As Londinia lurched towards her next degeneration, Peter was fortified: his Corinthian columns of hope now supported his entablature of resolve. For years he'd been filled with dismay as the iconoclasts built an unbrave new world. He'd long yearned for the calm surround of yesteryear, but today he had discovered the promise of a tomorrow. As the last crumbs of day were being eaten by the night, Peter noticed a man ahead with a guitar. His thin greying shoulder-length hair looked the colour of melting snow in an urban gutter.

His clenched the neck of his statement of rock cred with a closed fist. It had never been tuned, so he didn't bother messing about with those fiddly frets. His right hand bashed the strings with the finesse of a pile driver, and from a stubble adorned mouth he bellowed a string of grunts with the purity of a blocked sewer.

To the unindoctrinated ear it sounded like a stuttering camel with flatulence and hiccups, but it was affirmed as cool my neophiles of all colours: from dappled acne pink through alcoholic crimson to cardiovascular purple.

As Peter drew near he noticed a white stick hanging from the music strangler's arm, and dark glasses that covered his eyes; so he took the change from his pocket that hadn't been plundered by Honest John, and dropped it into the upturned hat. His respect for Alice sweetened his charity; but he may have responded differently if he'd known that the eyes behind the shades enjoyed twenty-twenty vision. The cacophonous counterfeit had found a walking stick abandoned on a bus, and he'd coloured it white with the remains from a paint tin that he'd rescued from a builder's rubbish skip. But his motives were pure.

Jamie 'Crackhead' Pugh did have a perfectly guiltless explanation for his unimpeachable conduct.

The ungilded truth was that he'd been a lifelong victim. He'd been a victim of society: a victim of the system. Victimised by his parents who'd neglected to create the wealth to fund the leisured lifestyle that he deserved; victimised by his school teachers who refused to accept his self-defensive right to cut others with a blade; hounded by the police with charges of theft, extortion, and assaults decent and indecent; discriminated against by magistrates who didn't endorse his victimhood; unjustly treated by social workers who didn't have degrees in victimology; ill-treated by juries who didn't accept his solemn, sincerely held, earnestly expressed visions of truth; oppressed by laws that restricted his freedom; maligned by a libellous press whose skewed reports ignored his victimisation; harassed by women who'd clung to their handbags when he'd only offered to lighten their burden of money; persecuted by children who'd complain when he aided their development by confiscating their corrupting mobile phones. Was he the only person to have the enlightenment to recognise hard-wired determinism and reject the myth of free will?

He'd been a lone innocent subjected to the anamorphic projection of a world filled with pernicious paranoia: but now society was paying its debt to him. Although he was disappointed with the gruel generosity of Plumham's community, it would keep neglected body and victimised soul together until he could sell his heartrending story to a sympathetic newspaper; preferably one with a vertiginous neo-liberalist leaning. He had *The Sentinel* in mind.

Dusk was now ascendant, and Plumham's hijab and burka clad citizens retreated behind closed doors to preserve their advertised respectability; shortly to be followed by those displaying the kumkum. In an hour or two their places would be taken by others whose personal shop windows gave unrestricted displays of what was on offer. When the year 2011 arrived, Plumham would then swell the ranks of the Slut Walkers with many befitting volunteers, their modesty and virtue doubtlessly on a par with the pure integrity of Jamie Pugh's self-exoneration.

Peter walked down a street where the past fused with the present. The vintage Hogarthian excesses remained; and blended with sophisticated Beardsleyan indulgence. He reached a bus stop, and made himself as comfortable as possible on the narrow plastic seat in the shelter. His only companion was a petite octogenarian who placidly looked at a tabloid in which gossip and celebrity antics surrounded photographs of big tits. She offered the news-lacking paper to Peter.

"A young man gave me this a while ago, but I've left my spectacles at home. I think it might be a church magazine. Would you like it?"

During her long life Hermione Wilmott had never had an alliance, platonic or otherwise, with a man: nor with a woman. Her interests lay in knitting, dusting her collection of bric-a-brac, creating new vegetarian delights, polishing her father's and brother's war medals, and fulfilling her duties as secretary of the Society for the Preservation of Nineteenth Century Knitting Patterns. Her only youthful cavalier desire had been to ride a motorcycle, but that had never happened and probably never would.

Five years ago, however, she'd discovered the love of her life when Wibbly moved in and lived with her. She waited on him hand and foot, attended to his every need, provided the best food that money could buy. He was not a vegetarian, but that was his only fault. Each month she sent him a card: for the New Year in January; for St Valentine's Day in February; for Easter in March; for St George's Day in April; for the spring festival in May; for his birthday in June. She could never think of one for July, so she sent him a get-well-card, irrespective of his state of health. The cost of postage was growing, but it was all worth it to open the envelopes before him. Some blinkered people may have thought it warped to lavish that much attention on a cat, but it was all perfectly straight. He was, after all, a creature of the opposite sex.

Peter accepted the paper, thinking that she might be taken aback when she found her spectacles, but later he'd discard it. He enjoyed newspapers when they'd comprised ninety per-cent news and only ten per-cent gossip. But those proportions now seemed reversed; and when opinions were expressed they were always contorted and didn't dovetail with his rational outlook, so he only listened to radio broadcasts.

They waited almost forty minutes for a bus to appear, and during that time cars filled with noise passed, their door panels juddering to the raw thuds as the drivers nodded and wagged their heads moronically.

Miss Wilmott grew tense as the delay lengthened. Peter seemed meek and kindly, so she confided her uneasiness.

"I don't like being out this late, you know. The streets fill with young hooligans. They push me aside as they walk past. Horrible it is. You should see them. Bodies all covered in tattoos. I think they swear all the time, but I don't know what the words mean. They drink out of cans and spit on the pavements. And the girls are just as bad. In fact, some are worse. Much worse."

He offered to escort her home, but she told him that he'd only need to keep her company during the bus journey. The road where she lived, she assured him, was close to the bus stop and lout-free.

Their transport eventually arrived: three identical buses on identical routes, all nose to tail. The first was packed, but the others empty, so Peter ran to the second and hammered on the door with his fist. The driver glowered at him for daring to intrude on his privacy, and his forehead knotted with fury as Peter stood at the doorway until the dainty but vascularly challenged legs of Miss Wilmott won through.

She need not have worried about her security, though. The only others to board during their homeward trip had mobile phones glued to their ears, grappled with cryptic crossword clues or drooled over porn magazines; but she thanked him warmly at her destination and invited him to call on her at any time and be introduced to Wibbly. "He needs to find new friends. He doesn't get out much now," she said in parting.

At home Peter made a drinkable cup of tea and an omelette sandwich, and then treated himself to a rare glass of Madeira to celebrate his newly found rose-strewn path. A bottle of that wine had always abided in their larder. It seemed to be part of his mother's bittersweet scrapbook, but she never explained its soulful identity.

From his relaxed seat on the sofa Peter looked at the Ultra radiogram which stood in the corner of the room. It had been his parents' only pre-war extravagance. He still regularly polished its walnut cabinet with its elegantly symmetrical Art Deco ebony inlay and harmonised mouldings which underlined the ugliness of successive waves of *dernier cri*. The radio had ceased to function, but the set's amplifying valves still stood defiant in their old age and allowed Christine's treasured but worn collection of shellac discs to give voice with a resonance still unmatched in a shallow digital age.

Peter raised its lid, took a record off the pile and one of the few remaining needles from the metal bowl by the turntable, and lowered the arm.

'What a difference a day makes,
Twenty-four little hours...'

He unexpectedly found himself dancing around the room, unknowingly retracing the steps his parents had taken fifty-nine years earlier. Within those years Plumham's culture had slithered from big band to broadband, but Peter's verve now embraced one and faced the other. Perhaps Christopher and Christine's reunited spirits were inspiring his normally clumsy feet.

During a hollow lifetime he'd fallen on his nose, on his ear, on his head, on his back, on his knees; but never on his feet: until now. The thought that he might also have fallen on Cupid's dart never entered his heavily inhibited mind.

Although his psyche's censorship closed the door on Eros, his memories had been rearranged. Like a canny grocer's counter display, the fresh filled the front and the not-so-fresh was pushed to the back.

For the next record he chose an uptempo number.

'Happy feet.
I've got those happy feet...'

He astonished himself with his new nimbleness, and wondered if he might take dancing lessons. Could Alice dance? He now realised that his ideas were racing ahead of likelihood, and that he had to get a grip on reality. For years he had clung to hope by his bitten fingernails. Now he had a foothold, but the top of the mountain was still distant. He vacated his dream world and vowed to spend the rest of the week making down-to-earth plans for his next meeting with Alice. It might be their only one, but he still had to squeeze every ounce of enjoyment from it: not for himself, but for her. He truly empathised with her. She was the one who now mattered, and she deserved better.

The next morning he breakfasted on toast and marmalade, his favourite. Although he'd noticed a tear in his mother's eye sometimes when he served it to her, he knew not why. His standard quota of one cup of tea was followed by two more, and with each he toasted Alice.

His priority was to buy a local newspaper and discover events in the locality suitable for Alice. As he walked past the Victorian terraced homes in his road he neared a property that stood aloof from the rest. It was a Regency villa, admittedly of a below par quality, which originally stood in acres of landscaped gardens. The then owner had invested heavily during a stock market bubble, became insolvent and faced a term in the Marshalsea. The bailiffs ensured that he didn't skip the country, so he sold his surrounding pleasance to a money-grubbing property dealer, who had the impudence to erect lines of hovels for the ill-bred on his doorstep.

Those abodes had now been rebranded 'bijou residences' by estate agents, but the present owner of the denuded manor was no more pleased with its location. Mrs Odelia Nash lived alone, her husband having escaped her tyranny by dying ten years before. Apart from her part-time gardener, part-time chauffeur and full-time maid, she never communicated with anyone in this locality. When she occasionally drew back the brocade curtains of her mind to glance at the world, it was always through the ornamental cream coloured nets of insularity. Now, perhaps for the first time ever, she stood at the black and gilded wrought-iron gates of her house and looked condescendingly for assistance. As Peter approached, she summoned him with an imperious gesture.

"I say. You there."

He wasn't at all sure how to address her. Should it be Your Ladyship? Or Your Highness? Or Your Upmarketness? Or Your Top-drawerness? Or Your Millefeuilleness? He decided to stick to madam.

"I have trouble with a leaking water pipe. I've been through the whole list in the telephone book. They all refuse to work on my glorious lead pipes, and want to replace them with those hideous copper things. The impudence of these men. How can they violate my home in that way? You'll have to help." In Plumham her closely clipped vowels sounded as natural as a topiary hedge. Peter thought of suggesting that she could phone Poland, but the steel in her eyes disciplined his tongue.

"I'm very sorry, madam, but I'm not a plumber."

"Well you must know somebody." She had already marked him out as one of the lower orders, that class of people who only seek *panem et circenses*. All of those frightful men who drop their aitches and have dandruff on their collars must know each other, surely?

"I think that I do, madam. I'll be back in a moment."

He pliantly ran back to his home and climbed the stairs to the spare bedroom. He'd inherited his maternal grandfather's 'come-in-handy' credo, but transformed it from a collection of nails, screws, clock springs, light switches and curtain hooks into archives of information. An office where he'd formerly worked scrapped their card index systems when computer records usurped them, and Peter had taken one of the cabinets home and diligently recorded everything that might have a future use. His file included a list of tradesmen who didn't have to advertise their services because the quality of their work ensured personal recommendations, and he copied it quickly and returned to Mrs Nash.

At her impressive entrance he was greatly honoured when she answered the door to him personally. Normally he would have been met by the maid. She took the list, showed her gratitude with a hemi-demi-semi quaver smile, and closed the door quickly to block out the degrading tone of the proletarian backdrop.

At the newsagent's shop Mr Singh offered him *The Plumham Times*, *The Plumham Gazette*, *The Plumham Advertiser*, *The Plumham Chronicle* and the oddly named *Newsoholic Shop*. He bought them all.

As he returned to his house he saw Mrs Jessop, his neighbour who'd been condemned by Modesta White as a traitor to her sex for treacherously conjuring a euphemism for Peter's receding hairline.

"There's an exciting letter in my post this morning, Mr Goodwin." She addressed everyone formerly. Even her husband was 'Mr Jessop' during their eleven months of matrimonial inertia before he ditched her in favour of a busty barmaid who excelled in every field of horizontal athletics.

Mrs Jessop was just as enthusiastic as Mrs Nash to preserve the traditional dignity of her home. It was the Victorian fear of miasma which placed her lavatory in the back yard, and her sentimentality which kept it there. Like Peter she had inherited the house from her parents, but a lifetime apprenticeship was now needed to flush the high-level cast-iron cistern. It had to be coaxed with soothing words. Assured that it would not be ill-treated. Then, with a sudden snatch of its rusting chain, taken by surprise and pulled quickly.

She was an isolated mortal but, unlike Mrs Nash, not by choice. A harmless, well-meaning person whom many apathetically avoided. Even her letter box remained lonely. Mrs Jessop's name had never appeared on any circulated junk mail list, so she never received offers of replacement windows at a generous twenty per-cent discount; appeals from charities, genuine or not-so-genuine; an invitation to invest her savings with a financial advisor from Peru; details of the excellent weight-reducing facilities available at the local gymnasium; menus of the excellent weight-gaining facilities available at a multiplicity of takeaways; helpful propositions for personal loans with interest rates shown in unreadable minute print. Now, at last, some enterprising promotion manager had discovered virgin territory, and her letter flap had been deflowered.

"What's it about, Mrs Jessop?"

"I don't know. I haven't opened it yet. But it says on the envelope that I've been specially selected. That's a great honour, isn't it?" The letter had, in fact, landed on her 'welcome' doormat the day before, and she'd since spent the time admiring the buff envelope, the neat typing of her name and address, the postmark, the stamp, and most of all those words that marked out her distinction as a person of note.

"Shall I open it for you?"

"Oh, please do. I'm all a quiver."

Peter opened the envelope with care and fitting ceremony. He didn't wish Mrs Jessop's great day to be an anti-climax. He pulled out a luxuriously printed catalogue of deceptively presented merchandise aimed at a dupable beau monde. Its pages held pictures of anorexic mannequins in surreal poses wearing little clothing at a lot of money; a 'must have' ivory toothpick for a mere five thousand; an executive mobile phone inlaid with poached rhinoceros horn, a gift at only half a million. Rags and riches were no longer strangers.

Mrs Jessop was delighted.

"I'll never be able to afford any of these lovely things, but I'll keep this book for ever. It's such a privilege to have it. It's like having a knighthood, or something."

She was the inveterate ingénue. She was a total innocent even in Peter's uncorrupted eyes; but he thought her a fine neighbour: quiet, well-intentioned and eager to please.

For the rest of the morning he searched the newspapers for inspiration, but found none. A class to teach basic plumbing skills, another to unfold the delights of origami. Mr Smithers was to help the distressed by using his powers to contact the dear departed: Miss Mudge would exhibit her prize turnips. Those curious about the future could explore metoposcopy, palmistry, austromancy, pessomancy, oneiromancy, graphology, I-Ching or a Ouija board séance: and those who wanted to bury the past could join the New Age Rehabilitation Group. Many and varied were the kinds of mysticism, occultism and weirdism, but Alice was too level-headed for any of those truths.

At St Mark's Church Hall a fundraising tiddlywinks championship was to be fought, a street parade would raise funds for free breast implant surgery for the destitute, and in the park there would be a world premiere of drum 'n' bass Morris dancing.

Plumham's Londinium University, now proudly at position number one hundred and seventy-two in the grade table, were giving a series of open-invitation lectures. Doctor Andrew Williamson would discuss the structural analysis of Inuit poetry; Doctor Angela Martin would demonstrate the range of economic benefits that would come about if all men were compulsorily castrated at the age of thirty; and Professor Diallo Ngoimgo would feature at the Robert Gabriel Mugabe Centre of Excellence to assert that all universities should be compelled to include Black Studies in their curricula and how vitally important they are to academic progress. Peter briefly wondered why there were no white studies, then dismissed the thought as totally evil. It must have risen from his left side, so he rapidly wiped the slate clean of impurity.

He had hoped to find something that might appeal to her remaining but heightened senses; a music concert or the scented medley of a flower show. Then it registered that such a plan of campaign would only rob him of his vital function: he was, after all, to be her eyes. But what were they to look at? He suspended judgement on that case and turned to another.

Refreshment would be needed, but where to go? It would be precocious, even impertinent, for him to invite her home for tea; but the gruesome sullage offered by Monsieur Patel was out of the question. Why, though, stop at tea? She might enjoy a glass of wine, perhaps? He couldn't imagine her with a can of lager, though.

He decided to research the ground that evening. His intake of alcohol had been infrequent and modest, and his knowledge of local boozers was long outdated. Great Uncle Archie, his mother's kindly perfume giver, had lived to a well-ripened age and had introduced Peter to the delights of the Crown and Anchor for his eighteenth birthday. They had repeated the jaunt on his nineteenth, but then Archie had succumbed to a stroke and Peter's tuition at the College of Bacchus concluded, without graduation.

He started his tour with the Crown and Anchor, but it was there no more, dismantled by the smoking ban, tax duties and supermarket loss leaders. His last memories of Great Uncle Archie were now rubble at an infill site. In recent decades churches had gone, local shops had gone, and now it was the turn of those Victorian cornerstones of the community where people and opinions mingled. The plot now only hosted a large block of apartments, their windows imprisoned by unusable balconies fabricated from galvanised offcuts of scaffolding iron.

Swimming against that tide a new bar had opened a mere hundred yards away in a former branch of the Plumham and Scottish Bank, recently swallowed by one of the financial juggernauts and then closed by its bonus-grabbing chief executive. The place was now owned by a giant 'pubco', which had installed plain glass in the window and ignored the time-honoured convention of using acid etching to protect innocents from the allure of strong drink and its aftermaths. Its name was not without humour though: 'The Overdraught'.

Peter entered, and the ambience was not what he was expecting. A single room had swept away the class barrier between the spit-and-sawdust and the carpeted saloon; but gone also were the intimacy of the snug-bar and the inclusiveness of a family room. The plain white walls were hung with mass-produced black and white photographs in plastic frames, showing images of people nobody knew and places nobody recognised.

At the bar he bought a small glass of orange juice which carried a nine-hundred per-cent mark up, and cautiously surveyed the facilities. Nowhere to be seen were the well-worn chairs where a pensioner might nurse his pint all evening in the warmth before returning to the chill of an empty home. Absent were the small tables where mates and newcomers might linger over a game of dominoes, rummy or shove ha-penny. The owners wanted only perpendicular drinking to promote consumption on a production-line scale; although some of the customers wouldn't be vertical by the end of the night.

The bar had a narrow choice of beer, with only Danish lager, German lager and over-chilled bottles from the USA on display. Luke warm English ale, the pulse of stout English hearts for centuries, was nowhere to be seen. John Bull would not have been pleased. At the food bar, doorstep sandwiches of British beef had been conquered by Spanish tapas. Sir Walter Raleigh would not have been pleased.

Peter felt very much out of place, and not only because of his age. The small car park had been crammed with sleek cars and the bar room was packed with the upwardly mobile. This was the place to be seen, and Peter didn't need to be seen. The clientele made fashion statements by casually holding open their jackets so that the extravagance of the labels could be identified, and slowly checked the time on Swiss watches with clockwork movements that cost thousands, but were less accurate than the lowest priced quartz model. Those timepieces had some of the ugliest features that Peter had ever seen. Faces crowded with four sweep hands and five secondary dials; cases made from unpolished steel surrounded with prominent bolt-heads. For those who practised public preening, bling had gone, but so had good taste.

The drinks in their hands were mostly alcopops and parasol shaded cocktails. As the evening wore on they would change to wine and then to spirits.

Admittedly fragrances had improved. Aftershave and discreet perfumes now dominated. The old public bar brew of tobacco smoke, stale sweat and fermented malt and hops had gone; but so had the aura of relaxation. For Peter that was a vital ingredient, so he finished his drink and left.

In the next road The White Horse was also closed down. Its windows shuttered with sheets of corrugated steel, doors sealed with anti-squatter mesh, once polished brasswork invaded by verdigris and gutters choked with weeds, it awaited demolition.

On the far corner The Carpenter's Arms had become the Cuisine de Epicurus, and Peter glanced through the window. In this gastropub, traditionally tatty furniture had been replaced with fashionably tatty furniture. Chromium steel tubing now supported the buttocks of connoisseurs rather than planed oak or steamed bentwood. A copy of the bill of fare was displayed by the entrance. Apart from soup-of-the-day, Peter didn't recognise any of the dishes. Embarrassment engulfed him easily, and gaucherie over the menu needed to be avoided at all costs, so he continued his expedition.

Half an hour's walk brought him to the Green Man, which had changed sex and was now the Anne Boleyn, and Peter entered hopefully.

Although the building retained its Edwardian shell, the interior had been garnished with fake antiquity, and it was no pearl. Long hunks of blackened and malformed expanded polystyrene had been glued to the ceiling with irregular spacing to supposedly recreate adze-hewn and tarred Tudor beams; horse brasses made in Taiwan were nailed to the walls; plastic jugs and tankards with a dull pewter finish paraded on bracketed shelves; fibreglass logs in a fireplace were licked by blued flames from gas jets; uncomfortably ridged slabs of concrete covered the floor to unconvincingly reproduce the flagstones of an ancient alehouse. It only remained fitting that the designer's neck be placed on an execution block.

Although urban taverns hadn't been socially divided until the nineteenth century, here the 'Royalty Bar' and the 'Commoner's Bar' posed an unrecognised anachronism. Peter knew his place, and joined the commoners, where he bought another glass of ye olde orange juice.

In this bar the sixteenth century imagery was further challenged by a row of gaming machines with flashing lights. King Henry the Eighth would not have been pleased.

Even though these walls had been artificially aged, the people within them had been artificially youthed; but Peter was not too uncomfortable.

As he stood by the bar, one other man was close to him, but the rest were at a distance. As Peter paid for his drink, he discovered why: the man was the quintessential barroom bore.

The man held his glass at a high level and looked at in intently, as if expecting to find living creatures swimming about in it; or perhaps looking into an alcoholic's crystal ball. As Peter pocketed his change the lone man turned towards him.

"This is a most curious thing, y'know."

"What is?" enquired Peter.

"Why should a pale yellow liquid be called white wine? The grapes they make it from are treated just as carelessly, y'know. Why are they called white and not green? It's a disgrace that their beautiful frosted green colour should be dismissed by calling them 'white'. It's the same with coffee, y'know. Why call it white when it's brown? Why has all our nourishment been whitewashed? What say you?"

"I must confess, I don't really know. But it's a most interesting thought." Peter's lie about interest was whitened also. The man always used this speech with a profound air as an opening gambit to trap another into conversation. A few unfortunate people had fallen for it, and had their ears bent for the rest of the evening. The drinkers of Plumham had all encountered him, and now kept at a safe distance.

The man was about to embark on another carefully scripted gobbet of wisdom when a karaoke machine started to blare and a tone-deaf trio hollered incomprehensible sounds into microphones. Conversation was impossible, and Peter recognised the opportunity, downed his drink at a single gulp, nodded to the disappointed buttonholer and made his escape.

On his way to the George and Dragon, he noticed that one shop had converted from pawn to porn, but the three brass balls remained, perhaps to denote an excess of testosterone. Nobody realised that a future recession would change it back again.

His next target looked hopeful, its full Victorian charm retained with no trace of decay. He now opened the door and cautiously entered. The bar counter was topped with an almost unending row of beer pump handles, a large array of barrels were at its rear, and an even larger display of bottles filled the shelving above.

Groups of real ale enthusiasts stood debating the merits of their favourites and the demerits of others. Bottle labels bore some treacherous sounding names: Peculiar Mischief, The Hangman's Noose, Spider's Den, Undertaker's Delight, Widow's Weedkiller, Rusty Treadmill, Parson's Downfall, The Sunken Wreck, Gravedigger's Axe, Highwayman's Plunder. The brewers seemed just as notorious: Scrimpshovel and Sludgepump, Snail Crushers, Hopscroungers, Grimbucket, Coffin Nail and Hammer, The House of Debauched Angels.

The booze buffs' esoteric themes were a blank sheet in Peter's manual. This was a club for the initiated so he quietly slipped away before anyone noticed his presence. It was a pity, however. This venue wasn't infected with piped music; and he preferred times long gone when the plop of a dart into dampened cork could still be heard above muted voices.

Another quarter mile and he reached The Red Lion, and by now his legs felt like saveloys that had been pushed through a mangle. If there were seats here, and if one was vacant, he needed to rest.

He surrendered two pounds for another small glass of orange juice, and thankfully dropped onto an unyielding chair. He was at the far end of the room away from a tiny stage, and a large crowd awaited the second half of an evening's entertainment. He sipped from his small glass slowly. His bladder had started to ache, but he didn't want to risk losing the seat if he moved away.

A man at a keyboard played a chord as Peter took his third sip, and he almost choked as a blubber laden comedienne entered, rolls of saturated fat spilling over every edge of a less than adequate costume. She made two lumbering circuits of the stage as the boards creaked in protest, her buttocks like two warthogs fighting in a sack and her unfettered breasts lurching like a pair of hundredweight sacks of cement.

After leering at the audience for a sludge filled minute, she took hold of a microphone and delivered a stream of obscene gags with the voice of a gravel-filled cement mixer in an echo chamber; then followed each punch-line with a guttural explosion form deep within a lard lined stomach and thrust her titanic pelvis forward and upward like a sperm whale rising from the ocean. Most of her bawdy rants weren't really jokes at all, but just strings of lewd words. As she slithered from one outburst of sewage to the next, the men continued to give laboured laughter, but the women grew restless and started to heckle her, mostly in language even more unsavoury than hers. As they were in the majority, and included several well-oiled hen parties, so the mega-sized artiste looked around the audience for a man to humiliate. That ploy always won over the unappreciative sows, and her eyes alighted on the forlorn figure of Peter. Her breasts looked ready to crush his skull as she barged her way through the crowd, so Peter left the rest of his drink and absented himself to the toilet, where he relieved his anxiety and his bladder, and waited until the performance had finished.

As he exited his refuge he realised why the women had been so impatient. The following act as a well-endowed male stripper, and they now whooped and cheered while the men looked uncomfortably inadequate. He now knew that this, also, was not the place to bring Alice.

The long walk back home was shrouded with hopes unrealised. Peter thought of those idyllic scenes in television dramas where people drank at pleasant inns, seated on lawns which ran to a sun-drenched water's edge where rowers rowed, scullers sculled and punters punted. That would have been the perfect setting for a relaxed encounter, brief or otherwise, but it would mean travelling to Oxfordshire or the narrow end of the Thames: not a practical solution.

One late discovery did then brighten the evening. Down a small side road Peter noticed a small restaurant he'd never seen before. *La Petite Fleur* actually listed 'Afternoon Teas' on its unpretentious fascia board. The close glazing bars of its bow window held small panes, some of which were reproductions of bottle-bottom 'bull's eyes', now upgraded as 'bullions' by the trade. If buyers had known the humble origins of these Dickensian relics, they'd have thought twice about fitting them.

Peter looked through the window and saw a modest interior, with spotless white tablecloths, quietly tinted wallpaper and shaded wall lamps. At least he'd found an oasis for tea drinkers in a desert of espresso, cappuccino and latte.

The sun rose feebly on the day of the planned meeting with Alice, but it outshone Peter's anchored imagination. Frustratingly no ideas had arisen there at all. He'd hoped that a record five cups of tea after breakfast would inspire his inert thought, but they didn't.

He began his wait at the bus stop almost an hour before the appointed time: nothing was to be left to chance. Then worries started to form. Did she really mean it about meeting him? Or was she just humouring him? The concern did nothing to prompt his dormant ideas about what to do that day, but he needn't have worried about either matter.

Right on time her bus arrived, and a kindly driver helped her onto the pavement. In a fraction of a second Peter was at her side.

"Hello, Alice. It's Peter."

"I know. I recognised your smell."

"I smell?"

"Most people do. You only notice it when you can no longer see them."

"What do I smell of?"

"Freshly ironed cotton."

"Is that a pleasant smell?"

"Of course. It's all part of your quiet charm."

This unexpected overture set Peter back into the centre of Saturnia Regna. She was as genial as before, and her sunlight flooded his darkest abyss. He guided her to a small bench at the roadside, and they sat for a while.

"Since we last met, I've tried to find something that you might really enjoy, but I haven't had much luck. I've read all the local papers, and there's nothing really special anywhere. I'm sorry to be such a failure."

"Then perhaps it's luck that I've found something."

"Really? That's marvellous. What is it?"

"You know the library in the town centre?"

"I go there every month. Sometimes more often."

"They have a little local history hall at the side. Well, it was extended last year, and now they have touring exhibitions there on all sorts of subjects. The one there at the moment I'd like to see; through your eyes, of course."

"How did you know about it?"

"Frank told me."

"Is he a boyfriend?"

"He lives next door. He's ten years of age."

"What sort of exhibition is it?"

"It's art, but I don't know what kind. When I was in my teens, looking at paintings was something I really loved doing. I think that I must have gone to most of the big London galleries. Sometimes with my school, sometimes alone. It's probably what I miss most. Will you take me? Or will it be just a bore?"

"It's a brilliant idea. I can't think of anything nicer. But I'm no expert. Are you sure that I'll be able to tell you what you need to know?"

"I'm sure you can. You're not insensitive, I know that for a fact. Have you ever dabbled in art yourself?"

"The only pictures I've ever made have been with a camera. I used to develop my own. Only black and white, of course."

"That's an art form. You're the perfect person. Won't you lead me to it?"

She took his arm and they walked steadily on their way, he guiding her around the *skoria* of an unrestrained community which littered the pavements.

Through the library and into the local museum Peter found it much the same as when he was a child. Chests of pull-out drawers contained collections of moths and butterflies, now decidedly frail and flagging; a few fossils, some now cracked; pressed flowers, faded and weary; a few Roman coins in varying states of tarnish; some bones of pre-historic animals, their identifying labels now faded; documents from ancient Plumham, blemished with fungus foxing and curling at the edges; a small selection of early dental equipment; and a display of nineteenth century tickets and a timetable of the Plumham and District Railway, long since overmastered by a succession of power steerers.

Shelves held a moulting owl, a brass fireman's helmet, a half inflated Victorian football, some coronation and Royal Jubilee chinaware, an array of wigs and hats, and a number of empty spaces where some more valuable exhibits had been unofficially relocated by opportunist visitors. On the walls were a large selection of old photographs far more relevant to Plumham than anything at The Overdraught.

"Nothing here has changed since I was a lad, except for the empty spaces."

"In that case I'll have seen it all as well. Shall we move on?"

"The notice on the new hall says 'An exhibition of challenging contemporary art'."

"Oh dear. That's what I feared. Still, we'll give it a try, shall we?"

The first challenging work of unfine art was a row of rusting buckets containing animal entrails topped with a wide diversity of excrement, around which swags of tinsel and strings of supermarket till receipts had been draped. It was entitled *Where is the market for life before death?* Peter read the title to Alice.

"What is it?"

"It's containers filled with fleshy bits, some shiny drapes around it, and some unmentionable stuff on top."

"Unmentionable? Don't be coy. You can mention it to me."

"It's what usually gets flushed down the toilet. I'll read you what it says. 'Gabriel O'Neill navigates a multiplicity of concept and not a linear progression. He explores a trajectory of subcultural denominations, at once attractive and errant, to subvert material images of unstable stability, uncertain certainty, mistrustful trust. His anger percolates the correlation of attrition and massification, and reconfigures reality to transform the viewer into a visionary. The plain of ephemeral immortality conjures a reclaimed philosophy of alter-modernism. His mission statement transcends the formalist anchor of definition to challenge complacency and humanity's flight from reality'."

"Just as I thought. It's Delphic obscurity."

"I'm not as well read as you. Does that mean you like it?"

"It means it's complete bollocks. Sorry, does that shock you?"

"Not at all, but I never thought I'd hear you say it."

"I only do when I'm furious. I don't mind it when the rich toss their wealth away on junk that masquerades as sophistication. In fact, some of them deserve it. But when taxpayers' money is thrown at this worthless rubbish, it's so unfair. That money might otherwise have paid for an operation on my eyes."

"Is there one for your problem?"

"I'm told that one has been developed in Scandinavia; but the NHS can't afford it."

Again Peter was dazzled by her insight. In the Country of the Sighted, the blind ought to be king. He had read art critics in papers and had struggled to believe in their impenetrable jargon, and now the quackery of it all flooded in on him. But he also shared her rage, and it doubled his already considerable sympathy for her. To the Arts Committee, however, the notion that the cutting edge was cutting into the public purse could only have come from ungrateful reactionaries. It was unthinkable that today's 'Wow' factor might become tomorrow's 'Yuk' factor.

"Perhaps there might be something here somewhere that's worth looking at. Now we're here, shall we move on and give it a try?" added Alice, her poise restored.

The next avant-garde creation was *My Blue Heaven* by one Laura Johnson. She'd pieced together a collection of comforters politely advertised in postal-sales catalogues as 'personal massagers', along with other sex toys, and had set a large crucifix at the centre. The whole was surrounded by a border of condoms filled with raspberry jam. As Peter scanned the barren profanity he didn't read the abstruse puff beside it but pressed on to the next artless-art sham. Alice sensed that he'd evaded something, and rightly diagnosed a tied tongue.

A large sheet of plywood, sawn crudely into the shape of two pendulous breasts and painted yellow was covered with photographs placed at haphazard angles, some upside down. They mostly seemed to have been taken accidentally, or while the camera was in the hands of a mischievous toddler. Those that could be recognised included a garden shed, the bottom of an empty shopping basket, the top of somebody's head, a damaged traffic light, a bottle of laxative and some fish bones. Scattered between them were a few aged sepia portraits of family groups and, pasted at the side, strip cartoons cut from newspapers.

Peter described it in some detail, and then read from another masterpiece of lucidity.

" 'Eric Picclesden's *The Ultimate Tragedy of Being* is at the epicentre of artecontemporanea. His work challenges our perceptions of form and matter with an evolution of sublime delineation to contradict contradiction. His symbiosis redefines historical determinism, the stochastic images infusing and diffusing beyond the boundaries of their own dimensions, and the exuberant dialectic between the spiritual and the seductive recontextualises the state of being with pro-active revelance. The vibrant tensions take us beyond space and beyond ourselves, and its vitality and immediacy raise the material presence to confront our sense of the world and our experience of time'."

"The scribblers who wrote this propagandist twaddle must be the greatest charlatans of all time. And our money is paying them to do to it." Alice's uncommon sense standpoint on the meaningless drivel was unwavering. To her, Josef Goebbels had been the master manipulator of truth; and now art critics and promoters had snatched his crown. But the honest, dedicated and politically correct Arts Committee knew otherwise. The trusted platoons of art dealers, trend directors, glossy and unglossy columnists, ad-men, con-men and assorted henchmen had unselfishly striven to heighten the cultural awareness of Plumham's cabbage brained. That motive was paramount: if they had unexpectedly widened their profit margins, that had no relevance.

On the next wall hung a very large, very old and very battered picture frame, but it contained nothing. There was little to describe, so Peter read another chapter from the annals of obscurity.

" 'Antranig Ozmanian's *Reality VIII* is a sensory meditation of reconsidered space, blurring the boundaries of non-painting, hyper-painting and beyond, directing the filter of sight through a sense of temporal displacement which collapses categorisation. It captures the essential fragments between being and not being, and the transference of energy defines a black hole in which non-systems perish. The accentuated border escalates the spatial truancy to become a tangible void of geometrical wholeness. It is a subtle and immaculate critique of the formal rhetoric of imaginative projection as we attempt to situate ourselves within the dynamic creation of an invisible visibility. Ozmanian's genesis of art without the brush and palette of an artist is the unholy grail that sets art beyond the self-denial of expression. We are liberated from representing anything other than ourselves, and we become a fertile void for the escape of meaning'."

"This would be hilarious if it wasn't for the damage it endorses. It's not just a waste of money. If this sort of anarchy is officially recognised and praised, then how can vandals be criticised for kicking things to pieces?" Alice's world of darkness was brightly lit. Her viewpoint might have been a forewarning of rioting in the next decade, but vogue thinking is rarely lateral.

They intrepidly marched in a lonely *kulturkampf* with the impenetrable inanity of the trendy illiterati. They battled against 'exquisite equivalents'; 'organic and synthetic states of embodiment'; 'resonant surfaces'; 'fusions of perceptual presence'; 'transitory permanence'; 'traditions of scions'; 'semiotic revolutions'; 'searches for placement'; 'multidirectional movements'; 'parallel worlds'; 'reassuring correlatives'; 'interactive mutable moments'; and waded through a swamp of delineations, discourses, re-posturings, substrata, transformations, dialectical pathways and elegiac entry points.

The allies of mystification had put up a barrage of supposedly shrewd gems, but they'd fallen on deaf ears. Alice and Peter didn't retreat from their rebellious line of battle: 'vacuous jumble'; 'tosh'; 'pretentious rubbish'; 'gimmicks'; 'absurdities'; 'putrid'; 'nonsensical'; 'the cant of pseudo-sociology', and, most irreverently, 'bullshit'.

At the final skirmish Peter noticed an overturned bucket of mouldy bananas on the floor. He stooped to tidy the mess, but the uniformed attendant called, "Please don't touch the exhibit." And only then he noticed the placard with a bizarre title.

"Oh, I can surely sympathise with your feelings. You just can't help yourself, can you? You just have to reach out and be intimate with these beautiful, beautiful things. It's quite, quite irresistible. You just have to immerse yourself in the whole wonderful experience. Isn't it just too, too delightful?" Peter looked behind him and saw the man with the blue-rinsed hair from the literary discussion group.

"I long to stay, but I must tear myself away to meet a very close friend. He's one of those who just can't be kept waiting. Now, you two lovely people must stay and lose yourselves in these sublime delights. We simply must have a long, long chat about it all at our next literary meeting, and relive the whole glorious experience. Until then, my dears, I bid you both farewell."

"That gives me another good reason not to go to any more of those literary meetings," commented Alice as flamboyancy minced out of earshot. "What about you?"

"That's also a definite 'no'."

"It seems to me that there's nothing to choose between those meetings and what we've just read. They're both flytips of nonsense. The words are obese and flatulent. It's an intellect born in nephelococcygia."

"You've lost me there."

"Sorry, I do show off at times. It means cloud-cuckoo-land. So, what do you think of it?"

"It's crap." The word fell from Peter's lips leaving him aghast. He'd never said anything like that before: and in front of a woman!

"That sums it up perfectly. Your tongue is loosening nicely now. Have you had enough of all this?"

"Most certainly. What shall we do now?"

"How about a nice cup of tea in that special place you found?"

"Perfect. But are you sure that's all you want to do?"

"Absolutely."

As they left the library Peter noticed that the elegant Edwardian gauged and moulded brickwork had been sullied by graffiti. Normally he was appalled by such groundless spite, but he now wondered if it was any worse than what was inside the building. The defacers had, after all, given their labour for nothing, and the results were perhaps less untalented.

The service and wares at *La Petite Fleur* exceeded Peter's expectations. A waitress in a black dress and white pinafore served tea and pastries, brewed and baked to perfection.

"I suppose that's one advantage of being blind. I can't see the ugliness that grows all around me. That exhibition was a good example of what I'm happy to miss. I only remember the nice things from the past."

"You're very knowledgeable and very well-read, though," observed Peter. "You must have been outstanding at school."

"Not really. I was about average I suppose. But since losing my sight, or most of it, I've read a lot to try to improve the parts of me that still work."

"How do you manage that?"

"There are lots of books in braille and on tape. My mum reads to me as well, and there are plenty of interesting radio broadcasts."

"If only I'd known you in my formative years. You could have been my tutor, or psychotherapist or something."

"I don't think I'd have been much use to you. I still had a dummy in my mouth then."

"Yes, I am a lot older than you."

"I'd already worked that out. If you'd been born during the war you couldn't be otherwise."

"And you don't mind?"

"Of course not. You're a fine friend to have."

"Perhaps I might be more? A substitute father or elder brother."

"Let's just leave it at friendship, shall we?"

"Of course."

They ordered another pot of tea, and Alice demonstrated her accomplished dexterity in serving it.

"I wish that I'd had your courage and bettered myself."

"Then why don't you? You've got all the basic ingredients. All you have to do now is bake yourself a richer cake."

"I think I might have left it a bit late in life for that."

"Nonsense. A few grey hairs don't matter. It's what's underneath that counts. What about further education? There are plenty of opportunities. Some universities offer very good facilities for all manner of disabilities. I know: I've been there. In my financial position it was all subsidised. It didn't cost me a penny; not that I've got many pennies."

"You've been to university?"

"That's right. And I enjoyed it. But it's been a disappointment since."

"Why's that?"

"I had hoped that it would open doors for me. But blindness is still a barrier. So far, I've not found a way around it."

"You deserve better. If only I had contacts with some people who might be able to help. I'd love to help you, I really would. If you can think of a way, please let me know. And I'd never expect anything in return. I couldn't even think of doing something that might harm you."

"I know that too. I don't think that you could harm anyone. And I'm sure you're genuine. It's just that I've made some bad friends in the recent past, one in particular."

"What happened?"

For the first time Alice looked uncomfortable, and rapidly changed the subject. He realised that he'd touched an open sore.

"So, what shall we do next week?"

"You're happy to meet me again?"

"Why not? You're my eyes on the world. My mum used to take me places, but she's not been well recently. Where would you like to go? It's your turn to choose."

"I'm not much good at that. I tried to think up something all last week, but failed."

"What do you usually do?"

"Housework; go shopping; tend the garden, though there's not much of it; do a bit of cooking, I'm not bad at that; read a lot; watch television when something good is on, which isn't very often; a bit of home maintenance; listen to music; go to a concert from time to time; go for walks; and tend my mother's grave at the cemetery. That's about it, really. Not very exciting."

"Well, to start let's visit the cemetery. After that, I'll see if I can think up another idea."

"You really mean it?"

"Of course. We could lay some flowers there together. You were very fond of your mother, weren't you? You've joined in my sorrows, now I'll share in yours."

"That's really kind. Would you like some more tea?"

"It's very nice, but I ought to be getting back. Mum needs my help."

"Maybe that's another way I might be of use. I could give her a hand sometimes. It must be very difficult for you to cope with it all."

As soon as he spoke, Alice again showed silent concern, and Peter realised that this was another forbidden pathway: so he changed route.

"Perhaps next week we might enjoy a meal as well. What food do you like?"

"I've never ventured far away from basic English, but I'm willing to try. We'll decide then, shall we?"

On the journey home, it dawned upon Alice how much her feelings for Peter had leavened. He was kind, considerate, gentle, helpful, unselfish, modest and sweetly innocent. He was everything she'd ever looked for, and perhaps he might be more to her than an occasional friend. Then she dismissed the absurdity from her mind. Age difference wasn't the only obstacle. There were at least two others.

Peter had already bought a large bunch of flowers and two potted plants before he once more helped Alice from the bus, and they walked pensively towards the cemetery.

He'd spent the last week worrying about where to take Alice for a meal. Apart from the rare visits to Miriam's fish and chip shop, he'd mostly fended for himself and had never explored the far flung gastronomic lands of Plumham. When he'd reconnoitred the tipple wells last week the experience had been daunting, and he couldn't face seven days of stomach stuffing. He wondered about offering her home cooking, but that was far too brazen.

With Peter's direction Alice laid the flowers and placed the plants, then she asked an unexpected question.

"Will you read me the inscription on the headstone?"

"Sure. 'The loved are never forgotten. Your joys and devoted sorrows linger until we meet again'."

"You composed that yourself, didn't you?"

"Yes, I did. How did you know?"

"Those aren't off-the-peg sentiments. There must be a lot of tenderness in you."

"I suppose there is, but it's all bottled up and buried away somewhere. Before I go, I usually say a silent prayer. Will you excuse me for a moment?"

"I can do better than that. I'll join you. We'll be silent together."

As she closed her eyes, Peter saw soft moisture glaze their sightlessness, and a drop of his bottled-up tenderness escaped.

"Are you religious?" asked Alice after opening her eyes.

"Not really. I don't feel like going through a lot of ritual. But I've every respect for those who do. I suppose I've got my own private religion now. How about you?"

"I've never had religion at all. I find it hard to believe in an Almighty who took away my sight, but perhaps now you've converted me. I'll join your private denomination, if you have room for another." The sparkle had returned to her voice: maybe Christine's youthful spirit abided, *Deo volente*.

"I'm glad to have saved your soul," replied Peter, echoing her humour.

"Where is your dad buried?"

"In Malayan clay somewhere, and I wish that they could have been buried together. She really loved him," answered Peter with a wisp of sorrow, then he returned to the well-being of the present. "So, what would you like to do now?"

"I'd like you to take me around the rest of the cemetery, and read some of the inscriptions on the monuments to me."

"You must be kidding?"

"Not at all. I know a lot of people's feelings about burial grounds are morbid. I think that's the fault of ghost stories, horror films and myths about Dracula. To me, they're full of love.

Unaffected love. I'd like to drink some in, if you'll help me. There aren't any headstones in braille."

"You really are a lady of hidden depths. Now it's your turn to show me the light."

"You don't need redeeming. Only awakening. Lead on, kind sir."

They made their way between the plots; some carefully tended, others sadly neglected. Where the mixed passions of clay undersoil had heaved and sank, there were collapsed graves and monuments that leaned perilously or lay shattered. The detritus of abandoned obsequies spoke of endearment lost or forsaken: overturned urns, rusting wire frames that had once clutched wreaths, bouquets or crosses. The apathetic weather had washed away inlaid lead letters and gilded engravings to dispatch the dearly departed into an anonymous eternity.

As Peter guided Alice along pathways narrow and broad, he felt her body shudder and her arm tighten a few times as he read from the graves of children. The inscriptions he read varied, from clichés taken from stonemasons' catalogues to others with originality, and a few were quite poetic. At the cemetery's Victorian edge stood a tall, magnificent monument of a weeping angel, its epitah *Sunt lacrimae rerum et mentem mortalia tangunt.* That said it all, and perhaps had never been bettered.

"Well now," asked Peter as they approached the exit gate. "Are we ready for that meal?"

"I'm very sorry Peter, I should have mentioned it earlier. But I have to get home to be with mum. The district nurse is calling, and she likes me to be there. Shall we have it next week?"

"Marvellous. Perhaps it's just as well. I haven't thought of anywhere to go yet. That gives me another seven days to crack the problem."

They stood at the bus stop, and a bold thought hammered impatiently at his door of inhibition, but paternal genes of reserve kept it closed.

As a bus approached the lock of shyness sprang open; which was a piece of luck. Peter didn't have the youth or the energy to chase after it as his father had done.

"Alice, may I ask... er... what I mean is, well, sort of, you know, can I... no... I mean will you, that is..."

"Go on, spit it out. I promise not to kill you, whatever it is."

"Well, you see, if you could see your way clear to..."

"Get on with it. I don't bite, you know."

"Well, what I wanted to say was..."

"Yes?"

"Would you like to have a meal at my house next week? I could cook for us both."

She thought for a moment, but to Peter it seemed like an hour as the bus drew in.

"Can I trust you?"

"Of course. Of course. I'll..."

"It's all right, I'm only joking. Yes, I'll be happy to sample your cooking. You can give me a guided tour of your house as well."

That evening at home, Peter's repressed hormones again relented and he danced around the room. His mother's treasured records sang with new meaning. Mood Indigo was now 'On the Sunny Side of the Street'.

In the midst of spurious intellectualism, shop-till-you-drop consumerism, plastic celebrities, New Age neuroses, untalented talent, venally generated inelegance, corporate greed, crotchets and quiddities, he'd found an angel.

But like the angel in the cemetery, this one now wept. As she lay in bed that night, Alice was divided. Her dexter segment glowed with the discovery of forgotten gentleness and honesty in a wilderness of inflated hype and deflated meaning; but her sinister schism eclipsed it with the gloom of inevitable defeat. She wanted to stay, but she had to leave. Time was growing impatient.

Peter guided Alice to his home, carefully but over-optimistically describing the route so that she might be able to find her own way if she ever wished. During the past week he'd studied his recipe books and borrowed others from the library. Knowing nothing of wine he'd bought eight different types to give her a choice, and some new finely cut and engraved glasses.

He'd looked at some fancy candles to place on the table, but then realised that strong lighting would be better, so he replaced the light bulbs with others of higher wattage. Although she couldn't see it, he meticulously dusted and cleaned the house from top to bottom, got out his mother's best china and table linen which had last been used for Christopher's and Christine's final meal together, and rearranged the house so there was nothing she might trip over.

Alice sat serenely at the table. She too had risen to the occasion, putting on her best dress and just a touch of perfume.

Peter's diligently prepared four-course meal, attentively served, was savoured by Alice with unanticipated relish.

"This is wonderful. Absolutely wonderful. You should have been a chef."

"I don't think I'd have liked doing that. I enjoy cooking as a hobby. Then I can take my time and please myself. But as an everyday job I think, for me, it would lose its appeal."

"Well, you certainly please me. I've never tasted anything as good as this." Her words were wholehearted, and not just empty praise, although her experience of fine food had never really existed. She'd had a few encounters with wine, though, and was able to choose from Peter's collection.

"Not only are you my window on the world, but you make my taste buds happy too. What more could a girl want?" The twinkle in her voice now shone brightly.

"I think you deserve a whole lot more. I'm sorry I can't deliver it."

"You do your best. That's more than anyone else is doing at the moment."

After they'd eaten, Alice asked to be shown around the house, and Peter obliged with fond descriptions. Then they sat on the sofa and he offered sherry, port, martini or Madeira. His cellar had suddenly expanded during the past week.

"I've never heard of Madeira before. What's it like?"

"It used to be my mum's favourite. She and dad drank it on special occasions."

"Then that's what it'll be. We prayed for them last week, now we'll drink to them."

"May I ask a favour?"

"Ask away."

"May I take a photograph of us both?"

"How can you take a photograph and be in it?"

"I place the camera on the sideboard and used the self-timer setting. Then I've got ten seconds to get back in place before it exposes."

"Sounds fine. I'd ask you for a copy only it won't be any use to me."

"It will be when they restore your sight."

"There's no hope of that in the near future. Anyway, I'll be honoured to be in one of your portraits. Snap away."

Peter set up his camera and took eight photographs of them both. Alice smiled sweetly throughout.

"Would you like me to take you anywhere?"

"It's alright. I feel safe here. Have you any music? I like classical, but I don't mind trying something else, although I can't stand heavy metal, or anything like that. To me it's just a load of noise."

"I've no classical, I'm afraid. My mum's old collection of records are a bit scratchy, but I still like them. They're all popular music or light music, but about fifty or sixty years old."

"Let's give it a try."

The trusty turntable spun, and the sturdy old speakers repeated, in habanera rhythm, Cole Porter's warning that his father had heard on abdication day.

'I'd sac-ri-fice an-y-thing, come what might,
For the sake of hav-ing you near,
In spite of a warn-ing voice that comes in the night
And re-peats and re-peats in my ear...'

"Yes, I like it. It's melodious and lyrical. And both are quite subtle. It's better than I expected, and so different from the thumping boredom that's being churned out now. We seem to get only the odious without the mel. Each time I go in a supermarket to help mum I'm forced to listen to it."

"In that case, here's something by the same composer. He was mum and dad's favourite."

'Do – you love me as I love you?
Are you my life to be, my dream come true…?'

He refilled her glass and pinched himself a couple of times to verify the reality. As she sat on the sofa she looked contented and tranquil, her quiet dreams misted around her slender figure.

'Bless you for be-ing an an-gel,
Just when it seemed
That hea-ven was not for me…'

An unfamiliar and fragile happiness bloomed within her, like an orchid in a deserted garden. For a while she luxuriated in its fragrance and beauty.

"My mum and dad used to dance to these records in this very room. Playing them again still gave her happiness."

"Shall we join them in a dance?"

"I can't dance."

"Neither can I. But we could shuffle around for a while."

He took her gingerly in his arms, in what he believed to be the correct hold, and they moved around the room with surprising co-ordination. This was the first time he'd embraced a woman, albeit formally, and he now stood on Everest's top of euphoria.

'If I had my way, dear,
For ev-er there'd be
A garden of ros-es
For you and for me…'

Alice basked in his protective touch, and the absence of lust. She felt as sheltered as a babe in a father's loving arms, but adult enough to enjoy a deeper affection. She was in a land she'd never visited, one where fear was unknown, pain was unfelt, sorrow didn't exist, and tomorrow would always be today.

They returned to the sofa, and Peter emptied the last of the fortified wine into their glasses. Alice edged closer and rested her head on his shoulder, and he astounded himself by boldly, without invitation, putting his arm around her shoulders. He expected her to pull away, but she didn't.

'Al-though he may not be the man
Some girls think of as hand-some.
To my heart he car-ries the key...'

The natural fragrance of her hair reminded him of one of his favourite smells: freshly cut cucumber. But he didn't mention it in case it offended her.

"Happy?" he asked.

"Never been happier." Peter couldn't be sure if it was the alcohol or her judgement that spoke, but it was the perfect reply. And the perfect end to a perfect day.

"Now I must leave before I get carried away."

He agreed. And that was the difference. Other men would have enticed her to get carried away.

"Perhaps you're the nicest man I've ever met."

"There are a lot of years between us."

"There's more than years between us, I'm sorry to say," she added mysteriously with a slight shudder. Peter noticed tramlines of concern appear above her nose, and he didn't delve deeper.

As they reached the stop her bus arrived, she stood on tiptoe, whispered, "Until next week," and kissed him lightly but expressively on the cheek.

Back at home Peter washed the dishes, heedfully put away the celebration china and tablecloth, played again all the records they'd listened to and slowly finished the remains of the dinner wine. It was by far the greatest alcohol intake he'd ever imbibed, but he relived the day passionately, just as his father had done after meeting Christine. This was another gene that he'd inherited, and a joyful one.

Alice didn't do the same. As the wine wore off her affection remained, but melancholy descended. She had reached decision point, and again she cried herself to sleep.

As Peter waited again at the bus stop, mulish splinters of unease refused to be drawn from his contentment. There were rocks of distress lurking beneath Alice's calm waters; he was sure of that. Why had she deflected his offers to take her home or call at her house? Why didn't she want him to help her mother? Was she ashamed of him? The idea that Alice might have opaque glass in her cabinet of Dasein never crossed his mind. He'd always made a full disclosure to her: he couldn't adopt even the benevolent concealment used by Charlie Chaplin's tramp towards a blind girl. His analysis, though, had always been in terms of self-blame and never self-pity.

Helping her from the bus, those unquiet shards were driven deeper. The fleeting moments of concern that had visited her face before were now permanent residents; and drought was far from her eyes.

"What are our plans for today?" asked Peter as he guided her from the pavement's edge.

"It's a fine day. I thought we'd take a walk in the park. You can tell me about the flowers and the trees."

"What about food? Home or away?"

"I've already taken care of that."

"You have?"

"I've brought a small picnic with me. Nothing up to your standards. It's all very humble, but I hope you'll enjoy it."

"Of course I will. But you shouldn't have gone to all that trouble. I could easily have made us something like that."

"I'd like to do something to repay your kindness."

"Just your company is good enough. I like to do things for people: you especially."

"I just thought that this would be an atonement."

"Whatever for?"

"Oh, it's well… I'll tell you in a while." It was the first time he'd heard her fluency falter, and as rainclouds darkened her eyes he placed her hand over his arm and cradled it reassuringly as they walked to the park. To raise her spirits he romanticised the splendour of the blooms, the leaves, the grass, the sky and the sun. Although he'd never been infused with the rousing oratory of Lysias or Hermogenes, he pulled away his spigot of inhibition and out flowed a sonorous maiden speech. Modest hyperbole, encouraging allusion, unmixed metaphors and hopeful compliments were marketed: but they sold like cold cakes.

They sat on a bench shaded by an almond tree in the otherwise deserted park. Peter picked up a fallen almond nut, still in its green casing, and gave it to Alice.

"You have this. It brings good luck, you know." He'd invented that myth on the spot hoping to gladden her, but she pocketed this novel talisman without faith.

Alice took a paper napkin and cardboard plate from her plastic bag and passed them to Peter. Then she unwrapped small parcels of aluminium foil and took out ham sandwiches, a sliced quiche and a prepared salad, and urged Peter to take as much as he could manage. Then, with Peter's help, she unscrewed a half-bottle of white wine and poured it into two paper cups.

"This is magnificent. You did all this yourself?"

"Most of it. It takes time, but I got up early and worked slowly."

"I don't deserve all this. After all, I'm only your temporary replacement for Humphrey."

"I feel you're a little more than that now, as I think we both know." Those words would have delighted Peter, but her tragic tone told him otherwise.

They ate their food silently for a while. Alice desperately needed to unburden a bleak decision, but her stalling larynx wouldn't oblige.

Peter searched to find a waxing moon that might lift her darkened tide.

"You mentioned that you liked classical music. Does the romantic period appeal to you?"

"Very much."

"I've discovered that there'll be a concert of Chopin's music later in the year at the Albert Hall, and another at the Royal Festival Hall for the work of Tchaikovsky. You've listened to my music, now I'd really like to share in yours. Shall I book tickets before they all sell out? It would make a lovely evening."

"I don't think that we ought to be making plans like that. Sorry."

"Well, here's another idea. Next year will be the Queen's Golden Jubilee. From what I've read it'll be a great event. I went to the Silver Jubilee, and the atmosphere was marvellous. Strangers were talking to strangers. I'm sure you'll like it, and we could take your mum along too."

Peter had fond memories of the Silver Jubilee. It was about the only occasion when he'd been able to overcome his natural reserve. In an often fractured Britain, only two things seemed to unite most of the people and make many speak with one voice: the 'Blitz Spirit' of warfare, and royalty. Of the two, Peter preferred royalty.

"I'm really sorry, Peter, but it has to be 'no' again. Could we leave it at that, please?"

Peter's tree of ideas had unexpectedly burgeoned above par, but now it was root bound.

"Are you sure I can't help in any way?"

"Yes, yes. We'll talk about it all in a minute." But that minute didn't arrive.

Alice unwrapped a bar of chocolate, Peter broke it and they shared the segments as they made another circuit of the park. They passed a large ornamental pond where the beauty of the water lilies had been augmented by three bald tyres, a flotilla of empty crisp packets and a bent supermarket trolley. Much of the oak tongued and grooved matchboarding had been kicked away from a hipped-roofed shelter, the gaps incongruously filled with now rotting chipboard, but then helpfully redecorated by the ever-present graffiti restorers. The bandstand had been rededicated as a temple of Dionysus, and its floor was now reverently covered with bent beer cans and broken bottles. Peter didn't include any of those adornments in his eulogies, but his inspiriting moon was now waning.

They reached the bus stop and sat alone on the little bench, with the words still immured within Alice. Then her restrain gave way and tears flowed freely.

Peter placed an arm around her trembling shoulders and his other hand wiped away her tears with a neatly pressed handkerchief. He was on the threshold of awareness, but it didn't have a welcome mat.

"Alice, why don't you tell me what's wrong? You know you can trust me, whatever it is."

"Oh, Peter. I'm so, so sorry. I wouldn't hurt you for the world, but I have to say this."

"Whatever is it?"

"We – we mustn't meet again."

"Why ever not? Oh, I suppose I'm too old and too feeble. But all I ever wanted was to help you. I ask for nothing more. I'm sorry I'm not good enough, but I'd still like to give you a hand."

"No Peter, age has nothing to do with it. To me your voice sounds young and handsome. That's all I can see. Please don't think that you're not good enough for me. You are. You're too good. It's the other way round."

"How do you mean?"

"I'm not good enough for you."

"Alice, that isn't true. You're a marvellous person. I've never been so happy as when I'm with you. What I'm saying sounds a bit corny, a bit sentimental, but I really mean it."

"I know Peter, I know. But you'll find happiness somewhere. I hate doing this, I really do. I should never have let it go this far. You've made me happy too, but there are things you don't know."

"Whatever they are, I can take it."

"I just can't bring myself to tell you. Believe me, it's for the good. It's the only thing that we can do." Alice heard a bus approaching, and added, "Promise me just one thing."

"Anything."

"Forget all about me, please. Go find yourself a really nice girl."

"But I –"

"Please don't say any more. It's too painful." She got to her feet, drew Peter close and kissed him gently on the mouth. "Bye, bye, Peter dear."

He helped her board the bus and stood silently looking at it until it was out of sight. Her tears had dampened his face, and he wished they'd never dry: they were all that he had left of her.

As he made his way home the spring in his step had been relegated to January. Euphrosyne had forsaken him, but Janus did not open a new door.

So few pages had been written in his life and so many remained blank, probably now never to be filled. A vast lacuna remained, but his pen of hope was dry.

On the doormat at home Peter found a small note from the voyeur Cyril Nudwick, who was now terrified as a financial tsunami approached his ogler's laboratory. It read: 'You haven't phoned me yet. Does it strike a chord in your memory?' Peter's mind was in fact full of chords, but all were in a minor key, so he screwed up the paper and threw it away.

His frame of mind had been devalued from a million dollars to a million Zimbabwean dollars. He looked towards the radiogram for solace, but the nostalgic memories of the past had now been joined by the desolation of the present.

He'd never read Ernest Dowson, but if he had he would have agreed that *vitae summa brevis*.

There would be nothing to tell his father that night.

Chapter Eight

On Christopher's train journey into central London, he sat back and pondered. Events over the last two days had pushed reflections aside, but now he tried to make sense of his unusual posting.

He'd completed eight weeks of 'square bashing' at an Initial Training Camp, secured his 'AG' wing at gunnery school and his 'sparks' badge at radio school. Most of the other trainees had then been sent to one of the Operational Training Units where they joined the haphazard 'crewing up' process before being allocated to a squadron. Christopher had expected to march in line with them, but going straight to Malaya put him out of step.

Now he opened his travel pass and found another oddity. His final destination was not a port where he might board a troop ship, but RAF Tangstone in the heart of Norfolk. Was Malaya a mistake? Was he to stay within reach of Christine after all? His hopes expanded like a lottery winner's bank balance.

The guardroom at RAF Tangstone directed Christopher to the orderly room, where the duty clerk assigned him a billet, and told him to return the following morning for an interview with the Administration Officer. The twelve-bed Nissan hut was damp and unoccupied, so he selected a bed close to a window, stowed away his kit and sat down to write a letter with a gleeful hand.

My Darling Christine,

I miss you so much already, and it's only eight hours ago that I last held your lovely hand. But now – Oh yes! – I just might, just might, have better news.

I'm not on a ship to Malaya, but in Norfolk, less than a hundred miles from the sweet girl who means all the world to me. No, not just the world. The moon and the stars and the whole universe.

Tomorrow I'll find out what's happening, but if I stay, and I can't see any other reason for being here, then I should be able to feel the touch of My Darling's lips again soon.
Until then, sweet dreams My Angel.

Your own Christopher

XXXXXXXXXXXXXXXXXXXXXXXX + a million, million, million, million more.

After an ample breakfast the next morning he drank three cups of mess tea. Cookhouse tea was usually regarded as less palatable than water which had cleaned a urinal, but that day it tasted delicious. At that moment, everything seemed delicious: the air, the sun, the birdsong, the whole planet. To hell with the enemy, to hell with the Air Ministry, to hell with Malaya. His feet were still on good old Blighty. That's where Christine was, and that's where he wanted to stay.

He was still on an escalator between an eighth heaven and cloud twelve when he accepted the proffered seat at the front of the Administration Officer's desk.

"Do you know why you're here, Goodwin?"

"No, sir. After trade training I was told that I was being sent to Malaya, but then directed here. I assume that Malaya was a mistake."

"It wasn't. You're not being shipped out. They need more aircraft in the Far East. We'll be sending some from here, and you're to be part of the crew to ferry one out. They may keep you there, or send you back for home duties. That will be decided there and then. Any questions?"

"When will I be leaving, sir?"

"Not for a while yet. We can't spare any of our aircraft. We're waiting delivery of one from somewhere in the north. In the meanwhile we've arranged for you to be familiarised with the aircraft type. Sergeant Haynes will give you the necessary information. Have you met Haynes yet? He's in your billet."

"I haven't seen anyone in the billet, sir."

"Oh, that's right. I forgot. He's on compassionate leave. Lost some of his family in the bombing, poor chap. He's due back today. And before you leave, Goodwin, fill in these documents in the outer office and give them to the Orderly Clerk. That's all. Good luck."

"Thank you, sir."

The forms he'd given Christopher asked for details of next of kin, and what his last wishes were for the disposal of his personal possessions and estate in the event of his death. His moving staircase was now descending to a grey sub-basement.

Christopher now regretted writing that premature letter, and again put pen to paper with a forearm now less than joyful; although some hope was coaxed from the fingertips.

My Sweetest Dearest Christine,

I'm sorry. So sorry. My letter yesterday was a bit mistaken. I am going to Malaya after all, but I may not have to stay there. And it won't be for a while yet, so I'm sure that I'll get a day or so's leave before we're off.

Until then, My Darling, please promise me that you'll stay happy. I can't wait to see your lovely smile again soon, and...

Christopher was just stoking the stove at the centre of the hut with fresh coke when through the door a grieving figure entered and slumped onto a bed. Christopher made a sympathetic approach.

"Hello. I'm Goodwin. Chris Goodwin."

"Nice to meet you. Derrick Haynes."

"I hear that something sad happened to your folks. I'm very sorry for you. Would you like to tell me about it?"

"Mum and little sister. They were in the Anderson shelter. Thought they'd be safe there, but it received a direct hit. Dad was away on fire watch that night."

"How is he?"

"Terrible. He seems to think that it was his fault for not being there. Now he says that he wishes he'd been with them, and they'd all gone together. He seems almost suicidal. I wish I'd been able to stay with him longer."

"Is someone taking care of him?"

"He's staying at his brother's at the moment. Aunt Queenie is very good. If anyone can pull him through, she can. Normally dad is a tough old bird. I've never seen him fold up like this. Sorry, this isn't a very bright introduction, is it?"

"Please don't worry about that. I'm always glad to help. I'm lucky, really. My family and my wife's family are all unharmed. I hope it stays that way. But I've just been home on a forty-eight, and things are pretty rough there."

"Where are you from?"

"Plumham."

"I know it. From the other side of London myself, but I know it well. Got a cousin from those parts. Name of Fielding."

"Not Colin Fielding?"

"The very same. You know him?"

"Used to go to school with him. And we often went to the same dance hall. How's he doing?"

"Serving in north Africa. Got a commission. I think he's a captain already."

"He always was one for getting on. I'm not surprised. By the way, when you were in Plumham, I don't suppose you ever met the girl I married. Her name was Christine Groves."

"I didn't know any girls from that neck of the woods. Why do you ask?"

"She once told me that she hated the name 'Derrick'. I assumed it was because she'd known someone with that name, but I know it couldn't have been you."

For the first time Derrick raised a slight smile. Christopher was surprised that he'd been able to comfort a new face so readily, and a grain of sugar was stirred into his porridge of blighted hopes.

"Shall we go to the mess for a bite to eat?"

"I don't really feel hungry."

"When did you last eat?"

"Can't remember. Yesterday, or day before perhaps."

"Well you need to build up the inner man. Hope I'm not being a bore. Am I?"

"Not at all, Chris. You're right. Sorry, I forgot to say welcome aboard."

They ate a small but nourishing lunch, and freely swapped fragments from a recent past, but Derrick's were jagged, blackened and bloodied. He was now in a ten per-cent minority: he'd actually completed a tour of duty of thirty missions and was still alive and physically unscathed. If his nerve had suffered, he didn't show it: but it had. Through a chink in Derrick's natural veil of modesty Christopher caught glimpses of outward flights in cramped, freezing isolation, weaving between tracer shells, machine gun bullets, bursts of flack, shards of shrapnel and the unwelcome publicity of a searchlight: homeward journeys spent comforting a dying comrade on the floor, the fabric of the Geodetic fuselage torn with gaping holes, the aircraft limping on one engine, the rear turret and its occupant shot away. He'd spent eight months surrounded by the familiar smells of hydraulic fluid, rigger's oil, Av-Gas and fear: and by five others who'd donated their youth to blood-drained weariness. All had volunteered to become aircrew: but none could volunteer to leave it. In their evenings they'd gladly shared their bottles of ale: at night they'd kept their bottles of dread tightly corked. If those corks were removed, they'd be classified as having 'Lack of Moral Fibre', and would spend the rest of the war humiliated and cleaning lavatories. Many moustaches now covered lips that were losing their stiffness.

"What happens when you've finished a tour of duty?"

"You're given leave, then you spend a while at a training school instructing new entrants, or some do an admin job. Then if the medical officer passes you, you're on another tour."

"So, you're here for admin work?"

"No. I'm supposed to be instructing."

"But this isn't a training unit. It's an operational station."

"That's right. But it's being used as a rendezvous point for kites being flown out to the Far East. They're all coming from different squadrons that are being re-equipped. It's all a bit chaotic, because they'll be arriving in dribs and drabs, and we don't know when. I'm here to familiarise new crews with their machines."

"So I'm not the only one going to Malaya."

"There are others destined for the Far East, but I don't know where. It's all being done gradually. You're the first."

"Do you know what aircraft they're sending us?"

"Blenheims. That's why I've been chosen. I've had a bit of experience there."

"You've flown Blenheims?"

"Only for three sorties. Then I got transferred to Wimpeys. I'm glad I was. Otherwise I'd be dead by now."

"That's not very encouraging."

"You've nothing to worry about. They're good reliable kites, but they're no match for German Messerschmitts, and you won't meet up with those in Malaya. Are you staying there or coming back again?"

"I don't know yet."

"You're probably better off staying. You'll be able to spend all your days sunbathing."

"I'd rather be back near my wife, though."

"You're one up on me there. I've never taken the plunge. Now I've not much family left, I suppose I ought to think about starting my own."

A pigment of concern again repainted Derrick's face, so Christopher thinned it with the turpentine of distraction.

"Do we have to wait delivery before instruction starts?"

"No. They want you to be ready for the off when that happens. There's an old Blenheim in the maintenance hangar. It doesn't fly, but I can show you all you need to know. We'll start tomorrow. OK?"

"Fine."

"Meanwhile, how about a game of billiards?"

The table in the billiard room was free, which was unusual; but most of the squadron crews were at a briefing at that time. They played two games of hundred-up, and Christopher led a brisk conversation to keep Derrick out of his trench of grief. He squeezed every possible theme from his pannier of popular topics: the music he enjoyed, films he'd seen, books, radio comedies, the few jokes that he could remember. He was glad that Derrick didn't mention sport: Christopher had bequeathed that subject to his brother when he'd married Christine.

The briefing sessions over, queues started to form to use the table, so Derrick went for a walk to the local village to try to traipse away his heartache. Christopher returned to the billet to find a letter on the table. He opened it and kissed every page.

My Darling Christopher,

I read your first letter over and over again. I started to reply, but screwed it up when I got your second one.

Of course it's disappointing, but we have to look on the bright side, don't we My Love? The Germans will never get as far as Malaya, so you'll be much safer there. I don't mind waiting a while as long as I know you'll be safely home again one day. I'll write to you every day. I'll just lock myself away and do nothing else.

Darling I love you so much, and...

Christopher followed Derrick through the Blenheim's narrow entry hatch and they made their way rearwards, past the observation ladder and into the poky constriction of the dorsal turret. His instructor showed him the rack on which to stow his parachute, and they stooped low as he demonstrated how to raise and retract the turret. Then he explained how to manoeuvre the Bristol hydraulic rotation motor; the elevation and depression of the twin belt-fed Browning machine guns, and how the retractable seat rose and fell to maintain the target sightline.

"The one I saw at the Training Unit only had a single Lewis gun."

"That was a Blenheim mark one. Bloody useless. This is a mark four. An improvement, but can't compete with a Messerschmitt's cannons. And many of the Jerry fighters' cockpits are now armoured. They can't be pierced with rifle-calibre bullets."

That afternoon they moved forward in the aircraft to examine the radio equipment. Christopher was glad that it had a fixed long-wave aerial on top of the fuselage. Working a manual trailing one would have been difficult for his tall frame in such cramped conditions, as would a hand-cranked turret.

Derrick then went for another stress shedding walk. He preferred to be alone on these hikes, so Christopher returned once more to his hut.

"Are you Goodwin?" asked a pilot officer who stood just inside the door.

"Yes, sir," replied Christopher, springing to attention and saluting.

"OK, old chap. At ease. We can dispense with the formalities I assure you. You're to be my wag, I believe."

"Beg pardon, sir?"

"Sorry. My weird sense of humour. W-A-G – wireless air gunner. Pledger is my name. I'm your skipper." Pilot Officer Pledger offered his hand, and Christopher was dumbfounded. He'd never shaken hands with an officer before; it was an unexpected honour. "Look, this whole set-up is a bit of a nuisance. We're not on a squadron, we've no crew room in which we can have a chat; and you're not allowed in the officers' mess, and I'm not supposed to be in the other ranks' messes. But we need to get to know each other. What say you if we have a drink at the local tonight? Not averse to a pint, are you?"

"Not at all, sir."

"Good man. We'll go early, before the bar gets crowded. There's a nice little place down the road a bit. Called The Crown. Shall we meet at the main gate and I'll show you the way? Six o'clock suit you?"

Christopher agreed, and was taken aback once more. The officer had said 'six o'clock' and not 'eighteen hundred hours'. It was like being back in civvy street.

My Dearest Darling Christine,

It was lovely to get your letter today. But you mustn't worry about me. I'm sure I'll be alright now, I've just met the officer who'll be my pilot. He's a smashing chap. We're going for a drink tonight, so I should have more to tell you in my next letter.

So, what of your news? How are mum and dad and big sister? When I...

The saloon bar of The Crown was empty. Mr Pledger bought two pints of best bitter, and they took seats at a small corner table.

"What's your first name?"

"Christopher."

"Do you prefer 'Christopher' or 'Chris'?"

"My wife always called me Christopher. Her name's Christine. If we called each other 'Chris' it would be a bit of a muddle. But to most others I'm Chris."

"Fine. Now here are my ground rules. When we're at the station and others can hear, then it's formal: I'm 'sir' and you're 'Goodwin'. When we're in the kite or relaxing over a pint, you're 'Chris' and I'm 'Frank'. How's that?"

"Marvellous, sir, er, Frank."

Like Derrick Haynes, Frank Pledger was also a survivor of a duty tour of thirty missions. Then he'd been a sergeant pilot. He was no socialist, but he loathed the idea of elevated privilege. The distinction between officers and other ranks was, he thought, a long outdated aristocratic legacy in which some were treated as humans and others as sub-humans. He'd held his non-commissioned rank with radical pride, but at the close of a tour pilots were automatically commissioned. He had no choice in that process, but he was still determined to unofficially reject the aloofness of rank and treat all as equals.

"I understand that they're giving us a Blenheim, Frank."

"Yes. I flew one for a while. Bloody awful things. Tiny little cockpit, and pilot and observer sat side by side. Almost in each other's laps. All very nice I suppose if one happens to be a poof, but no bloody good for flying. Lucky that I'm a skinny sod. I don't know how fat buggers could cope. Anyway, that was the Mark One. We're getting a Mark Four. In that kite they've put the observer forward in an extended nose section with a little navigation table. But they tell me that the cockpit layout is still far from ideal."

They swapped personal reminiscences, and Christopher relaxed in this man's company. After a second pint he was able to confide family details, including the desire for children and the frustration of having none.

"Where do you live, Chris?"

"Plumham."

"They got a terrible pasting the other night. I read about it in the paper."

"I know. I was there on a forty-eight. That's what worries me. Leaving Christine in such danger."

"I can sympathise with that, I really can."

"Are you married, Frank?"

"I was. Wife and only child killed in one of the early bombing raids. That's why I volunteered for this job, to get my own back on the bastards. Revenge isn't the best motive, I suppose, but it's something that I can't shake off. Helps me to cope with all the sorties, too. I don't care now if I die. I'll never find another girl like my Hannah; nor another little lad like Tommy. So I don't get the shakes like some of the others." Frank noticed a look of concern cross Christopher's face. "Oh, you needn't worry, old chap. I never take chances. My own life is worthless now, but I still take care of my crew, especially when there are good guys like you among them."

Christopher saw the look of hopeless despair that now haunted Frank's face, and he immediately felt a rising tide of compassion for this tragically courageous man. It formed a strong bond of understanding between them, and would remain for the rest of their lives.

The bar was starting to fill, so they finished their drinks and arranged to continue the conversation the next evening: same time, same place.

My own Beloved Christopher,

I do miss you so, and I'm so afraid of wasting just a few minutes without you. But that mustn't stop you doing the safest thing. I can still put my heart on paper. And I can do more than that. I kissed this letter all over, and I know you'll do the same.

I went to visit your mum and dad yesterday, and they're really fine, although they miss you also, especially mum. She told me that...

As Christine had predicted, Christopher did kiss the whole surface of the paper, eight times.

Christopher spent the next morning again in the battered Blenheim, where he plugged in a newly-charged 'trolley-ac' to boost the aircraft's failing batteries. In the radio compartment he donned a test headset, pushed home its jack plug, checked each crystal in the recently installed high-frequency set, and explored the full range of medium and long range frequencies on the trusty eleven-seventy-two. Then he practised all of the drills and routines previously demonstrated by Derrick in the gun turret.

Derrick was nowhere to be seen when he returned to the billet, so he kissed Christine's letter three more times. His instructor seemed to be on an even longer walk that day.

My Own Wonderful Sweetheart Christine,

The only way I can think of heaven is to be as close as possible to my dear and only one for the rest of my life. I just can't wait for it to happen, but I'm luckier than some.

Yesterday I had a long chat with my new boss. He calls me Chris and I call him Frank. I can't believe what a really nice chap he is, but I feel very, very sorry for him. His wife and only child...

Christopher entered the bar of The Crown just after six. Frank was already there and had a pint of best waiting on the counter for Christopher. With him was a lean, muscular man.

"Chris, I want you to meet Jimmy. He's our third Musketeer. Jimmy Evans, this is Chris Goodwin." They shook hands and retired to their usual corner.

"Jimmy is observer and bomb-aimer. We won't be carrying bombs, so he'll try to be our full-time navigator."

"The crew of a three-man kite used over Europe doesn't include a full-time nav-man," explained Jimmy. "They only feature in the big crates. The pilot still does most of the map work in a Blenheim and I help him a bit, but that won't be much use going halfway around the world."

"And neither of us have been outside of Europe before. Don't want to put the wind up you, Chris, but it's only right that you should know all the facts."

"Will I be able to help?" offered Christopher.

"Not while we're still in Europe. Nor near North Africa. You'll be busy keeping your eyes open for the Hun. After that it should be quiet, so we'll try to fit you in somehow."

"Don't worry though," added Jimmy. "I'm getting a bit of tuition from a very experienced bod on this station, and Frank and I will spend much of our time genning up on charts."

"But we'll still have time for a pint or two," confirmed Frank.

For the next hour they swapped life sketches. Jimmy was another of the unblest. He'd lived with his parents, and the proximity of a bombing raid had induced a stroke in his mother and now she couldn't speak nor use the right side of her body. Being an only child he'd applied to the authorities to excuse him from military service so that he could help his father care for her, but his request was refused. Now he too had anger with those who were enemies, but with it was mixed with annoyance against those who were not.

My Very Precious Christine,

I did kiss your letter, eight times, and then three more for luck. That makes a total of eleven, and that might be our own lucky number. It falls between ten and twelve, and 10/12 was the date of the day when we first met. Abdication Day. Remember how clumsy I was then?

As eleven is between those numbers, then it must also keep us together. And as today is the eleventh, and I got that idea on this day, then what could be luckier?

I know it all sounds a silly superstition, but the crews who've been on a lot of missions all seem to have good luck tokens, so I thought if I found one now then it's bound to work.

As well as a lucky number, I'd like to have something personal of yours to carry with me at all times. If you can spare it, can you send me one of your stockings to keep in my pocket? One that you've worn, but haven't washed? Then you'll always be with me.

So, My Darling, how was...

In selecting his lucky number, Christopher had overlooked the fact that at 'the eleventh hour of the eleventh day of the eleventh month, we shall remember them'. Not, perhaps, such a good omen.

Twelve more letters, one enclosing a neatly folded stocking, seven more practice sessions and eight pints of bitter later, the aircraft had still not arrived, so Christopher plucked up courage and knocked on the Station Warrant Officer's door.

"I'm sorry to disturb you, sir, but there's no sign of our Blenheim yet, and I wondered if I might have a day or so's leave. My wife is getting a bit worried as I haven't been home for a while, and I'd like to put her mind at rest. A forty-eight would be just the job, but a thirty-six is fine. There doesn't seem much for me to do around here."

"Out of the question, I'm afraid. The aircraft could arrive at any time, and you need to be ready to leave immediately. The only exceptions we can make are if a very close family member has died, or is in hospital in a critical state. Otherwise you're on permanent standby."

My Very Own Sweetest Christine,

I tried the SWO today to see if I could get a bit of leave, but it's not on at the moment. But take heart, My Darling. We'll be together again soon, I just know we will, and then we'll face the future whatever it has to hold.

When you wrote that...

He spent another morning going through a practice routine that now seemed a waste of time. On entering the billet he found Derrick talking to two newcomers.

"Ah, Chris. This is Charlie Stevens and Bill Mitchell. We're all of the same trade. They'll be taking flights out after yours. I'll leave you to get acquainted."

"Where are you going, mate?" asked Charlie.

"Malaya. What about you two?"

"I'm off to Burma. He's going to North Borneo, wherever that is."

"So, what is there to do around here?"

"Just practise on an old Blenheim. Derrick instructs you. He's quite good."

"What about the evenings? Any cinemas?"

"Not for miles. There's a nice little pub down the road. I'll show you the way this evening, if you want."

At the mess they lunched together, and then the new men went for an afternoon's instruction with Derrick, and Christopher passed an hour at the billiard table with a couple of the squadron lads.

Frank and Jimmy were not at their usual seat in the bar of The Crown as Christopher entered. They were elsewhere pouring over the charts and making detailed notes and almost endless calculations and recalculations.

Charlie and Bill had glasses of black 'goodness' from the underground springs of Dublin, and Christopher moderated his order to half a pint. His boozometer had risen too sharply recently.

"I'm not looking forward to this, you know," confessed Charlie.

"Why's that?"

"Well, they don't eat proper food out there. I was told they have fried rice. Have you ever heard of such a thing? Rice is alright with custard, but that lot spoil good grub. I'm going to make the most of good old bacon and egg while I'm here."

Charlie was the Messiah of English cuisine. If he had his way he'd bring the delights of tripe and onions, faggots and pease pudding, bubble and squeak to the rest of the world, and save them all from the perdition of foreign food. If the Germans hadn't stuffed themselves with sauerkraut and funny shaped sausages, he reasoned, they'd never have gone to war with us.

"You could always get yourself a bit of Oriental skirt to take you mind off it," consoled Bill.

"Not on your life, mate. I'm not going to do that. I'm going to keep it in my trousers. They've all got the pox out there."

"What about pubs?" queried Christopher. "I don't suppose you'll find any of those either."

That set off Bill's reminiscences of taprooms he'd tanked-up in, and Charlie's aggrandised tales of the piss-ups he'd survived. Their company was cheerful, but Christopher's penny-watching life had strictly limited his knowledge of Bacchus, so he excused himself and made his way back to camp through the evening's chill air.

The Royal Mail had faithfully delivered six more packages of love from Tangstone to Plumham and five more from Plumham to Tangstone when the message was received: a Blenheim was on its way.

Christopher and his crewmates stood at the side of the dispersal area as the aircraft taxied in, parked and a rigger ran forward with chocks.

The pilot emerged and approached the trio. As the green cloth oxygen mask was unfastened, lipstick appeared. Raising of the celluloid goggles displayed pencilled eyebrows; and when the brown chrome leather flying helmet was taken off, shoulder length blonde hair fell downwards. Frank and his crew stood open mouthed.

"What's the matter with you lot? Never seen a woman before?" asked the pilot, then indicated the aircraft with a polished fingernail. "She's all yours now, laddies."

"I'd rather have you, my love."

"Jimmy! We don't address ladies in that manner!" Frank's respect for the fair sex was paramount.

"Don't worry, skipper. I've met dirty old men like him before." She made her way to the office with the aircraft logbook in her hand, and called back over her shoulder, "They're all mouth and nothing in their trousers." It was game, set and match to the ferry pilot.

As the ground crews moved in to refuel and arm, Frank went to see his commanding officer.

"As soon as the mechanics and armourers have finished, you'll be off."

"I don't think so, sir."

"Pardon?" This senior officer wasn't used to having his orders questioned.

"I've no experience on a Mark Four, and my two crewmen have no hours logged on Blenheims. We need to practise for at least a day, even if it's only a few circuits and bumps. If all goes well, we'll leave in the morning."

Wing Commander Butcher knew of Frank's nonconformist reputation, but he also knew of his exemplary war record, so he agreed.

As soon as the fitters and riggers moved away, the three flight crew took their places. Some pilots' pre-flight checks consisted of walking around the aircraft, kicking the tyres and waggling the ailerons; but Pilot Officer Pledger was meticulous.

He spent a long time adjusting the seat-raising handle at his left to try to get the best view of the impressive array of instruments and be able to manipulate the awkwardly placed controls, and came to the conclusion that the cockpit layout was far from convenient. He was grateful for the redesigned asymmetric fuselage nose which improved his forward vision, but he spent a full twenty minutes swearing at the inexpedient and unwieldy format of the knobs, levers and switches. His short arms could cope with the throttles and mixture controls; but he had to bend double to reach the elevator and rudder trim wheels. He had to lean out of his seat to manipulate the hydraulic controls of wheels and flaps; and the oil cooler shut-off and the carburettor heat and cut-out switches were all out of reach. The four magneto switches were too far forward and obscured by the selector handle, and with the control column in standard position the compass couldn't be seen. Worst of all was the position of the propeller pitch controls. To change from fine to coarse Frank had to reach far behind him. As these knobs needed to be grabbed quickly in an emergency, it did not inspire confidence; but he kept that detail to himself. He did not wish to alarm his crew.

Jimmy crawled through the tiny entry to the nose section, and tried out the navigation table.

"This bloody seat is the most uncomfortable thing I've ever sat on."

"Perhaps you've got the wrong shaped arse."

"Then whoever designed this thing must have a really weird bum."

Christopher's check was relatively brief, so he stood at the rear of the aircraft to report back to Frank on rudder and elevator movements.

After an hour and a half Frank finished his careful appraisal, started the engines and they taxied around the peritrack. Christopher tuned to the control tower frequency and received clearance for take-off. Frank reduced drag by changing the gills from wide open to trail, adjusted the flaps, reached behind him to set the pitch control to fine. At the runway's starting point, with wheel-brakes locked on, he pushed forward the dual throttles, slowly released the brakes and advanced the throttles further as the Blenheim sprang forward. Juggling the rudder pedals with both feet he aligned aircraft to runway, pushed the throttles through both final gates and returned his right hand to the control column as they became airborne.

They completed three circuits and landings, then climbed to ten thousand feet and headed south. At the Thames estuary Frank turned west and followed the river. Some light fog still shrouded London's suburbs, dappled with darker smoke that still rose from the previous night's bombing. That distant glimpse would be the last that Christopher would see of Plumham. In the evening they had their last drink at The Crown, bade farewell to the landlord and assured him they'd return soon. It was a promise they'd never be able to keep.

The next morning Frank completed another scrupulous inspection of their Blenheim. The auxiliary outer-wing tanks had been filled to capacity, increasing weight by more than a thousand pounds, and so the crew's personal kit had to be kept to a bare minimum, although Christopher made sure that his included pen, envelopes and paper. To save weight the commanding officer had ordered the plane to fly unarmed, but again Frank rebelled, and the armourers reinstalled the ammunition belts.

As an anaemic sun peeped briefly between early snow clouds, they waved goodbye to the ground crew, ran the full length of the runway and slowly climbed. It was the day before Abdication Day anniversary, and so Christopher was certain that this odyssey would have a delightful outcome, just as it had five years before. As they flew out of sight, a Royal Mail van made a delivery to the main gate. It included one very special letter.

My Own Dearest Christopher,

At long, long, long, long last I've got the best news we've ever had. Darling, it's wonderful! Wonderful! Wonderful!

I've just returned from the doctor's, and he confirmed that in only seven and a half months' time, you're going to be a daddy!

My precious, there have been two absolutely miraculous days in my life; the day I met you, and the day we married. Now there are three!

What about names? As you know, I don't like 'Derrick'. I used to work with a man of that name, but he was horrible. But now I think of it, I dislike 'Malcolm' even more. But I do like Peter. What would you say to Peter, plus a family name? Perhaps Peter James, after your dad.

If we have a girl, I'll let you think of some names, but I don't want any of your old girlfriends included (it's all right, I'm only joking). I wondered about putting our two mums' names together, either 'Ruby Sally' or 'Sally Ruby', but as they both end in 'Y' it sounds a bit clumsy. What do you think?

Darling, I'll let you know all my other news tomorrow, but I had to get this in the post today. Now God's speed, and deliver you back some day soon. Till then, I love you with all my heart, and I'm yours for ever and ever and ever.

I'll give you the biggest hug possible when I see you next, and at least a hundred kisses.

Until then, sweet dreams, My Darling. All my fondest love and devotion.

*Yours to have and to hold.
Always and for ever,*

Christine.

XXXXXXXXXXXXXXXXXXXXXXXXXXXXXXXXXX (36 – that completes the date for Abdication Day – and the wonderful day we first met. All luck be with you).

A week later, that letter was forwarded, but never reached Christopher. Also that morning newspapers fell on doormats across the world with news of another beginning: Pearl Harbour.

The Blenheim climbed to its service ceiling of twenty-two thousand feet. The draughty, unheated cabin was even more uncomfortable than Frank had anticipated, and they were thankful for their 'teddy bear' jackets, Sidcot flying suits, thermal socks and zip front boots. They stayed within English air space until passing Cornwall, then made a wide sweep around occupied France but flew close to neutral Spain. Through the Straits of Gibraltar they passed high over the spot where HMS *Ark Royal* had been torpedoed and sunk four weeks before, and Christopher kept a very alert eye open for the vengeful forces of Erwin Rommel or Benito Mussolini. Christopher saw the contrails of distant aircraft, but to his immense relief none grew nearer. The Mediterranean sun had raised the temperature a little, but it was minute after minute of anxiety that caused the palms of Christopher's hands to sweat.

As they lost height and touched down in Malta, the visions of devastation were beyond belief. Thirty continuous nights of bombing had reduced most of the island to rubble, and the week before they'd passed their thousandth bomb alert. One runway was usable thanks to some very swift and energetic repair work, but the rest were littered with the smouldering hulks of burnt-out aircraft and pock-marked with bomb craters. An astronomer might have mistaken it for the surface of the moon.

A flight-sergeant fitter ran forward to greet Frank and his crew as they emerged through the awkward hatchway, and was disappointed to discover that this wasn't a replacement aircraft for their use. Nevertheless, they were treated very hospitably during their refuelling stop and overnight stay.

In spite of being very short of food, they shared their meagre rations with the newcomers, and apologised for having drained the last of the beer two weeks before. Fuel was also in short supply, but they topped up the Blenheim's tanks willingly.

Every single one of the sleeping quarters had been flattened, and all personnel had to make do with mattresses on the floor of an underground shelter, which also served as a makeshift hospital; and three more mattresses were squeezed between the others to accommodate their guests. Officers were no longer segregated by privilege, which pleased Frank: but a rope line was hung with blankets to wall off the women's section, which didn't please Jimmy.

Frank, Jimmy and Christopher all had enthusiastic audiences to hear news from home. The men and women were doubtful about the carefully doctored news broadcasts on radio and the official information distorted by omission. They wanted first-hand accounts. Christopher felt immediate sympathy for these war weary people, and withheld some of the more heart rending sights he'd witnessed in Plumham. In return, the Blenheim's crew learned about Pearl Harbour, but it didn't worry them unduly. Hawaii was a long way from Malaya. They didn't then know that the new aggressors were advancing on more than one front, but it warned Christopher to be wary of the now notorious Mitsubishi Zero-Sen as they neared the Pacific.

My Own Darling Christine,

I've reached Malta, and the poor people here have had a terrible time. Almost everywhere is bombed, and they're almost out of food and supplies. Perhaps London isn't so bad after all.

I don't know if this letter will reach you. Many of the supply ships have been sunk and not many are getting through. But I just have to tell you every day how much I love you. That's all I can do at the moment to make you happy, My Darling. Let's hope that soon I'll be able to do a lot more.

This is the furthest that I've ever been from you, and tomorrow it will be further still. So if...

After a benevolent but strictly rationed breakfast the Blenheim's crew shook hands with all those who'd helped them. The rapidly repaired runway was quite short, but Frank's skill managed to coax the heavy fuel tanks into the air just before its end, and they climbed away from an isle of dust, destruction and dogged resilience.

They flew westwards over the Mediterranean, keeping their distance from the former Italian colonies to the south. Although the Italian army had retreated from them, they were now being retaken by Rommel's panzer division. That may have been to the aircrew's advantage. The Luftwaffe were probably fully occupied giving air support to their troops, and were too busy to bother about a lone Blenheim apparently minding its own business. With an endless expanse of soft whiteness below, they flew beneath a blue sky of confidence.

High above Suez they flew south-south-east towards the Horn of Africa and then east to their destination: Aden. Frank was annoyed with this official flight plan. He'd calculated that with their sizeable fuel load they could have reached India and saved a day; but he didn't question the authorities. Adding to his defiant reputation was best avoided.

As they approached Aden, Christopher took his seat by the radio installation, but couldn't trace this station on medium or long wave frequencies, so he turned on the high frequency and found it dead. He checked all of the leads but found them secure, then tested the fine tuning of the crystal channels but none responded; so he reported loss of contract to Frank.

The Blenheim made four circuits of the airfield to see if Christopher could raise life in the set, but resuscitation didn't work. Frank flew low over the control centre and seesawed the wings to indicate wireless failure, and made an uninvited landing.

"The H/F R/T set is U/S, sir," truncated the flight mechanic to Frank. "We've no spares for that gear, sir, but I can modify the aircraft to accept a different model. It'll take about a day." Frank always put safety of his crew first, and agreed. But the 'day' estimate was optimistic; and almost three days passed before the work was completed. An aircraft in transit did not take priority here.

This station was relatively unscathed, and the class distinction between officers and other ranks was still intact: which didn't afford pleasure to Frank. And the personnel were all male. There were no WAAFs present, which didn't afford pleasure to Jimmy.

At dinner, Christopher shared a table with one disgruntled airman and his more phlegmatic colleague.

"Are you posted here permanently?" asked the less-than-happy one of Christopher.

"No. I'm on my way to Malaya. After that I might be returning home."

"Then you're lucky. I wish I was back in Merry England."

"It's very cold there at the moment."

"That's just what I need. It would all be worth it. If I was back home, I wouldn't have to put up with this fucking heat, nor the fucking flies, nor the fucking dust, nor the fucking mosquitoes, nor the—"

"And I wouldn't have to put up with a moaning bugger like you," interrupted his stolid friend, breaking through his phlegm of composure.

Christopher agreed with his view of the heat, though. Coming from chilly England at freezing altitudes the contrast was insufferable. Luckily the colony had a plentiful supply of water, so he took cold showers three times a day, but the balm evaporated in minutes.

As the hours passed, news of the Japanese invasion of north Malaya arrived.

"It's a pity that we're holed up here," remarked Frank. "They obviously need more aircraft now. It's a shame we're not already there."

My Very Own Darling Christine,

We're at the tip of Arabia now, surrounded by desert. The heat is terrible. As you know, I'm not fond of winter weather in London, but I'd much rather be there now, and not just for the weather, My Darling.
One of the wireless sets has broken, and we've got to stay a while to have it replaced. I've heard about the Japanese invasion of Malaya, but it seems quite a long way from the spot where we're going, so I don't think that we need to worry about that.
I love you more and more as each day passes, and I...

The time rolled by, and Frank grew more and more restless by the hour.

"What on earth are they buggering around at?" Then completion of the work was announced, but he didn't prune his rigorous pre-flight checks, and at last they were on their way to India. The flight schedule specified a base in the west. They'd calculated that they could easily reach the east, but orders are orders and they obeyed, and touched down in the early evening.

They reported to flight control and there was more dismal news: the tankers had got stuck in some unusually wet winter-monsoon mud, and wouldn't arrive until the next day. At dinner, Christopher picked his way through a bony and unappetising kedgeree. Perhaps Charlie had been right about foreign food.

Jimmy and Frank made a lot of intricate calculations that evening, and decided that if there was still no delivery the next morning they had sufficient fuel to reach east India, and perhaps complete the full journey. There was one consolation, anyhow. There was beer on offer at this place, so they bought pints from their allotted messes and sat on some scorched grass beneath a withering tree. Perhaps Vishnu had transhipped this venue's rain ration to where the tankers were stuck. They sipped their febrile ale slowly, and watched the tropical sun hide itself hastily below the horizon.

My Own Dearest Christine,

I'm now in India. The food is awful and the beer is halfway to boiling point, but being further and further away from you My Darling is so hard to bear.

There's a hold-up about petrol – they haven't got any. Frank wants to press on, but I'm a bit worried about it. Nonetheless, I don't like to disagree with him. He's such a terrific man and such a great, great friend; and he always puts us before himself.

So, My Darling, I've got another good reason to get home – your marvellous cooking – as if I didn't have enough reasons already! When you next see...

The following morning the bowsers were still empty and Frank reported to Wing Commander Green.

"There's still no sign of fuel."

"Actually, sir, my observer and I calculated last night, and we're sure that we might have enough to complete the journey. If we look like running short on the way, then we can land at a base in east India."

"In that case, I'll reveal some more news. The Japs have advanced south much faster than expected, and they're now just north of Penang. That's not far from your destination. If you get that far, then there won't be enough fuel left for turning back."

"I appreciate that, sir. But if we delay longer, then we'll be denying them the use of an aircraft that might help to hold back the advance."

"You're very courageous, Pledger, but there is another aspect. Aircraft are in short supply everywhere. If you waste one, that isn't going to help. I can wire London and request new instructions, if you wish."

"That will also waste time. If you'll allow me, I'll discuss it with my crew and come to a joint decision."

"Certainly, if that's what you want. You're very democratic."

"I try to be fair to everyone, sir."

Frank saluted and left, and took his two crewmates into an empty crew room, where he laid all the facts before them for their opinions. Jimmy and Christopher were both apprehensive of the idea, but didn't reveal their feelings to Frank. He was always so keen to help others and contribute to the greater good that they didn't attempt to contradict.

They lightened their load as much as possible. The thermal clothing certainly wouldn't be needed, and they changed their flying boots for regulation black leather shoes. They also took their personal kit and left it in the stores, hopefully to be collected on the return journey; but Christopher did not part with his writing paper, envelopes and pen. As they took off and headed east, a fleet of fuel tankers entered the airfield; but radio silence had been agreed, so the commanding officer couldn't recall them.

At the far east of India Jimmy and Frank carefully studied the gauges, reassessed their calculations and with Christopher's agreement decided to continue. Through the Bay of Bengal there was no sign of the Rising Sun insignia, and they crossed the northern tip of Sumatra, turned south east along the Straits of Malacca and entered Malayan territory just to the south of their destination.

As they approached the Malayan airfield, Jimmy saw a line of aging biplanes with two-seater open cockpits arranged along the tarmac.

"What the hell are they?"

"Vildebeests," answered Frank, whose knowledge of aircraft was encyclopaedic.

"It looks as if they came out of the Ark."

"And now it looks as if they're going back again." They were now close enough to see that every aircraft was damaged beyond repair, and three were burning.

"The poor blighters must have been bombed to hell before they could get off the ground."

"Not much use those things getting off the ground. They've only got a maximum airspeed of eighty-two miles an hour."

"Bloody hell. The place is overrun with Nips." Jimmy had noticed the smoke of anti-aircraft fire rising, and Frank yanked over the control column to head southwards, and pulled it back into his lap to gain height as quickly as possible.

"Jimmy, study the chart and find the next airfield to the south."

"It's about a hundred and twenty miles, Skip. Steady as you go, you're right on course."

Frank looked at the instruments and saw that the fuel gauges at the right were both perilously low, each needle hovering just above zero.

"I'm sure that we've got enough to make it," said Frank, with a tone of confidence that was far above reality. "Chris, just in case we don't, stand by the radio to give distress calls."

The fuel gauges hit bottom, but the engines continued for another half an hour. For the first time in his life Frank was grateful for an instrument's inaccuracy. Then the starboard engine started to splutter.

"How far away, Jimmy?"

"Another twenty-four miles, Skip."

"Right, I'd better find a clearing to put her down. Chris, start those calls. Jimmy will give you the chart bearings for your signal. If I don't find the right spot to put her down, then prepare to bale out."

Christopher started to tap 'dot-dot-dot: dash-dash-dash: dot-dot-dot' on the Morse key with his right hand, while he manipulated the high frequency set with his left and called "Mayday" with equal relentlessness, but neither received a response.

The engine picked up for a brief while, then both started to falter.

"There's a clearing ahead. Now I'm going to make a wheels-up belly landing. Hold on really tight."

Frank circled the clearing losing height rapidly, then aligned with the clearing as the engines coughed their last. He manipulated the awkwardly placed controls with the dexterity of a juggler that brought the Blenheim in for a bumpy but immaculate landing, and it juddered across the forest floor as the Pitot head and the mirror-sighted ventral blister with its twin Brownings were ripped away. They had lost half their speed and all seemed hopeful, but then a pernicious Vitis Amurensis tangled with the twisted starboard propeller blades, which slewed the lurching fuselage to the right. The trunk of a tree caught the wing tip, which spun them through ninety degrees, and the nose of the aircraft collided with the trunk of another, bringing the crumpled Blenheim to a savage halt.

Frank's retraining straps kept him in his seat, but the impact thrust a surge of blood through his brain and he blacked out. A minute later his eyes eased open, but purple whales swam before them. Neither vision nor brain had completely cleared when concern for his crew took command. He tore off his parachute harness and seat straps, and turned to his rear to see Christopher crawling painfully across the centreplane with blood running down his face from a cut on his forehead.

"You all right, Chris?"

"I think so. A bit bruised, but I can move around."

"Oh God, what a bloody mess. I can't tell you how sorry I am, old friend. If only I'd listened to the CO, we'd have had enough fuel to get us back to east India. I'll never forgive myself for this."

With the loss of Frank's family, his crew had become more than a band of brothers: they were successor kinsfolk. In the short time he'd know them he'd recognised the best friends he'd ever known, and their survival was his supreme concern: possibly his only concern. He was devastated, and deeply regretted his hasty decision, but he was determined to make amends and somehow get them safely back.

They crawled through into the battered and buckled nose section to find Jimmy lying on the floor nursing his right leg.

"I tried to stand, but this bloody thing gave way on me."

One glance at the leg told Frank that it had multiple fractures, and his imagination raced with ideas about breaking off tree branches and tying them to form a makeshift splint.

"We'll soon have you out of this, old man. Then we can patch you up, put together a rough and ready stretcher, and carry you to the next base." Frank's voice soared with a confidence miles above its stratum, but it was a tool necessary to slacken his over-tight remorse.

"Don't be bloody ridiculous. It's another three miles at least. And it's thick jungle all the way. Leave me here. You'll stand a better chance on your own. If you make it, then send back a search party to fetch me. It's your only hope."

"We won't leave you, Jimmy. We need to listen to your jokes to cheer us on our way. We're the Three Musketeers, remember?"

"All for one and one for all," echoed Christopher.

Jimmy protested, but his fellow crewmen stood shoulder-to-shoulder in resoluteness. They moved him across the nose compartment with difficulty. The low headroom usually prevented an upright stance, but the distorted floor kept Frank and Christopher bent double as they carried Jimmy.

The restricted opening to the cockpit was even more awkward. They had to lay Jimmy on the floor and push and pull him across the jutting fuselage ribs and around functional metal brackets. The entrance hatch was blocked by the heavy landing, so Frank and Christopher toiled for ten minutes to try to open the sliding top of the cabin, but they couldn't budge it.

Christopher crawled back across the wing root, climbed the observation ladder and, after a struggle, succeeded in opening the hinged hatch cover. Frank unwrapped a parachute, cut off a length of nylon cording, wound it into a rope and fastened it to Jimmy's harness. Then they hauled him diagonally through the hatch, where his muscular shoulders jammed for a while, but he wriggled his way free. From the top of the fuselage they lowered him onto the trailing edge of the wing, and from there to the ground.

They rested for a short while, then Frank caught the smell of escaping high octane fuel.

"We'd better move away, the kite might go up in flames soon. We'll make it to the edge of the clearing, Jimmy. There you can rest while we splint your leg and botch together a stretcher. We'll take the rest of the parachute with us, and use the cording and the canopy for that job."

Frank checked his pocket compass and found due south. Jimmy placed his arms around the shoulders of his fellow comrades at either side, and they moved away from the fated hulk of twisted aluminium alloy.

As they neared the edge of the clearing, the malignant vision of a concealed cancer materialised from between the trees, and a patrol of ten Japanese soldiers surrounded them with menacing rifles and fixed bayonets. A corporal stepped forward and searched Frank, found the compass and threw it away. Then he turned to Christopher, found the writing material in his tunic pocket, ripped up the paper and envelopes, broke the pen in two and tossed them over his shoulder. That spelt the end of distant love for Christine.

"Supai!" shouted the corporal, and slapped Christopher viciously across the face. From Christopher's other pocket he took out Christine's stocking, looked at it, sniffed it and stuffed in into his own jacket. That spelt the end of distant love for Christopher.

On the corporal's orders two of the soldiers pushed Frank and Christopher away from Jimmy with their bayonets. Jimmy tried to balance on his left leg, but he hadn't realised that the ankle at that side was broken also, and he collapsed on the ground.

While Frank and Christopher were held at bay, the corporal stepped forward and slowly thrust a bayonet into Jimmy's lower abdomen with a joyful leer on his face. The wound was shrewdly placed. It would ensure eventual death, but extend life so that Jimmy could endure the maximum pain for the maximum time. The whole patrol laughed and applauded, and to heighten the entertainment the corporal joggled the bayonet to coax out further screams of agony, before withdrawing the blade.

Christopher and Frank were instantly soaked with a deluge of hatred for their vile captors, but it was only a brief taste of what was to come.

Chapter Nine

Nature is a remarkable thing. The weather always obligingly follows mood. When Dracula stalks Transylvania, lightning complaisantly rents the night sky and thunder rolls; when a murderer is on the prowl, clouds conveniently cover the moon; when people are sad, it willingly rains; when knavery is on the loose, fog abettingly closes in; when people are poor and hungry, it uncaringly snows; when an optimistic corner is turned, the sun cordially breaks from behind the clouds; and when a heroine dances with joy, the sun shines gleefully in a cloudless sky, birds sing, butterflies fly, bees buzz and sweetly scented flowers bloom.

But not so in Plumham. There the raindrops, snowflakes, rainbows, the four winds and the gods and goddesses of nature just refused to co-operate. As Helios radiated across a sky of unsullied blue, so Peter Goodwin's melancholy remained in a paperweight snowstorm.

As he walked through the gate of Plumham Cemetery with the pathos of a family entering Auschwitz, the sun had the impudence to brightly shine in opposition. On this June morning his life was as incomplete as a recurring decimal. In spite of the barren ground, he was determined to plough on, but his coulter was now wedged in an increasingly lonely furrow.

The warm gentle breeze whispered comfort but dissuaded sweat. It was one of those rare days on which an even rarer breed of altruist might have persuaded the hordes of globe-trotting sun-chasers that it was better to stay at home than to pollute the ionosphere with millions of gallons of burnt kerosene: but for Peter twelve hours of guiltless daylight now waited meaninglessly.

The decay of Victorian monuments, and the neglect of the more recent, lamented in harmony with his elegy sighed in an urban graveyard; and as he knelt by his mother's final sanctum, the sight of the infant shrubs planted by Alice tolled the knell of departing happiness.

He unfastened his small bag of cemetery kit, clipped the edges of the grass verge, cleaned the headstone, tidied the soil, and was repacking when he heard familiar footsteps and the tapping of a stick.

"Alice!" he exclaimed as he turned, leapt to his feet, guided her to a nearby bench and sat beside her.

"I thought I'd find you here. I've come to apologise."

"Apologise? Whatever for?"

"What I did was not kind. I owe you an explanation."

"Alice, you owe me nothing. But if you want to share your thoughts, then I'm here with you."

"Peter, I'm sorry, but I have to tell you this. I should never have allowed this friendship to happen. You're much too nice. The truth is," Alice hesitated, then blurted, "I'm pregnant, deserted and scared stiff."

The glass aound Peter's miniature blizzard evaporated, and he now felt the sunshine. Perhaps the literary deities had discovered Plumham. The welcome flowers of May had belatedly bloomed. Orphean harmony pushed the dirge from his ears, and his mind glittered with thoughts of loveable babies with chubby cheeks, the innocence of an infant's chuckle, the joy of hearing those first words. A disc from his mother's collection spun in his memory, this time to embrace the news he'd just heard, and not to avoid it.

'He's washing dishes and baby clothes
He's so ambitious he even sews.'

Peter would be delighted to help with it all, and wouldn't dream of expecting to 'make whoopee'. He even thought of the prospect of changing a soiled nappy as a part of happiness.

"I can feel that I've offended you. I'd better leave. Thank you for listening." Alice was unable to see the glow on Peter's face and had misunderstood his prolonged silence. She rose from the seat and started to tap her way back along the path. Peter awoke from his baby-filled daydream and caught her by the elbow.

"No Alice. Please wait. I can help."

"Why, are you an abortionist? I've already arranged for a termination. I'm going to the clinic next week."

"I didn't mean that. I think there might be another way."

"Are you one of those pro-life freaks?" Unknown to Alice, a temporary clerk at the clinic was a dedicated active group member of The Guardian Warriors of Life, and had copied her name and address onto a circulated list. She'd already received anonymous hate mail, including two death threats, from London's brave new vigilantes. Her mother had opened those letters to read to Alice, and her misandrist volcano erupted. Mrs Screep hadn't known of the pregnancy, let alone the planned abortion, and her rage added to the poor girl's massive burden. It was little wonder that Alice reacted sharply to any like-minded plea.

"No, it's nothing like that, I assure you."

"Well I don't want to listen. It's impossible to even think about doing anything else in my circumstances."

"Alice, you said you owed me an explanation. Don't you also owe me a hearing?" In all his life he'd never said anything as hastily nor as firmly as this, and he surprised himself as the words left his mouth. Alice was equally surprised at hearing his determination.

"Oh, all right then. But you won't change my mind."

"This place is a bit public for a personal conversation. What about a cup of tea?"

"A café is just as public."

"Suppose we go to my house. I promise not to twist your arm while you're there."

"Go on then. But you'll only be wasting your time." Alice would never have consented to listen to anyone else, but she admired Peter's well-intentioned tenderness, and couldn't bring herself to be abrupt with him.

She held his arm as they walked to his house. He talked almost without pause about every irrelevant topic he could think of: the weather, the local news, the national news, the international news, people he'd known, people he'd never known, how Plumham had changed, the parts that hadn't changed. Anything other than Alice's pregnancy or her plans to finish it. That he kept on an upper shelf and out of reach until they were alone. Alice grew impatient with his evasiveness, gave pithy responses, but kept her annoyance tightly caged.

He settled her on the now familiar sofa, and gave her tea and biscuits.

"Now, Peter, you've beaten your way around every bush in Plumham. What is it that you want to tell me?"

"How did this happen?"

"You don't know about the birds and the bees?"

"Of course. What I mean is, you're an intelligent girl. You're very sensible. I can't imagine you not taking precautions. Were you raped?"

"No."

"Then what happened? I'm not being nosy, Alice. But I'd like to know so that I can help you in the best possible way."

"I don't see how you can. Like the former Prime Minister, this lady's not for turning."

"But what of the father? Doesn't he care?"

"You'll remember that awful literary meeting? The reason I went there was because he used to attend those meetings. I thought that I might recognise his soft-centred chocolate voice once more."

"Couldn't you have gone to his home?"

"I had already done that. At his lodgings they said he'd moved on without leaving a forwarding address. He'd performed a moonlight. They were anxious to find him as well. He owed three months' rent."

"What was his name? Perhaps I could trace him."

"It's a lost cause. He said it was Ken Hemlock, but now I'm sure that it wasn't. He told me that he had a swell job in finance, but his landlord said he was unemployed. I enquired at the Social Security Office, and they'd never heard of anyone with that name. It was obviously false."

"Didn't you use any, er…"

"Contraceptives?"

"Yes."

"He told me he did, but he must have lied about that as well. Now, to put it crudely, I've got one up the spout, and I need to unload it."

"There is an alternative."

"No there isn't. Don't talk nonsense, Peter. I get a little low-paid work from time to time, but mostly exist on disability benefit. My mother has only a state pension. She used to do a part-time job, but for the past year she has had a nervous disorder. I expect my pregnancy will only add to that."

"Could you raise money by selling your house and moving to a smaller one?"

"We could if we owned the house, but we don't. When my rotten father walked out on us, he left the mortgage with more than a year's arrears. He'd already received a repossession order from the building society which he'd never mentioned. He paid alimony for a while, and I still had my sight then, so the council wouldn't consider social housing for us. We had to rent from a private landlord on a short lease. Then my father disappeared along with his monthly payments, and the lease expires next year, which can only put up the rental. Now that our circumstances have changed, we could apply to the council again, but mum won't hear of it. She's no snob, but she is cautious. We'd almost certainly be rehoused in that dreadful place at the rear of Plumham Wood. It's full of drug dealers and criminals. I'd be mugged every day if we lived there. Peter, what is the point of all this interrogation? It's not leading anywhere."

"I think it might be, but one final question. Do you dislike children?"

"No. As a matter of fact I love children. What difference does that make? It would be sheer cruelty to bring a child into the world in these impossible circumstances. Those people who are completely against abortions are hypocritical sadists. By condemning children to lives of inescapable misery they're just putting their own vanity above everything else."

Peter now saw this as the final chance to put meaning into his hollow life. Maybe Ruby Goodwin's longing for family survival arose, either genetically or spiritually, and planed his vigour, glass-papered his innovation and polished his resolve; but he spoke with a new-born lucidity and cogency which crowned the Goodwin virtues.

"Your love for children makes a world of difference, Alice. Because I can help in so many ways."

"How?"

"Firstly, your accommodation. You can forget about leasing costs and move in here."

"What as? Your concubine or your lodger?"

"Neither, as a friend. No, not just as one friend. Your mother comes here also. This house has three bedrooms. I can only use one. You can have another, and mum uses the third. There's a second reception room. I'll stay in this one, and you use the other. You can bring your own furniture if you wish."

"We don't have much. And what we've got is worn out. So, how much rent would we have to pay?"

"Nothing. You'll be here as my guests for as long as you want. For always, if you wish."

"Why are you offering us this?"

"Because my life has been empty and lonely. My mother was my only relative. Now she's gone, you're in need, and you deserve better. I'll keep out of your way, and you can live your lives as before."

"I'm not sure I want to live my life as before. What you say is very kind, Peter. I'll certainly think about it. But you haven't met my mum yet. She's kind to me, but otherwise she's a bit of a dragon. Ever since my father walked out on us, she's been a complete man-hater."

"Then perhaps I can convince her that all men are not the same."

"If anyone can, I suppose you stand the best chance. But what difference does that make to a pregnancy termination? Without eyesight, I could never cope with looking after a child. My mother's health isn't good, and she seems to be getting worse. It's all I can do to care for her. Yes, I do love children, but that's why I must go ahead with my plans. I couldn't commit a child's young life to my clumsy care."

"We'll come to that in a moment. But firstly, your mum. Without the financial worry of having to find the rent, her health could improve. And once I've won her confidence, then I'll be able to look after her. I've had plenty of practice there. I cared for my own mother for years."

"But you can't throw your life away like that, Peter."

"I'm not throwing it away. I'm putting it to good use. When I'm dead, people won't be able to say 'he lived for nothing'. I'm not giving, I'm taking. I'm taking my last chance to get my life together and find some happiness. I know that sounds like a line from a slushy novel, but I can't think of a better way of putting it."

"If I refuse your offer that makes me seem cruel, doesn't it? You're very good at persuading. You've hidden talent, Peter. You should have been a barrister. Anyhow, it sounds very nice, and I'll try to convince mum. But I'm still not having a baby. That's impossible."

Peter had entered his plea, presented his argumentum ad hominem to a jury of one, and now he threw himself into a summing-up with every energy that he could muster. This was his last and only opportunity to convert that recurring decimal into a meaningful fraction.

"I think that it is possible, Alice. I could look after the baby as well as mum. I think I'd make a good nurse. After all, I've nothing else that's worth doing. I've always been fond of little ones, but for a bachelor it's difficult to be near them. If women like children, they are virtuous. But if a lone man shows an interest, he's suspect. If you're likely to be branded a paedophile, it's a great deterrent. The authorities would never allow me to adopt one, but I could look after yours."

"Suppose something happens to you?"

"You mean I die?"

"Yes. How do I cope then?"

"Here I can help also. I'll level with you, Alice. I've never told anyone else about this, but I've quite a bit of money saved. The house I inherited, so I've never had to spend on a mortgage, and as I was the only breadwinner, I got into the habit of saving. Now there's a sizeable nest egg, and we could use it to repair your sight. It would pay for you to go to Scandinavia and have private treatment."

"Peter, I can't rob you of your life savings. Some day the National Health will provide, and I'll get it all for nothing. Then I can think about having children, and eyesight will help me to choose a more suitable man."

"It could be too late by then. You're thirty-eight years of age now. Having a child in ten years' time won't be easy."

"How do you know my age?"

"When I took you into hospital for emergency treatment. Remember? You had to give personal details then. If you have a baby now it'll be much safer. And you'll be giving me what I've always wanted. I'd like to be part of the happiness. And I'll never ask for anything in return."

Alice hadn't thought of her pregnancy as 'happiness'. A 'happy event' was just a Victorian euphemism. But Peter's bubbling, almost naïve, enthusiasm made a slight dent in her determination.

"But why is my baby so important?"

"You're an intelligent and right-minded girl. I know that for certain. There are enough bad people in the world already. We must give a good one a chance to live. With your bloodline and my help, we'll create the perfect child." Peter could think of many who should have been put down, but not Alice's. Her beautiful inner wisdom had to be preserved. The perfume of her mind was the sweetest fragrance he'd known.

"What if the father's genes dominate? We'll just have another opportunist rogue."

"I don't think that nature counts for much. With the right nurturing, our child will be just right." Alice's feelings received another jolt. Peter was already thinking about her pregnancy as 'our' child.

"Peter, why on earth do you want to take responsibility for another man's child? You've not been physically involved."

"I'm the last of a line, a line that was once a wide one. My father's family all died, so did my mother's. My father's death and my mother's life of sorrow have all been for nothing so far. Time's running out for me, and I need to turn nothing into something." Peter's feeling of ascendancy gave him the confidence to wax lyrical, and the courage to add, "A donation of money and care is far more important to a child's welfare than a donation of sperm."

Peter's comment on the triviality of semen startled Alice. Its profundity published another strength hidden within his scroll of gentleness. And perhaps something of Ruby's cataractous vivacity found its way behind Alice's quiescent cornea. She was now uncertain about the termination, and the possibility of another future glimmered at a distance. But it was a far distance.

"Peter, tell me honestly, why are you doing this for me?"

"Because you're worth it." As Peter said the words, they sounded as insincere as a cosmetics advertisement. "No, it's more than that. Much more. It's because I want to look after you."

"Why?"

"Because I love you." Peter had never exhumed anything so deeply buried before, and he couldn't believe he'd said it.

"Ken Hemlock said that to me."

"Well, I mean it. And I don't mean carnal love. You need to be looked after. You deserve so much better. I'd be honoured to take care of you. And it isn't binding. When all is well, if you find a really nice man, I'll be happy for you to join him."

"Peter, I think you really mean it." Alice reached across, and for only the second time in his life Peter was kissed on the mouth by an unrelated woman. Tears rolled down his cheeks, and he was thankful for Alice's blindness. Images of masculinity were difficult to dismiss.

"I'm still not convinced, you know," added Alice, resting her head on his shoulder. "In a way, I'd like to do this for you, but there must be snags somewhere. I'd like to think about it for a while."

"Of course."

"Have you any other ideas?"

"Only two. First I'd like you to be a little dishonest. Tell a white lie."

"That's not like you. What exactly do you want me to do?"

"Record my name as that of the father."

"Why?"

"If you use the name of Kenneth Hemlock, and he doesn't exist, it'll make you seem dishonest. If you state 'father unknown', it makes you look like a tart, and it won't do the child any favours with that on a birth certificate."

"You think of everything. It's almost as if you'd been planning it for weeks."

"I've surprised myself. I have never been able to think this quickly or this clearly before. It's probably because nothing as important as this has ever happened before."

"And what's the other idea?"

"The other one? Well first I must make it very clear that they'll be no strings attached to this at all. You're a free woman, and always will be."

"OK, tell me all about it."

"You won't be cross?"

"I'll try not to be."

"I'd like us to be married. Just in name only. I promise I won't force myself on you. Then when I die, you'll inherit the house and you'll all still have somewhere to live. Otherwise it'll only go to some distant relative I've never met, and he'll probably spend the money on booze or expensive foreign holidays. Also, little one will be born in wedlock. I know that doesn't mean much these days, but it must count for something. And you'll get rid of the name 'Screep'. You once told me you'd like that. I won't interfere with your life in any way. You can go out with other men, and if you want to marry one, I promise you an instant divorce. My only request is that baby keeps the name of 'Goodwin'."

"Peter, would you have asked me this if it hadn't been for the baby?"

"I'd like to have done, but I wouldn't have dared. I wanted to keep you as a friend. If I'd said anything like that, then you'd probably have thought I was mad and I'd never have seen you again. That's an honest answer, I assure you."

"I know it is. Oh, you are a dear. I wish I'd met you before Mister bloody Hemlock, or whatever his name is. But I still need to think about all this. Now, my mother will probably phone the police if I'm not at home soon. Will you take me to the bus stop?"

As they stood waiting for a bus to arrive, he felt Alice's arm tighten around his.

"Are you agreeable to meeting my mother?"

"Of course. I'd be delighted."

"Shall we say in two days' time? Early evening?"

"Fine."

"Have you a pen and paper? I'll give you the address."

"Is it sixty-three Constitution Road?"

"Yes. How do you know that? Have you been spying on me?"

"You also gave that information to the hospital when we were there."

"And you remembered it?"

"Of course."

Alice heard the sound of a bus approaching. She wrapped her arms around Peter, and kissed him with a passion he'd never thought possible.

"Peter, if you can persuade mum about your ideas, then I'll agree to them. But I warn you, you're in for a tough time with her." She kissed him briefly again. "Bye bye, my darling."

He helped her board the bus, then held his arms aloft and jumped joyously in the air. Passers-by looked at him with curiosity, but he didn't care. On his way home he jigged along a child's chalked hopscotch site; and although it wasn't raining, he imitated a few of the dance steps he'd seen Gene Kelly perform in a film. People walked by, but his inhibitions slept. He felt an excitement like a child watching a first firework display.

At home he had a light lunch, and celebrated with four cups of tea followed by a glass of Madeira. It seemed fitting. The old Goodwin traditions might now be bestowed upon a new generation.

Peter laid out the carefully preserved black and white family photographs on the table, and administered the most elaborate and divine rites and laudations of his private religion that he'd ever performed. He needed their help for the task to come. He told the best news he'd ever confided to his father, and then to his mother. His prayers extended to grandparents Jim and Ruby, and to Uncle Jack and Auntie Anne. His mother's family were also entreated: Harry and Sally Groves, Aunt Janice, and finally Great Uncle Archie, who'd introduced him to his very first pint of mild and bitter. He kissed all of their heliotype images, and then added his picture of Alice seated on the sofa to the collection. That symbolic gesture, he was certain, would ensure her embrace into the heart of the family.

He meditated a while over another glass of wine, and reached a weighty decision: now was the time to open his mother's collection of memories.

Her boxes of remembrance were placed on the table, and he untied the white ribbons which encircled them, making sure that he memorised the knots used so that they could be returned exactly as Christine had left them. The first was the one on which his father had written 'These Foolish Things'. On the top was a packet of unsmoked cigarettes, into which a tram ticket had been placed. The dry dusty tobacco started to spill from one of the cigarettes, so Peter scooped it together and scrupulously funnelled it back into its original paper tube. Everything needed to be preserved at this stage.

For the next three hours he reverently studied letters, personal and official; newspaper cuttings; diary entries; birthday and Christmas cards; and countless souvenirs whose significance had been taken to the grave.

Christine had only outlined family history to her son, but had never gone into details. It upset her far too much, and Peter didn't want to worsen her sorrow by pressing for more. Now, piece by piece, the whole picture emerged, and it ached with the hunger of loss.

He had never known the radiant light-hearted woman that his mother's family and girlhood friends remembered. For Peter's memory a tear never seemed to be far away from Christine's eye. She had received news that Christopher was missing only days after the difficult birth of Peter, and it had thrust her into a bleak post-natal depression from which she never fully recovered. Christopher's family had lived nearby, and they helped nurse Christine and care for Peter. By the time that he could toddle across the floor, his mother's sorrow started to lighten; but a telegram confirming Christopher's death thrust her into Stygian depths.

When Peter had reached his second birthday a faint smile broke occasionally across Christine's face. Then she cheered a little to the news that Christopher's elder brother, Peter's Uncle Jack, was due home on leave. The family had saved their meat ration coupons for weeks so that they could afford a joint of beef to celebrate the homecoming. Then little Peter caught measles, and he and his mother disappointingly had to forsake the reunion. His grandparents, his Uncle Jack and his Aunt Anne, who no longer played hopscotch, settled down around their small dining table without them, and toasted 'absent friends' with a rare glass of port. The cherished and caringly roasted joint of beef was about to be carved, when a *vertgeltungswaffe* exhausted its alcohol and liquid oxygen fuel supply, completed it trajectory arc and fell silently back to earth, where its nose cone tore through the roof of their little home as if it were paper, and its two-thousand pounds of high explosive blasted the rest of the building to brick dust and rubble, crushing the fragile bodies, the tender memories and the fond hopes of four loving people.

Peter's mother slid back into a ditch of despair, and lived with her parents for a while at Plumham Wood until she regained a little strength and could return home. The end of hostilities brightened the horizon for a while, but fate had not yet played her full hand: a black ace was still to be dealt.

Not all destruction came from afar. A blind leviathan now stalked the land in the name of progress, and its lumbering foot was to stamp on little Peter's surviving grandparents. A new extension to the estate at Plumham Wood was planned, and their house stood in the path of its access road. A Compulsory Purchase Order was used, which compensated them for the land value only. Because they had ventured into house purchase late in life, the payment was less than half of the amount owed on their mortgage. With nowhere to go, a future of unpayable debt before them, and not wanting to burden anyone else with their troubles, they found their own solution, and were discovered lying hand in hand on the floor of their gas-filled kitchen. They had given their lives for the building of 'homes for heroes'; but the twenty-first century's heroic drug dealers now occupied them, and it was the place where Alice feared to tread. The prudence of a modest family had been sacrificed to the grand plan of quack equality.

Peter's mother was comforted by her unmarried elder sister, until Janice yielded to cancer at the untimely age of thirty-six, leaving Christine and her son alone to cope with the world on a war widow's pension.

In the midst of loss beyond repair, hurt beyond belief, grief beyond cure, it would have surprised few if Peter had become morbid, alienated, withdrawn, malicious; but he did not. An affinity grew between him and his mother which had immeasurable depth. He instinctively knew that the sadness which she endured was rooted in love, and he felt comfortable sharing it with her. That empathy was now unabridged, and through tear-filled eyes Peter saw the full picture. He'd returned to a period when toil meant making things rather than making money; when poverty was genuine, not relative. He'd held fragments from a time when the Spirit of Ecstasy could only be found on the bonnet of an unattainable Rolls Royce and not in teenagers' blood streams. Those foggy, bitter-cold, hungry, hand-me-down years seemed so distant from today's unholy trinity of hedonism, liberalism and consumerism. Then, when the shy King George replaced the extrovert King Edward, it seemed as if the day of the meek had arrived: but it hadn't.

At the bottom of the final box rested an old buff envelope with 'waiting to be reunited' written in his mother's hand. Within it was a single, carefully folded stocking. With it were two telegrams. The first read:

REGRET TO INFORM YOU THAT YOUR HUSBAND 2753648 GOODWIN CHRISTOPHER IS MISSING AS A RESULT OF AIR OPERATIONS STOP ANY FURTHER INFORMATION WILL BE IMMEDIATELY COMMUNICATED TO YOU STOP PENDING RECEIPT OF OFFICIAL NOTIFICATION NO INFORMATION SHOULD BE GIVEN TO THE PRESS

The second was no less formal:

MADAM I AM DIRECTED BY THE DEPARTMENT TO INFORM YOU THAT THE RED CROSS COMMITTEE HAVE CONFIRMED THAT YOUR HUSBAND DIED WHILST A PRISONER OF THE JAPANESE STOP I AM TO EXPRESS THE DEPARTMENT'S DEEP SYMPATHY WITH YOU IN YOUR GRIEF

Pinned to the second were a number of press cuttings about Japanese atrocities and the maltreatment of prisoners. All still carried the stains from tears shed more than half a century before, and Peter's tears now rested beside them. He was now more than ever aware that he was the sole survivor of two dear families annihilated by the hatred of war and by the indifference of peace. He had shouldered a conscience of obligation which had seemed to have no answer, until this moment. Now he knew that he had to succeed.

The next morning Peter rose early. Like St George, he had to prepare to meet the dragon, and concluded that his most practical armour would be to plan a polite but persuasive speech. He couldn't rely on the impromptu skill he'd mobilised for Alice's ear. Faced with the dominant Mrs Screep, his tongue would probably seize, and a carefully prepared and thoroughly rehearsed script was the only answer.

He spread a number of writing pads across the table, and with the mindfulness of an academic preparing a doctoral thesis he postulated an opening argument, mustered all of the salient points and supportive evidence into a structured order, and reached a reasoned but compelling conclusion. He rewrote it at least twelve times, discarded the doubtful, polished the hopeful and emphasised the substantial until he had a thirty page oration that would have won over the green leather benches of the Lower House.

After reading it through eight times, he set it aside, but could only remember the first line. His memory had always found learning by rote difficult to master. A year before he'd thought of joining an amateur dramatic group. The preponderance of female members was an attraction, but his inability to memorise a dramatic part was a deterrent. Then when he attended the first meeting, some of the men seemed more interested in him than the women, and that decided him to abandon the idea.

Self-analysis over a thoughtful lunch left him with no alternative but to seek help: but whom to ask? There was only one person in Plumham, in England, in the world, who could assist: his reliable neighbour Mrs Jessop. She welcomed him into her parlour, and he tactfully explained the situation.

"Oh! Mr Goodwin! You're to be wed. What marvellous news. It's wonderful. Wonderful. It really is." She was so exuberant he thought for a moment that she might hug and kiss him, but even on an occasion as this she could not bring herself to yield to such intimacy.

"Well, it's not settled yet, Mrs Jessop. I need to convince the lady's mother first, and I believe that she can be a bit difficult. So I've prepared what I'm going to say to her, but I'm not good at memorising things like this, so I wondered if you might help me to learn it."

"Oh, Mr Goodwin, I'll be honoured to help in any way that I can. If we succeed, can I come to the wedding?"

"You'll be the guest of honour, I promise."

"In that case I must buy myself a new hat."

"I think we ought to wait until I get mother's blessing."

They toiled for more than an hour, but Peter only managed to remember the first page, and he was not word perfect with that. Mrs Jessop suggested that it might be easier to relist the most important points, and return that evening to see if he could master those only. He thanked her handsomely, and spent the rest of the afternoon preparing a précis and baking a cake to reward her kindness.

On the morning of the planned interview, Peter recited the words Mrs Jessop had helped him to learn as he washed and shaved. Then he recounted them again as he pressed knife-edge creases into the trousers of his best suit.

As a token of his good faith, he drew five hundred pounds from his savings account to offer Alice and her mother.

"Going on a spree, Mr Goodwin?" asked the building society cashier as she handed him the money. Unknown to Peter, she had always fancied him, but only because of the size of his account balance.

"I might be doing something much more worthwhile," answered Peter without explanation.

From a florist he bought a large bunch of flowers as *drachenfutter* for Mrs Screep. He pondered about buying her a box of chocolates as well, but changed his mind. He wanted the gifts to be a token of friendship and not be construed as an embarrassing bribe.

That afternoon he again prepared his altar of family photographs and graciously entreated their help. He found his father's posthumously awarded war medals, gave them a final polish, and slipped them into his jacket pocket as an amulet of other-worldly protection. After reciting his scripted notes for a final time, he pushed a 'thank you' card through Mrs Jessop's door and set out for Constitution Road.

As he passed the degraded manor house with the troublesome lead pipes, a disgruntled plumber emerged, slammed the door of his van and drove away in a furious temper. Mrs Nash had found another unsatisfactory tradesman.

Through the High Street, nothing had altered. Nico prepared for another cavalry charge on his rotating hunk of reconstituted lamb, and the fascia board of the Starlight Introduction Agency still drooped. It was only Peter who had changed, and he strode along the littered pavement with the confidence of one who is prepared to do right.

His walk took him past The Red Lion, and here the contrast was sensual. To Peter, the smell of baby oil was innocent. To the female audience within, awaiting the performance of another male stripper, it was anything but innocent.

As a final tribute to his family, he took a slight detour to the green where Plumham's war memorial stood, and Christopher Goodwin's name was engraved as one of the fallen. Being careful not to spoil his pressed trousers, Peter knelt and offered a prayer of thanks to his father and all of the other departed heroes; but unknown to him a vicious trio approached.

"He's the bastard who lost me my job," growled Modesta White, late of the Starlight Agency, with vengeance in her voice, white rum in her belly, heroin in her arteries and cocaine in her nostrils. She addressed her two sociopathic confederates. Mathew and Luke had torn off their saintly labels on becoming born-again Satanists, and were now Hornie and Scratch. They were equally shot up, snorted up and swilled.

"Hello, bastard. You're going to die," announced Ms White into Peter's left ear, the engine of her larynx fuelled by disdain and lubricated with alcohol, marijuana and not infrequent squirts of semen.

A startled and still kneeling Peter turned towards the unexpected voice, and as he did, Hornie and Scratch kicked him viciously to the ground from his other flank. The *sans-chaussures* of Plumham now wore Doc Martens.

Nobody was in the area, no houses overlooked the green, and the Cyclops eye of a security camera was absent, so the two diabolists took long breaks between their kicks to relish Peter's agony. They choreographed their dance of death to leave his head until last, and prolonged his life with the same care exercised by a certain Japanese corporal fifty-eight years previously.

The only distant intruder was Maurice Slupp, alias Honest John, on his way home from another fruitful day's fee gathering. He saw what was happening, but retreated rapidly. His caring philosophy was that the loss of a client was preferable to the loss of his own blood.

"Are these for his fancy woman?" asked Hornie as he stamped on Peter's bouquet of flowers.

"More likely his fancy man," retorted Modesta.

"So he's ginger, is he? I hate irons," declared Scratch, and gave Peter a particularly hard kick above his left kidney, which rolled over the limp and battered torso so that he now lay face upwards.

It inspired Modesta, and she told the others to stand aside. Lifting what little there was of her skirt, she tore off her thong and cast is aside. Placing a foot on either side of Peter, she emptied her bladder on his face. Years of snorting, freebasing, hitting up, shooting up and pill-popping had desensitised her sphincter and slackened the muscle walls, so her capacity was bloated and it splashed from her urethra for almost a minute.

Hornie's name was inapt in one respect. Heroin dependency had anaesthetised his potency. But now, for the first time in months, the sight of Modesta's bacteria loaded fountain aroused that dormancy, and the erectile tissue began to dilate and his ischiocavernosus tightened. He pushed Modesta back against the war memorial, loosened his trousers and pushed his inflamed manhood into the wet, clammy, freely available sauna between her legs.

Droop wasn't the only symptom of his scag mainlining. The routine had also marred output of the seminal vesicles, and it took more than half an hour of pelvic pumping before a droplet of fruition trickled alone Hornie's vas deferens. But Modesta was ecstatic. She'd never know such prolonged vigour, and she climaxed eight times. On the seventh, the rapture induced loss of bowel control, and she defecated on the memorial behind her, filling Christopher Goodwin's engraved name with a quagmire of untold excesses.

While they were engrossed, Scratch took the opportunity to search Peter's pockets. He found the medals and pocketed them. They could be pawned and yield the means to buy a day's supply. Then he discovered the money, and kept that also. It was a great find, and would keep his drug larder filled for at least a month.

The rest of the action he watched closely. As far as sex was concerned, voyeurism was his all-consuming interest, and his pulse rate matched the tempo of the studiously observed genitalia.

To celebrate the triumph, Hornie and Scratch moved towards Peter for the *coup de pied*, but Modesta stopped them.

"Leave the mother-fucking Fascist to die slowly. It's what he deserves." The others agreed, and spat on Peter's broken body before leaving. What Modesta didn't admit was that she was now secretly grateful to Peter for a unique experience that would never be repeated.

They walked away from the memorial and took a short cut through Plumham Cemetery. Modesta dropped her soiled skirt on the ground and left it. She was now on a high that she'd never reached before, and cared about nothing.

Scratch walked behind, and the sight of a half-naked woman awoke a slumbering inner man. He'd only been interested in scopophilia, but now he wanted to involve himself.

Bounding in front of Modesta, he pushed her back against the nearest headstone, fondled her saturated vulva, and then entered the sudatorium vacated by his fellow nihilist. Hornie assisted the novice stud by tearing a bough from a yew tree and flailing Scratch's bare buttocks. The ends of the branch stung Modesta's widely spread thighs, and she climbed to the peak of Astarte's mount four more times.

As they walked away, the headstone against which they'd writhed leaned sharply on its shallow foundation, then fell to the ground and shattered into three pieces. It was the grave of Christine Goodwin.

Through the evening Peter's tortured body lay untouched, surrounded by young trees previously uprooted or killed off within their wire protection by youths 'expressing themselves'. Passers-by assumed him to be a drunk or a tramp; or just didn't care. Many in Plumham were keen to read celebrity gossip, watch people make fools of themselves on 'reality' television shows, or any other means of not minding their own business; but they kept their noses out of corners where someone might need help.

As dusk fell on the leaking roof of Miriam's fish and chip shop, a house alarm wailed for half an hour unheeded by neighbours or police. A war-torn tom cat, one eye closed and one ear bent, looked briefly at Peter, and then returned to tormenting a bloodied sparrow as it tried to escape. Society did not respond, nature did not respond, and the sounds of unshackled sensualism floated by on the summer breeze.

It seemed to be the end of nothing: nothing done patiently and lovingly cherished. Alice sat quietly waiting for yesterday to return; and spiteful fate sat by and smiled.

Chapter Ten

As she did in Plumham, when Mother Nature watched over the Far East she could never have become a popular novelist or screen writer. The sun shone brightly in the heavens, vividly plumaged birds filled the sky and scented flowers sweetened the air; while under the patronage of mankind a period of sadistic terror was about to unfurl, the like of which the modern world had never seen.

Frank and Christopher were pushed at bayonet point to a hastily erected compound, and within the barbed wire they befriended two other airmen, Barry Parris and Spike Buckman. It was a friendship that would become close, comradely and mutually supportive until it was murdered by inhumanity.

Barry had been a solicitor's clerk, and had studied every moment of his spare time to graduate as a *legum baccalaureus*, but was conscripted just weeks before his finals. His application for postponement of service was rejected by a callous official, and five years of intense part-time study was castrated. Both he and his wife Alison longed to start a family, but she needed to keep her job as a shop assistant to raise his meagre income above hunger level. Hope was now a butterfly trodden under the heel of pitilessness.

Spike was a contrast. A cockney born and bred, he'd become a docker; but instead of his money finding its way into publicans' tills or bookmakers' pockets it had been judiciously nudged into a building society, and now he was the East End's rara avis: a homeowner. With his wife Vera he'd enjoyed the bliss of two healthy, bouncing babes; until his call-up papers arrived. For them hope was still on the wing, but was destined to be shot down in six months' time.

Barry and Spike were soon to discover that they had a common handicap. For them, the hatred the Japanese had for all Westerners was intensified. Barry was especially tall, and his captors reserved a particular loathing for anyone who towered above them. And Spike had a face which naturally looked cheerful. Even when he wasn't smiling, he appeared as if he would laugh at any moment; and that would be a provocation to his tormentors. In the coming months the Japanese temperament would reveal its total vindictiveness and perversion. They delighted in the looks of misery, helplessness and hopelessness that surrounded them, and any prisoners who hadn't sunken to the depths of despair were to be singled out for extra rations of humiliation and torture.

Within this compound though, for the next two weeks life was relatively relaxed. At the close of Malayan winter, it was pleasantly warm, and there were trees above them for shade. The intense, intolerable heat was still weeks away. There were no huts or facilities, and they had to sleep on the ground in the open. But the ground was dry. The drenching of a monsoon deluge was still months away.

At morning roll-call, the Japanese commandant listened to the names of almost a hundred internees. He spoke good English, and over the next few days he instructed the prisoners on their duties. He didn't mention rights: they had none. But by Nipponese standards, this man was a great humanitarian. The captives were told that they must salute and bow to all of the guards, whatever their rank. Those who disobeyed would be punished. But under his command this only entailed a slap around the face, and with an open hand: totally different to the closed-fist, full arm-swing that was practised elsewhere. The guards resented this restriction that stopped them giving the very cowardly, very effeminate, weak spirited, inferior Westerners what they deserved, but they obeyed.

At one side of the compound a trench was dug and a bamboo pole placed across it for prisoners to lean on to answer the calls of nature. By the end of that week it was filled and another latrine was dug, but that one filled far more slowly. The diet of rice and almost nothing else caused chronic constipation, and some of the prisoners didn't have a bowel movement for almost a month.

Christopher and Frank had no kit to use, so they shared the use of toothbrushes, razors and soap with Barry and Spike. Barry's pen also had a little ink left in it, so all four used it to fill tiny cards that were supplied the following morning. The commandant told them to write their home addresses on one side, and dictated the message to be written on the other. Christopher obeyed, and wrote:

To Christine,
I am alive and healthy and being well
looked after. Soon I'll be doing some
work for the Japanese. Please do not
worry about me.

From Christopher

Each card was carefully inspected to ensure that no secret codes had been used. It would be the last message that Christopher would ever write, and it wouldn't reach Plumham until three months later.

Each morning they would receive, courtesy of the Emperor Michinomiya Hirohito, a saucer of grey, glutinous rice, and another in the evening. At midday four spoonfuls of a watery onion soup were provided, and once every five days that diet was supplemented with a single sardine, or half a pilchard, or a tiny piece of unrecognisable gristle about the size of a matchbox. Those who were reported for disobeying orders had that generous ration cut in half. The prisoners had yet to learn how to improvise, fend for themselves and live off the jungle. Each glorious feast was washed down with half a mug of water, and every third day a weak cup of tea, without milk or sugar, could be had by those who'd behaved themselves. Again, the four friends had to share eating utensils and tin mugs.

Each morning the commandant, Captain Kurofuji Yukid, gave the assembled men a lecture. He started by explaining that they were exceptionally lucky that he spoke English, and that when they were transferred to a working camp, it was most unlikely that any of the guards would be able to do that, and so they'd all have to learn some Japanese. He added that his master race were shortly to conquer the world then everyone would be obliged to learn the heavenly tongue. All other languages would be annihilated, so these prisoners were doubly lucky in having a head start over the rest of the world.

All future numbering at parades had to be in Japanese, and each prisoner was obliged to shout a number in the correct order. 'Tenko' was roll-call, and numbering started: iche, ni, san, yon, go, roku, nana, hachi, kyu, ju, juchi, juni; and concluded at sanju, number thirty. As working parties were unlikely to be grouped in units that exceeded thirty, they were not obliged to learn other numerals, but those who couldn't swiftly count that far would receive 'no mercy'. At that moment they didn't appreciate just how unmerciful the Japanese could be.

At the next tutorial he outlined the Code of Bushido, or the way of the warrior. All Japanese soldiers fought to the death. To surrender was unthinkable. Because the English had allowed themselves to be captured, they had shamed themselves and thrown away their status as human beings. They were now beasts: contemptible and expendable. But they still had a chance of partial redemption. If they committed themselves to working hard, diligently and earnestly for the great Japanese cause, then they would continue to earn entitlement to the gracious gifts of food that would be offered. The prisoners had already experienced how frugal those bestowals would be. They were yet to discover that this phoney largesse could plummet further still.

The guards conducted two days of counting practice, and then Captain Kurofuji conducted another lecture of indoctrination. Bushido was not only the code of the Samurai warrior, he asserted; it was also the equivalent of the European word 'chivalry'. But over the last century the Japanese had developed the finest civilisation the world had ever known; whereas the West had become corrupt and debauched. The Knights of Bushido would save the morality of the world before it was too late. His manner was so unshakeable and convincing that a few of the prisoners started to believe the propaganda; but the paradox between words and reality would soon be thrown open.

Three more days of numerical rehearsal, muted face slapping, viscid rice, meagre driblets of skilly and colonic immotility passed, and the ideological captain gave one more deceitful address of Nipponese credo.

The history of the East for three hundred years, he contended, had been one of oppression and brutality by the imperial West on the native races, and Japan had stood alone and repelled them. Now, he assured them, those people were going to be freed from the atrocities and despotism of an Anglo-Saxon empire. For those who listened, the quality of that 'freedom' would become apparent at their next camp.

He concluded by showing them a manual which had been issued to all Japanese troops, and told them that it was a major work of chivalry to which only the Japanese could aspire. The sordid little book was actually an inflammatory rant against the West intended to induce optimum cruelty and sweep away any last vestige of humanity. Captain Kurofuji added that although they must learn to speak Japanese, they must not try to discover how it was written. Any prisoner who attempted it would be convicted of spying and executed.

The next three days of tenko practice was augmented with learning the 'soldier's oath' as composed in the previous century by the Emperor Meiji. The parade had to turn towards the east, stand rigidly to attention and chant:

'A solider must honour loyalty as his most important virtue.
A solider must be impeccably polite.
A soldier must be courageous.
A solider must treasure his principles.
A soldier must be frugal.'

That ceremony would then have to be repeated at dawn each day for the rest of their captive lives. As the months passed any meaning that it once might have had would become extinct in bewildered minds as they all unwillingly plumbed the depths of human misery.

The final day of comparative calm arrived. The commandant told them that, due to the benevolence of their hosts, they were all now in good health: a contention that, for many, lacked accuracy. It was now, he said, the individual's responsibility to keep it that way. To become sick was a shameful deed. To lose health was a crime, and criminals must expect punishment.

As they marched out of the gate they sang 'Rule Britannia'. They'd already been told that to sing the National Anthem was an act of high treason; but the words 'Britons never shall be slaves' were about to be questioned.

An eight mile march over very uneven terrain brought them to the railhead. They'd started with heads held high and arms swinging, but torrid heat, lack of water and vitamin starved muscles soon turned it into foot-slogging drudgery. Halfway there, a weary marcher asked the guard in the best sign language he could muster for a rest and some water.

"Kyushi kinzuru. Mizu kinzuru," retorted the guard, and struck the enquirer a heavy blow across the shoulders with his rifle butt. The moderations of Captain Kurofuji no longer prevailed.

"Bastard!" shouted Frank.

"Ochitsuku. Shizuka ni naru," bellowed the guard. Fortunately he understood no English, otherwise Frank would have been bayonetted on the spot.

Three metal goods wagons, previously used for cattle transporting, rested against the buffers at the end of the line; and the marchers slumped wearily to the ground on the shaded side. They were each given a charitable mugful of unholy water, and a benevolent ten-minute rest before being prodded into the trucks.

Thirty-two men were crammed into each wagon. There was no room for anyone to lie down, and most had to stand. Those who were the most fatigued sat on the floor for a while, then changed places with those who stood, and a jointly agreed rota system was kept alive. The aging locomotive plodded at a slow pace. The now scorching sun heated the sheet-steel walls and they became too hot to touch, so the passengers had to huddle closer. As the wheels pitched along poorly maintained track, the wagons lurched wildly, and the prisoners had to support each other to prevent falling. It was the genesis of comradeship in which compassion and brotherhood would endure and become life-saving precepts. A merciful system was to evolve in which the fit looked after the sick, the young looked after the old, those with surplus took care of the needy. For the great majority, the principle of 'every man for himself' disappeared; but for a tiny few it lingered, as they were yet to discover.

"Christ. I can't hold out any longer. My bladder's bloody well bursting!" The speaker was a small man with receding ginger hair and a lopsided moustache.

"Do it on the floor. There is nowhere else. The doors at both sides are locked."

"There is no free floor space."

"What about using those slots?" suggested a chubby man in a bush hat, and indicated openings that had been cut about thirty inches below roof level for cattle ventilation.

"I can't reach up there."

"You might if we lifted you up." Two muscular gunners took a leg each and hoisted him high. By bending his head and shoulders as low as he could, the owner of the aching bladder managed to align with the slot and empty onto the trackside bush. As the day wore on, five others with plights of distension used the same facility, but one missed the target and soaked himself and his helpers.

Six evacuated bladders from a total of thirty-two was a phenomenally low number, but lack of water and rapid dehydration starved the bodies' reservoirs. And that imbalance spawned other frailties. The interior of the wagon was now at oven temperature, and shirts were black with sweat. The heat, the stench and the lack of water now made many look on the point of collapse. Changes between the seated and the standing had to be swifter, and often those in want had to be supported by their less sickly comrades until a sitting space was vacated.

The train lumbered on its way for the rest of the day, and as evening arrived the heat lessened. The steel walls were less injurious, and the men could now give each other a little more space and take it in turns to rest against them. Then another pitfall opened.

"Sorry, chaps, but it's a necessity. I need the lav."

"We'll lift you, mate," offered the gunners, who were now dry on the outside as well as within.

"No, I don't mean that. It's the other thing. So sorry, but I've been holding on for more than an hour hoping that we'd stop."

"He can't be held against the vent slot for that. He'll have to go on the floor."

"But if that happens it will smell absolutely awful," protested a corporal with a fastidious air that seemed completely out of place.

"If he doesn't, he'll shit his trousers, and you'll still smell it."

A vote was swiftly held and most agreed that there was no alternative. Although the rice diet had anaesthetised nature, the long march followed by hours standing in a swaying truck had rewoken peristalsis, and several sphincter muscles now began to twitch, so approval was partly out of self-interest.

The sitters shuffled along to make space in a corner and the sufferer painfully relieved himself, but the stench of a fortnight's compressed faeces in such a hot, confined space agonised nostrils as if they'd been douched with sulphuric acid and iron filings. As others had to add to the nauseous heap, most of those resting on the floor tried to get closer to the high vent slots. Another two hours passed and three had fainted. There wasn't room to lay them flat, so they were propped against the wall with legs outstretched, and a sapper who'd been a member of St John's Ambulance checked their pulses. As the fetor worsened, several diaphragms heaved, and bile saturated vomit was added to the fly-covered mound. But the experience was also preparatory. It was an undress rehearsal for the months of dysentery that awaited.

A mosquito barbed night crash dived with tropical haste, but a bright moon gave a cataractous view of the wagon's interior. The trundling metal coop now magnified the night's chill as it had done the day's heat. Sweat soaked shirts had given a droplet of scant relief during the day, but now their dank folds clung to exhausted bodies, and all began to shiver, some convulsively. Apart from those who fainted, none slept.

The train made three stops on its journey for the locomotive to take on more coal and water, but the doors remained locked. Now thirty-two desiccated tongues painfully rested in thirty-two saliva abandoned mouths, thirty-two heart rates and breathing rates soared, and for some dizziness, confusion and eventual fainting was the only release from the agony of cramped muscles.

After a journey of twenty-five hours the train rasped to its final halt, but the prisoners had to wait another hour before the door slid back and three guards stood menacingly with rifles and fixed bayonets.

The corporal at their centre looked disapprovingly into the wagon, his callous eyes slowly surveying the gaunt shadows before him. Then he noticed the vile heap in the corner.

"Obutsu!" he shouted. "Katazukeru," and indicated with his hands that he wanted the mess cleared. Another guard at the rear held a bucket of drinking water, but then moved it behind him to demonstrate that none would be given until the order was fulfilled.

"Have you a shovel that we could use?" asked the finicky corporal, miming the action of shovelling to the guards.

"Ife," was the response, and the Knight of Bushido cupped his hands and made a scooping motion, a command that was very clear. The bayonets of the other guards moved intimidatingly closer to reinforce the order.

"Right. Let's get it done and keep the bastards happy," said Frank. As always, he led by example, and pushed his hands deep into the graveolent sludge-heap, climbed down from the wagon, and dropped it into the bush a few feet from the track. Christopher, Barry and Spike did likewise, as did the rest of the standing prisoners from the truck. The sight of closing bayonets even galvanised the cream-puff corporal into carrying his share. A number added to the load by vomiting bile, but empty stomachs disgorged nothing more substantial.

They cleaned their hands on the long leaves of an amur grapevine as well as they could, and then dipped their enamel mugs into the bucket of bacteria-flavoured water that was proffered. It was soon emptied, and a second one was produced which looked even less hygienic, but that didn't deter the desperately parched. Frank and Christopher now had their own mugs, Frank having bartered his last packet of cigarettes for two spares hoarded by an infantryman.

Spike noticed that two comatosed bodies still lay unattended on the hot metal floor of the wagon, so he filled his mug for a third time and made his way towards them, but two guards held him back at bayonet point. The corporal of the guard looked into the truck and saw the helpless men.

"Tsukaenai!" he bellowed. "Nonashi no."

Two guards entered the wagon, bayonetted the two pitiless frailties where they lay, and with malicious leers on their faces carried the bodies to the side of the track and dropped them on the heaps of faeces and vomit which were already seething with fat maggots. The corporal and the other guards looked delighted and started to laugh.

"I wish I had a gun. I'd like to slaughter the little yellow bastards!" smouldered Spike with a tone of hatred in his voice that didn't match his perennially cheerful face. Frank, peace-loving Christopher and legally constrained Barry all nodded in firm agreement.

"We can't try anything bare handed," cautioned Frank. "They'd mow us down and probably murder all the others as well. They'll get their comeuppance some day." That was a prophesy that would never materialise.

The prisoners were marshalled savagely into a long line, and ordered to march, led by a guard still smiling at the thought of unworthy corpses being laid to rest on piles of excrement. Ahead lay a twelve-mile ordeal for nutrient starved muscles, sleep starved brains and hope starved spirits.

As they slogged through tangled brush and rocky outcrops under a relentless sun, their recent intake of water quickly vanished as sweat, and mouths and throats were again arid. When they did pass the shade of trees, the air was black with flies, which entered nostrils, ears, gasping open mouths and painful waterless eyes. Passing through a shallow swamp several emerged with leeches clinging to their lower legs, but weren't permitted to stop to try to remove them. Instead they had to continue to march until the annelids had stolen their blood and fell engorged back onto the earth.

Two were stung by scorpions as they passed through long undergrowth. Within an hour their hearts were fibrillating and their cardiac contractions lost their strength. Panting for breath and reeling with dizziness they fell behind the others, and were bayonetted by two guards who followed at a distance to deal with stragglers. Their corpses were left to decompose and serve as a grim warning to any who'd not respect the canons of Bushido.

Hunger now gnawed painfully at their shrunken stomachs, but ceaselessly they were driven onwards. Revolting blubbery flies and hoards of mosquitoes harassed the toiling bodies incessantly, but it was as nothing compared to the remorseless torment inflicted by the disciples of the Rising Sun.

"Supido!" yelled the guards, and flayed any prisoner who looked like slackening pace. With rifles in one hand, each carried a bamboo rod or a wire whip in the other and used them vigorously and viciously.

"Hayaku naru!" Christopher felt the sting of a riding crop across his shoulders, neck, head and waist, and as the miles passed, his bruised flesh intensified the agony of each additional blow, and the tears in his shirt exposed blooded skin that was targeted by his zealous flagellator.

"Zensokuryoku de!" The tall frame of Barry was a special focus for the fanatical ogres, and he was assaulted with rods, whips, fists, canes and boots until blood ran from several wounds and flies covered them hungrily.

"Ningen no kuzu!" Spike's work as a stevedove gave him greater strength and vitality than most, but his determined pace wasn't good enough for his captors, and his sweating body wasn't overlooked.

An onlooker might have said that they were driven like animals, but no farmer or herdsman would have treated their beasts with such appalling ferocity.

A number succumbed to the beating and could no longer be driven by it. They staggered to the side and collapsed, where they were dealt with by the guards bringing up the rear. As the bedraggled column reached their destination, eighty-four remained of the ninety-six that had started. The rest were already being eagerly sampled by flies, centipedes, mosquitoes, rats, snakes and maggots.

After twelve miles of cold-blooded merciless torment, twelve miles of shouting, screaming and bellowing, twelve miles of sweltering heat and harassment from all manner of tropical insects, eighty-four palpitating hearts dragged eighty-four aching, bloodied, sweating, famished, dehydrated and bewildered bodies into their work compound. They all had to stand to attention and perform another tenko ritual. One prisoner was too befuddled to remember the next Japanese number, and a guard beat him relentlessly with a rifle butt until he fell to the ground.

"Okiru!" yelled a guard corporal, but the battered man was unable to rise. A bayonet was poised above him ready to thrust, when Frank and Christopher broke rank, ran forward, lifted the man to his feet, dragged him back to the line-up, stood him up and supported him at either side. It was a gesture of defiance and a development of comradeship that impressed and inspired the others, and stimulated a spirit of mutual help and protection that would endure. They were still eighty-four in number.

The parade was dismissed, and they all were pushed towards a single, partly built hut, where they slumped onto a floor of bare earth and most fell into a fitful, hungry, thirsty sleep. Two hours later Frank and Christopher were awoken by someone gently shaking their shoulders.

"Welcome to hell-on-earth, fellas." Denny Hughes introduced himself. He'd been one of the first to be captured, and had worked at this camp for almost three weeks. "I've brought a bit of refreshment for you. I saw what you did on parade. That was really brave. This stuff is only the usual stingy muck that Nips provide, I'm afraid, but I thought that you two deserved first choice. The water's been boiled, so it's a bit safer than what's often dished out."

"Is it alright if our two mates join us? They're really good men too, I assure you."

"OK by me."

Frank woke Barry and Spike, and they all guzzled several mugs of water.

"The grub is just the usual rice, but I've also scrounged a bit of boiled rat. We catch them from time to time. Not a lot of meat on them, but it tastes better than you'd think. There are also a few leaves. I forget what the plant is called, but when you find some in the jungle, snatch a few for eating. They help make up for the vitamin deficiency of a rice diet. That's what the MO told us."

"There's a medical officer here?"

"Yes. We're lucky in that way. Some of the places have got Japanese doctors, and they couldn't care less. Our man is English, and he's really good. He works hard all the time, but there are no medical supplies, so it's all very primitive treatment. He stands up against the Nips as well, and tries to protect the men as much as possible. You'll meet him in a short while."

"What is the work here?"

"There are only sixty of us here at the moment, so work hasn't got very far. They're planning to build an airfield four miles away, and working parties have to march out each day."

"Build an airfield. That doesn't sound too bad."

"It's nothing of the sort. God knows why they've chosen that place. Most of it is thick jungle. The rest is all solid rock that has to be hammered away. I've not been there yet. So far I've only worked around the camp. I helped to build this hut. But the others have told me what it's like. They're not back yet. They won't return until dusk."

"Is this hut supposed to be finished?"

"Not yet. There are sides to be put on, and they're going to make some sort of raised platform to sleep on when the monsoons come. There are only a few of us working here. They wanted most to go out and work on the airfield. Now there are more here, perhaps they'll spare a few others for work on the camp. The MO also wants a separate sick bay built. He calls it a 'hospital'. Bit optimistic, but I suppose that's a good thing. He tries to persuade the Nips every day, but so far they've just ignored him."

"How do you know that there are Japanese doctors at other camps?" asked Barry, whose legally trained mind always enquired about information with loose threads.

"There's one next door."

"Next door?"

"Yes. There's an adjoining compound to this where the native workers are kept. They're even worse treated than we are. As the Nip doctor does nothing for them, our MO wanted to help out, but they wouldn't let him. Now I'll leave you to enjoy your grub. I won't wake the others yet. I don't want them to know that I've given you double rations."

"This is double?"

"Afraid so. As I said, we have to try to add to it as and how we can."

Denny waved and left, and the others ate their food as slowly as they could, worried that a rapid intake might cause them to vomit; but four nagging stomachs couldn't be kept waiting for too long. They'd all have normally been repulsed by the very idea of trying to consume a dead rat, but such refinements were now at a distance. Denny had left behind the bowl of boiled water, and they all had four more mugfuls. They were just scraping up the last grains of food as Doctor Mick Tidnam entered, looked around the sleeping hut, noticed that they were the only ones awake and approached them.

Christopher was the first to notice him, and he immediately recognised a welcome face from Plumham. He was a little more drawn and ashen than when Christopher had last seen him, but he was sure that he was the very helpful houseman who'd treated his mother at St Agatha's Hospital when she'd tripped and injured her leg. As the former junior hospital doctor neared them, Christopher got to his feet as fast as painful muscles allowed and stood to attention.

"It's all right, old chap. We don't stand on ceremony here. Please be seated, and I'll join you on the floor if I may."

"Thank you, sir."

"Forget the 'sir'," added the medical officer as he squatted beside them. "To most, I'm just 'Doc'. OK?"

"Actually, Doc, I think that we've met before."

"Really?"

"At St Agatha's Hospital in Plumham."

"Why yes. After graduation I went there as a houseman. Did I treat you there?"

"No, but I was with my mother when you attended to her injured leg. She used to tell everyone afterwards how nice you were to her."

"I'm delighted to have pleased the lady. Do give her my regards when you next see her."

"If that ever happens," commented Barry.

"Not in the near future, perhaps. But we mustn't lose hope. All will come right in the end, I'm sure." Dr Tidnam spoke with a reassurance that he did not personally share.

"Now," continued the doctor. "I have a question to put to you all. I'm trying to improve facilities here as much as I can. Have any of you experience in building work?"

"I used to be a surveyor," answered Frank. "I was studying to be an architect, but the war disrupted that."

"Just what I need. The name is?"

"Pledger, Frank Pledger. And my three comrades here also have building experience." He glanced quickly at their faces to ensure that they didn't contradict his deliberate lie.

"Excellent!" The doctor took a note of their names on card torn from an empty rice packet. There was no paper available here.

"Down to business. I'll just give you all a quick once-over." He examined each in turn and confirmed that none of the wounds were infected. By that time Denny had re-entered, awoken the others and started to distribute more food, so the medical officer moved away to question and examine them.

"Why did you say we'd all been builders, Frank?" asked Spike.

"He obviously had me down for his list. I thought it was a way that we could all stay together as a team."

"But supposed it's discovered that you've been fibbing?" queried Christopher.

"It's not likely. Take a look at this place. There are no conventional building materials used here. It's just a lash-up. Make it up as you go along, that's the solution."

"Brilliant thinking," added Barry admiringly. It was to be, in fact, a far more beneficial idea than they realised. Working on the camp for the next three weeks would save a forced four-mile march twice a day, and would spare them from any of the beatings and whippings: but only for a while.

As the sun started to dip, forty-eight forlorn, exhausted and bedraggled figures entered the hut from a day's toil, gathered their eating utensils and made their agonised way out again. Unlike the fortunate newcomers, food wouldn't be brought to them, but they had to gather at the far end of the site where the rice was being crudely and unevenly boiled and sit there on the ground to eat it.

A short while later, they all returned. A sergeant pilot who'd previously flown the outdated Vildebeests noticed their RAF uniforms, and limped over to speak to Christopher and his friends. His blistered feet had no footwear, but were covered with large jungle leaves and bound with strips of tree bark and dried rushes. He introduced himself as Tom Beaven. They swapped details of experiences for a short while, and then the ever curious Barry asked, "Whatever happened to your shoes?"

"When we were at our first detention point after being captured, we were all commanded to remove shoes and boots and give them to the Japs. They made some phoney excuse that it was more healthy to have bare feet. It was obvious that they were lying. They all had boots on. Those who refused were bayonetted. I think that they had some sort of scheme to sell them on and make money, but they also enjoyed stamping on our bare feet. Luckily we were only there a few days, but many of the feet of the men here are in a sorry state."

"Did you have far to march to get here?"

"Only about a mile. We were well to the north. One of the first sites to be taken."

"Why couldn't they use your old airfield instead of building a new one?"

"The position of the new one is said to be more strategic, and they'd need much longer runways than we had. A Zero needs more than twice the length to take-off as our old crates used. And they couldn't extend out runway. It had a hill too close to one end and the sea at the other."

In spite of their twelve mile march, most of the new arrivals looked fitter than those in the returned work force, so they mingled with them, helped where they could, and offered their last cigarettes to them. It was the start of a friendship union that would seldom be equalled elsewhere. They listened with sympathy to hardships worse than their own, and the mutual help that was freely given in the months to come would extend and even save the lives of some.

At the tenko the next day the now familiar numbering was completed and they all turned eastwards and fruitlessly chanted the 'soldier's oath'. Then Sergeant Hideki Makoto, the camp commandant, strode in, and he was accompanied by another face from Plumham which Christopher instantly recognised, but this was not a welcome one. It was Malcolm Screep, Christine's former neighbour and constant pest, and the man whose bowler hat brim Christopher had filled with whelks. He looked totally different to all of the other prisoners: well fed, healthy, fresh and wearing clean clothing which looked similar to the Japanese army uniforms.

The commandant made announcements to the parade which Screep translated. These were all thunderous complaints. The work wasn't fast enough, it wasn't efficient enough, and they were all insulting the glorious civilisation that the Japanese had created. Unless immediate improvements were made, punishments would be increased and privileges withdrawn; though quite what those privileges might be nobody could guess.

Then Screep reminded the commandant that the medical officer needed to speak, and Doctor Tidnam stepped forward, bowed, and announced the names of those who were to remain at the camp to do construction work. The names included Christopher and his three companions, and four others whom he'd found to have experience in building trades. The parade was dismissed, and the eight fortunates accompanied Doctor Tidnam as the others were marched away to the site four miles distant for another day's agonising toil and unending brutality.

"At long last I've managed to convince the Japs that we need a medical centre," said the doctor to his eight new helpers, and Denny Hughes who had now joined the group. "Denny will explain the crude construction methods that we've used so far, but if anyone can suggest any improved methods we'll be most grateful. Frank, can you devise some plans for us?"

"I'll be delighted, Doc."

"Splendid. What I need will be quite a large building. Some of the men are in a bad shape already, so I think that we'll require quite a lot of space for them when they need it, and that time's not far away. For perfection I'd like the hut divided into two wards. Dysentery will strike sooner or later, and those patients should be separated. I hope that we'll avoid cholera, but if it does arrive, then a separate building will be needed. We'll leave that for the present. Finally I'd like another small space partitioned within the hut. I've found two medical orderlies among the men, and I'd like them to be billeted with the patients at all times when things get rough. That section will also double as an emergency operating theatre."

"You're going to do surgery?"

"I'm not a pessimist, but we need to prepare for the worst. Also, I'm not a surgeon, so I'll just have to bodge my way along as best as I can. But we can't just leave men to die without making an effort. There's no medical equipment or supplies, so I'm going to have to improvise. I've managed to salvage a couple of bits of broken bayonet. Anyone here with engineering experience?"

"I have, Doc," confirmed Christopher.

"Good. Do you think that you could grind some really sharp edges on them?"

"Sure. I'll look around the compound for some suitable stone to use."

"Fine. One last detail, Frank. The living section in the hut should be large enough for three persons. I intend to move in as well."

"Where are you billeted at present, Doc?" asked the ever inquisitive Barry.

"At the far end of the compound there's a separated section, and a much more substantial building in it. It used to be the local village chief's house until he and his family were murdered by the invaders. That's where the Japs live. Also the English commander, Brigadier Woodhams, and his adjutant, Lieutenant Ridge are there. As well as being near the patients I need to get away from them. My advice is to keep your distance from them. They're easy to spot. Unlike the other officers, they're well fed, well dressed and do no work all day."

"I know the sort," said Frank, gritting his teeth. "I'll take your advice, Doc. If I meet them I might say what I think of them."

"Well, be careful, Frank. They're both dangerous men. Oh, and there's also that interpreter bloke billeted there. Name of Screep. I think he's from Plumham, Chris."

"Yes, Doc. I know him." Christopher didn't go into details of his knowledge of Malcolm.

"Right, well I'll let you get on. I won't use any driving force, but there are always a few Japs about the place. If they see you resting, we'll all be punished. Now I must go and try to knock up some makeshift medicine. I can remember a few herbal remedies. Luckily I'm allowed out of the camp, so I can look around at local flora to see if I can find something useful."

The new construction team went with Denny to the existing hut, where two of his companions were working on side panels, and looked closely at its framework. It had a frame of bamboo poles, the whole stabilised by shoring up with other poles, and the roof and sides were clad with atap-palm shoots woven together like raffia matting. Denny and his two colleagues demonstrated the techniques used, and seven of the newcomers helped to complete the wall coverings. Meanwhile Frank looked around the compound for a suitable site for the doctor's 'hospital'.

At midday the doctor returned with armfuls of medicinal plants, and they all sat on the ground with the standard dollop of sticky grey rice, supplemented with more of Denny's vitamin enriched leaves.

"I think I've found a good site," reported Frank. "It's far enough from the other hut to inhibit spread of infection. The ground is firm but not impossible to dig out. It's fairly level, but a little higher than the rest, so it shouldn't suffer too much from flooding when the monsoon comes. If we can find bamboo poles long enough, then I think that the roof pitch should be raised to fifty degrees to help shed rain water. Also, if we can find the right wood, then timber ridge-pieces would add to strength. They can be supported with central posts if needed. An ideal timber would be ramin, which grows in these parts. It's a hardwood, light, very strong and easy to cut. If I can get permission to go outside the compound, I might be able to find some."

"Excellent, Frank," exclaimed the doctor. "Don't worry about permission, I've already got that for you to go out this afternoon.

We'll need to gather bamboo and other materials. Denny knows his way around. He can show you the best spots."

That afternoon, while six remained to finish the wall coverings for the billet, Frank and his crew went into the jungle with Denny. The guards had grudgingly loaned them three knives for cutting the bamboo, but they were all very blunt, so Christopher spent an hour sharpening them on a nearby rock while the others gathered the best specimens they could find. Four return trips were made with their initial building materials, but Frank couldn't discover any ramin trees, although they didn't have the tools to cut it down if one had been found.

The work proceeded briskly over the next few days, with frequent trips into the jungle for more supplies, and Denny made sure that they had plenty of boiled water nearby. He suggested that he might try to wangle some extra food, but Frank though it unfair to possibly deprive others. Then they managed to trap a snake to eat, and rats weren't scarce. At the close of two weeks the main structure was complete, and the partition walls were started while Frank designed small raised platforms that would serve as beds. During all of that time, the Japanese had, remarkably, not interfered, although they did keep a distant eye on them from time to time. That was doubtless because their slave-driving priority was to make war on, rather than comfort for, the corrupt Westerners.

"Two more days, Doc, and you'll be able to perform your opening ceremony," said Frank at the close of the day. "What name shall we give your hospital?"

"What about Saint Michael?" suggested Barry. "He did manage to conquer Satan."

"I don't think I'm that vain. But thanks for the testimonial," smiled Doc. "You've all done really well, and I think it'll be just in time. From what I've seen of the men, there are quite a number of serious cases coming to boiling point."

Frank, Christopher, Barry and Spike remained to talk to the doctor while the others left to gather their evening's paltry allocation of stodgy rice.

"I've been trying to get the Jap's permission to build a separate isolation ward, but they won't agree. However, I'll keep trying. I know that they're scared stiff of cholera, and at least they've agreed to do something about the possible source of an outbreak. And that's why I wanted to have a quiet word with you."

"Tell us more, Doc," invited Spike.

"Well, there's a very nasty job that needs doing, and I was going to ask if you could spare the others to get it done."

"Perhaps you'd like us to do it, and leave the others to finish the job. It's all fully planned now," offered Frank, always willing to lend a hand at whatever the task.

"I'll describe what needs to be done, and then I'll leave it to you to choose."

The medical officer outlined the task, and how it had arisen. In the nearby compound, where the enslaved Asian citizens were incarcerated, Japanese ill-treatment, starvation and disease had killed a number already. Their captors would not spare any of the workforce to bury the dead, and their bodies now lay in a heap in varying states of decomposition. Because that mass of decay was close to their own compound, then plague was a probability, and the corpses needed to be cremated as soon as possible.

"I'm game," agreed Frank. "But I'll need to consult my team first." They all nodded reluctantly. Had it not been for their admiration for Frank, they'd all have avoided that job.

The next morning they met Doc, and he'd already cut up some old tenting material, the only cloth that he could find, and tied strips around their noses and mouths. Then he wrapped other pieces around their hands to form a crude barrier against contamination by gas gangrene. He prepared himself the same way, and the five of them made their way towards a harrowing and nauseous task.

Entering the civilian compound they were immediately confronted by a vision of how these courageous, beneficent Nipponese liberators had freed the local population from the cruel bondage of the vile Anglo-Saxon empire. The British, Dutch and American flags of corruption had been swept away, and now the native peoples of the Far East could enjoy their new-found freedom under the flag of the Rising Sun. The honourable Nobility of Bushido had brought them the joys of death, the delights of starvation, the rapture of being tortured, the luxury of slave labour, the jubilation of disease without treatment, the exuberance of being sliced by a bayonet.

Before them was the sight of almost fifty bodies in rotting ranks of putrefaction. The tortured had been murdered by inhuman sadism; the sick had been murdered by inhuman indifference; the serfs had been murdered by inhuman brutality. Almost half of the corpses were women: the old and unattractive having been worked to death, the more beautiful had been gang-raped and then killed by having their breasts cut off or disembowelled. The Japanese had also devised an amusing new form of gambling. They had bet on the sex of the child within three mothers-to-be, and then sliced open their pregnant bellies to settle the wager. The bitter irony of Captain Kurofuji's lecture was now all too apparent.

Rats had already torn away much of the decaying flesh, and now maggots and flies covered the rest. The stench was vile, worse than they'd lived through in the railway wagon, and even the medical officer felt queasy, but he worked just as hard as the others.

They gathered a lot of dried wood and dead vegetation from the floor of the jungle and built a large pyre. The bodies were lifted, and several dripped a foul grey-green liquid as they were carried to the makeshift crematorium. When the top of the funeral pile was covered with the pitiful remains of abused and battered mortals, Frank lit the fire and they set about gathering more faggots to belatedly dispatch more tragic reliquiae. None could face a midday meal, so they worked until sunset when the task was finished.

After the evening rice pittance, Christopher was slumped on the earth floor of the now finished billet hut when the disagreeable face of Plumham entered through the open doorway.

"Hello Mister Goodwin, or may I call you Christopher?" asked Malcolm Screep in a smarmy voice like adulterated engine oil.

"Of course," said Christopher, raising himself on his elbows as the faithless toady squatted beside him on the mud floor. "How did you get here?"

"I was a clerk with the Royal Artillery. I didn't like the job. I wanted to be fighting in the frontline with the others. But they made me do it because of my administrational experience with the Ministry. Then they found out about my fluency with the Japanese language, so I was flown out here urgently to be a negotiator. But by the time I got here it was too late; war was declared and the invasion had begun. I was captured along with the rest."

"Well, you seem to have fallen on your feet. You're smartly dressed and look much healthier than everyone else."

"Don't you believe it, Christopher." He looked cautiously about him for prying ears, then lowered his voice. "Look, I know that I can trust you, so I'll tell you what I'm doing. But don't breathe a word of this to anyone. Alright?"

"Yes, of course."

"I'd really like to be in it with the rest of the men and doing my bit, but I figured that I could help everyone much better if I pretended to help the Japs, managed to get them to listen, and then plead on behalf of everyone to try to get conditions made better than they are. I work at it night and day, but they're very difficult people to get along with."

"Yes, I can imagine they are." Malcolm had, in fact, already told this gallant saga 'in confidence' to all others on the camp, and intended to gradually inform all the newcomers one by one. He'd mastered the craft of deceit, the mask of a cardsharper, the insincerity of a corrupt politician, the fraudulent spiel of a confidence trickster. His phoney integrity made Uriah Heep honourable. His caring façade concealed a pitiless imposter who designingly ingratiated himself with the Japanese by spying on the prisoners, and who would be instrumental in sending many to their graves to further his own interests and ensure self-preservation. His principles blended perfectly with the practised ethics of Bushido. But his well-rehearsed deception worked, and even Christopher, who'd known him previously, began to believe that his soul might have been decontaminated.

"There is another way that I can help," continued Malcolm with a slight-of-tongue comparable with a thimble-rigger's little finger. "When you start work on the airfield, the Japs will pay you twenty-five cents a day. That's very little in the local currency, but if you save it for a week you'll be able to buy an egg which will improve your diet. I've managed to make contact with a supplier on the outside, and I can usually get them at that price. But whatever you do, never let the Japs know about this. If they find out that I'm helping the lads in this way, they'll kill me without thinking twice."

"Thanks, Malcolm. That's good of you."

"Also if any of your friends can be really trusted, I'll do the same for them. But make sure they keep it to themselves. I'm really taking one hell of a risk here, and I get nothing out of it apart from the gratification of knowing that I'm doing what I can to help the men. But if I get found out, I'm sure they'll take it out on others too."

Again, reality was somewhat different to the patter. The Japanese knew all about his dealing, and secretly condoned it. He made ninety per-cent profit on the sales, and shared half of that with the camp commandant. But while Sergeant Hideki spent his gains on saki and visits to brothels, Malcolm Screep was far more frugal. When any prisoner was desperate for food, he told them that he had contacts where he could sell gold, and offered to negotiate for a 'secret' sale of a gold ring or watch at a price that proved to be abysmally low. The starving man almost always agreed, but Malcolm actually bought the goods with profits made from egg dealing, and carefully buried his hoard outside the camp in sealed packets. He knew that the fragile local currency could plummet in value at any time, but the troy ounce would always remain stable. Whichever side won the war, he'd dig up his treasure and be a rich man.

"How's Christine, by the way?"

"I hope she's all right. I haven't heard from her since I've been here."

"Oh, I know. I believe that there is a great deal of difficulty for the mail to get through," lied Malcolm, knowing that all letters were being withheld by the Japanese, and any parcels sent by relatives would be ransacked and kept by them. "I see that you're working with Mick," he added with fake familiarity.

"Mick?"

"The medical officer. Very nice man. We're both doing all we can to help. Now, I've still got much to do, so I must press on. Remember, Christopher, anything I can do for you or your friends, just let me know."

"Sure." As he left, Christopher wondered about Malcolm's supposed close friendship with Doctor Tidnam. The way in which the doctor had pronounced Screep's name didn't sound at all amiable.

The next morning they went again to the almost completed sick quarters. The others had heard about the previous day's work in the adjoining compound, and insisted that the four should take it easy that day. But after an hour of resting, Frank's conscience told him that he wasn't pulling his weight, and out of respect the other three also completed a full morning's work. On their way to high noon's low food, a pompous, arrogant voice snorted at them with vowels clipped by privilege, public school contempt and the brittle self-importance of the upper crust.

"You there. Halt, and stand properly to attention."

They did as commanded, and were approached by an officer with a puffed-up moustache, a puffed-up belly and a puffed-up ego. Brigadier John Woodhams strutted towards them with a swagger stick and conceited ostentation, closely followed by a fawning Lieutenant Eric Ridge. Both were immaculately dressed in spotless clothing that had obviously never been used for work of any kind.

"Who of you has the senior rank?"

"I have," replied Frank.

"Then I demand the proper military courtesy of a formal salute, and you'll address me as 'sir'." Frank saluted, but with little reverence.

"Why are you wearing shoes? Only officers are allowed to wear shoes."

"I, sir, am an officer, sir." Each time Frank said 'sir', its tone deliberately conveyed a lack of deference.

"Then why do you wear clothes in which you've obviously done grubby work? Officers should command their men, not demean themselves with physical labour."

"Because, sir, I believe in leading by example, sir. If I don't do that, sir, then I'm neglecting my responsibility to ensure the survival of my men, sir. I also believe, sir, that no one has a divine right of authority, sir. It is wrong, sir, to insist on privilege of rank, sir. I am convinced, sir, that a genuine officer should earn the trust of his men, sir, and not demand it as a God given right, sir."

"Good God!" shrieked the brigadier, his face crimson, his body trembling with rage. He was close to the verge of hysteria. "What is your name?"

"Pilot Officer Francis William Pledger, sir."

"Well, Pledger, I'm going to strip you of your commission. I'm going to reduce you to the ranks."

"You, sir, cannot do that, sir. You, sir, have no authority over my rank, sir. Only the Air Ministry or a senior officer appointed by the Air Ministry can alter my rank, sir."

"You're impudent and lying. I can and I will."

"Mr Pledger is right, sir," Barry leapt to his comrade's aid.

"Who are you to tell me what to do?"

"I, sir, am a lawyer, sir. I know military law as well as civil law, sir." Barry imitated Frank's tone of mild but obvious disrespect. He lied about a knowledge of military law, but Frank was the finest man he'd ever known, and he'd have risked anything to support him. It was a glowing example of an officer having earned respect.

"I'll find out about that. You, Pledger, are insolent, as well as letting down the officer class by doing menial work."

"In that case, sir, all the other officers are also betraying their supposed status, sir. All the officers I've seen are working alongside their men, sir. Except you, that is, sir."

The brigadier looked unable to restrain himself, and was about to strike him when he saw the gleam in Frank's eye and realised that this officer's eloquence had the upper hand.

"Now you're adding more lies to your insolence. Officers under my command are true gentlemen." It wasn't surprising that he didn't know about conditions in the camp. He'd commandeered all supplies of paper for his own use, and spent every day in his quarters waited on by the obsequious Lieutenant

Ridge and a very unfortunate batman. All the time he concentrated on writing his verbose and vacuous memoirs. He was determined to outstrip the recently published five-volume biography of the Duke of Marlborough written by Winston Churchill. The brigadier was, after all, far more important. The Japanese were content for him to have abdicated his command in everything but name. Most commanders stood up for their men, but he presented no such obstacle.

"My notion of a gentleman, sir, is one who recognises that we are all prisoners of war, sir, and that privilege is immoral in the circumstances, sir."

"That is blasphemy. It is mutinous. You are a disgrace. You are insulting British history, the British nation and the British Monarchy. You are on a charge. Are these other men officers?"

"No, sir, they are not."

"Then they must all remove their shoes and give them to Lieutenant Ridge for the use of officers. You know that only officers are allowed to wear shoes. This is dereliction of duty. You have allowed your men to be improperly dressed. They must wear boots."

"They, sir, are properly dressed, sir. In the Royal Air Force all aircrew wear shoes whatever their rank. These men, sir, are all valiant flying personnel."

"I don't care what they do. They're under my command now, and they'll do as I say. You three, remove your shoes."

"I'll do no such thing, sir," said Spike pluckily. "I support Pilot Officer Pledger, sir. So you'll have to put me on a charge as well, sir."

"That goes for me too, sir," seconded Christopher.

"And me too, sir, " confirmed Barry.

"You're going to sorely regret this, all of you. Take their names, Lieutenant, and prepare a charge sheet." From that moment, a hate-affair would simmer between Frank and the windbag brigadier.

When they returned that afternoon to the medical hut, Doctor Tidnam had lost his look of jubilation and was now crestfallen.

"I've heard about your confrontation with our unworthy brigadier. I warned you about him, Frank. Your opinions of him are absolutely right, but I still think that you should have held your tongue."

"Don't worry, Doc. He's put us all on charge. What punishment can he give anyone in the present circumstances?"

"That's just it, Frank. He doesn't dish out any disciplinary action himself, but reports you to the Japs. He just stalks around the camp full of pomp and self-importance, and picks on anyone for the most trivial reason, and leaves the Japs to do his dirty work for him."

"That's dreadful! It's treachery of the worst kind! It's betrayal!"

"I agree. The man's a complete bastard. He reported one poor soul a few weeks ago for failing to salute. The Nips executed him. As soon as I heard about this latest catastrophe, I went to see him to ask him to drop the charges against you all, but he'd already reported the matter to the Nips. I think you'll receive a summons at any moment."

"God, I'm sorry I've done this to you, chaps," said Frank, turning to Christopher, Barry and Spike. "This is the second time I've let my men down, first about the fuel in the aircraft, and now this. I can't begin to tell you how much I regret letting my mouth off. But I can't stand by and let this happen. I'm going to plead guilty to everything, and I'll tell the Nips that you were just innocent bystanders who weren't involved in any way. Just remember to stick to that story yourselves. I've already got too much on my conscience, I can't accept any more."

"I'll do no such thing, Frank," countered Spike, "If I'd had your guts and your way with words, I'd have done exactly the same. I'll be honoured to go to the gallows with you."

"You can't throw your life away like that. Your wife and little ones need you to stay in this world. I'll be happy to join my family in the next one."

"You won't change my mind. I know what's right."

"So do I," said Barry. "I'm with you."

"So am I," agreed Christopher. "Remember 'all for one and one for all'? You stood by Jimmy in the kite. We're four musketeers now, no longer three. That's the only difference."

For the first time in his life Frank didn't know what to say, and undignified tears ran down his face. It was like a scene from a classical tragedy, but neither Sophocles nor Virgil could have written sentiments so deep and inexpressible. The poets and dramatists of the Romantic period elegised emotion that seemed hardly credible, but here it was in sincere reality. This loyalty was like something only conjured in fantasy, but here it was a fact.

Frank was groping for words to make another protest when two guards entered with rifles and fixed bayonets, and indicated that the accused should follow them.

The four stood before the commandant's desk and bowed. Frank was glad that they were all together. If each had been interrogated separately then individuals might have admitted to more than they had actually done. Also, one idea scorched into his frozen mind. He swallowed his pride, and determined to put on a performance of servile reverence. He would now scramble his every standby squadron of stagecraft to ensure his friends' survival.

Malcolm Screep stood at the commandant's side, wearing a persona of tragedy, but behind it was an anima of glee. He held grudges for life, mostly about imagined wrongs. Christopher had snatched Christine from out of his arms, and he wanted revenge. Now it seemed likely that he would taste its sweetness, and he inwardly hoped that Christopher's end would be long and painful. Through his interpretation, the commandant read the charge of disrespect and insolence to a senior officer, and asked how they pleaded.

"With the greatest respect to you, sir, I would like to recount what happened." Frank bowed his head after ever sentence, and his Thespian portrayal of humility could have won him an Oscar. "I have great admiration for your leadership, and for the integrity of Bushido, and for the pre-eminence of the great Japanese nation. But I do not think that Brigadier Woodhams shares my enthusiasm, because he does not commit himself fully to your just and noble cause. I told him, sir, that he evaded his responsibilities, that he was not a fitting leader of his men, and that he was conceited, uncommitted to your just cause, and put his interests before those of your nation, whose glorious victory deserves every encouragement and every support. I did it for the greatest good of all people. I also, sir, told him that he was lazy, vulgar and cowardly. I did so, sir, because my men work ceaselessly for the benefit of our new masters, and I sincerely believe that they deserve better leadership to inspire them. Thank you, sir, for letting me speak. I am sure, sir, that your faultless judgement will find the fitting solution so that we can all better serve our new flag, the Rising Sun, and ensure its success throughout the world."

It was very fortunate that the brigadier was not present to contradict his account, but he was too busy writing the most important literary work of the century, and assumed the result of this hearing was a foregone conclusion.

In petto Sergeant Hideki concurred with Frank's opinion of Brigadier Woodhams. He particularly liked 'conceited', 'lazy' and 'cowardly', although his own savage grain made 'vulgar' difficult to fathom. Through Screep's translation he announced that he found them guilty, but because they were hard working and less dishonourable than most Westerners he'd give them only a minimal punishment. They would all have to kneel to attention on the parade ground for six hours, and be supervised by a guard who'd whip them if they moved or tried to rest on their heels. He added that normally this punishment would last for twelve or twenty-four hours, but he wanted to reward prisoners who worked hard, so they were being treated with exceptional clemency, and couldn't expect it again if they misbehaved. Malcolm Screep's Jungian concepts were now reversed: he wore a mask of relief but inwardly boiled with chagrin. His acting was below Frank's standard, but he practised it through every waking hour.

Under the broiling and unremitting sun they knelt rigid and motionless. Like Malcolm, the Japanese guard was also disappointed. He'd had no entertainment all day, and he watched intently for the slightest movement so that he could use his whip, but they remained stock-still.

Christopher endured the ordeal by remembering Christine. However cruel the present, nothing could hurt the past. He'd previously found happiness by featuring her on the silver screen of his memory with their own incidental music; and now he salved pain with re-runs.

'Stay as sweet as you are,
Don't let a thing ev-er change you.

Christine's slender figure stood before him in the sumptuous imitation silk dress, its indigo off-set with roseate and eau-du-nil bouquets. He relived his faltering invitation, their first dance, the first touch of her hand, her heavenly perfume. He retraced every step of his two clumsy foxtrots and then the gauche bolero. Each second of his anxious search to find her after the dance interval was spun out to make her last-minute return more joyous. As he journeyed towards her home, the present agony of his legs was now transformed into that feverish eleventh-hour sprint after the trolley-bus and the rapture of her departing assent to another date with him.

'Night and day I pray
That you'll always stay,
As sweet as you are'.

The amusement-starved guard gave each of them a farewell clout across the shoulders with a bamboo rod, and they knew that their purgatory was over. As the frustrated tormentor left them, Doctor Tidnam approached from the rear and helped them to their feet. Straightening their legs took almost ten minutes and walking seemed impossible, so Doc gave them some on-the-spot physiotherapy and they hobbled back to the medical hut.
"Tomorrow the work here will be finished, and then you'll all have to join the others working at the airfield. There's nothing I can do about that. But you're good men, and you're adaptable and inventive, so I'd like you at my side again in the future. This afternoon I went to see Sergeant Hideki, and told him that I expected an epidemic of sickness soon, and that I'd need more help here to cope with it. He refused, but when I suggested that fever could spread to the Japanese quarters, he relented. I told a

white lie, I said that you'd all had medical training. So don't let on that you haven't."

"We certainly won't," affirmed Barry. "Thanks Doc. Thanks a million."

"And I promise not to let you down again," added Frank. "And while I'm confessing my sins, I'll level with you Doc. I also told a white lie. These men hadn't had any building experience. I made that up."

"I know," smiled Doc. "I realised that at the time. But you seem to be able to turn your hands to anything, and that's what I need, and that's what the men need."

Two days later, after tenko, they were herded together with the working party, and as they passed out of the camp they saw the latest example of the malice prepense of the great new Nipponese culture.

A lurking Malcolm Screep had overheard a prisoner speak of 'little slant-eyed yellow bastards', and reported it to his overlords. A sharpened meat hook had been skewered through the base of the offender's tongue, and the other end tied to a rope which was looped over the branch of a tree and he now hung with his feet just clear of the ground and his hands bound behind him with barbed wire.

As the marching column neared, his body convulsed with suffering, and the uncontrolled movement wrenched out his tongue by its roots and he fell to the ground. His quivering body was unable to respond, he lay on his back as his mouth and then his lungs filled with blood and he slowly drowned. Christopher tried to think of one adjective to describe his captors, but none seemed bad enough. 'Barbarous' was not apt: the most primitive people didn't sink to those depths. And 'bestial' didn't fit: animals were not that sadistic.

As the column struggled towards the worksite, the pitiful state of many of the men was displayed before the newcomers like a canvas of a vile apocalypse, but it was a vision that neither John Martin nor Hieronymus Bosch could have painted.

The feet of most were blistered and swollen, and ulcers had started to erupt on the legs of some. Their backs, arms, legs and necks were covered with lacerations, bruises and dried blood from whippings and thrashings, and the faces of some were scarred where they'd been caned and punched viciously. Dermic parasites bored into the unwashed skin, and infected wounds wept. Some navigated their way by holding on the shoulder of one in front of them, their vision blurred by the sun's glare and vitamin dearth. For two, optical neuritis had advanced and they were almost completely blind; and retinal scotomata inflicted others. Ringworm troubled many and the medical officer had covered the affected skin with wet clay: he had no other treatment available.

All of the guards gloated and many laughed at the spectacle, but one didn't. This revolting, hateful troop of men were completely insensible to any sort of decency: but there was one exception. Private Matsuo had much more than a shred of compassion within him, and he loathed his present duties; but within a short while that would be his undoing.

A small number cried with the pain of walking on red-raw bleeding soles and heels where severe dermatitis had struck; and grossly swollen, weeping almost skinless feet were driven forward by incessant flailing with wire whips and bamboo rods. Spike picked up the poorest wretch and carried him on his arms for the rest of the journey. It wasn't difficult: the man's emaciated body only weighed five and a half stone.

Christopher, Frank and Barry helped some of the others by carrying each in turn for a short way to give their limbs brief respite, and as the heat climbed above one hundred on Gabriel Fahrenheit's scale, they all fought their way through pyretic misery, thirst, hunger, torture, humiliation, filth, sickness, pain and despair towards the retreating hope of survival.

They came to a small hillock, and the weakest had to crawl up one side and slither down the other. Again Frank and his crew helped them, and in a short while they reached the site of the proposed airfield, where less than a sixth of the ground had been cleared.

A rest was desperately needed, but none was given. Most had to clear the scrub and chop down and uproot the trees with hopelessly inadequate tools, and as the four new arrivals looked the strongest, they were taken to a rock outcrop to try to break it.

Barry and Christopher held chisels while Frank and Spike wielded hammers. When a boulder eventually broke away, they had to shatter it into manageable pieces and carry them to fill a depression in the ground. It was arduous work, and although they toiled unflaggingly, the guard was not satisfied, and gave them occasional blows to drive them faster with yells of *"Supido."*

At midday a mugful of dirty water was generously dispensed with the usual quota of rice, but this serving contained the added delicacy of rat droppings. They were trying to pick them out from between the grains when the English sergeant who'd carried the food whispered a warning.

"Don't bother to do that, mates. Time you've fished it all out they'll send you back to work and you won't be able to eat it." They took his advice.

Spike had seen a hibiscus plant growing nearby, and when the guard wasn't looking he picked up a few of the leaves recommended by Denny and shared them with the others. The slimy taste of that supplement was worth the unsavoury moment. It would protect them from the ulceration that afflicted many, and from the haemorrhages of scurvy that were emergent in others.

The afternoon of forced labour brought the ground clearers close, and more cataclysmic murals of callous oppression were unveiled in the gallery of suffering. The blistered and ulcerated feet were now matched by raw and bleeding hands; three limped severely with strained Achilles tendons; wrists, arms, ankles, knees, backs, shoulders and four hamstrings were sprained; bruises spread, cuts bled, sun-scorched skin peeled; and fractures from beatings with rifle butts were countless: broken fingers, wrists, toes, ribs, collar bones. One brave second-lieutenant had a broken arm but continued to slog on in the fear that he'd be bayonetted if he stopped. Like Christopher, he tried to anaesthetise the pain by concentrating his mind on images of his wife and family.

At the focal point of this artwork of inhumanity stood a man more emaciated than the others with maggots feeding on the pus that exuded from his wounds. Lefty Springfield had been a sickly child, and the ghost of a heart murmur should have been detected at his recruitment medical, but it wasn't. Now the heat of the sun, his starved and battered body and his deficient blood supply placed him at the doorway to delirium, and his work slowed and faltered. The closest guard lashed him with a horsewhip, but he couldn't respond, so Lefty was disciplined for slacking. He was made to kneel, a sharpened wedge of wood was placed behind his knees to prevent him from resting on his haunches, and he was forced to hold a heavy rock above his head with straightened arms. Each time he dropped it or tried to lower his arms he was whipped until he collapsed altogether, and no amount of beating could rouse him.

Throughout the afternoon two beautiful kingfishers darted from tree to tree, their vivid brown and blue sparkling in the sun; and on the ground a peacock paraded its brilliant colours. Mother Nature could still paint exquisitely within the same frame as man-mad ugliness.

At cessation of work Spike gathered Lefty in his arms and the column hobbled back to the prison camp. Again the semi-fit assisted the unfit, but now each group was a little more frail; one individual fatally so. Throughout the painful return journey Lefty remained in a coma, and as they re-entered the compound, his floundering heart stopped. They had slaved for a total of nine hours. In three weeks' time, as the workforce was depleted by sickness, that would increase to twelve hours; and then to sixteen.

As they passed the entrance barrier, the body of Malcolm Screep's latest sacrifice still lay on the ground, his severed tongue beside him, and the evening roll-call took place in view of his bloodied remains. As the parade was dismissed, the medical officer approached rapidly.

"Have you got a patient there for me, Spike? Let's get him to the hospital."

In the medical hut Doc failed to find a pulse, listened through his substitute hollowed-out bamboo stethoscope, and tried every technique of cardio-pulmonary resuscitation, but all failed.

"Looks as if the bastards have claimed another one. They wouldn't let me move that other poor soul today. Obviously they wanted it there as a grisly frightener for when you all got back. However, I've one bit of brighter news. Instead of heaping our dead on a bonfire, we're now allowed out of the camp to bury them. We've been allotted a small cemetery area to use. I saw the commandant today, and got his permission. Now we've got two to put to rest. Would you like to organise a burial detail and just a few of their mates as mourners? I thought we'd carry out a really civilised ceremony before the sun goes down and show these diabolical scum what fellow feeling is all about."

"I'll be delighted, Doc. Leave it to me."

As the sun started to abandon this tragic land and seek a less wretched place to shine on, an impressive cortège slow-marched towards the gate. The two dead were carried on two of Doc's bamboo stretchers, and they were covered by a tattered Union Jack which had previously been carefully hidden away. Spike and Barry had preceded them and a grave was already dug. Almost every walking man stood to attention at either side of the parade area and gave a final salute as they passed. Malcolm Screep was hypocritically in their midst. He needed to maintain his guise of comradeship.

No padre was among the prisoners, so a flying officer who had served as an acolyte at his local church led the procession and delivered the burial service which he had memorised.

"I am the resurrection and the life, saith
the Lord: he that believeth in me…"

The bodies were lowered with vine stems intertwined to form ropes and a few handfuls of earth followed them.

"Forasmuch as it hath pleased Almighty God…"

After a minutes silence, all of the mourners recited in perfect unison.

"Our Father, which art in heaven,
Hallowed be thy name.
Thy kingdom come…"

At the close, a sergeant who had attended many Remembrance Day services and parades concluded with the well-remembered words of Robert Laurence Binyon.

"They shall grow not old,
As we that are left grow old…"

When the assembly had left, Spike and Barry retrieved the flag for future use before replacing the earth. It would lamentably be utilised again: innumerable times.

In the hut that evening an unusual thing occurred. None of the men had received a letter or parcel since capture, and that perhaps was their greatest torment. All cherished memories of home. Those simple pleasures, previously taken for granted: reading a book, taking a bath, wearing clean clothes, having a bed to sleep on, listening to the radio, looking through a newspaper, smoking a cigarette; they were all now rapturous delights from a distant and inaccessible land. Some still had photographs of family, but these only heightened the poignancy. It was simply not knowing that was a constant nagging anxiety, and added overburdening weight to the leaden crosses that each had to bear. Were their families alive or dead? Sick or well? Injured or unharmed? Were their homes standing or flattened? Had England been invaded, or was it still free from goose stepping jackboots?

But now Joe Richardson held a newly delivered letter in his hand. Others gathered around him just to admire the white paper of the envelope, the once familiar face of King George on the postage stamp, the dependable image of a British postmark. A few wept silently: now, perhaps, they too might get yearned-for news from home.

Joe sat and looked at the envelope for half an hour almost delirious with excitement; then he opened it and his sun-scorched face turned ashen and his body shuddered with anguish. The letter was from his wife: she had grown tired of waiting for his return and had left him for another man. What was left of his battered and abused spirit vanished, he sobbed himself into to fitful and poisonous sleep.

Christopher, in contrast, slept well and deeply, but only for an hour. He was awakened by a new source of annoyance: two rats had found their way under the mosquito netting, and one was gnawing at his toes while the other had started to eat his earlobe. After that he had difficulty returning to sleep, so he screened another epic memory starring Christine.

'In the still of the night,
While the world is at slum-ber...'

***

During that tram ride towards Plumham Wood the memory of Christine's *Sans Adieu* perfume lingered in his nostrils, and on the trolley bus in the final leg of the journey it strengthened his resolve to try to impress her parents when he'd now meet them for the first time. He'd spent a week writing scripts for his possible opening lines, and he'd rehearsed them daily, but as the destination grew closer his memory faded and became confused. The long walk through the suburban roads didn't help. Should he say 'You have a wonderful house'? That sounded a little envious. 'What do you do for a living, Mr Groves?' Too artificial. At their door only his longing for Christine prevented him from retreating back down the road. As the door opened his paralysed lips refused to move, but Harry Groves shook him warmly by the hand and Sally gave him an arousing peck on the cheek. Their daughter had already forewarned them of his bashfulness, and from that moment he felt entirely at ease. But he still didn't dream that in only a few months all of his family would be there to celebrate his engagement. Neither did he know that Malcolm Screep skulked resentfully in the adjoining house.

'Do – you love me as I love you?
Are you my life to be, my dream come true...?'

***

As they marched, limped and hobbled out of the compound the next morning, another sample of the graciousness of Bushido confronted them. Malcolm Screep had reported another miscreant, but this one's wrongs were entirely fictitious. When this man had been offered the chance to participate in Malcolm's egg-buying scheme, he had the effrontery to call Mr Screep a 'racketeer', and now he was paying the price of not buying an egg. The ever inventive guards had tied his thumbs with rope. He too had then been hoisted at the same spot as the previous day's sufferer, and the tips of his toes just tantalising touched the ground.

For the workers the morning passed much as before, except that the tenderness was sorer, the limbs were weaker, the bruises and wounds were larger, more blood flowed and the sun was even hotter. The rice that day was flavoured with a new bonne bouche: mealworms and weevils. But all consumed this munificent and unexpected meat allocation.

That afternoon two more were accused of failing to pull their anorexic weight, and they were corrected by being bound to the trunks of trees with barbed wire for the rest of the day, and every time a guard passed he would hit each one across the face with a malacca cane.

On arriving back at camp, the morning's martyr now lay dead, having been beaten throughout the day, but next to his displayed body lay an even more formidable exhibit.

The ever vigilant Malcolm had discovered that one man had a small undetected hoard of paper and was secretly keeping a diary. This was a massive wrong in the eyes of the Japanese. They didn't want any unedited or unsanitised records to remain of their activities, so they took the opportunity to enhance their archive of monstrosities with an apt penalty.

He was dragged from the tenko that morning and taken to the side of the compound where he was bound, laid on the ground and the pages of his diary pushed into his ears and nostrils and set on fire; and then they obligingly doused the flames by slowly pouring three buckets of boiling water over his face. He was left under the sun for the rest of the morning while the committee of evil debated their next diverting depravity.

The pillars of Bushido had quickly become bored with the short-lived amusements of bullets and bayonets, and their appetites had been whetted for longer lasting recreations. Their creativity was now at its most resourceful. Ingenious ideas occurred daily, and now they practised one on the diary writer.

"Nodo ga kawaite iru?" asked one holding up a bottle of water, and the prisoner nodded. Then while one guard pinched the victim's nose, another poured pint after pint into his mouth, forcing him to swallow it. When his stomach had become grossly distended, they took it in turns to climb onto a table and jump down on his abdomen while the others beat and kicked him fiendishly. Assisted by a little intrusive surgery with a bayonet eventually his belly burst, and his entrails spilled out to the laughter and applause of the onlookers. His body now lay at the parade area, and his greyish-blue intestines had been spread across the entrance so that all of the returning workers had to step on them as they passed. The commandant announced through the voice of Malcolm Screep that this loathsome man had been guilty of espionage, and a similar fate awaited those who were found to be spying.

That evening another funeral service took place. The men were determined to show their captors what decency and respect really meant; but the message fell on deaf ears. They did not know that the practice was being ridiculed. At the burial site there was another freshly dug grave which nobody recognised. During the day Denny Hughes had been convicted of failing to salute a guard, and was then forced to dig his own grave and was buried alive. His absence was noticed at the hut, but he was only the first to mysteriously 'disappear'. Not announcing his death added another facet to the widening Nipponese macabre sense of humour.

As the procession returned to the compound, smoke arose from the adjoining area where the *jimoto no hito* were interned. They were now allowed to cremate their own dead, and their number was already reduced to almost a half.

Throughout the day, after reading that letter, Joe Richardson had become even more feeble than his half-starved body confessed. That evening he was totally dispirited and gave away his ration of rice and water. The following morning again he relinquished his food and drink. He said nothing and his eyes were vacant. He had abandoned hope, determination, positive thinking and every thought of camaraderie. At the airfield site he stood aimlessly and refused to work. The guards beat, kicked, punched and whipped him until he fell, and they continued to assail him but he didn't move. Within an hour his brain started to haemorrhage, and by evening he'd be dead. A guard rifled his pockets and confiscated his personal possessions, leaving him only with a photograph of his estranged wife. If his captors had realised the significance of that unintended irony, it would have added to their repertoire of humour. Spike now had another memento mori to carry back to camp, but on their arrival they were again presented with yet one more.

Alf Hosier had been determined to survive. So much and so many depended on his return. His wife now cared alone for their five children, the youngest of whom had Down's Syndrome, and she struggled to keep their Norfolk smallholding productive. Alf's disabled mother lived with them as well, and needed constant attention.

The adage of ends justifying means seemed morally clean, and he'd found many Red Cross food parcels destined for the prisoners but retained by the Japanese for their own use. A small amount of the unwanted and stale remains he'd pilfered. He'd also discovered the massive stocks of undistributed medical supplies, and he'd helped himself to a few vitamin tablets and some quinine. His body now appeared a little less unhealthy than the others which aroused suspicions, and the theft was uncovered. For the guards it was a case of double rejoicing: they'd completed their investigation without the prying nose of Mr Screep, and now had another day's innovative fun to enjoy.

Ruthless ingenuity had been active, and they'd perfected the previous day's inventions to fit the crime. Alf was asked if he needed more food, and he nodded; so he was given a large container of raw rice and forced to eat it. Several lengths of barbed wire were wrapped tightly around his body from waist to chest. Then he was pushed onto the ground, the previous day's water treatment repeated, and over the next two hours the rice swelled within his stomach. To add to the delicate art of schadenfreude, others hammered short lengths of bamboo into his ears. No abdominal surgery was now needed. Those incisions were all competently performed by the barbed wire. Sadism was now practised with great innovation, great efficiency, great enthusiasm and great relish.

That evening another double burial ceremony was undertaken, but the spirit of live-saving comradeship did not diminish: it increased. The prisoners were all the more resolute to help each other, and those who died did so in a milieu of brotherhood. However, the absence of self-interest did not align with the conceits of Malcolm Screep, Brigadier Woodhams or Lieutenant Ridge; and the bonus-grabbing fraternity of the following century would also have difficulty adjusting to it. Their laws of their jungles would sustain. For them the frail must be squashed underfoot, the sick must be abandoned or despised, the dead consigned to oblivion.

The mosquito and fly infested light of dawn broke on another day of misery. At this noon the Cordon Jaune rice would be enhanced with fat yellow maggots, but on the trek back to the *keimusho no sensohoryo* welcome help would come from a very unexpected quarter. Sadly, it would be short lived: as was the helper.

The humane and unhardened Private Matsuo had been ordered to accompany the workers on this day, and as they limped back nursing their sores, he went from one prisoner to another and helped the weakest to walk. He was a strong man, and for those with the most ulcerated legs he carried each in turn for a while to help relieve their agony.

After tenko in the camp, Corporal Hagiwara, the overseer of the workforce for that day, reported this man's felony to Sergeant Hideki. The tender-hearted private was summoned to the front of the parade where he was beaten mercilessly about the face, arms, back and legs with a rifle butt until he slumped to the ground, and there the honourable sergeant gouged out his left eye with the heel of his boot. The battered and bleeding private was ordered to his feet and dismissed. That evening he would commit suicide by thrusting a bayonet into his viscera. For the warriors of Bushido, comradeship and compassion were images beyond their field of vision. They had absolute power and no scruples about exercising it.

The following day was welcome and unwelcome. It was a *yasumi*, a rest day, which occurred once every ten or twelve days. It was hardly a day of recuperation: more like a brief respite from slavery, torture and the seemingly inevitable path towards death. But that morning a feared spectre appeared in two guises: bacillary dysentery swept through the closely packed hut, and amoebic dysentery which had been loitering for some days also sprang into action. By evening, almost a quarter of the men were infected.

Doctor Tidnam responded quickly. He transferred all of the patients into his new hospital, and summoned his emergency medical team. Spike and Barry set about digging another large latrine trench, and Frank and Christopher helped on the ward. Those who had the energy to stagger to the latrine by themselves did so: the ones who were too weak were helped by Frank and Christopher, but they were not rapid enough to cope with all those who needed aid, and some fouled themselves and lay in their own excrement until they could be attended. Doc found some very large jungle leaves nearby, and placed them under the patients as a temporary measure.

Christopher was helping one sufferer who could no longer control his bowels towards the trench but they didn't get far enough: the man sullied the ground with diseased diarrhoea. Sergeant Hideki was passing at that moment, and forced the man to eat his own faeces. The patient died two days later.

That afternoon Doc entered the accommodation hut and lectured the men on emergency hygiene. As no water was available for washing hands he advised them not to touch their mouths. Thanks to that and his swift action to isolate the dysentery victims the epidemic was largely contained, but of those who had already entered his ward few would emerge alive.

The medical officer then visited the commandant to beg for drugs to treat the condition, but Sergeant Hideki lied that he had none available. Doc pleaded with him to search the Japanese store for magnesium sulphate, but the deceitful sergeant said he knew that none was there.

Through the usual channel of Screep's translation Doc asked what treatment he could give his patients for this disease.

"Don't give them food."

"How long for?"

"One week."

"In that case they'll all die."

"Good. It will save on the rice ration."

"But it will also deplete the workforce."

"Prisoners are an expendable commodity. I'll simply request more. Our glorious armies are advancing across the world. They will not stop in the east. Soon they'll free the native tribes of America from the vile tyranny of the white man, then we'll have plenty of workers. With Emperor Michinomiya Hirohito as our leader, we cannot fail. The Emperor is number one, King George is number ninety-six." With that rousing speech he concluded the interview and waved Doc away with a peremptory hand.

The ingenuity of Doctor Tidnam exceeded that of the Japanese, and he put his resourcefulness to the opposite use. He ground charcoal to give them orally, and utilised clay to try to absorb the mucus. It was all he could do, but it was of restricted benefit.

The novice medical team worked throughout the day and slept for only two or three hours at night. Some men ceased to care quite quickly, lost bowel control altogether and with it their self-respect, their spirit and their will to live: but most battled on and clung to life. Possibly their now intense hatred of the Japanese gave them an additional motive to beat them and survive; but few would achieve victory over the bacteria and parasites that infected them.

The commandant issued an order that all sick should only receive half of the rice ration given to workers, and all of the miserly supplements would be withdrawn from them. Again, comradeship and benevolence excelled. Many of the workers donated a much needed part of their paltry rations to friends in the sick ward.

To try to retard dehydration the medical officer managed to coax additional water supplies from the parsimonious Sergeant Hideki, but the hopelessly deficient diet and lack of effective medication yielded incessant bowel movements that contained little other than blood, pus and slimy intestinal mucus.

Another request to the commandant was to construct additional support above the dysentery latrine trench, but it was refused, and that was another measure to humiliate and degrade the cowardly Westerner. Several of the patients were too weak to be able to brace themselves on the single bamboo strut which spanned the length of the trench, and fell into the foul, stinking pit of excreta, blood, pus, slime and writhing hordes of slithering blubbery maggots. A sizeable audience of guards assembled to enjoy this new spectacle, and kept at a sufficient distance to avoid personal infection. But one of the entertainers was disappointing, he managed to grab the rail to prevent complete immersion. The onlookers weren't satisfied with that performance, so a guard whipped his hands to loosen his grasp, and then held him under the revolting quagmire with a wooden pole until he suffocated. Christopher and Barry had the not pleasant task of recovering the body.

At evening many visited their sick friends and did their utmost to cheer and comfort them, but in contrast none of the citizens of the great new civilisation of the Rising Sun entered the ward. Now that Private Matsuo was dead, the flagrant brutality of the remainder excluded that type of courage. For them, it was far easier to take than that save life.

For the first few days the full burial ceremonies continued, but as the death rate increased they had to resort to mass graves and hasty funerals. Barry, Frank, Christopher and Spike now laboured almost without sleep. Doc's two trained medical orderlies had succumbed to the disease quite early, and now only the quartet remained to back up the medical officer's epic struggle.

The stench was now beyond description, and the usually quiet night air echoed with the groans and screams of the dying slaughtered by cold-blooded indifference, but was matched during the day by the cries and howls of those tormented by cold-blooded inhumanity.

Youths of twenty had now metamorphosed into wizened old men, their faces grey and their brains scrambled. Doc and his exhausted crew moved rapidly from one emaciated wretch to another to hold these haggard featherweight bundles of skin and bone over a crude bamboo bucket, only to have to return perhaps moments later to repeat the task. All the while clouds of blowflies, horse flies, gnats, bluebottles, caddis flies and midges settled on those too weak to brush them away; and swarms of bedbugs, lice, giant centipedes, maggots, grubs, flukes and spiders crawled in and out of every orifice of every helpless man and fed hungrily on the giant tropical leg ulcers, some of which were turning gangrenous.

In spite of the unceasing and diligent labouring of the lay disciples of Hippocrates, only eight of the sick would survive the epidemic. The arduous toil started to lessen as the dead were cleared from the ward, but then another sea of troubles surged into a tsunami of suffering.

The monsoon started, and rain hammered down continuously for three days and nights. The billet flooded and water rose above the level of the bamboo sleeping shelves; but Frank had found higher ground to build the medical unit on, and although water entered it did not reach to that height.

Work at the airfield continued unabated, but now men with sun-blistered skin had to wade eight miles each day through mud that was ankle deep, and in places knee deep. On that water a whole fleet of new diseases sailed in.

Two cases of beri-beri appeared on the first day, but these were due to lack of thiamine caused by vitamin deficiency. In the deluge the team gathered as many hibiscus leaves as they could find, and Doc waded into this flooded ward to feed the patients on them. One responded well, and the patient's fluid accumulation broke; but the other also had pellagra, and his swollen tongue made eating almost impossible. His legs, trunk and face rapidly swelled like grotesque balloons, his pulse quickened and heart failure vacated another bed space a few days later.

Before the rains started the medical officer had also harvested rhododendron leaves and buffalo grass which he'd dried under the still shining sun, and he'd then powdered them to treat other illnesses: some effectively, some not.

The mosquitoes had also been active, and several men showed signs of dengue fever, but the commandant insisted that all were fit enough to work. The early symptoms of malaria were also dismissed by Sergeant Hideki as 'only influenza', but when the sufferers were carried back from working in a coma or convulsing they had to be admitted. The remains of Alf Hosier's hidden stock of quinine was donated by Alf's friends, and it saved the lives of some, but not all. When the quinine was exhausted, Doc improvised with herbs gathered from the jungle.

Skin infestation with mites delivered scabies, but the commandant dismissed this ailment with instructions to simply 'scratch it'. He also refused to recognise diphtheria, and sent invalids to work; but one died of heart failure and another of paralysis of the throat.

Beri-beri infected more and Doc's treatment was effective on many, but some others were now half-demented wrecks alive with vermin, and a few died thankful to be set free from the horrors that surrounded them. Unlike prisoners of war in Europe, for these men death was the only means of escape.

Avitaminosis, scrotal dermatitis, weil's disease, yellow fever, oedema and cholera also put in appearances, but by far the most numerous affliction was ulcerated legs. The commandant had ordered that those who could not walk or stand should be carried to work, where they would sit on the ground and break rocks; but now there were too many sitting workers, and for the first time he asked for the medical officer's assistance. Doc managed to coax him into providing a few dressings, but he deceitfully denied the very existence of other medical supplies. It was, though, a small step forward. Previously wounds could only be covered with leaves or the skins of wild bananas and bound with strips of tree bark.

Lack of attention and forced labour had enlarged many of the ulcers and the men were agonised with the never ending pain. Soap was absent, so men had cleaned themselves with sand which only aggravated the condition. For some, the whole flesh from knee to ankle had been stripped by ulceration, and in the worst cases bones were starting to rot. The smell of putrefaction was sickening. Shin bones were now totally exposed, and as they decayed maggots feasted on the uncovered bone marrow and flies laid eggs in the decomposing crevices. Before resorting to amputation, Doc tried several treatments.

With each patient he ethically explained what he intended, but they were all in so much pain that none withheld consent.

Doc needed a replacement for plaster of Paris. Spike's father had been in the building trade, and he thought he'd recognised some limestone nearby. With Christopher he ground it on harder rock, mixed the powder with sand and water to make a crude and lumpy paste, and it sufficed. Ben Hinde, an infantry lance-corporal, had been given a small bottle of iodine by his mother before his departure to the Far East. She'd insisted that he should take it, and he'd kept it more as a memory of home rather than an item of utility. He was not infected himself, but donated the bottle to Doc when he had heard about the treatments and lack of medical supplies. It was another instance of the comradely fusion of empathy and selflessness.

Christopher had previously ground a piece of broken bayonet into the shape of a curette under Doc's direction, and a cut-throat razor, a pocket knife and a spoon with a sharpened edge were the only other substitute instruments at hand. All were sterilised in a bucket of boiling water. The patient's two closest friends asked to assist, and with Barry and Spike they held him down – no anaesthetics were available.

Frank and Christopher helped with the treatment. Doc cleansed the area with almost scalding water, then he scraped away what skin that there was left, removed pus and flesh with the edge of the sharpened spoon. With the rough and ready curette he scraped and chipped away the blackened bone, and told Christopher to compress the leg with his hands at either side of the ulcer so that he could excavate more pus with the spoon. At that point the patient fainted, which was timely. One of the friends who was restraining him had to rush from the hut to vomit, but bravely returned to his duties immediately after. Doc concluded with a sparing wipe of the precious iodine, applied a rice poultice and secured it with a narrow length of bandage made from torn strips of tenting material that had been cleaned by boiling.

After a ten minute break, the next man was hoisted onto the bamboo platform. His ulcers weren't so extensive, but the weakened bone had fractured. Here Doc performed an attenuated cleaning exercise, wiped on a smear of iodine, and encased the whole leg in plaster and left the ulcers to airlessly coddle in their own ichor. When the cast was removed weeks later, scar tissue remained but the ulcers had disappeared. Unlike many, that man would survive, and on eventually reaching home he set about discovering Doc's address and then sent him a Christmas card every year until he died at the age of seventy-five. Throughout the day eight more ulcerated legs were treated, and the following day another twelve: but now they reached the final invalid. For him, there was no alternative. Amputation was the only answer.

The team spent the morning looking for fresh supplies. In the rubbish thrown out by the Japanese parachute cords were found. The guards had taken the silk canopy for their own use from a wrecked aircraft but could think of no use for the cording: it was too fine and too smooth to be an effective means of torture. Doc was overjoyed with the find. It would be a good replacement for catgut stitches. Meanwhile, Barry managed to locate three soldiers who still had their 'housewives' with them, and he borrowed and sterilised the darning needles.

Frank, whose hobby had been woodwork, used a razor to carefully sharpen a small piece of bamboo to use as a cannula; and he secured it to a length of vine tendril as a drip-feed for Doc's improvised saline solution of salt and boiled water.

Before the War, Sam Hastings had worked with his father in the family's greengrocery shop. He'd married, and his wife and child also lived in the flat above, but there was continual friction between his parents and wife. He longed to buy his own home, but on the wage that his father paid that was not a possibility. His one hope rested on his athletic prowess. He'd become a star amateur performer because his footballing skills were remarkable, and he'd been offered a place with a professional team shortly before he was conscripted. Now he faced amputation, and his only candle of prospect had been snuffed out.

Sam consented to Doc's advice readily. He couldn't stand the hell any longer. The pain was driving him mad; but the medical officer was concerned that his depressed state of mind might lessen his chance of pulling through a very risky operation. Frank and Christopher visited him to attempt to boost his morale, and Frank showed him a dried branch of Ramin that he'd found on the forest floor. He told him that this wood was strong and light, and that he could make a very good artificial limb. If fact, he was going to start work on it that evening. Christopher took measurements of the leg, and assured him that the medical officer was a brilliant surgeon. The counselling therapy worked well. They left Sam in much higher spirits than they'd found him, but neither let on that Doc had never attempted a major operation before.

Barry also made a lifesaving discovery. As well as law books, he was well read in a range of subjects: the closest Christopher had met to a polymath. In the jungle he'd found a rare pomelo tree, and seemed to remember that its fruit might be useful. He took some to Doc, who scraped away its exterior fungus and mixed it with boiled water to make an effective antibiotic. The iodine bottle was almost empty, and this was just what was needed. If Aesculapius lived, he had smiled on them that day.

But if the god of health was benevolent at that time, the gods of the weather weren't. At noon the rains returned, and by the time the operation started the floor of the medical hut was ankle-deep in water. A fierce wind started, and grit from between the atap-palm covering of the walls swept across the room when gusts blew. It was a rest day, and eight of Sam's friends offered to help. Four stood around the bamboo operating table holding sheets of canvas to deflect the swirls of dust, and another waved a palm frond to shoo away the swarms of flies, bluebottles and mosquitoes that filled the air. The operating team had no gloves or gowns: their only infection shields being the masks Doc had previously made when the dead were cremated and sweatbands around their foreheads to stop perspiration dripping on the patient. The one addition to Doc's sparse surgical instrument array was a saw that had been used to fell trees at the airfield site. Christopher had sharpened the teeth with a chip of granite and then it had been sterilised by boiling. Again there was no anaesthetic, so three of the team held him tightly, but Sam had Spartan resolve. Sergeant Hideki had been asked if he'd like to attend the operation, mainly because Doc wanted him to witness the primitive conditions under which they worked. Doc thought it might induce the sergeant to release medical supplies. Not surprisingly he refused the invitation.

Emaciation had whittled away the flesh of Sam's lower leg. That remaining was about half the diameter of his knee joint: little more than skin and bone, and much of that skin was absent. The shin bone was exposed for almost its entire length, and another ulcer revealed the ankle bone. After Doc's incision through the withered debris he tied each artery as it appeared, then used the saw with Brooklands circuit speed and applied swabs and bandages. The whole coup d'eclat was completed in twelve minutes.

During the ordeal Sam sweated and swore profusely, biting his arms while tears ran over a face contorted with pain. His mates held him tightly and heartened and encouraged him for every second. At the close he heroically uttered, "Thanks Doc. That feels better already."

Over the next few days he received many visitors, and they all contributed a little of their near-starvation food rations to his convalescent diet. Two days after the operation Frank brought in the artificial leg that he'd finished carving, and Sam responded well to the unselfish care he was shown. He forgot about football. He forgot about his other troubles. He even dreamed of plans to open a greengrocery business of his own one day. But at that moment he was alive and pain free, and that was all that mattered.

His recovery was astonishingly rapid, and he gratefully asked Doc if he could be a member of his medical crew as soon as he'd mastered the use of his new leg. His gesture was aptly timed: the days of the four *mousquetaires médical* were now numbered.

Some days after the deluge eased, the compound was still waterlogged, and Frank was helping a frail patient through a morass of mud towards the latrine trench when a voice of plush-purple snobbery halted them.

"You men. Stand to attention and salute." The egotistical, vainglorious Brigadier Woodhams swaggered towards them.

"This man is at death's door. If I don't hold him he'll fall."

"I am the most senior officer here. Do as you're told," blustered the overfed and underworked blowhard as he closed within an arm's length of Frank and scrutinised him haughtily along the length of his toffee nose. Frank's crater cone of restraint could contain his magma of rage no longer and, in spite of his promises to Doc, a verbal Krakatoa erupted.

"You selfish, hateful, greedy, self-indulgent, lazy bastard! You shameless, mean, evil, loathsome heap of shit! You brainless, over-privileged remnant of a corrupt, outdated, worthless, undeserving elite of pipsqueaks! You swollen-headed mass of muck! Your men work themselves to death and you sit on your fat arse. Your men die of starvation and you don't give a damn! They face the cruel enemy every day, and you hide. You've abandoned your men and you care only about your good-for-nothing self. You obscene, cowardly, skiving, ridiculous, supercilious, patronising, bragging moron! You belong in a sewer! You are –"

The brigadier's physiognomic canvas was already primed with yellow ochre which had a sfumato of alcoholic blue, but as Frank's denunciation surged it was glazed and over-painted with every florid pigment on the artist's palette: rose madder, vermilion, cadmium, scarlet, carmine, crimson lake; and his neck and jaw were scumbled to a chiaroscuro of distillery indigo while his ears were highlighted with brewery mauve. His blubbery body trembled, his bloodshot eyes flared, his yellowed teeth gnashed, his lardaceous buttocks rippled as his anus emitted a gale of gourmand gas. He could contain his wrath no longer, raised his hand and slapped Frank hard across the face. Frank sat the patient gently on the ground.

"You've asked for this, and it's long overdue." He swung back his arm, the brigadier was too slow witted to take evasive action, and Frank planted a heavy punch into the centre of the petty tyrant's flabby face. As the brigadier fell to the ground,

Frank turned his back, carefully lifted the skeletal man back on his feet and helped him towards the latrine trench.

Less than an hour later, Frank was taken away by two guards. Sergeant Hideki had been very amused when the brigadier reported what Frank had said, but when he was told that the junior officer had struck the senior he knew that swift remedial action had to be taken. This man was dangerous, a potential mutineer. He had to be quashed: publicly.

Weary bedraggled human scarecrows returned from the day's work, and after *tenko* they were ordered to remain on parade. Doc was told that all of the sick must attend as well, and he and his helpers had to carry out barely living skeletons with skin and place them on the ground. Through Screep's subservient tone the sergeant announced that mutiny had been committed, and that they must all bear witness to the punishment for this despicable act. Frank was pushed to the front of the parade and on the commandant's orders his hands were untied.

"Are you Christian?"

"Of course," confirmed Frank.

"Then I am going to do you the great honour of letting you follow your Saviour."

Frank was stood on an ammunition box so that his shoulders were level with the timber crossbeams of the hut's entrance. Two guards held his arms along the joist, and another gave the sergeant a hammer and a handful of nails. It was obvious what was going to happen. Pilot Officer Pledger wasn't frightened. He'd wanted to join his wife and son, now it was going to happen. His only regret was that these poor, sickly, starving men would have to watch it.

Before raising his hammer, the sergeant rifled Frank's pockets. This was unusual. He normally did that after his victim had died. Frank's last and only possession was found: his late wife's wedding ring wrapped in a lock of her hair. Hideki unwound the hair with a spiteful, derisive laugh, spat on it, threw it away and pocketed the ring. Frank didn't care about dying, he was prepared to put up with the pain, but to see his wife's memory insulted in that way detonated an explosive charge of loathing within him. He had to avenge her beloved immortality.

He easily wrenched his arms away from the guards who held them against the beam at either side, they weren't expecting this outburst, and from his raised vantage point he struck the sergeant an ardent blow on the side of the neck with a clenched hand and felled him instantly. The two adjacent guards were unarmed, and another pulled back the bolt on his rifle, pushed a round into the breech, rapidly took aim at Frank and squeezed the trigger: but at that moment his target jumped down from the box and fell to his knees to retrieve the ring, and the bullet hit the guard at Frank's right and killed him instantly.

All attention was focused on Frank, and Christopher, Spike and Barry broke ranks simultaneously. It was almost as if a telepathic message electrified each one. Christopher snatched up a spade and ran towards the Japanese who now had their backs to them, raised the tool as he ran and sliced the closest guard through the side of the neck with the blade's edge. Barry was next to him and caught the guard's rifle as it fell. Spike's brother was a commando, and he'd shown him some of the more ferocious methods of unarmed combat. The next guard turned as Spike closed in on him, received a powerful kick at the base of the kneecap and Spike snatched his rifle and turned towards the largest group of Japanese and opened fire.

Barry concentrated on the other guard at Frank's side, who was kicking at his kneeling body, and managed to down him with three rapid shots. Christopher tore towards the loathsome Corporal Hagiwara with his spade. Before he reached him the corporal managed to fire four hasty rounds, two of which missed him, one passed through his left thigh and the other crashed into his chest but the ribs deflected it slightly and it just missed his right lung as the spade's blade knocked the gun from the corporal's hands and the return swing sliced him across the face.

Doc longed to join them, but knew that it would be certain death and that many sick men would then die untreated. He knew that the men needed him, but the memory of his inaction would needle his conscience for the rest of his life. Many others would like to have given their support, but were too sickly, and the emptiness of their spirits would never pull their slow and dragging legs very far. Some stood or sat hypnotised and dazed:

sights and sounds were absented from their minds. Some of the lesser unfit started to move forward, but Doc waved them back. He knew it was a lost campaign.

Barry and Spike ran towards the Japanese line firing as they went, and managed to hit three before exhausting the ammunition magazines of the commandeered rifles. They carried on running towards the line, but eventually fell in a hail of bullets. Frank joined them, armed only with the sergeant's hammer, and was cut down also.

Christopher, still armed with the spade, had been momentarily forgotten, and as blood flowed freely he staggered towards what he saw as the most deserving quarry: Brigadier John Woodhams. The brigadier stood with his mouth agape and his burgundy streaked eyes wide open. This was the first military action he'd ever seen. By opportunist manoeuvring his military career had been spent bullying men on the parade ground and propping up the bar in the officers' mess. Christopher was hit in the arm with another bullet but still managed to summon the energy to strike Woodhams across the side of his supercilious face with the flat side of the spade. A bruise would remain on that craven mien for two weeks. It would be the only war wound that he'd ever receive. If Christopher had known of Malcolm Screep's malevolence and treachery, he might have made him his objective.

As blood drained from his limbs he no longer had the strength to hold the spade, and it fell to the ground. The guards moved towards him with fixed bayonets. He was now harmless. They didn't want to shoot; he deserved a slow death. The nearest looked him over to decide what would be the most prolonged and painful method, when a voice rang out from behind Christopher.

"Tomaru. Ki wo tsuke." Christopher turned his head and saw Captain Kurofuji, the commandant of the previous detention camp. The military hierarchy had heard about the inefficient progress made at the airfield site, and had sent the captain to relieve Sergeant Hideki of his command. As he'd entered the compound he'd seen the action, and was clearly impressed.

The guards lowered their rifles and came rigidly to attention, and Captain Kurofuji stood in front of a panting Christopher.

"In the code of Bushido, captivity is the utmost degradation of the male spirit. You and your comrades are brave men. You have overcome the shame of surrender. It is a pity that you had to serve under such cowardly leaders. England should be proud of you all. In view of what you've done the Emperor would not allow me to spare your life, but I can give it an honourable close at the hands of an officer and not by this uncouth rabble. Will you take a cigarette with me before I complete my duty?" Christopher nodded and the officer drew a packet from his pocket, offered one to Christopher, then lit it and took one himself. This was Christopher's first ever cigarette, and seemed so timely, so absolutely right, so perfectly entwined. He remembered Mr Mubby's smiling face when he'd bought the packet on that beautiful day when he'd first met Christine. The packet had remained in his box of memories throughout their treasured lives together, and now one would be at its closure.

"You speak remarkably good English, sir." Christopher decided to address him courteously, and return his formal but thoughtful tribute.

"I attended London University for three years. It is a fine institution. The tuition is good, and it is not spoiled with the outmoded snobbery of your ancient universities. It is a pity that most of your politicians haven't been educated there. Your country might have been better led." Christopher didn't interrupt or try to argue. He knew nothing of universities, although he did respect many British statesmen. But these moments were reserved for Christine. When the cigarettes were finished, the captain told him to kneel, and for the last time in this world a song brought Christopher and Christine together and held them together.

> 'How many times a day do I think of you?
> How many roses are sprinkled with dew?'

***

Christopher was the precise opposite to the conventional image of a bridegroom. Fabled wedding day jitters were nowhere to be seen. As he stood before the Reverend Donaldson he'd never felt such confidence as Christine gracefully came to his side on the arm of Harry Groves. Behind her stood bridesmaids Janice and Anne, all three dressed in fashionable creations from the sewing machine of Sally Groves aided by her bargaining power with the material suppliers of Plumham market.

"Dearly beloved, we are gathered together here in the sight of God, and in the face of this congregation, to join together this Man and this Woman in holy Matrimony: which is an honourable estate, instituted of God in the time of man's innocency, signifying unto us the…"

As he slipped the ring on her finger, she gave the sweetest smile he'd ever seen, and its recollection remained, as did the fragrance of her *Sans Adieu* when he kissed his bride for the first time. Friends and family smiled sincerely as the newlyweds walked slowly down the aisle, but behind Malcolm Screep's sham lay a vat of boiling jealousy. Confetti showered, and the photographer arranged the congregation for commemorative portraits.

***

'How far will I travel
Just to be where you are?
How far is the journey
From here to a star?'

***

It was only a ten minute walk from the station to the honeymoon boarding house, but Christopher insisted that they took a taxi. A lingering dinner that evening, with two glasses of Madeira wine: then his first vision of Christine in her soft flowing nightdress. She looked like a painting by Lord Leighton or Alma-Tadema, and he took her slowly in his arms.

***

'How much do I love you?
I'll tell you no lie.
How deep is the ocean?
How high is...'

Captain Kurofuji's accurately aimed sword sliced through Christopher's neck as a large flock of gossiping parakeets flew overhead and a crimson butterfly settled fleetingly on his slumped body. At the spot where his blood fertilised the soil, a beautiful rare orchid would bloom a year later, only to be trampled on within the hour. The captain turned to Doc.

"Are you the medical officer?"

"Yes."

"Please move your patients back to the medical section, and take as many helpers as you need. The remainder of you dismiss and take rest. The funeral of these honourable men will be held this evening. Can you arrange that, Doctor?"

"Of course."

While he spoke one of the guards had spiked Christopher's head onto the top of his bayonet, and held it aloft. As the captain turned and saw him, the man started laughing. He was ordered to remove the head and place it next to Christopher's body. Captain Kurofuji them slapped his face and told two other guards to relieve him of his rifle and escort him away.

From that moment changes were made. Vile tortures were banned, although the guards still beat the prisoners when out of the new commandant's view at the airfield site. A small amount of medical supplies was released, which delighted Doc, and rest days were now to be at weekly intervals: no doubt a legacy of the captain's experience of the English Sabbath. Although food rations were still insubstantial, they were increased a little, and small portions of meat or fish were served on alternate days. Malcolm Screep now had to conduct his egg supply racket in secret; the new commandant was obviously incorruptible. That had the advantage that he could keep all of the profits to himself, but the commandant's good command of English made Mister Screep less indispensable. Brigadier Woodhams was relegated to superintendent of latrines, but still spent all his days writing the memoirs, which would now include an account of how he was wounded as he gallantly and single-handedly put down a terrible mutiny. Doc was appointed new British commander, and Sergeant Hideki was posted to the Russian front, where he surrendered almost immediately, and then spent the rest of the war in a Soviet labour camp. It was one of those rare instances of natural justice.

The enormous hoard of undelivered mail was also distributed, and some wept as they opened letters written almost a year before. Belatedly, Christopher would have had thirty-six letters from Christine, twelve from his parents and eight from Harry and Sally Groves. They'd also sent him parcels of tinned meat and new underwear on which precious food and clothing coupons had been spent; but they'd all been pilfered long ago by the Japanese.

As the funeral cortège passed slowly across the parade area a tall heron flew reverently overhead. The route was lined with every man who could walk and many who couldn't. Doc had been asked by many of his patients to help them to attend, and he willingly agreed. The few dysentery sufferers who'd survived stood in clothing gruesomely soiled but too valuable to discard and paid grateful homage to the four who'd selflessly helped them to remain alive.

Much to the astonishment of the Japanese, and to the concealed annoyance of some of them, Captain Kurofuji attended the burial and marched out with the small procession. As a Japanese officer was present the two guards at the gate had to salute a funeral for the first time. It was a tiny victory for Christopher and his close comrades.

It was not a common grave that had been excavated, but four adjoining plots. As part of his punishment, the guard who had insulted Christopher's severed head with his bayonet was ordered to work with the party who'd dug the graves.

As each of the dead was lowered solemnly beneath the trusty Union Jack, Captain Kurofuji saluted. As Frank and Christopher were laid to rest, a large flock of hornbills flew across the cemetery, the sound of their heavy wings not dissimilar to the throb of a Blenheim's engines.

As the funeral service was read from memory, the brilliant green, red and blue plumage of a group of ground thrushes could be seen darting about in the nearby undergrowth.

At the conclusion of the ceremony small swiftly-made wreaths of balsam and cannas flowers were thrown into each grave, and the sergeant with the good powers of recall recited Rupert Brooke's soulful poem:

"If I should die, think only this of me:
That there's some corner of a foreign field
That is forever England..."

As those plaintive but inspiring words resounded, in a far distant corner of England a new life began. Peter was born.

Chapter Eleven

"You stupid, stupid, stupid girl. Haven't I always warned you what men are like?"

"But Peter is different, Mum. He's the nicest person I've ever met, man or woman," Alice pleaded.

"Then why didn't he come to see us last night? Answer me that."

"Something must have happened to him. He'd never let me down, I just know it."

"Well, I don't. How long did it take this one to get into your knickers?"

"Mum, I keep telling you, he's never tried to take advantage of me. He's not like that."

"Perhaps that's the answer. He didn't get anywhere with you, so he's taken his interests elsewhere."

For Mrs Screep, all men were boastful, beer-swilling, self-centred idlers who couldn't keep it in their trousers. They were born out of a woman, and then spent the rest of their lives trying to get back in again. They should all be put down by drowning in raw sewage was her considered verdict.

"If he was going to do that, then why did he want to marry me? And why did he offer us both free accommodation in his house?"

"That was all just part of his chat-up line. He only wanted to get you into bed, that's all."

Alice's mother had always pitied her daughter for her blindness, but it also seemed to have a hidden benefit. The daughters of all the other women she knew were either anorexic, or schizophrenic, or drug addicts, or binge drinkers, or single mothers, or had one or more of the venereal diseases that were on offer. Alice's disability had inoculated her against all that; until now. Now she'd been corrupted by men: not just one, but two. Two in quick succession. How many more would follow if Mrs Screep didn't put her foot down?

"Mum, you just wouldn't say that if you'd met him."

"And why haven't I met him? Because he didn't show up, that's why."

"There must be a very good reason for that."

"Well if that was so, then he could have phoned to let you know. But the telephone didn't ring all night."

There had been nothing in that day's newspapers about the attack on Peter. For the popular press, their front pages had been reserved for a heart-warming, cuddly and profit expanding story about a veterinary surgeon who had performed, without payment, a life-saving operation on an urban fox. Tabloid editors had featured, with photographs, the disclosure of the century: a premier league millionaire footballer who was a transvestite. Peter was the most uncelebrated person in the world: they'd no space to spare for him. Similarly for the politically-correct liberalist readers, Peter wasn't from an ethnic minority, not homosexual, nor a fashionable interior designer, and he hadn't been bludgeoned by the police, so he didn't deserve sympathy. Peter's attack, like his life, had passed unnoticed.

"I don't know why he didn't make contact. But there must have been a good reason. Perhaps he was taken ill."

"You mean he got the wind up at the thought of meeting me."

"I think he deserves a second chance."

"Well I don't." A loud knock sounded on their front door as she said it. "Leave it. It'll only be someone trying to sell something. Nobody else calls here." The knock was repeated. "Yesterday you telephoned the clinic and asked them to postpone the termination. Well, today I'm going to telephone them and ask for it to be reinstated. If we leave it any longer, it'll be too late." Again the door knocker was hammered. "Oh, I'd better answer it and clear them off."

Mrs Screep opened the door and was confronted by two men, one young and of medium height; the other with receding hair and exceptionally tall. Both wore businesslike suits with white shirts and neatly knotted ties. Both had conventional non-vogue haircuts. Obviously high-pressure pushers. She hastened to verbally put a foot in their groins before they could put a foot in her door.

"Whatever you're selling, I'm not buying it." The taller of the two men was about to reply when Mrs Screep launched another anti-sales missile. "And if you're Jehovah's Witnesses, I don't believe in your God or anybody else's God, and I don't want to. If there is a God then he must be a rotten type who doesn't give a damn; otherwise I'd never be in the mess that I'm in. Good morning to you."

"Mrs Screep?" the taller man managed to thrust the question through the rapidly diminishing gap as the door closed swiftly.

"So you know my name. It doesn't make any difference. I'm still not buying anything."

"We're not selling anything, Mrs Screep."

"They all say that." The door was only inches from the frame when the shorter man used his penetrating voice to infiltrate the Screep fortress.

"We're police officers." The door opened wider and they both displayed warrant cards. "I'm Detective Constable Spencer, and this is Detective Sergeant Pierce."

"Oh God!" Mrs Screep beseeched the being she didn't believe in. "Have my nosy neighbours reported me for being a witch? Have you come here to burn me at the stake?"

"Actually, it's Alice Screep we wish to talk to. Is she your daughter?"

"Yes, she is. What has she done now? I hope that she's castrated a few men. That would please me no end."

"This is rather serious. May we speak with her please?"

"You'd better come in." The door was held wide open, and the hawk's plumage whitened to that of a dove. "Look, I'm sorry I let my tongue run away with me. My Alice is a good girl. The best in the world. She couldn't have done anything wrong or harmed anyone, I assure you."

"Good morning, gentlemen," greeted Alice as she heard them enter the room. "You'll have to forgive my mother. She's got a lot of troubles on her mind. Her bark really is worse than her bite. In fact, she's no bite at all. You're quite safe here. Now, what can I do for you?"

Both detectives were amused by her ready wit, and when they noticed her white stick and almost sightless eyes, admiration was added.

"Won't you sit down, please?" said Mrs Screep, anxious to atone for her arrogance. They both instantly sat: they didn't want her to start barking again.

"Miss Screep. Er, it is 'Miss', is it?" began Sergeant Pierce.

"Yes, I'm not married."

"Tell us, Miss Screep, do you know a Peter Goodwin?"

"Yes, I do."

"I knew it. The man's a criminal. What has he done?" The hawk was again in the ascendancy.

"We're coming to that. But first, Miss Screep, did you know him well?"

"Actually, we might have been going to get married, but mum objected. He was going to come here last night to try to win her over, but he didn't arrive."

"Just as I thought. He's run off with another woman and left you in the lurch. Probably robbed a bank as well. All men are the same," the hawk continued to screech.

"I assure you, Mrs Screep, that it's nothing like that. The reason he didn't arrive yesterday is because he was badly injured last evening, and he's now in hospital."

"Oh, dear, I'm sorry sergeant. I've let myself get carried away again. Was it a road accident?" The dove had flown back, this time to stay.

"Nothing of the sort. He was viciously attacked and beaten. By the injuries he received, there must have been more than one assailant."

"My poor dear Peter. Who did this to him?"

"We don't know."

"Didn't he recognise any of them?"

"We can't ask him. He's in a coma. That's why we're here. Do you know anyone who might want to harm him?"

"That's impossible! He's the kindest, gentlest man in the whole world."

"Yes, that's what his neighbour told us."

Alice started to cry, and within seconds she wept de profundis. Her mother moved closer to her on the settee and put her arm around her shoulders. Mrs Screep continued the conversation.

"If he isn't conscious, how did you know about us?"

"There were several things which led us here. He had Miss Screep's name and address written on a piece of paper in one pocket. There was also a bouquet of flowers near to him which had been trampled into pieces. On it was a card which read 'To Mrs Screep from Peter Goodwin'."

"If he didn't have any enemies, why did they do this to him?"

"We think the motive might have been theft."

"But Peter didn't carry anything worth stealing," Alice managed to utter between sobs. "He didn't even have a mobile phone."

"On this occasion it looks as if he did have something valuable with him. Also in his pocket was an envelope. On it he'd written 'For Mrs Screep. I hope that this will help you'. We think it contained money."

"How could you know that? It might have been a greeting card or some little present."

"We're fairly sure about that. The envelope is the type that one particular building society uses when a customer is withdrawing cash. We made enquiries at the local branch and found that he had an account there, and had withdrawn five hundred pounds on that day. It seems, Mrs Screep, that he was going to give you quite a valuable present."

"Oh no! What have I done?" Mrs Screep also started to cry, but for different reasons. "I'll never get over this. I'm so sorry darling," she added, turning to Alice.

"You're not to blame, Mum. You didn't attack him."

"No, but I shouldn't have been so obstinate about the poor man. You see, Sergeant, I married a man who was a complete swine and who abandoned me, and my poor daughter was abandoned by another. I didn't trust any men after that. I suppose you'll think me a right bitch."

If Alice hadn't been devastated by the news, her mind might have wondered about her mother's uncharacteristic reaction. Mrs

Screep had never been heard to call any member of the male sex a 'poor man', and she'd certainly never shed sympathetic tears over one. Could she be on the road to Damascus? Or disappointed not to be on the road to El Dorado? Sergeant Pierce and Constable Spencer both weighed such thoughts, but kept them behind the curtains of tact.

"I don't think anything of the sort, Mrs Screep. After what you've been through it's perfectly understandable. Miss Screep, I'm sorry to have to trouble you after you've received this awful news, but do you feel up to answering a few questions? We need to get as much background as we can to try to find whoever did this."

"I'll be pleased to help. I'm not a vengeful person, but anyone who could do such a thing to someone like Peter deserves to be punished."

"Thank you. It seems to us that this may not have been a chance theft. Perhaps someone knew he had all that money on him. Also, his injuries don't correspond with a mugging. We think it might be a hate crime as well. Please tell us what you know about him, and the names of anyone he might have known."

"I don't think he knew anybody very well. He was very shy, and from what he told me he had never had much chance to socialise. His father had been killed during the war around the time he was born, and his father's family all died shortly after, and so did his mother's parents. His mum became very depressed, and he had to spend most of his adult life looking after her. I only met him quite my chance. I had an accident, and he took me to hospital. He was very kind to me, and a friendship developed from there."

"Did he have any interests or hobbies? Could he have belonged to any clubs or groups where he met people?"

"I'm sure he didn't. He did a little photography, and he also liked popular music. But he didn't like modern music, only the sort that his parents listened to. He still has their record collection, and he often played some of them. I think that was partly sentimental, but he also genuinely liked it. He once said 'I like music that kisses your face, not slaps it'."

"That sounds almost Shakespearean."

"Inwardly I think he was quite creative, but he'd never had the opportunity to develop it."

"Did he owe anyone money?"

"None. He had always been careful with money. I think his savings were quite healthy."

"They were. The building society confirmed that. I'm sorry to have to ask this, but might he have been involved in anything underhand?"

"You mean like drugs or crime? Never. He was probably the most temperate and law abiding citizen in Plumham. It was almost as if he still belonged to a make-believe age when people did nothing wrong."

"I'm sorry about all these prying questions, but we have to explore every possibility. Were there any other women in his life?"

"Apart from his mother, I think I was the first woman he'd ever kissed. He was innocent in every meaning of the word." Alice suddenly realised what she'd been saying. "No, that's wrong. Why are we all talking in the past tense? He *is* innocent. He is still alive, isn't he?"

"Yes, yes. He's just unconscious, that's all."

"Will they let me see him?"

"As you're close, almost family, then I'm sure they will. Miss Screep, I'm so sorry to have brought you such awful news, but if you can think of anything that might help, please let us know. I'll leave you my card."

"I apologise for being so rude earlier," said Mrs Screep quietly as she opened the front door for them. "I've so many other troubles on my plate at the moment. I won't bore you with all the miserable details, but it all makes me a bit short tempered at times."

"That's quite all right. We do understand."

"Don't worry, Mrs Screep. We've met far worse than you," added Detective Constable Spencer, who often phrased his sentiments somewhat clumsily. As the police met many villains, Alice's mother assumed that she was being classified as a lesser criminal. The sergeant recognised the hurt look on her face and smoothed her feathers in the right direction.

"Your daughter wouldn't be so nice, Mrs Screep, if she didn't have a good-hearted mother." It worked, and the born-again dove cooed goodbye.

Soft rain fell gently as Alice and her mother walked along the approach path to St Agatha's Hospital. A forlorn tomcat sat to one side, and Mrs Screep stopped to stroke it, which was remarkable. In recent years she'd usually kick male cats out of the way.

"Are you relatives of Mr Goodwin?" asked the ward sister. "He's in a deep coma. I'm afraid that we can only allow close relatives to visit him."

"We're the nearest he's got to close relatives," announced Mrs Screep in a dominant voice. "My daughter is engaged to Mr Goodwin, and they were soon to be married. I'm his future mother-in-law." Alice's eyes no longer functioned, and now it seemed that her ears were floundering. Mrs Screep was again in control, and this lady had definitely turned: by one hundred and eighty degrees.

Mrs Screep placed a chair at the bedside and guided her daughter into it. Alice felt Peter's face, then held his hand tightly as liquid lament filled her eyes, slowly ran the length of her face and dropped onto the bedclothes.

"I'm so sorry this had to happen, my dear. It must have been a dreadful shock for you." The vision of Alice at the bedside filled the sister with pity. "If there's anything I can do, please let me know. May I get you both a cup of tea?"

"That is kind of you. Yes, please." Mrs Screep had now dismounted from her high horse. In that moment she too had awakened to her daughter's depth of feeling. "I'll come with you, Sister, and help to carry it back.

"What are his chances?" asked Mrs Screep after the door of the intensive care room had been closed. "You can give me your honest opinion. I promise not to tell my daughter the news if it's bad."

"He has a fifty-fifty chance. If he does recover, he'll have his full mental faculties. His head is almost undamaged. But there are many other internal injuries. If we can build up his strength then he'll need extensive surgery. When he recovers consciousness we'll know that the initial shock has been overcome, and then we can make plans for further treatment."

"Here we are, darling. Here's your tea," Mrs Screep announced in an encouraging voice as she placed the cup on the bedside locker and guided Alice's hand towards it. "I've just been chatting to the sister, and she's sure that all will be well. There's no brain damage, which is the most important thing, and he'll need one or two operations to put him right again when he comes round. So it looks like you're going to be Mrs Goodwin after all."

"Thanks Mum." Although Alice couldn't see the tubes feeding into Peter's body, she could hear the bleeps of the nearby monitors, and realised that her mother's sanguine expectations had been gilded.

"I expect you'd like to be alone with Peter. I've a little shopping to do. I'll be back in about an hour. OK?"

"Sure Mum. Thanks." Alice now felt reassured over two things. For the first time her mother had said 'Peter' instead of 'That Man'; and Mrs Screep's confidence and spirit had moved well away from her recent unstable mood swings between melancholy and bile explosions.

Over the next hour Alice spoke continuously into Peter's ear in the most buoyant, optimistic and elated voice that she'd ever used. All her life her thoughts had been realistic and rational, but pragmatism was now pushed out of sight, and hope and reassurance only were on display. She spoke of their forthcoming marriage, the future happiness of their lives shared together, and made plans for 'their' child.

Mrs Screep returned unnoticed, and overheard some of Alice's words. Her eyes again moistened as she became fully aware of the full length, breadth and depth of her daughter's devotion, and the dragon's fire was converted to considerable warmth. She placed her hand on Alice's shoulder.

"Shall we come back again tomorrow? And the next day? And the next day?"

"Yes please, Mum."

"Before we go. We must both kiss Peter goodbye. I haven't kissed my future son-in-law yet." Mrs Screep brushed her lips against Peter's forehead noisily. She wanted Alice to know that her assent was genuine, and they made their way home, both now closer to each other than they had been for some while.

Peter remained helplessly in a world of his own, a casualty of his own seven deadly virtues; but his mind remained active.

'I'll be see-ing you
In all the old fa-mil-iar plac-es
That this heart of mine em-brac-es
All day thru…'

***

Alice walked arm-in-arm with Peter, and smiled at him sweetly. Her vision was fully restored, and she told him that now she could see him, he was even more handsome than she had imagined.

They walked blissfully through a garden where they had never been before, along a path of white Carrara marble, interlaid with strips of pink tinged *Giallo Antico* and dark red *Rosso Antico*. A soft breeze ruffled the high branches of pine trees, embroidering ever wavering patterns of sunshine on the ground.

Spring flowering rhododendrons and camellias bloomed alongside autumnal roses. Every shade and hue of primula, gladiolus, dianthus, pelargonium, dahlia, paeonia and anemone stretched to the horizon. The perfumes were immaculate, and petals from all species of orchid glided across the pathway as they strolled together into a past beyond the future.

***

Alice and her mother returned through the refashioned corridors of St Agatha's. The original ornate dust-gathering Edwardian ceiling mouldings had been hidden away in the name of hygiene, and were now concealed behind bacteria-gathering plastic panels in the name of progress. The old glazed ceramic tiles had been prised away in the name of betterment, and walls were now featureless white-painted surfaces in the name of obligatory fashion.

But in spite of these virus and parasite conquering measures, the people of Plumham had yet to be domesticated. One unflagging cleaner tried to scrape several lumps of squashed chewing gum off his newly cleaned floor; another resignedly gathered used drink cans, sweet wrappers and empty cigarette packets from areas that had yet to be cleaned.

A consultant who cared for his own voice more than he cared for his patients led a small flock of awed students around a ward giving them his indisputable opinions. Two overworked nurses hurried from one needful patient to the next, while two others lounged against a wall exchanging gossip.

Three housemen laboured resolutely in a surgical ward to resuscitate a fading patient. In a medical ward a disinterested wife sat reading a magazine by the bed of her terminally ill husband. He tried to attract her attention by waving his hand feebly, but she ignored it. As death-rattle resonated she glared at him with a look of disgust and left. His lungs filled with a yellow liquid until it spilled from one corner of his mouth. Curtains were not closed around the bed for almost an hour: not a comforting picture for the ward's other ailing inmates.

Mrs Screep settled Alice in Peter's bedside chair and was trying to think of an excuse to leave her alone for a while when the ward sister appeared in the doorway.

"There's another lady here to visit Mr Goodwin. Do you mind if she joins you?"

"That's fine. Show her in," answered Mrs Screep without consulting her daughter. She was curious to know who this other woman might be. The sister ushered in a hesitant elderly woman in neat but humble clothing.

"I'm sorry to intrude. I hope you don't mind? I'm Mrs Jessop, the next door neighbour of Mr Goodwin." Mrs Screep was pleased to see this nondescript figure who wouldn't be a hindrance to her daughter's future with Peter. What's more, she might be a valuable source of information about her future son-in-law.

"Please come in, Mrs Jessop. I'm Mrs Screep, and this is my daughter Alice."

"Oh, Miss Screep, I'm so pleased to meet you. Mr Goodwin told me so much about the beautiful lady he hoped to become engaged to. This is such a terrible, terrible thing to have happened. And right on the eve of happiness for you both. I just can't begin to tell you how sorry I am. How is Mr Goodwin? What have the hospital told you?"

"We think that all will be well, I'm glad to say," replied Mrs Screep before Alice had a chance to speak. "I'd very much like to tell you more, and I think that Alice would like to be alone with her fiancé for a while. Would you care to join me for a cup of tea in the hospital canteen?"

"I'd be most honoured, Mrs Screep. I don't get the chance to meet nice new people very often."

Over four cups of tea and two muffins they chatted for almost an hour. During that time Mrs Screep succeeded in ferreting out every knowable detail of the Goodwin family's history. She had found the perfect person. Mrs Jessop had lived next to Peter and his mother for more than forty years. She was the world authority on the subject. She had been neighbourly and helpful to Christine during her depressive years, and eulogised the family and wrote Peter's curriculum vitae on a parchment of twenty-four carat gold. Mrs Jessop enjoyed talking, but it was never gossip. All of the detail was factual and well meaning. Her lack of scandal bored many people, but for Alice's mother she was the perfect find: accurate, sincere and without malice. Finally she told Mrs Screep all about Peter's script, and all of the reasons why he thought that he and Alice should marry. Mrs Jessop had a good memory, far better than Peter's, and could quote much of it verbatim. Alice's mother was very impressed, and if any doubts had lingered in her mind, this swept them away. She was now single-minded about the marriage, and resolved to do everything to arrange it as quickly as possible.

As they returned to Peter's intensive care room, a large group of doctors and nurses stood around the bed, and Alice now stood behind them.

"Oh God," they both exclaimed simultaneously, and ran into the room.

"Alice, darling, what's happened?" As Alice turned towards them they saw tears running down her face and feared the worst. For Mrs Screep was it the end of her chance for a new place to live? Was she back with all her old difficulties? But for a moment she hadn't realised that tears of unreserved joy now soothed Alice's care-lined face.

"Oh Mum, it's wonderful. Peter has woken. What they said was right. There's no damage to his mind. He recognised me instantly."

"What a relief. Am I allowed to talk to him?"

"Just for a moment Mrs Screep," replied the ward sister who stood nearby. "Just say hello, and then we've got much to do, and he must not yet talk for any length of time. It'll be too tiring. Also the police are on their way here. We've given them permission for a short interview."

Alice, her mother and Mrs Jessop made their way to Peter's bedside.

"Why hello, Mrs Jessop. They didn't tell me that you were here. Have you met Alice?"

"Yes I have, Mr Goodwin. And I'm so pleased to see you well again."

"Who is this lady? Is she your friend?"

"I am now, Mr Goodwin. And I'm also Alice's mother."

Mrs Screep drew close to him, and his fear almost sent him back into a coma. Was The Dragon about to incinerate him?

"I'm so pleased to meet my future son-in-law at long last." She bent forward and planted a heavy kiss on the centre of Peter's forehead. "How are you, Mr Goodwin?"

The words were as unexpected and improbable as hearing a vegetarian recommend cannibalism, a Marxist fervently reciting passages from *Mien Kampf* or Richard Dawkins admit to believing in Father Christmas. He pinched himself a couple of times, and it took him over a minute to disentangle a reply.

"I seem to be alright, but I feel very numbed. And call me Peter, please. Should I call you Mrs Screep? Or Mum?"

"I think 'Mum' would make me feel old, and I hate the name 'Screep' just as much as Alice does. Is 'Hilda' alright with you?"

"That's fine, thank you."

"We've been told that we mustn't stay any longer. But we'll be here again tomorrow after you've had a good rest, and then we can have a nice long talk. The police will be here soon to find out who did this dreadful thing to you. It's a pity they've abolished hanging; that's what they deserve."

Mrs Screep would normally have advocated hanging, drawing and quartering, but she moderated judgement to fit the subdued occasion. Alice became a little restive about her mother hogging the final moments with Peter, so she carefully nudged her aside.

Bending low over her man, she gave him a long and reassuring kiss, and then whispered in his ear. "We really are engaged now, Peter, and you're going to be a father: I promise you that. All is going to be well, so get plenty of rest, don't worry about a thing, and we'll be back again tomorrow."

An elderly staff nurse was disappointed that Alice had whispered her goodbye. In the present day everybody said 'see you later' when parting, and she wondered what words a blind person might use.

"Will you be visiting again tomorrow, Mrs Jessop?" asked Hilda as they walked back along the hospital corridor.

"I'd love to, but I don't want to overstay my welcome."

"Not at all. Of course you'll be most welcome. After all, if we're going to be neighbours, then we ought to get to know each other." Alice's mother was already making plans of reinforced concrete for her future.

The powerful analgesics flowing into Peter's body muffled all physical pain, and now his final mental anguish was healed. Although the Goodwin bloodline was probably lost, the family virtue would survive: he'd make certain of that. Ruby Goodwin would surely have approved.

He now had so much to tell his father. He had to reassure him that his sacrifice had not been in vain, that the Goodwin family love would be immortalised, and that he would certainly achieve that end. Peter was also conscious of his mother's dilemma. She had needed him to look after her, but she also wanted him to marry and have children. Now he could put her at ease. There would be at least one Goodwin child and, just possibly, he might be able to sire another himself. The warmth of Alice's voice had told him that day that her whole person wanted to be with him.

The reverie and ritual of Peter's private religion were interrupted as Sergeant Pierce and Constable Spencer entered the room.

The following day Hilda Screep entered Peter's room under full sail, with Alice at her side and Mrs Jessop following in her wake. She presented her future son-in-law with a very large bunch of grapes and two cartons of orange juice.

"Lovely to see you again, Peter. My, you're looking well. Firstly, is there anything that you need?"

"Hello, Mrs Screep. Er, sorry, Hilda. Yes, there is, if you wouldn't mind. In my coat pocket are the keys to my house. Would you bring me in some pyjamas, please? These National Health ones are very uncomfortable. Mrs Jessop knows her way around the rooms, she'll be able to show you where things are."

For the next hour Peter gave them all of the soothingly euphemised opinions that the doctors had disclosed, details of the police visit and a long description of the assault. Alice grew impatient, and at long last her mother invited Mrs Jessop for another cup of tea.

As soon as the door was closed they embraced as amorously as the cannulae and tubes allowed. Peter confessed that he had never been so happy, and Alice avowed that she was even happier. She told him all about her mother's amazing transformation when the police called, and they talked of plans for 'their' child. Peter made her promise to use his savings for a Scandinavian eye operation as soon as possible. He wasn't sure when he'd be fit enough to help with baby, and he wanted her to be able to cope alone.

In the canteen over four more cups of tea and two rock cakes Hilda and Mrs Jessop exchanged endless personal dossiers. As soon as Peter's neighbour revealed that she too had been abandoned by her husband, a bond of friendship was forged that was unique to both women. Hilda Screep no longer saw her merely as a font of information, but as a kindred spirit. She found her honesty and innocence so refreshing and so good-natured that an affinity was launched which remained afloat for many years.

"Actually, Mrs Jessop, I've something to confide. I hope that you'll keep this strictly to yourself."

"Of course."

"Alice is expecting a baby."

"Oh, how lovely. When is the happy event?"

"In about seven months."

"I'm sure that Mr Goodwin will be ever so pleased. I know he likes children so very much. And I like them too, but I never had any of my own. I'd love to help with the baby when you move in next door. Mr Goodwin must be delighted that he's going to be a father."

Hilda didn't mention about the true fatherhood, and she intended that nobody else should know. It was what Peter wanted, and that's how it would be.

"But I'm sure you'll understand that I'd like them to be married as soon as possible. It seems the right thing to do. Alice wants to wait until he's fully recovered, but I think that special arrangements ought to be made. Do you agree?" Alice's mother was the only one who knew about Peter's 'fifty-fifty' chances, and she didn't want her last train to freedom from worry to be derailed.

"I do agree. If you wish to try to persuade them, I'll do all I can to back you up."

"You're very kind, Mrs Jessop. That is most helpful."

As they sipped the last of their tea, this private exchange unfurled a banner of fidelity. For the first time in her adult life Mrs Jessop became Betty; and Betty and Hilda walked arm-in-arm back to Peter's room. These two birds' feathers were very different, but they still flocked together.

"Mr Goodwin, I'm so very pleased for you both. You're going to be a father. What wonderful news." Peter looked startled, and then Hilda Screep gave him a long slow wink, and he knew that his secret was safe. "Now I'd like both of you to listen very carefully. Hilda has something most important to ask you."

It was a fine introduction for Mrs Screep, and she presented her case for an immediate marriage with care and conviction. Her cogency and lucidity were well practised: as Peter had done days before, she'd spent the previous evening preparing a script. Much to her relief Peter agreed with every word, and although Alice would like to have waited awhile, she was a lone voice in this committee, so she agreed.

Hilda Screep was hooked on Peter's house as soon as she crossed the polished brass doorstep plate. It reminded her instantly of the home of a close school friend she'd known. She had envied that girl. The happy atmosphere there was in that house was so different to the perpetual bickering between her own parents. That contentment she now saw again; in the trusty, traditionally-fashioned, carefully preserved furniture; in the disciplined fluency of the drapery; in the concinnity of the ornamentation. The tight budget of the Goodwin household had immunised them against the meaningless treadmill of the avant-garde, and over the decades an affordable evergreen elegance of homely charm had been fondly orchestrated. Now it sung to Hilda Screep with words she'd never known, and another key change was written onto her vital score. No longer did she see this house as a means of survival: she now wanted to immerse herself into his history, its serenity, its honesty, its tenderness.

With the equally determined Mrs Jessop she entered the Plumham Registry Office early the next morning. She explained and emphasised the tragic and desperate reasons why an urgent marriage was needed; her daughter's disability, her pregnancy, the savage assault on her fiancé, and all troubles and disasters were ably authenticated by Betty. Alice and Peter's birth certificates were produced, and the necessary forms completed. But, in spite of the sympathy of the staff, they said that by law marriage could only take place at the office, whereas Mrs Screep had hoped that a registrar might be able to visit the hospital to conduct the ceremony. The two ladies had an emergency conference over morning coffee, and two bubbling imaginations captured an audacious stratagem.

At the offices of *The Plumham Times* they enacted their rehearsed drama to the editor, and offered him exclusive rights to coverage of this breathtaking story if the newspaper could sponsor transport for Peter to the registry office. He agreed to foot the bill for a private ambulance, but stipulated that in view of the serious nature of the injuries then hospital staff would have to agree to accompany the patient.

The stalwart duo didn't pause for food, but went straight to St Agatha's. For Mrs Jessop this was the greatest adventure of her cloistered and uneventful life, and her adrenal medulla gave surges that she never knew existed. They pleaded for an immediate interview with the chief executive, but in spite of their now barnstorming narrative, he told them that, much to his regret, hospital staff couldn't be spared. But he'd underestimated the resourcefulness of the passive looking Betty Jessop. Her magazine of innovative ammunition was now fully loaded, her new friend looked defeated, so she led a fresh charge.

"Mr Chief Executive, sir, there is one thing that we haven't mentioned. The newspaper who are sponsoring the private ambulance are also sending a journalist and photographer to report on the ceremony. They've told us it will be front page news, and that your wonderful hospital will get lots of fine publicity if the event does take place." She neglected to tell him that it was only a small local newspaper involved, and he assumed it was a national daily. St Agatha's had received a lot of bad press recently: two botched operations, one midwife stuck off for negligence, almost bottom of the London league for MRSA preventative hygiene, top of the London league for budgetary overspending. Favourable publicity could only do the hospital some good, and perhaps his job might depend on it.

He asked the ladies to wait in an anteroom, and then telephoned the consultant to ask if Peter was fit enough to make the journey. The doctor agreed, as long as adequate staff could accompany him with the equipment essential to the patient's health. The administrator had only three years to retirement, he needed to cling to his office chair until then, so he emerged to tell the anxious pair the good news. The two triumphant women hugged each other: it was the most vivacious thing that Betty Jessop had ever done, either in public or in private.

At visiting time Peter and Alice listened in wonder for almost an hour to the blow-by-blow account of that morning's victory for the allied forces of Hilda and Betty. Then the conquering heroines retired to the tea room, where they celebrated their honours of battle with fresh cream cakes.

On the wedding day they assembled with the medical team on the entrance steps to the hospital for the press photo-call. The chief executive found a prominent position in the group, and then took a reporter to one side and told him that this occasion was his idea, and that it was typical of the sympathetic all-embracing care that his patients received at his hospital. The newspaperman already knew otherwise, but decided on diplomacy and included an abridged version in his report. The following day the administrator bought thirty-six copies of the newspaper, sent one anonymously through the post to each of the hospital governors, and left the others conspicuously at every waiting area throughout the hospital.

Mrs Jessop was blissfully appointed matron of honour, and she bought not only a new hat, but also a new suit, new blouse, new shoes, new gloves, new stockings, new underwear, a new broach and a new necklace. She shed several tears during the ceremony into a new lace handkerchief.

Peter lay on a hospital trolley throughout, closely attended by four nurses, two doctors and a porter, and still coupled to mobile drip-feeds. One doctor volunteered to be best man, and kept the wedding ring chosen with great care by the Hilda-Betty alliance. The other doctor and one nurse brought cameras with them, and another nurse immortalised the event on her video recorder. The registrar didn't normally allow photography in the room, but they made an exception for this occasion.

The press photographer was very busy. He noticed another rare tear rolling down Hilda Screep's cheek as she gave her daughter away. He zoomed into close-up on her face, and cunningly sold the poignant picture to a national newspaper the following day. Fleet Street were now making amends for their unconcern about the assault on Peter, but for profitable rather than altruistic reasons.

As Peter kissed his new bride for the first time, all cameras closed on them. The registry office didn't allow confetti to be used within the premises, but as the press were present they relented. For them also it would be positive publicity, although the cleaners complained afterwards because almost everyone there had thrown some.

While Peter and Alice were away from the hospital, Peter's room was decorated by the nursing staff. Some loaned souvenirs from their own weddings, and six silvered cardboard horseshoes now hung on the walls. Others hung swags of silver tinsel between them, and one student contributed his parents' Christmas paper chains and garlands. The strict demands of clinical hygiene were set aside for that day. The nurses had clubbed together to buy an impressive bouquet of flowers, and several of the night staff had forgone that day's sleep to join them.

Two days earlier Betty Jessop had baked an enormous wedding cake which she'd smuggled into hospital and the ward sister had hidden it in a cupboard. Hilda Screep rose early that morning to prepare platefuls of sandwiches, and the hospital's catering contractors had risen to the occasion by supplying a few other buffet delights.

A consultant and two registrars looked in for a while, and each brought two bottles of wine. The chief executive made a grand entrance, and conspicuously presented two bottles of champagne, making sure that the press were aware of his generosity. What he didn't disclose was that he'd included the cost of his gift on his expenses account.

For the first time ever Betty Jessop's hair came tumbling down. After two glasses of wine she kissed the bride and groom, the bride's mother and several people she'd never met before; but the press never realised the immensity of this seismic tabula rasa. The writing on her slate would never be quite the same again.

The best man displayed his oratory prowess with a rousing speech and a toast to the happy couple. Peter made a valiant reply, in spite of his shyness and physical state; and the mother-of-the-bride concluded with a purple-tinted gush of thanks for all who'd helped.

Quite a few patients visited briefly to give good wishes to the newlyweds. Some sampled Mrs Screep's sandwiches, then decided that they preferred hospital food.

After most had left, Alice quietly asked the ward sister if she could spend the night with Peter, not in his bed, but sitting at his bedside. The sister sympathised, but recommended that Peter's long term interests were paramount. He'd had a long and tiring day, and now he needed rest.

Hilda and Betty considerately left Peter and Alice alone for an hour. Alice kissed him as passionately as his fragile health would allow. She repeated all of her plans and wishes for their life together, assured him that they would have a belated honeymoon as soon as he was well, and gently placed his hand on her breasts as a token of her commitment.

That night there was so much to tell his parents that he only managed to relate half of it before falling into a deep sleep.

'In that small ca-fe,
The park a-cross the way,
The chil-dren's ca-rou-sel,
The chest-nut trees, the wish-ing well'.

***

Alice and Peter now walked with their arms around each other through another part of that divine garden. Butterflies of every pattern and colour danced on the soft breeze and settled trustingly on the ground before them. The pathway led them to a balustrade overlooking a celestial view of perpetual devotion. Below them were verdant meadows never deserted by the sun but never scorched or wilting. The trees were habitually in blossom and exotic birds flew between them. The couple descended a long curving stone staircase, bordered by rock gardens filled with plants from all of the world's mountain ranges, and reached an ornamental lake teaming with twenty-four carat goldfish.

***

'I'll be see-ing you in ev-ry love-ly sum-mer's day,
In ev-ry thing that's light and gay,
I'll al-ways think of you that way.'

Visiting time again, and Mrs Screep arrived brimming over with ideas. Alice just had time to kiss her new husband before her mother detailed her schemes.

"Peter, my love. Is it alright now if we move into the family home?" Peter and Alice were both surprised of her phrasing 'the family' and not 'your family'; but this was all part of her grand plan.

"Of course."

"I've looked over the house so many times with Betty, and I think it's just perfect as it is. What I'd like to do is throw away all of our rotten old furniture, because it all reminds me of my rotten old ex-husband, and use all of your lovely things instead. We'll need another bed, of course, and we'll bring our clothes and personal bits and pieces, but otherwise we leave the home exactly as it is. Are you happy with that solution?"

"Of course. I'm sure my parents would be happy with that plan as well."

"Good. And that brings me nicely to my next question. Can you tell me all you know of your family's history? There's a special reason why I ask."

For more than an hour Peter told her all her knew, in great detail, and included all of the facts he'd discovered from the recent opening of his mother's boxes of memories. Hilda was completely engrossed.

"Thank you so much Peter. It's perfect. One final question. What was your mother's maiden name?" Peter and Alice were now thoroughly mystified.

"Groves."

"That's perfect too. Now, my dear, I'd like to ask your permission."

"Please do."

"I think you know that both Alice I and hate the name Screep. It's not just the sound of the word, but it's part of my awful husband and I want to leave it all behind. Alice is now Mrs Goodwin, so her problem is over. I'd thought of reverting to my maiden name, but I didn't like my parents much, either. I've considered changing my name by deed poll for some while, and I've got the forms already. Would you be agreeable if I changed it to 'Groves'?"

"I'm sure the Groves family will be delighted to welcome you."

"That's a nice thought on your part, Mum."

"Well, I can't help it now. I'm part of such a nice family."

Hilda felt doubly pleased about her decision. Many people adopted abandoned children, now she'd adopt an abandoned family: a family abandoned by uncaring outsiders. She wasn't just joining this family to escape, it was also an act of restoration of a sensibility that deserved to live on. She wanted to be part of it. She wanted to redeem it. She also wished that she'd thought of it before, so that a worthier name could have been written on Alice's marriage certificate. She was about to launch her next inquiry when the door opened and Sergeant Pierce entered.

"Good afternoon, everyone. I won't stay long, but I thought that I'd just update Mr Goodwin with the latest developments. Firstly, sir, do you recognise these?"

"Why yes. They're my father's war medals. How did you manage to trace them?"

"We've been calling on local dealers and pawn shops, and discovered them. Some have 'Christopher Goodwin' engraved on them. They were sold by a young man a few days ago. Unfortunately, he gave a false name and address. Normally we'd need to keep them as evidence, but we've taken photographs and we have the dealer's statement, so you can have them back."

"What about my descriptions?"

"We've traced the woman and arrested her. She's in custody. The curious thing is that she won't yet give us the names of the two men who were with her. Her parents are wealthy people and they've hired a very expensive defence barrister. One of the best. I think he's trying to negotiate a lesser charge if she co-operates and discloses who her accomplices were; but it's curious, she hasn't yet complied." The sergeant didn't mention it, but her reactions were even more curious that that. When she was interviewed, he'd told her that if the victim died, as was still possible, the charge would be raised to manslaughter or possibly murder, expecting that threat to prompt her into talking, but instead she'd looked pleased. Why? he asked himself. He didn't know that Ms White now regretted her leniency. The unique carnal rapture she'd thrilled to that night had induced an equally unique feeling of gratitude towards Peter. Now she wished that she had made sure of his death at the time, but knowing that he still might die and not be able to give evidence at the trial left her with the chance that she still might be able to distort the facts to her own advantage. She was as benign as a loaded gun with a hair-trigger, but she could embody the semblance of a helpless brutalised woman when it suited her.

"Now I must make my goodbyes," he concluded. "And many congratulations to you both, and to our new mother-in-law. I know I'm a bit late for this, but may I kiss the beautiful bride?"

"Please do," agreed Peter, and the sergeant gave Alice and then Mrs Screep a token peck on their cheeks.

As he left the room Betty Jessop entered and gave everyone a cheerful kiss. Although the effects of the wine had faded, so had her inhibitions. She'd never be an extrovert, but the handcuffs of formality had been unlocked.

After ten minutes of greetings, she adjourned with Hilda to their established custom at the tearoom, and that day treated themselves to iced fruitcake. Hilda outlined her idea about name change, and Betty thought it a marvellous scheme. Although her temperament lacked Hilda's wrath, she also wanted to untie the final loop of the marital knot, and with a dexterous hand of inspiration she built on Hilda's plan of escape from the Colditz of unfaithful marriage.

Neither Hilda nor Betty had enjoyed the company of siblings. Now, she suggested, if Betty also changed her name to Groves, then they could be sisters in name if not in blood. Also, they would break out of the corral of 'Missus' and again frolic in the open pastures of 'Miss'. Hilda relished the idea, they rejoiced with two more slices of cake, and the two future Misses Groves made their way back to the wards.

Peter and Alice both secretly thought the plan rather quaint, but they praised it, and Peter gave his permission and his blessing. On their way back to the bus stop, they passed a small barrier on the pavement where work was being done on an interceptor of a sewer, and the inspection cover hadn't been replaced. They performed an improvised ceremony at the side, and then Hilda and Betty solemnly threw their wedding rings into the sewer. Alice found it difficult not to giggle, but controlled the urge and applauded instead.

Peter had asked Mrs Jessop to buy him a will form from a stationer's shop. He completed it with the help of a nurse, leaving all to his new wife. The nurse's husband was a solicitors' clerk, and she took it home for him to check the wording. Two doctors witnessed his signature, and he gave the document to his mother-in-law for safe keeping. Alice protested that it was all unnecessary and assured him that he was going to live to enjoy his hundredth birthday, but Peter believed in avoiding all risks. As might be expected, Hilda supported his caution.

Over the next six days Peter seemed to gather a little strength, and while Hilda and Betty worked their way through a menu of Danish pastries, Dundee cake, meringues, cheesecakes, éclairs and puff pastry mince pies, Alice cautiously turned up the thermostat of amour. On the seventh, while slices of Battenberg cake were being consumed elsewhere, she unbuttoned her blouse and guided Peter's hand beneath it. She had deliberately left her brassiere at home that day. On the eighth day the three ladies arrived together, and Alice announced her latest maternity bulletin.

"Peter, I've been for a scan this morning. All is well, and we're going to have a little boy."

"That's wonderful news. And how do you feel?"

"Fine. Now that we know we're having a boy, what about names?"

"Don't use Robert. That was my lousy husband's name," interjected Mrs Screep, soon to be Miss Groves.

"And avoid Ronald. That was Mr Jessop's name," added Mrs Jessop, also soon to be Miss Groves.

"Actually, there were two names my mother didn't like. One was Derrick, and she said that she absolutely hated Malcolm."

"That's a coincidence. I had a smarmy relation named Malcolm. I think he was my father's cousin. I last met him when I was about twelve. He used to leer at me all of the time, as if he was mentally undressing me. I couldn't stand him."

"Was his surname Screep?"

"Yes, it was."

"Of course, that's it. I knew I'd heard your family name somewhere before. I remember now. Malcolm Screep was the name my mother once used. I'm pretty sure of that."

"It's possible," confirmed Hilda. "He used to live in Plumham. I think it was on the Plumham Wood Estate. I don't know much about his early life, except that his father died of cancer, and my ex-husband was scared stiff of his mother. I disliked him as well, but there was quite a mystery about him."

"What was that?" asked Peter, now curious himself.

"Everyone I knew thought him horrible, but apparently at one time he must have been a great hero. Like your father, he too was a prisoner of war in the Far East, but they say that he took a lot of chances defying the Japanese prison guards and getting extra supplies for the prisoners. Knowing what he was like it seems incredible to me, but he earned a knighthood for his troubles. Whenever we went to see him he insisted on showing me his citation. I saw it so many times that I can remember the words on it. His name had been put forward by a Brigadier Woodhams and a Lieutenant Ridge. He was always telling me what brave men those two were. They were some of the few survivors of that awful camp that they were in. So now he's Sir Malcolm, so it must all be true. But I still find it hard to believe."

"What was his job?"

"Something in the civil service, I think. But then after the war he suddenly had a lot of money. The family said he'd made it in business, but I don't know what that business was. With all his money he moved out of Plumham and bought a small mansion somewhere in Surrey. I lost touch with him after my ex-husband did a bunk."

"That's very interesting, Hilda. When I'm back home, I must look through all the old family records to see if I can find any mention of him."

"I'm glad you said that, Peter. It brings me to another favour I wanted to ask. Alice told me about all those boxes of family souvenirs. When I become Miss Groves, would you mind if I took a look through them. I promise I'll be very careful. It's not that I'm being nosy. Not at all. It's just that now I've found a nice family, I'd like to be part of it as much as I can. I'd like to soak up the Goodwin love to get rid of the Screep hate." She sounded very sincere, and unexpectedly romantic.

"Of course you can, Hilda," confirmed Peter. "Do it as soon as you wish."

"That's a nice gesture, Mum. I'm sorry that I can't look through them with you."

"You soon will be able to. Remember your promise?"

"Can you get it done now on the National Health?" asked an astounded Hilda.

"No Mum. But Peter wants me to use his savings to get it done privately."

Hilda and Betty were ecstatic. They hugged each other, hugged Alice and finally Peter; then they left to celebrate the splendid news with another fresh cream bun fight.

When they were alone, Alice raised the warmth of Venus by another degree. She again unbuttoned her blouse, then slid her hand under the bedclothes, unfastened his nightwear and softly caressed his body. He was no longer an older friend, he was no longer older. Now he was her cherished husband, and she wanted to have him and to hold him.

"Peter, my love, please get better soon. I can't wait for you to come home and to be with you all the time. And after our son is born, I'd like him to have a little sister. So think up some girls' names as well."

"I can't think of a name lovelier than Alice. And we'll buy her a blue gown and live together in wonderland." There was so much to tell his parents that night. Not only would the Goodwin name survive, but there was a chance of the bloodline continuing. It was beyond his wildest dreams.

> 'I'll find you in the morn-ing sun;
> And when the night is new,
> I'll be look-ing at the moon,
> But I'll be see-ing you'.

***

Peter again walked through that garden, along a pathway strewn with rose petals. Clutching his hand was a three-year-old boy, whose name Peter instinctively knew to be Christopher. Beside him Alice pushed a pram. In it was a baby girl: he also knew her name to be Christine. They walked towards a high ancient wall, and the path led to a solid oak doorway. As they neared, the wall changed to red brick with lime-cement pointing, and the doorway reduced to a dark green panelled door glazed with Art Deco sunburst pattern. Alice smiled, took a key from beneath the baby's shawl and handed it to him with a loving kiss. He opened the door and entered alone. On the other side of the wall was light, only light, bright but not blinding. At the centre of the light stood a radiant seventeen-year-old girl, arm in arm with a handsome eighteen-year-old boy. She wore the dress that hung in his mother's wardrobe at home, but not here carefully protected with layers of tissue paper. The young man was dressed in a brand new suit of clerical-grey herringbone pattern. Behind them, just visible, were two family groups: one with a son and daughter, the other with a girl.

"Hello Peter," said the beautifully dressed girl at the front. "I'd like you to meet your father."

"I'm so pleased to meet you, Peter, at long last," greeted the young man. His voice sounded as if it were a harmonic blend of all the singers' voices in his parents' record collection.

***

The noonday sun warmed the faces of Alice, Hilda and Betty as they walked together to the hospital entrance. The same cat sat at the side of the path, and all three stroked him as he rubbed his head affectionately around their legs and purred loudly.

St Agatha's was no longer just a hospital; no longer a place to be feared. It was even more than a place of recovery. With a few exceptions the staff were friendly and helpful, and the patients were as cheerful as their health allowed. It was a place of new beginnings: a new marriage, two new quasi-sisters who had both found new and happier lives. It was a temple of new hope, new futures, new warmth, new fondness. For the three women, one was to be a new mother, another a new grandmother, and the third a new honorary aunt.

Hilda carried more grapes and cartons of orange juice, Betty had a fresh bunch of flowers to replace the now wilting wedding bouquet, and Alice had bought a bottle of Madeira wine. She wasn't sure if they'd let him drink it, but if they didn't she'd keep it for a later celebration.

As they emerged from the lift the ward sister met them. She'd seen them approaching when looking through a window. They were ushered into the sister's office and asked to take a seat. The sister left them for a while, and then returned with a young doctor.

"I'm so very sorry to have to tell you this, Mrs Goodwin, but your husband had to be rushed to the theatre last night for an emergency operation. The surgeons worked on him for more than ten hours."

"Well, we were told that he'd probably need surgery. Perhaps it's better to have it sooner rather than later," commented Hilda.

"He will be alright, won't he?" asked Alice.

"I'm afraid not," began the sister, then buried her face in her hands as she sobbed uncontrollably. The doctor had to continue.

"It distresses me a great deal to have to tell you this, Mrs Goodwin, but your husband passed away earlier this morning. We did all we could to save him. I'm so very sorry."

The whole of Alice's body shuddered, she opened her mouth and let out a agonised scream, got to her feet, took two steps forward and collapsed in a faint.

Alice and Peter's life together ended as it had begun, with her lying unconscious on the floor. Modesta White, aided by the Avenging Furies, now wore the laurels of victory.

Chapter Twelve

London 2012. A city still dragged at the chariot wheels of trash. Still the world centre of trashy modernity. Self-interest and hedonism still trashed precious fabrics and values. Fake intellectualism's pointless abstractions still trashed reality.

But the metastasis of trash now spread secondary tumours further into the city's flesh. The one-time stable, trustworthy, honourable heart of finance had been trashed by the malignant growths of avarice, unscrupulousness and insincerity.

London was no longer for Londoners. The freeholds were lodged within the tiers of politically conniving Russian dolls; or beneath the robes of leisurely Bedouin sheiks whose wealth had been thrust upon them by a quirk of geology. Leaseholds of prime sites were in the pockets of money manipulators, money launderers and those celebrities whose role modelling had pushed two generations of youth into narcotic quicksands.

But somewhere within Londinia's castellated crown a few resistance patriots still waged a valiant rear-guard action, although one of these blameless die-hards had been annihilated eleven years previously. A cynic might have said that he was a ghost before he died. A romantic writer might have concluded that he never reaped the harvest of his dreams; but the writers of Plumham were all preoccupied with harvesting the royalties of soft porn, hard porn and medium-rare porn. All, that is, except Alice Goodwin.

Peter's savings had been sufficient to fully restore vision in one of Alice's eyes, but that was enough to lower the drawbridge to a new future. Inspired by Peter and his memories, she had tasted every deep-rooted emotion, joyful and sorrowful, that the family tokens of remembrance held; and that kindled a new poetry collection which was at last successful. Of itself it earned little. In the twenty-first century it was the closest that a book of poems could be to a bestseller; but it was noticed and applauded, and she was offered a part-time post at Plumham's Londinium University as a tutor for a creative writing course.

And that wasn't her only new-born writing breakthrough that drew breath from her brief life with Peter. With vision returned she reawakened her interest in art, and became an art correspondent for a not unpopular newspaper. Among critics she was almost alone in condemning the heaps of bilge, dross, slag and offal that posed as contemporary art. Among the fashionistas she was a pain in their artlessness, but her column was popular with a down-to-earth public, and it was another small but sturdy sea wall against the rising tide of trash.

The parched details about the final days of her father-in-law also raised her thirst to know more of his fate. Through the Far East Prisoners of War Association she luckily traced Doctor Tidnam, and interviewed him during the last year of his life. Although his health was failing his memory wasn't, and he painted for Alice a perfectly lit picture of Christopher Goodwin's life and death in captivity. That not only filled a vacant space on the Goodwin canvas, but it also added another pigment to Alice's literary palette.

The dauntless but modest doctor had only been awarded an MBE for his valiant work, and compared to Malcolm Screep's knighthood it was a grotesque inversion of sweet and sour. Yet when he heard of the Screep award, he didn't challenge it. His interests lay with his patients, not in his self-esteem.

And that iniquitous reversal between the noble and the ignoble wasn't the only one that Alice witnessed, and the legacy of Peter's death wasn't entirely wholesome. Modesta White's spite was no longer clamped by the risk of a court testimony from Peter, and she gave the police the supposed names of her two confederates. She said that she'd been too frightened to reveal their names before because she was terrified of retaliation; but now she'd become heartbroken at the news of Peter's death, and had plucked up the courage to unmask the culprits. They had forced her to watch their horrible attack, she claimed, and her account was dilated by her skilful barrister and enriched by her acting. In return for being 'helpful' to the police she was given a mere thirty hours community service, most of which she avoided by feigning ill health.

But the names she gave to the police were not those of Hornie and Scratch. Instead she pointed a vengeful finger at two innocent young men whom she hated because each had refused to climb into the rancid bed of Plumham's Messalina. She knew that they couldn't give alibis because she'd seen them alone together that night. Each was sentenced to fifteen years: one committed suicide in prison; the other became severely depressive and never recovered. She'd expected her two cronies to be grateful for their deliverance, and to repeat the erotic voracity she'd once wallowed in; but their sensual powder kegs were dampened by snorting, mainlining and cowering, and failed to ignite.

Nevertheless the sword of Nemesis succeeded where the gilded personification on the roof of The Old Bailey had failed. In two years' time liver failure made certain that Hornie alias Mathew joined His Satanic Majesty.

Similarly, rough justice dispatched Scratch née Luke. His drug dealer withdrew supplies due to a large unpaid debt, and the remaining Satanist attempted blackmail by threatening to tell the police of the dope peddler's trade if he failed to continue deliveries. Scratch was given a deliberately adulterated fix, which also fixed the threat.

In the glorious sunshine of Thursday 28th June Alice Goodwin entered Plumham Cemetery, hand-in-hand with an eleven-year-old Christopher Peter. There was no other man in her life, and never would be. Only Alice and her mother knew the true fatherhood of her son, and under no circumstances would they ever tell him that the name on his birth certificate was bogus. Some might think that deceptive, but Alice knew otherwise. Billions of sperm were slaughtered daily by contraception. Why should one count when it had been delivered by deception? Peter was not the man who'd carelessly given her son life, but he was the man who'd allowed him to have life. He was the genuine draughtsman of creation: not the barbarian marauder, but the renaissance architect of the boy's being.

Young Christopher was not at school that day because of a teachers' strike, and he carried a carefully selected bunch of flowers which he laid on his chosen grandmother's grave; then he and Alice said a silent prayer just as she had done with Peter eleven years earlier. She had commissioned a stonemason to replace the shattered headstone with an exact replica, to which she added the words:

> Here lies also the spirit of her beloved husband,
> CHRISTOPHER GOODWIN
> 1918-1942

They then walked a short way through the ranks of memorials, some remembered, others forgotten, until they reached the best kept and sublimely touching plot of final rest. A local stonemason had read of Peter's hospital marriage and his tragic death, and was deeply moved. He was close to retirement, tired of hammering out clichéd monotony, and wanted to leave his career with a final flourish, so he offered to make Alice a bespoke monument at an off-the-peg price. Knowing Peter's preferences, she collaborated on its design. At the top was a carved weeping angel holding a music score, and on the staves was minutely engraved the notation of Jack Strachey's 'These Foolish Things' written, fittingly, in 1936, and was the melody and the year that had brought Christopher and Christine into harmony. Crushed beneath the angel's right foot was a crumpled book of saw-edged avant-garde literature, a symbol of the discord that had brought Alice and Peter together. The inscription was followed by the simplest but most deeply felt verse that Alice had ever written. She wrote it with a rhythmic metre to attune with his melodic sensitivity.

> In loving memory of
> PETER JAMES GOODWIN
> 1942-2001
>
> A devoted husband and loving father.
>
> So few hours together, so many years apart,
> I can't hold back the dusk of yesterday.
> Requiescat in pace, though heavy in my heart,
> This precious love of ours will always stay.

Alice arranged fresh flowers in the containers at the foot of the memorial while her son tidied the plot. When their labour of love was done they both stood with their eyes closed. Peter had been right about the hidden hand of ancestry. Nurture meant almost everything, and nature really did count for very little. During young Christopher's silence he spoke earnestly to that beneficent father he'd never known, just as Peter had done before him. Alice's words and thoughts, just like Peter's, now included melody.

'Follow my lead,
Oh, how I need,
Some-one to watch o-ver me'.

Alice now owned a car, but they walked home that morning partly for the benefit of exercise. She'd got into the habit of not driving for short journeys. Originally that was because finding a kerbside space in Brunel Terrace was difficult, and she didn't vacate her parking spot unless it was really necessary. She'd never want to move to another house: those bricks and mortar held the repose of the Goodwin soul; the quintessence of all that she loved; the perfect shelter for her happiness.

The car parking difficulty had been partly resolved. The front fence had been taken down and the tiny front garden paved. But nudging her car in and out of that barely adequate space took a deal of time and concentration. A smaller vehicle would have been easier to manage, but she needed one with five seats that would accommodate her family. With Christopher Peter, there was also Nanny Hilda Groves, Aunty Betty Groves, and as she crossed the still brightly polished doorstep plate of number thirty-six the fifth family member ran to meet her.

"Hello, Mummy," greeted eight-year-old Christine Alice Goodwin, flinging her arms around the neck of a now stooping Alice.

"Hello, darling."

"Did Daddy talk to you today?"

"Yes, he did. And he told me how proud he is of his own little girl."

Christopher looked fleetingly quizzical, but said nothing. His respect for Peter was unbounded, but he now viewed his little sister's quaintness with an eye approaching adolescence. He often spoke to Peter's spirit, but he was adult enough not to expect a reply.

The ward sister and the doctor at St Agatha's rushed to Alice's side and straightened her limp body.

"Please be careful. She's expecting a child. It's been bad enough losing her husband. She mustn't risk losing her baby as well."

"Yes, we know, Mrs Screep. Please don't worry, she'll be safe now. I'll make sure of that."

They lifted her onto a trolley, then placed her attentively onto a bed in a vacant room. Another nurse brought in an oxygen bottle and mask in case they were needed, and the doctor paged Dr O'Neill, the hospital's senior obstetrician.

It was unusual for a lowly houseman and a consultant to be on close terms, but they were both music lovers and sang in the same amateur choir. They were also both 'real ale' enthusiasts, and sometimes enjoyed a pint together after choir practice.

As Alice regained consciousness, she convulsed into tears, and the now enlarged medical team and her mother worked intensely to console her. They talked ceaselessly in encouraging tones while she was being examined, and it was pronounced that all seemed to be well.

"It's not well at all. My poor dear Peter gone, and he so much wanted us to have another child together. And so did I. Now it's all gone. Gone forever." She almost said 'our first child together', but checked herself. The doctor nodded to the sister, and she knew what he meant.

"Actually, Mrs Goodwin, there is something that I haven't told you. We promised your husband not to tell you this before. He thought you might believe he was just being morbid, and that it might upset you. But if you feel up to it, I'll explain."

"What is it?"

"You will, probably, be able to have his child."

"That's ridiculous!"

"No it isn't." Between them the sister and the young doctor gradually unwrapped the events of three days before. Quite an affinity had arisen between Peter, the houseman and the ward sister, and he'd asked for their help and advice. Whether or not he'd had a premonition about his imminent death nobody knew, but he'd asked if immediate arrangements could be made for him to donate seminal fluid that might be preserved and used for a future artificial insemination for Alice. It was a most unusual request, well outside the remit of a general hospital, but the doctor engaged the persuasive help of his singing and drinking friend, and he and Dr O'Neill confronted the chief executive with the request. To their astonishment he agreed without protest. The administrator was so grateful to Peter Goodwin for the recent favourable publicity that he decided to reward him with more than expense-account champagne. Peter's family continuity was frozen in liquid nitrogen at a distant clinic, and would be used by Alice three years later. The Goodwin blood was preserved as well as the name. Peter's wildest dream had come true. Ruby Goodwin's spirit was overjoyed.

After lunch the family of five mounted a train to central London. It was a special afternoon. Alice had promised to let the children have their first glimpse of royalty. She remembered Peter's suggestion in Plumham Park that they might attend the Golden Jubilee celebration the following year, and this was partly her apology for leaving him without explanation that day. But that wasn't her only raw feeling.

Alice was peace loving, but no pacifist. She'd always been repulsed by the carnage of warfare, but the interview with Doctor Tidnam had triggered her pity for those who'd suffered or sacrificed their young lives. She was especially incensed by the unjust bias of sympathy and reward. The undeserving honour heaped upon Malcolm Screep whilst genuine heroes lay forgotten was an abyss of injustice. She was powerless to influence those decisions, but she also reacted against the jaundiced lack of condolence shown for some groups of people; and two of those groups included her late father-in-law.

Remorse and sorrow for the Holocaust was universal. The perpetrators had apologised profusely, built monuments and given generous restitution. Nazism was now a dirty word.

But in the Far East the atrocities committed had been equal if not worse, yet the cult of Bushido remained unsullied. A nation's history had been deceitfully rewritten, apologies were refused, and present generations were kept ignorant of its ferocity and it's evil. That was a wrong still to be corrected, and Alice campaigned to straighten the warped pendulum of judgement with her writing.

That afternoon, though, amende honourable was being paid to the second band of neglect that included Airman Christopher. Although he'd never dropped a bomb, he'd been a member of Bomber Command. Those men had the highest death ratio of any of the fighting forces. Half of those who flew out never returned. Young men, some scarcely out of school uniform, were dressed in blue and winged into their unmarked and unlamented graves.

Although he'd never been a flyer, Doctor Tidnam had seen the intense and unselfish comradeship of those like Christopher and his fellow musketeers, and described every detail to Alice. She now believed that the sanctimonious post-war protests against bombing should have been aimed at politicians and officials who'd directed the strategy, not those who'd courageously followed orders and donated their lives to the eventual restoration of peace.

Alice and her family stood in Green Park, as close as they could to the Queen's unveiling of the neo-classical but meaningful Bomber Command Memorial. Alice felt a mixture of relief that a blemish on the conscience of humanity had at last been healed, and sorrow at the sadness of the event. She also knew that, through her gentle schooling, her family felt the same.

But in another corner of London the constipation of blind forbearance still needed purging. To coincide with a year of celebration, the Mayor of Plumham was bestowing Freedom of the Borough on one Modesta White. Her parents were no longer alive to contradict her, so she gave a convincing address to the assembly about her mythical childhood abuse, and how she'd struggled throughout her life to overcome its torment; and then she went into lavish and sparkling detail about how she was devoting her life to the care of others. She had, in fact, changed direction: but it was not towards virtue.

Her syphilis, drug and drink dependencies had all been treated. She no longer yearned for perverted sex, and she had even stopped smoking. Her image of care and concern for others had been sculpted by taking a job in an old people's home, but beneath that cloak of respectability festered her new-found thrill of debauchery. Those inmates who'd lost the ability to communicate fully and to be able to report her conduct had been carefully selected, and each day she enjoyed the rapture of humiliating and torturing them in ways that could never be traced. Three deaths had resulted, and she planned more. The buzz she felt was better than the habits she'd kicked.

Londinia's flowing robes still thirsted for disinfectant.